Meeting Mu

CW00454810

By Keith A P

For more information about the author and to receive updates on his new releases, visit …

www.keithapearson.co.uk

'The truth is rarely pure, and never simple.'

- Oscar Wilde

1.

"And they all lived happily ever after."

The man closed the book.

"That was brilliant," chirped the boy. "Can I have another story? Please, Dad."

"Not tonight, son. It's late."

"But it's still light outside."

"I know, but that's because it's the summer. It's way past your bedtime."

The man leant over and kissed his son on the forehead before ruffling his hair.

"And besides," he added. "You've got school in the morning. Nine-year-old boys need lots of sleep to make them clever."

"Do they?"

"Absolutely. So, best you head off to the land of nod."

"Okay," the boy sighed. "Night, Dad."

"Goodnight, son."

The man got up from the edge of the bed and returned the book to a shelf. With a parting smile, he switched off the light and closed the bedroom door behind him.

The boy lay there in the half light and listened to the sounds outside his bedroom window. He could hear older children still playing in their gardens, and somewhere in the distance, the chimes of an ice cream van.

"It's not fair," he whispered to himself.

Long minutes passed, and the boy fidgeted beneath the covers.

With sleep unlikely, his mind sought entertainment, and an idea promptly arrived—if his dad wouldn't read him another story, why not read one himself?

A mischievous grin crept across his face as he snuck from his bed and tip toed over to the bookshelf.

So many books and so many titles he recognised. He scanned the shelves looking for a book which hadn't featured in a bedtime story and, on the top shelf, tucked away at the very end of a row, he found one.

He quite liked the sound of the title on the spine and plucked the book from the shelf. It was old. He could tell by the cover, which was a faded shade of blue, and it smelt kind of musty like his granddad's house. Still unsure if it was worth reading, he studied the strange picture on the front cover. It wasn't like any of the books his dad had read to him, and that was good enough reason to give it a go, he thought.

Returning to his bed, he slipped back beneath the covers and, feeling just a little naughty, opened the book.

He read that book cover to cover; not because he wanted to, but because he desperately hoped there might be a happy ending.

There was no happy ending.

Suddenly, sleep felt a better place to be than awake. The boy closed his eyes, but he couldn't shake the story from his mind. He tossed and he turned, and thought of everything he could to force his thoughts elsewhere.

Tiredness eventually took over and he fell into a fitful sleep; the book sliding from atop his duvet to the rug on the floor.

An hour later, the man returned to the room in a fit of panic—the boy's screams so loud they could be heard at the opposite side of the house.

As he tried to comfort his distressed son, he happened to glance towards the floor, and that's when he noticed the book lying there.

In that moment, he knew it would be a long time before his son ever slept soundly again.

TWENTY-FOUR YEARS LATER

...

2.

Four miles from Heathrow Airport and the traffic has ground to a halt. The weather couldn't be less festive as we sit beneath sombre skies, and drizzle mists the windscreen.

I prod buttons on the stereo in the hope of finding a station playing something other than Christmas music. Misfortune prevails as I tune in to songs from Slade, Wizzard, Slade again, and Mariah Carey. Daisy slaps my hand away before I can try a fifth station.

"I love this song," she coos. "Leave it."

Unfortunately for me, *All I Want for Christmas Is You* has just started. I slump back in my seat while Daisy sings along. There are many things I love about my fiancée but her singing voice isn't one of them. I need to distract her.

"Do you think she means it?"

Daisy breaks off mid-screech and turns to me. "Means what?"

"Does she really not care about the presents?" I ask, referring to a line in the chorus.

"I guess not. All she needs is the man in her life."

I ponder her reply.

"I'd definitely buy her something. Nothing big, mind; maybe a chocolate selection box. At least she'd have something to unwrap."

Daisy rolls her eyes before pulling down the sun visor and studying her reflection in the mirror. A few flicks of her immaculate blonde hair and the visor is returned to its position.

"So let me get this straight, Adam," she frowns. "You'd buy the multi-millionaire, Mariah Carey, a selection box?"

"Yeah, just as a token. I mean, she said she didn't want anything, so it'd be a nice surprise."

"Like the bathroom scales?"

It's been precisely one year and nine months since Daisy's thirtieth birthday. At that point we'd been together less than a year, but I thought I knew her well enough. So, when she complained her favourite jeans were getting a bit tight around the waist and she therefore needed to lose a few pounds, I presumed a set of digital bathroom scales would be a practical gift. Turns out I was incorrect, and Daisy has never let me forget it.

"No," I grumble in response. "Not like the bathroom

scales."

"What about the lingerie you gave me last Christmas? Do you think Mariah would have liked that?"

Here we go.

"There was nothing wrong with that lingerie," I grumble.

"Apart from the size."

Whatever I learnt at school, and I must confess I didn't listen most of the time, I'm pretty sure they never taught us how to buy a bra. Therefore I was ill-prepared when I entered the lingerie store that fateful Saturday afternoon. Who knew tits were measured in cups? How does that even work? Do they use a china tea cup, or one of those giant novelty mugs? Either way, the vision of women squeezing their breasts into cups was beyond my comprehension as I stood befuddled in front of the sales assistant. With my hands outstretched, as if weighing up two imaginary grapefruit, I explained that Daisy's breasts were "a decent handful."

I was asked to leave.

Undeterred, I tried another three shops and eventually acquired the now infamous lingerie.

"The knickers were a decent fit, weren't they?"

"If I wore a belt maybe. And as for the bra …"

"It wasn't my fault," I protest. "How was I supposed to know you had to crack a sodding algorithm to buy a bra?"

"Anyway, it doesn't matter now," she concedes. "This gift more than makes up for it."

She leans over and kisses me on the cheek. "Thank you."

I can't help but feel just a little smug. Daisy absolutely loves Christmas, so what better place to spend it than in a snowy New York. Neither of us has been before, so, when I received an offer by email from British Airways, I knew it would be the perfect gift. And despite my reservations about sitting in a pressurised aluminium tube for seven hours, I have to admit I'm almost as excited as my fiancée.

"It's going to be amazing," I say. "Five nights in a five-star hotel. No cooking, no cleaning and no drizzle."

The traffic begins to move again and Daisy does a little dance in her seat—presumably in excitement and not because she needs the loo.

"You don't …?"

"No."

"Okay. Just checking."

The final few miles of our journey are tortuously slow but

we eventually reach the car park at Heathrow with half an hour to spare. After a panicked check I've got the flight time correct, we grab our bags and hop on the shuttle bus to the terminal. Two minutes later, the bus sets off.

"What time do we land?" Daisy shouts over the noisy diesel engine.

"Just after five o'clock, their time."

"What are we going to do first?"

"Um, we'll have dinner in the hotel and then I'll let you decide."

"Probably wise."

My fiancée knows me only too well. I don't have a great track record when it comes to making decisions; an affliction I can pinpoint to an episode during my first weeks at secondary school. My best mate, Joe, and I, were at the local chip-shop one lunchtime. As we waited for our chips, Joe spotted a jar of pickled gherkins on the counter and casually remarked how disgusting they looked. I don't recall the specifics but his observation became a challenge and a bet was duly placed. I could have accepted his bet as initially offered and eaten just one, but no. In a fit of youthful bravado, I foolishly upped the ante and told him I could easily eat ten.

Challenge set, the man behind the counter duly plucked ten turd-like gherkins from the cloudy vinegar and wrapped them in one diabolical package.

Outside the chip-shop, and with enthusiastic encouragement from Joe, I set about my task. The first three gherkins were manageable; the fourth hard going; the fifth and sixth gag-inducing. The seventh proved a gherkin too far and I admitted defeat after two bites. With my chips uneaten and pride dented, we returned to school and went our separate ways.

Thirty minutes into a maths lesson—while discreetly trying to pass wind—I shat myself.

Somewhere in my decision-making process I overlooked the potential laxative effect of consuming seven pickled gherkins in one sitting; a mistake I would never be allowed to forget, as my fellow pupils changed my surname from Maxwell to Shatwell for the ensuing three years of school.

I didn't like school much.

The bus pulls up outside the terminal and we smile at one another.

"Ready?"

"You bet."

We disembark and dart across the pavement into the terminal; stopping for a brief moment to savour the anticipation. While Daisy gazes across the sea of humans in transit, I take the opportunity to gaze at the human next to me. It would be fair to say I'm punching well above my weight, and I still have no idea what Daisy sees in me, or how she puts up with my crap. Sympathy, maybe, or some misguided maternal instinct I'd guess. I don't know, but I do know I'm a lucky man—in love at least.

She turns to me. "Have I got lipstick on my teeth?"

"Sorry?"

"You're staring at me, Adam."

"Oh, sorry. I was miles away."

"Soon enough, honey. Soon enough," she coos, pointing towards the British Airways check-in desk.

We hurry across the tiled floor towards the desk and join the queue. As we wait, I check our passports for the fifth time and locate the booking confirmation I printed from the British Airways website.

"You've definitely got the right passport this time?" Daisy asks.

Back in March, our weekend in Paris was almost ruined when I grabbed my out-of-date passport from a drawer, rather than my current one. On this occasion I know it's the right one because I checked three times before we left the flat, but mild panic still builds as I scrabble to extract my passport. I flip it open and breathe easy.

"That photo is awful," Daisy giggles. "You look like a convicted sex pest."

I stare down at my own face and concede she has a point. The day I chose to visit the photo booth in town turned out to be the windiest day of the year, and I might also have been suffering a mild hangover. As a result, my coffee-coloured hair resembles the nest of cables behind our TV, and my brown eyes are a bloodshot shade of misery. In truth, it's not the face of a man you'd ask to babysit your kids.

"Just as well you're not with me for my looks," I chuckle.

"Or your money," she replies with a wry smile.

I'm about to offer a feeble defence when we find ourselves at the head of the queue. One of the two check-in positions becomes free and we're beckoned over with a smile from the uniformed attendant.

"Good morning," chirps the young woman, who, according

to her badge, is Jessica.

"Good morning," we cheerfully reply in unison.

"Are you checking in?" she asks.

I confirm we are and ask if she requires the booking reference from my confirmation email. Jessica confirms she does and dutifully taps the keyboard as I quote the reference, one character at a time.

She strikes the enter key and her smiley expression dissolves.

"Sorry, sir. Can I double check that?"

I quote the booking reference again and Jessica taps the keyboard, confirming each character as we go. Striking the enter key does not invoke the relief I hoped to see.

"Is there a problem?" I ask.

"The system doesn't recognise that booking reference. Probably a glitch, so let's try your surname instead."

"It's Maxwell. Adam Maxwell," I confirm.

"And which flight are you booked on?"

"The two o'clock to New York, JFK."

More tapping, but no sign of a smile.

"I'm sorry, Mr Maxwell. I've just checked the customer manifest for that flight and … your name isn't on it."

"What? There's obviously been a mistake. I have the booking confirmation here."

To prove my point, I wave the sheet of paper in front of her.

"Can I take a look at that?" she asks.

I hand it over and fold my arms. I daren't risk even a glance at Daisy, so keep my eyes fixed on Jessica as she scans my booking confirmation.

Seconds pass before she poses another question. "Where exactly did you make this booking, Mr Maxwell?"

"Online. The British Airways website."

She stares up at me, eyebrows arched. "I don't think you did."

"I bloody well did. It had the logo at the top and everything."

"No, I think you booked on a website which *looked* like the British Airways website. It's what's known as a phishing scam."

"For crying out loud," Daisy mumbles to herself. I ignore her and shoot Jessica a glare laced with confusion and agitation.

"A what?" I snap.

Jessica places the sheet of paper on the counter and points out the address of the website. "You see this URL? It says *cheap-brittish-airway-deals.com*."

"So?"

"That's not the British Airways website. It's a fake made to look like ours, but if you'd checked the website address, it's pretty obvious it's fake."

"How the hell is it obvious?"

"For starters, we know how to spell *British*."

I check the website address.

Shit.

"And to be honest with you, Mr Maxwell, the price you paid is a bit of a giveaway too."

"Eh? It was a deal. The website said you had to fill a last-minute allocation of seats."

I can almost smell her glee as she points out what most people would have considered obvious.

"Five nights in a five-star hotel, and return flights to New York, at Christmas, for two people. Did you not think two hundred pounds each seemed a little on the cheap side?"

Oh.

I risk a glance in Daisy's direction only to find her eyes firmly shut.

"Um, so what can I do?" I ask, returning my attention to Jessica.

"I can't help with the hotel, but I can still get you on the flight. Did you want me to confirm a price?"

"Please," I gulp.

More taps of the keyboard. "Return flights are eleven hundred pounds. Each."

Any lingering hopes of salvaging the situation are dashed. Even if we spent five nights in New York's fabled drunk tank, the cost of the flights alone would swallow every penny of my overdraft.

"We'll leave it."

Jessica appears to have found her smile again—my stupidity has clearly added some colour to her otherwise dull day. She grins up at me as I snatch the fake booking confirmation and screw it into a ball. But, as bad as I feel, I know worse is to come.

I take my mute fiancée by the arm and lead her away from the check-in desk. Her silence, I know, is the calm before the storm. This is far, far worse than the bathroom scales or ill-fitting lingerie.

We come to a stop. "Honey, I'm so sorry …"

"Don't, Adam. Just don't."

Her usually radiant blue eyes are empty. She then shakes her head and walks away.

"Wait. I've got an idea."

She stops and her shoulders slump. Slowly, she turns around.

"What?"

I scurry over and grasp the final straw.

"We passed a hotel on the way in. I know it's not the same, but we could check-in for the night, and have a mooch around the area."

Her expression is unreadable.

"Honey? What do you think?"

"What do I think?"

"Yes."

The quickening rise and fall of her chest suggests a tantrum is brewing. Perhaps I've unwittingly managed to make the situation worse—a quite remarkable achievement considering the circumstances.

"You've got to be fucking kidding," she snarls. "I wanted to see Central Park, The Statue of Liberty and Times Square. What I don't want to see, Adam, is the inside of a shitty hotel in Heathrow. Nor do I wish to tour the various industrial estates and car parks of west-fucking-London."

Daisy rarely swears so this is not a good sign. In hindsight, I could have sold the idea a little better, but I don't think it matters now.

"But …"

"I want to go home. Now!"

Those were the last words Daisy said to me for the entirety of the Christmas period. Not even a word of thanks when she opened her present—a New York guide book I planned to give her when we arrived at the hotel I never actually booked. Seemed a shame to waste it, and I thought she'd at least enjoy reading about the places we planned to visit.

My mistake. Again.

3.

After one too many silent nights Daisy finally relented, but not before setting a new record. For nine long days she steadfastly ignored me; offering only the occasional grunt or scornful tut. I spent New Year's Eve in Coventry—not literally; that would have been truly awful—but she did mumble something about me being an "inconsiderate tosser," just before she went to bed at ten-thirty. Progress, I thought.

Unlike this bastardly cold January morning, relations did eventually thaw and we're now on speaking terms, but only on condition I re-book our New York trip for the spring. I've no idea how I'm going to pay for it, but that's tomorrow's problem.

Today's problem is getting Alan to start. I can't recall who came up with the name for my unreliable van but I kind of like it. On mornings like this, when Alan refuses to start, I can try to reason with him rather than kick his rusty bumpers.

"Come on, Alan. You know you want to."

I turn the key for the sixth time. The engine wheezes and whines like a fat man on a treadmill, but it ends in disappointment.

Nothing left but to beg. "Please, Alan. Don't do this to me."

At the seventh attempt the engine finally splutters into life.

"Yeah! Go, Alan," I whoop, thumping the steering wheel.

I'll assume the sudden screaming of the fan belt is Alan's way of joining the celebration.

I glance over my shoulder to check I've not forgotten anything and pull away. A quick trip across town and I arrive at the first house of the day.

When people ask what I do for a living, I tell them I run my own business. I always hope they don't press the subject because I'd rather not confess it's just a window cleaning round. It is what it is I suppose; and seeing as I've been fired from fourteen different jobs, self-employment was the only career option remaining. There are perks, however. I work the hours I choose and there's very little required in terms of equipment: ladders, a bucket, a cloth, a squeegee, and a spray bottle containing my homemade cleaning solution. Very little to break, fail, or crash; if you exclude Alan.

I knock on the door of the semi-detached house and wait. One of the first lessons I learnt in this business is to check if anyone is home before I make a start. Despite the popular misconception, my courtesy knock isn't to warn a sexy, scantily clad housewife of my presence. I'm far more likely to find a chubby man wearing his wife's underwear, or a teenage lad enjoying his first wank of the day. Awkward, for all concerned.

Mrs Carlton, a fifty-something housewife, opens the door.

"Good morning, Adam."

"Morning, Mrs Carlton, and a happy New Year."

And thanks for the three pound Christmas tip, you tight-fisted crone.

"To you too," she replies curtly, handing me the fifteen pounds due. "Let me know when you're done."

With a withering smile, she closes the door. I tuck the notes in my pocket and return to Alan.

I spend the next forty minutes diligently cleaning Mrs Carlton's eight windows and two doors. She is one of my more fastidious customers and actually checks my work upon completion. Her demanding nature suggests Mrs Carlton might be the type to critique her husband's sexual performance: *lacked vigour and the ending was a disappointment. Two stars.*

As satisfied as she's ever likely to be, Mrs Carlton completes her inspection while I load my kit back into Alan. I seem to spend an inordinate amount of time loading and unloading, but until the day I can move a twelve foot ladder without using a van, it's a cross I have to bear.

I move on to the next customer's house, just a hundred yards up the road.

By three o'clock I've completed the eight houses on today's schedule. Eight houses a day, five days a week, for four solid weeks—then repeat from the beginning. On average, I clean the windows of almost a hundred and eighty houses every month. At best, it's an existence. Many of my former schoolmates, except for Joe, have achieved their life goals: marriages, mortgages, proper careers, and kids—some of them are even happy. My list of life goals still has four empty boxes awaiting a tick.

The one I've come closest to fulfilling is a wedding. I proposed to Daisy in Paris last year and much to my surprise, she accepted. Then it began. I naively assumed we could get married in a registry office and then head to the pub for cocktail sausages and a shit disco. Fat chance. By the time I step down the aisle of a church, rather than a registry office, it will be more than two years beyond the date I first proposed. This is now a military-grade exercise in planning, with a budget to match.

The only consolation is I'm not picking up the twenty grand tab: a fact Daisy's father, Eddie, likes to remind me of every time I complain.

There are, however, some things in life worth waiting for, and Daisy is one of them.

With my round complete, I decide I'd better make a long overdue visit to my parents while I'm in the area. I promised, and promptly forgot, to pop in and see them on Christmas Eve so I'll no doubt receive a ticking off. Still, there might be homemade mince pies left over, so it's not all bad.

After another nervy attempt to start Alan, I make my way to their suburban cul-de-sac.

My parents have lived in Rosemary Gardens for as long as I can remember. It was my childhood home and, together with my younger sister, Kate, we were the very epitome of a nuclear family. My dad, up until he retired last year, was a financial planning consultant, and my mum a school administrator. We were, I suppose, boringly ordinary—at least up until the gherkin incident; the initial trigger after which I became the mildly dysfunctional element of family life.

Once I've abandoned Alan in the cul-de-sac, I plod down the path and unlock the front door.

For a man in his thirties to still have a key to his parent's house, and unfettered access to his childhood bedroom, is telling. Today I unlock the front door at an unusually stable stage of life, but many a time I've arrived seeking refuge from an angry partner or unforgiving landlord and, in both instances, usually skint. God knows how, but I've managed to stay out of that damn bedroom for almost two years now.

I open the door and kick my trainers off.

"Mum? Dad?" I holler down the hallway.

"Is that you, Adam?" Mum calls back.

"No. It's Kate—just popped in to say I've had gender realignment."

I make my way along the hallway and open the door to the kitchen.

"Oh, you remembered where we live then?" Mum chides, the second I enter.

I step across the lino to the breakfast table where she's seated, and plant a kiss on her cheek. "Yeah, sorry, Mum. Had a bit of a situation with Daisy over Christmas."

Her reaction to another of my situations is no longer one of surprise, or even disappointment. The crease across her forehead is now just a sign of resigned acceptance.

"Do you want me to make up your bed?"

"You always assume the worst, Mum," I complain, while taking a seat at the table. "And for your information, the situation is now resolved."

"Amicably?"

"Yes, amicably."

"So, if I call Daisy she'll tell me everything is fine will she?"

"Yes. Probably."

Eyes roll, and her scowl deepens. I'm pretty sure Mum is in her mid-sixties, but even so, her face bares more lines than it probably should. I wouldn't be surprised if her hair turning prematurely white was also down to my antics. She now looks like God's haggard elder sister, although I'd never dare tell her that—well, not again.

"So, did you have a good Christmas?" I ask, changing the subject.

Her face brightens. "Oh, we had a lovely time at Kate's."

"Great," I reply with a thin smile. "How is she?"

It's strange to think that Kate and I evolved from the same gene pool; such are the differences between us. She is everything I'm not, and I'm everything she despises.

"They're all wonderful. Little Arabella is taking piano lessons now and she's quite taken to it. She performed a lovely rendition of *Away in a Manger* for us."

I'm not going to lie and say it doesn't sting when I see the pride in Mum's eyes. I honestly can't recall the last time I saw that same pride for any of my accomplishments. Granted, I haven't accomplished much, but that's hardly the point.

"How old is she now?"

"Arabella? She's just turned six."

"And Kate forces her to take piano lessons? That's verging on child abuse."

"Don't be silly. She loves it. And besides, don't you remember how musical you were at that age?"

"No."

"Yes you do. Your father and I came to that recital in primary school."

"Did you?"

"Yes, you played … what was it?"

"The wood block."

"Ahh, yes," she replies, wistfully. "And beautifully too."

"Mum, I repeatedly hit a lump of wood with a stick. It was the beginning and end of my aspirations for a career in music."

Her eyes glaze over as she recalls possibly the last moment of pride in her son.

"And how's Ethan?" I ask.

I really couldn't care less about my pretentious brother-in-law's well-being, but it's preferable to Mum reminiscing over the model child I once was.

"He's very well. Did I tell you he's now a senior partner?"

"Yes, you did. Several times, as it goes."

"They're looking to move home soon."

"Why would they move? Their current house is too big for the three of them."

She ignores my question and gets up. "Tea?"

"Please."

I don't need Mum to answer the question, really—what's the point in having money if you can't use it to make everyone else feel inferior. Ethan is a golf-playing, sweater-wearing, Porsche-driving, smug-faced twat of the highest order. We don't get on.

"How are the wedding plans coming along?" Mum calls across the kitchen.

"Yeah, great," I reply with little interest.

"Have you chosen a best man yet?"

"Joe, obviously."

She puts the tea canister back in the cupboard and turns to me. "Really, Adam? Could you not find someone a little more responsible?"

"He's my best mate. He'd be mortified if I didn't ask him."

"You know who'd make a great best man?"

Don't even think it, Mother, let alone say it.

"No."

"Ethan."

"I don't like Ethan."

As she waits for the kettle to boil, she turns and faces me.

"Why not? He's a charming man."

"No, Mum. He's an arrogant prick."

"Adam! Language!"

"Sorry, but you made me swear. I'd rather have Dad organise my stag do than bloody Ethan."

"And what's that supposed to mean, young man?"

"Nothing. It's just that Dad is very … sensible. And who wants a sensible stag do?"

She scowls at me before returning her attention to the boiling kettle. Almost on cue, Dad appears in the doorway with a glass of red wine in hand.

"Someone mention my name?" he chuckles.

"Alright, Dad?"

He wanders over and pats me on the head like a wayward dog. "I'm good, son. How's life treating you? We missed you at Christmas."

He looks down at me with his kindly blue eyes; the spotlights in the ceiling reflecting off his bald dome.

"Yeah, sorry. Had a few complications at home."

Dad is far less judgy than Mum and simply returns a knowing smile. I put that down to his appetite for wine, and the fact he's perpetually tipsy. Seemingly, having an interest in fine wine is now the acceptable, middle-class face of borderline alcoholism. As Dad has to live with my mother, I'll forgive him.

"Adam was saying he'd like you to organise his stag party, dear," Mum calls across the kitchen.

Dad looks at me. I look at him. We both try to hide our respective horror before I turn back to Mum.

"Um, not quite what I said was it?"

She shuffles over to the table and places two cups down.

"You said you'd prefer your father to organise your stag party over Ethan."

Shit. Did I?

"I … what?"

"It's alright, son," Dad interjects. "I think I see the point you were trying to make. Don't panic."

"I've never liked that Joe," Mum continues. "He's a bad influence on you."

"He's alright."

"He's always been trouble," she adds.

"Drop it, Mum. I'm not having Ethan as my best man, or Dad for that matter."

I turn to my father. "No offence, Dad."

"None taken."

The discussion ends with one parent disappointed and the other mildly offended, or perhaps relieved. I'll chalk that one down as a victory.

We sit and drink tea, but there are no mince pies left, allegedly. Something tells me Mum is punishing my insubordination by withholding her baked goods. I'll have the last laugh though, as they're selling-off mince pies at the petrol station. They might be out-of-date, but I will not be denied.

Parental duties completed, I get up from the table and say my goodbyes. I almost make it out of the kitchen when Mum chucks a spanner in my plan to beat the rush-hour traffic.

"Oh, Adam. Did your father tell you about the bowls tournament?"

I look across at Dad. He takes a gulp of wine and shrugs his shoulders.

"No he didn't," I reply.

"Yes, he's made the semi-finals."

"Great. Well done, Dad. Anyway … better be going."

I turn to leave.

"It's this Saturday," Mum adds.

"Is it? Right."

Quick. Think of an excuse.

"I, um … think I might be going to a wedding fair with Daisy."

"All day?"

"Maybe. I don't know."

Mum gets up from the table. "I'll see you out."

I offer a final nod to Dad and scuttle back down the hallway with Mum hot on my heels. I make it to the front door but she grabs my arm before I can escape.

"You've got a very short memory, young man," she hisses.

"What?"

"Do you remember playing for that football team?"

"Ramsey Colts? When I was a kid?"

"Yes, that football team."

"Vaguely."

"And do you know how many seasons you played for them?"

"Dunno. Two or three?"

"Four."

"I'm not sure where you're going with this, Mum, but I'm in a bit of a hurry."

"I'll tell you where I'm going with this," she snaps. "Your father got up at the crack of dawn every Saturday during the season and drove you all over the place. He went out in all weathers and watched you play, yet he never complained, and never once let you down, did he?"

Mum's point is made, albeit in a roundabout way. A sudden sense of guilt descends, not least because I know she's right and I should have considered it myself.

"Okay, I get it. I'll be there."

"You promise?"

"Yeah, yeah. What time is it?"

"Two o'clock at the leisure centre, and don't let me down, Adam. He'd never tell you himself but he'd really appreciate your support—this means an awful lot to your father."

"Alright."

She plants a perfunctory kiss on my cheek and opens the front door. "See you Saturday then."

I skulk back to Alan and sit for a moment—the nagging guilt beside me in the passenger seat. Over the years, Dad has always treated my behaviour with a degree of empathy and pragmatism. Mum, on the other hand, tends to let her emotions rule. She's never left me in any doubt I'm a disappointment, especially when compared to saintly Kate. Dad though, is an eternal optimist and I suspect he still believes I'll turn my life around one day. I do love both my parents, but I feel more of a bond with Dad; and for that reason I could kick myself for not returning his support for once.

Under a now-dark sky, Alan starts on the second turn of the key and I reverse away from the kerb. At the same moment, my phone rings. I then simultaneously conduct a three-point turn while answering Joe's call.

"Alright, Joe?"

"Yeah, good. Got time for a quick pint?"

I try to turn the wheel full lock with one hand while considering Joe's offer.

"Um …"

"Come on. Just a quick one."

Having turned the wheel, I tug the gearstick backwards and reverse, while also trying to check the clock on the dashboard.

I've been told many times, by many people—I shouldn't multi-task. A loud thump booms from behind me.

"What the fuck was that?" Joe yells down the phone.

"Dunno. Give me a second."

I drop the phone on the passenger seat and open the door. As I look towards Alan's rear, I'm relieved not to see another car. However, the loud thump I heard suggests I hit something. After a quick look around to ensure none of the residents saw or heard anything, I get out and inspect the damage. Thankfully, I only find an upturned wheelie bin and a trail of rubbish strewn across the pavement.

Pick it up? No, fuck it.

After quickly checking I haven't added yet another dent to Alan's bodywork, I return to my seat and grab the phone.

"Hit a wheelie bin. No harm."

"Nice one. So, Red Lion in ten minutes?"

"Just a swift half?"

"Yeah."

"Alright. See you shortly."

Just popping to the pub for a swift half. In the league of lies we tell ourselves and our partners, that one must rank pretty highly.

Not tonight, though—I must resist.

4.

The Red Lion has amassed forty-seven reviews on TripAdvisor, with an overall rating of two-stars; a fact Vince, the landlord, is quite proud of.

"It means we're not absolutely shit," he once proclaimed.

I've always considered the two-stars a fairly generous rating. I actually gave it a solitary star, and that's only because Vince allows the occasional lock-in. Situated in a downtrodden part of town, it's frequented by too many overly opinionated, middle-aged men who won't stand for any of that 'foreign muck' the previous landlord naively tried adding to the menu. Yes, I choose to drink in a pub where lamb tagine is actually barred, but it's handy for my flat.

I squeeze Alan into a parking space and head in through the back door.

The saloon bar is devoid of charm, or patrons. I think it was Dad who told me that apparently many pubs originally had a separate public and saloon bar because women weren't allowed in the public bar. Not an issue in this day and age as very few women ever frequent the Red Lion. Daisy popped in once and, after experiencing the ladies toilets, vowed never to return. Beyond the odd guest appearance by a regular's wife or girlfriend, the only female faces we see are the landlady, Marion, and Handy Mandy, a toothless harridan who'll happily administer a hand job in the car park in return for a double gin.

Vince appears, looking as miserable as a wet weekend in Rhyl.

"Adam," he grunts.

"Vince. Usual please."

He plucks a glass from a shelf and pulls almost a pint of gassy lager. The glass is then unceremoniously dumped on the bar.

"Three-fifty."

I look at the pint and then at Vince. "I'll come back for the rest later, shall I?"

He mumbles something unintelligible before reluctantly topping it up. I hand over the exact change and check my phone to ensure I haven't missed a text or call from Daisy.

Relieved there are no messages, I grab my pint and head to the fruit machine.

It's a shame I never inherited my dad's aptitude for number crunching because it would be interesting to calculate how much money I've lost to fruit machines over the years. Although, thinking about it, perhaps I'd rather not know. Or would I?

Still undecided, I grab a handful of change from my pocket and deposit the first pound.

Five minutes in and a voice yells across the bar. "Adam. Pint?"

I turn around to find Joe stood at the bar; looking his usual scruffy self. His straggly ginger hair is typically left to its own devices, and his jowly chops bristle with translucent stubble. Daisy once suggested Joe might benefit from a thorough scrub in a bath of disinfectant. She's probably right.

I give him a thumbs-up before returning my attention to the fruit machine. Three spins remaining. The first spin delivers a bell, a cherry and a lemon, and the second spin two melons and an orange. The buttons flash for my final spin and I hold the two melons.

"What you got?" Joe asks, handing me a pint.

"Cheers mate. Got two melons on hold."

I hit the play button and the reel spins. The third melon plops into place.

"Nice one. That's a fiver isn't it?"

"Yeah. Exactly what I've put into the bloody thing."

I'm about to hit the collect button but the flashing lights offer temptation. It's a simple gamble—one tap of a button and I double my winnings to ten pounds, or lose the fiver. I can either walk away with the same amount of money I started with, or I walk away five pounds in profit. It doesn't even cross my mind I might lose.

I hit the gamble button.

"Bollocks."

"Bad luck, matey."

I let out a resigned sigh and step away from the machine. "Poxy thing is rigged."

We take our pints to a table and sit down.

"So much for a half," Joe comments, nodding towards my second pint.

He knows me too well. In fact, Joe knows me better than pretty-much anyone, as we've been friends since infant school.

"Yeah, well. I'm drowning my sorrows now."

"You lost a fiver. Get over it."

"It's the principle," I grumble. "Anyway, I'm only having

the two pints. I'm already in Daisy's bad books after the New York trip."

"The trip that never was?"

"Yeah, that one."

"You're an idiot."

"Am I?" I reply with mock surprise. "Because you've only told me that every week for the last twenty-seven years."

"Truth hurts, eh?"

"Fuck off."

I take a sip of my second pint, conscious it must be my last.

"Anyway, why have you dragged me out on a Tuesday evening?"

"Do two old mates need a reason to have a pint?"

"Not usually, but it's a Tuesday. When was the last time we had a beer on a Tuesday?"

"March 2014," he replies matter-of-factly.

"Really? You remember that?"

"Course I don't, dickhead. But, as it happens, there was something I wanted to talk to you about."

"Oh, God," I groan. "Not another one of your business ideas?"

"If you're going to be like that," he huffs. "I'll keep it to myself."

Joe thinks himself something of an entrepreneur. He would be correct if the definition of entrepreneur meant running a spectacularly unsuccessful web design business and developing a stream of terrible business ideas. Ironically, the window cleaning round I've operated for the last two years has proven more successful than any of Joe's ventures. If I was being honest, we're both fairly inept at everything, yet somehow—probably because the bar is set so low—Maxwell's Window Cleaning Service has become a shining light of success in the black void that is our mutual careers.

"Go on," I sigh. "What is it this time?"

He leans across the table and replies in a hushed voice. "Keep this to yourself, right?"

I slowly turn and survey the empty bar. "Joe, I don't think Richard Branson is hiding behind the pool table."

He glances around, just in case, and continues. "Okay, this is the big one."

"I'm listening."

"Dog crap."

"Dog crap?"

"Yeah—collection and disposal thereof."

I remain silent as Joe sits back in his chair. "What do you reckon then?"

I stare back at him, open mouthed. "Wow!"

"I knew you'd love it," he incorrectly assumes.

"No, Joe. That wasn't a good wow. It was a what-the-fuck-are-you-on kind of wow."

"Don't be too dismissive, mate. Think about it. There are millions of dogs in the country and plenty of owners who either can't or won't clear up all that mess. There must be tons and tons of dog crap left lying around every day. Somebody has to deal with it, right?"

"I'm not denying it's a problem but I fail to see how that makes it a business opportunity."

"Firstly, we offer a domestic collection service where we collect the waste from people's gardens. They could let their dog merrily shit away and then we pitch up once a week and collect it all."

"Are people really that lazy?"

"Yeah, course they are, but then there's the commercial market too. We could do work for local councils, schools ..."

"Schools?" I interject.

"Playing fields. People think it's okay to let their dogs shit in fields. That's a fact."

"Is it? Is it really?"

"Course it is."

I sit back and absorb Joe's literally shit idea. Is it really that ridiculous? I've lost count how many times I've trod in dog shit while walking home from the pub, so maybe there's something in it.

"And nobody else is doing it," he adds enthusiastically. "We'd have the market to ourselves, and then once it's proven, we could even look at franchising the business model. Think about it, mate—in five years' time we could have a hundred franchises up and down the country, all making us a tidy sum every month."

Keen not to get too swept away with Joe's enthusiasm, I consider a few of the more practical issues.

"What would we do with all the ... waste?"

"At first we'd just flush it down the loo."

"Is that legal?"

"Who'd know? I've calculated that three dog turds are roughly the same size as one human turd. You could probably get away with flushing four or five at a time. And once the business has grown, and that's no longer practical, we could invest in some sort of septic tank."

"You've obviously thought about this at some length."

"For a week now and, besides the labour and disposal cost, there aren't any other overheads. It's brilliantly simple, mate."

I empty my glass and let my imagination drift. A picture floats into my head; a fleet of liveried vans outside an impressive head office. Then I think about a big house, much bigger than Kate and Ethan's, with a Mercedes parked outside. My parents would visit my lovely house and Mum would shed tears of pride.

"So?" Joe interrupts. "What do you think?"

I pause for effect. "It's got legs. Definitely."

"I've even designed a brand, and the name."

"Go on."

He clears his throat. "Scoopy Poo."

"As in, Scooby Doo?"

"Yeah. Do you like it?"

"Not really."

"Got any better ideas?"

Before I can answer, Joe gets to his feet. "You want another beer while you're thinking about it?"

The third pint is the pint of no return. It leads to a land of bad decisions and worse outcomes. I should know by now never to venture there, especially when I'm expected home about now. Problem is: beer is moreish, and I'm weak-willed.

"Yeah, one more won't hurt. I'll walk home and collect Alan in the morning."

Joe wanders off to the bar, content to buy another round if it keeps me in the pub for another half hour. I check my phone again and there's still nothing from Daisy, suggesting she's not arrived home to an empty flat yet. I toy with the idea of sending her a message to say I'm just having a quick pint with Joe, but that will only pour fuel on a spark yet to ignite. If I pick up her favourite Chinese takeaway on the way home, I'm sure that'll make up for the fact I haven't cooked dinner. Again.

Content I've bought myself some time, I put my phone away as Joe returns with more beer.

"Come up with anything?" he asks.

"Um, how about … Super Scoopers?"

He ponders my suggestion, perhaps annoyed it's better than his.

"That's not bad," he finally admits. "I'll think about it."

"You do that and, in the interim, why don't you tell me what we're going to charge people to pluck shit from their lawn."

"It's a simple pricing structure—one pound per unit."

"Unit?"

"Yeah. I think it sounds better to call them units rather than shits."

"Fair point, but surely an Alsatian is going to create far bigger … units than, say, a Pug. Surely there should be a different pricing structure based on the size of the dog?"

"Let's not get bogged-down in the detail. There's always room to haggle if it becomes an issue."

"Right, and what about marketing? I can't see many people searching on Google for a service like ours."

"I'll deal with all the marketing and build a really cool website."

"Shouldn't we hire a professional?"

"Very funny."

For the next two hours, and another three pints, we discuss every detail of the new venture. It's not the first time we've sat in the Red Lion and enthusiastically downed beer while plotting our path to business success. Many ideas have been floated, fuelled by alcohol and naïve idealism, and deemed to be the next big thing. To date, no idea has ever gone beyond the drunken planning stage.

At eight o'clock I call an end to our meeting and leave Joe to reflect on the next stage of our plan. I've also had far too much to drink to think rationally; not that I'm prone to rational thought when sober, but the drink doesn't help.

I head to the Chinese takeaway and leave with two portions of Daisy's favourite Singapore noodles. She still hasn't called or texted which is either a good thing, or not a very good thing. I'll find out which soon enough.

Our rented flat is on the first floor of a converted Edwardian house in Mason Street. The street itself is lined with similar, once-grand properties, which have all been converted into either flats or bedsits; and the residents' lack of pride in their rented accommodation is obvious. Every property bears some scar of neglect: blown render, cracked windows, missing tiles, flaking paint and front gardens littered with … well, litter. It's hard to imagine now, but this was once a desirable street where affluent people lived. Even in the dark, under the soft glow of street lamps, there's no hiding the fact it's a shit-hole of a street. It's what we can afford, though.

I scoot through the communal hallway and head up the stairs; the scent of the noodles piquing my hunger with every step. After fumbling for my keys, I open the front door to darkness.

"Hello," I call out. "Sorry I'm late."

No response. Not a good sign.

I head straight to the kitchen and switch the light on. A note has been fixed to the centre of the fridge door where it can't be missed, even by me.

No dinner and no you, so I've gone out with my parents for a meal. Don't wait up. X

My immediate thought is to head back to the Red Lion. I'm actually quite annoyed Daisy didn't ring as I wouldn't have left in the first place if I'd known she was out. Still, I now have two portions of Singapore noodles to myself, and there's beer in the fridge. Every cloud.

I grab a fork from the drawer, a beer from the fridge, and wander through to the lounge. TV on, cushions removed from the sofa, I flop down and hungrily fork noodles straight from the container; only stopping for the occasional slurp of cold beer. The only fly in my manly ointment is the programme on TV— one of those property shows where unrealistic house hunters ignore good advice and end up staying where they are. Tonight's show features a deluded couple from Kent who turn down every property because they're convinced the market is about to crash and they'll soon be able to afford a mansion for the price of a new car.

I watch the final twenty minutes with more agitation than interest.

Once Karl and Sarah have smugly declared they're staying put, and both noodle containers are empty, I return to the kitchen and retrieve the three remaining cans of my four-pack. Rather than putting on warmer clothes, I turn the heating up a few notches and return to the sofa.

Two more beers are dispatched and, with no sign of Daisy, I slip into a dream world of gold-plated dog faeces and castles in Kent.

5.

"Adam! Get up!"

Judging by the edge in Daisy's voice, my assumption was correct.

I open my eyes to find my fiancée stood over me, still dressed in her pink pyjamas.

"Sleep well?" she snaps.

Slowly my brain processes sufficient information to answer. I'm lying on the sofa in the lounge, still clothed, and it's hotter than a Turkish sauna.

"I … what time is it?"

"Half-seven, and it absolutely stinks in here."

I tentatively sniff the air. She's not wrong.

The window is opened before Daisy corrals her precious cushions and returns them to the sofa. I'm clearly in the way, so I sit up and try not to appear as hungover as I feel.

"Did you have a nice evening?" I timidly enquire.

"Not the evening I planned."

"No, sorry."

"Would it have killed you to text me?"

"I … um."

"Save it, Adam. I've heard it all before."

With that, she turns and leaves. A few seconds later I hear the sound of cupboard doors being slammed in the kitchen. Clearly Daisy isn't happy with me, but perhaps if I explain what I was doing in the pub; it might calm her down a little. She desperately wants to move to a nicer flat and my new business opportunity might just offer us that chance.

I get up and head into a dragon's den far more intimidating than the one on television.

Besides the rumbling of the kettle, I'm met with a stony silence. Daisy is leant against the counter; her arms folded and expression hostile.

"Honey, can I at least explain why I was in the pub?"

"No."

"Come on," I plead. "Just hear me out. I've got some exciting news."

"Oh, Jesus," she groans. "Not again."

"Eh?"

"Do you remember the last time you announced exciting

news?"

Ah ... now she's mentioned it.

"This doesn't involve New York, honey."

"Neither did your last announcement as it turned out."

"You're never going to let me forget that, are you?"

"Never is a long time, Adam, but no, I'm not."

She turns around and pours water into a cup. For a fleeting moment I consider asking why she's not making two cups of coffee, but best not to provoke her at this delicate stage of negotiation.

"So, my announcement."

"I'm tired, Adam, and I feel like crap, so just spit it out will you."

"I'm setting up a new business with Joe."

With her back to me I can't see her expression. Maybe she's beaming with pride. She slowly turns around, cup in hand, and if there was ever a beaming smile, it's withered away.

"What?"

"I said, I'm setting up a new business with Joe—that's why I was late last night. We were making plans at the Red Lion."

"You're going into business with a serial loser who still lives with his parents?"

"Don't be mean."

"I'm not. I'm being bluntly honest."

Daisy's assessment might be blunt, but I can't argue it's not an honest one. I do wonder if the reason I'm friends with Joe is simply because he's one of the few people who've failed in life even more miserably than I have; a feat on anyone's scale. For all my many faults at least I don't look like an unwashed, seventeen-stone version of Ed Sheeran. I'm not exactly what you'd call handsome, but to some girls I guess the foppish, boy-next-door look appeals. But, in all the years I've known Joe he's only ever had two girlfriends, and for a combined period of nine weeks. I can't help but feel a bit sorry for him, and someone has to defend the poor bloke.

"Yeah, well, Joe's come up with a great idea."

"Go on then," Daisy scoffs. "I can't wait to hear this."

"We're going to offer a dog waste collection and disposal service."

A mouthful of coffee is promptly spat across the kitchen.

"Oh my days," she coughs. "You two have really excelled yourselves this time."

"Thank you," I reply with a smile. "It means a lot to hear

that."

Her eyes widen and she stares at me, incredulous. "I was being sarcastic, Adam. It's the worst idea in the history of worst ideas."

Pride dented, I launch into a minute-long defence of the idea.

Once I've blown myself out, she calmly puts her cup down and, in the same tone a mother would employ when chiding an errant toddler, offers her feedback.

"I admire your enthusiasm," she sighs. "But, it's … misdirected."

"Why?" I reply with a frown. "Nobody else is doing it."

"Probably for good reason."

"Didn't they say the same thing about Facebook? Nobody had done it before and I bet loads of people told that Zuckerberg bloke it would never catch on."

"Are you really comparing the world's largest social networking website to collecting dog waste from gardens?"

"No, but …"

"And, come to think of it, exactly how are you going to deal with all the waste, assuming anyone will ever hire you?"

"Initially, we'll just flush it down the loo."

A deep crease forms across her forehead. "Who's loo?"

"We'll split it."

"What? You're going to bring bags of dog waste home and …"

Her voice trails off as she stifles a burp.

"I'll do it during the day, when you're not here, and I'll use plenty of air freshener. I promise you won't come home and find any floaters."

I look for signs of positivity in her face but Daisy now looks quite pale, almost sickly. She burps again, followed by some strange gagging noise. Her cheeks then balloon and she darts out of the kitchen. It's only when she's gone do I notice a plate on the side, together with a half-eaten slice of toast topped with chocolate spread.

Oops.

Breakfast was probably not the ideal time to discuss my new venture. I'll try again tonight, and hope we're not having sausages for dinner. Daisy clearly needs a little more convincing.

I make myself a cup of coffee and finish the uneaten toast— it seems a shame to waste it and I think I've inadvertently taken the edge off Daisy's appetite.

By the time I finish my coffee, the sound of retching from the bathroom has been replaced by the whine of the shower pump. I toy with the idea of making Daisy some more toast but the kitchen clock tells me she won't have time. Beyond my misdemeanours, one thing guaranteed to irritate Daisy is being late for anything, especially work. While I can pitch up to clean windows any time I please, the firm of accountants who employ Daisy are less flexible with time keeping.

With nothing else better to do until my fiancée vacates the bathroom, I make myself another cup of coffee and scan the email in-box on my phone. It proves to be the usual fare and, if I suffered from erectile dysfunction or wanted to hook up with sexually frustrated housewives in my neighbourhood, a few of the emails might be of interest. But in amongst all the spam there's also an email from Joe. Sent late last night, he was clearly drunk and it makes my brain hurt trying to decipher it. As I work on unpicking Joe's lager-fuelled enigma, Daisy returns to the kitchen. As ever, she looks amazing, even in the dullest of grey business suits.

"I'm off."

She plants a barely worthwhile kiss on my cheek and turns to leave.

"Oh, and I'm going to be late tonight," she adds. "Probably an hour or so."

"Right. You okay, honey?"

"Fine. Why wouldn't I be?" she asks, a tad defensively.

"Because I discussed our venture over breakfast which probably wasn't the ideal time. Sorry."

"Forget it. See you later."

She grabs her handbag and leaves without another glance in my direction.

It's on mornings like this I'm grateful my career doesn't carry the same weight of responsibility as Daisy's. My job might be unfulfilling, but it never invades my personal life. I probably should have asked, but I suspect she's got a heavy day ahead of her; hence the mood. Saying that, perhaps it's her time of the month—it would explain her feeling crap and the chocolate spread for breakfast. If that is the case then maybe I'll play it safe and give it a few days before seeking further feedback on my new venture.

With Daisy now on her way to work I can get on with my first task of the day which involves an oversized bowl of Coco Pops and a couple of painkillers; both consumed on the sofa and surrounded by more cushions than I swear were here earlier. The damn things must be breeding.

Despite having almost two hours to get my arse in gear, I manage to leave the flat ten minutes late. In some way my lack of accountability isn't ideal because the devil on my shoulder forever taunts me with distractions. Some mornings it takes a Herculean effort not to return to bed for a few hours, particularly in the winter months. If it wasn't for the fact Daisy now checks my books on a weekly basis, I'm sure that's where I'd be about now.

Already late, Alan decides he doesn't want to go to work either.

"Come on, old boy. You can do it."

Apparently he can't. I try again but he steadfastly refuses to start. Time for a different tack.

"Nobody else will put up with your shit, Alan. Start now or your next journey will be to the scrap yard."

Alan coughs into life.

"Yeah, thought that'd change your mind."

We head off to the first house of the day.

An hour later I'm stood at the top of a ladder, frozen to the bone, when the first flake lands on my cheek. I turn my head and examine the sky—now the same depressing shade of grey as my old school jumper. They might have mentioned snow in the weather forecast if I'd had the foresight to check it. You'd think, being that I work outside, it would be part of my daily routine to check the weather. However, the app on my phone lied to me once too often and, in a fit of sodden rage, I deleted it after an unexpected soaking back in August.

"Looks like snow," a voice bellows from below me.

I look down and Mr Bailey, the owner of the house, and tone-deaf pensioner, is staring up at the sky as if awaiting the Four Horsemen of the Apocalypse. If I were him, I'd be more concerned about a visit from the Grim Reaper; such is his appetite for self-rolled cigarettes.

"Yeah, think it's already arrived," I holler back.

"You look frozen," he yells. "Can I get you a brew?"

"Yes, please."

"Sorry. Didn't catch that."

"Please," I shout.

"Cheese?" he mumbles while shaking his head. "I think I've got some left over from Christmas."

Before I can correct him, he wanders back inside while I

consider how to decline his mouldy Stilton … or is it supposed to be mouldy? I'm not sure. Either way, this day is not going well, and cheese isn't going to help.

I give the bedroom window a cursory wipe and clamber back down the ladder. By the time I set foot on the driveway the few flakes have developed into a flurry; whipping into my face courtesy of the bitter wind. If I were still at school, I'd have wet my pants with excitement at this point but as a grown-up, particularly a self-employed grown-up, snow is most unwelcome.

My phone rings. With barely-functioning fingers, I prod the screen to take Joe's call.

"Ah, it's Alan Turing."

"Eh? Who?" he replies, clearly puzzled.

"Your email last night. It was written in some kind of unbreakable code."

"Oh yeah," he chuckles. "I was a bit wankered and couldn't see the keyboard."

"Well, as much as I'd love to know, I'm stood on a punter's driveway at the moment and there's a lump of cheese waiting for me inside."

"Cheese?"

"Don't ask, but it's preferable to cleaning windows in this bloody weather."

"What weather?"

"Have you opened your curtains this morning?"

"No."

"It's snowing, mate, which means I can't work."

"Is it? Brilliant."

"Why is it brilliant? We're not going sledding, if that's what you're thinking."

"No, it means you can join me for the meeting at one o'clock."

"A meeting? With who?"

"One of my clients has a contact in the environmental services department at the council. Anyway, I called him this morning to see if we could meet, to discuss the business idea, and he agreed. I'm meeting him in town at one."

"Right, great … but what are we going to discuss in this meeting?"

"Dunno. Haven't thought that far ahead but maybe we can ask if our service would be of interest to the council. It'd be a bloody good start to get a council contract, don't you think?"

"Yeah, it would."

"Right, I'll meet you at the Wheelwright Arms at half twelve, and wear a suit."

"A suit?"

"Got to look the part. See you later."

He hangs up. Now, I don't know if fate is a real thing, but maybe the snow and the meeting are a sign I'm supposed to follow. I remember Dad used to have this poster in his office of a desert highway splitting in two directions. At the top, in big black letters, it read: you often find fate on the path you take to avoid it. I've never really given that poster any thought until now. Ordinarily, I'd avoid meeting Joe in a pub at lunchtime because it never ends well, but perhaps the poster I haven't thought about in years is a message in itself. I've got to do this—fate is sending me on a path I would usually avoid.

And besides, there's sod all on TV this afternoon.

6.

As it transpires, Mr Bailey's cheese was rather pleasant. Granted, it was a bit strange standing in the old man's kitchen while he watched me nibble on a chunk of Red Leicester, but at least I didn't offend him. I think he was secretly pleased to have some company and, as I left, he promised to have a better selection next time I call.

By the time I coaxed Alan back onto our driveway the snow had turned into sleet, and the little that had settled quickly became a grey mush. Typical half-arsed British weather.

Once I'm back in the flat and thawed out, I scour the wardrobes in search of my one-and-only suit; a charcoal number procured for weddings, funerals, and court dates—not that I've had any of those for a while. Amazingly, it still fits, but less amazingly, I still don't know how to knot a tie. I try following an online video but after delivering two uppercuts to my own chin, I give up. Sod it—ties are old hat these days anyway. I'll go without one, and people will just assume I'm nonchalantly cool, rather than incapable of tying a simple knot.

Knowing I'll be having a pint or two, and the town centre pub doesn't have a car park, I leave Alan on the driveway and take a brisk twenty minute walk. Another sure sign this day is fated comes with a break in the sleet. I'm definitely on a roll.

Despite being a generic chain pub, The Wheelwright Arms is several steps, and stars, up from the Red Lion. They even have such luxuries as hot water and toilet paper, and the food is near edible. I find Joe already propped up against the bar with a pint in hand.

"Nice suit," he remarks.

"Thanks. And nice … what is that exactly?"

"A cravat, obviously."

"I thought as much, but then I thought: why would Joe wear something only an enormous bellend would wear?"

"You really are behind the times," he grumbles. "All the hipsters are wearing them."

"Err, no. You're thinking of a bow tie, mate."

"What?"

"Hipsters wear bow ties, not cravats."

"Whatever. Pint?"

Joe hails the barman while surreptitiously removing the

lurid yellow cravat. He did make an effort though, and I feel a little guilty for pointing out his error, but someone had to tell him.

We take our pints over to a table. With only twenty-five minutes to spare before our esteemed guest arrives, a plan of action is urgently required.

"Tell me about this bloke then. What do you know?"

"Not a lot," Joe confesses. "He works in the environmental services department and his name is Gary Tomkins."

"Is that it?"

"Yeah."

"And what precisely are we going to discuss with him?"

"I've got some questions written down."

Joe then extracts a crumpled sheet of paper from the inside pocket of an equally crumpled jacket and lays it on the table. It doesn't take long for me to digest his list of questions.

"Is that it, Joe? Four questions? One of which is 'how are you?'"

He looks at me puzzled. "Shouldn't we ask? I thought it was polite."

"Eh … what? Yes, we should ask, but why write it down?"

"In case we forget."

I shake my head in despair and return to the three remaining questions.

"Assuming a question about his general wellbeing is a given, let's see what else you have here."

"Cool."

"Question two: what is the council's current policy on dogs crapping in gardens?"

"Yeah. That'd be useful to know, right?"

I scratch my head. "Would they even have a policy on that?"

"Dunno. That's why I put it down."

"Fair enough. Question three: who is in charge of dog waste in the council?"

"Makes sense. We need to deal with the top bloke."

"Or woman."

"You think it might be a woman?"

"I don't know. Does it matter?"

"Probably not."

"Question four: will you pay us to collect all the dog crap from the streets?"

"Good question, eh? No messing around."

"It's direct, I'll give you that."

Joe's sorry list of questions complete, I suddenly fear fate might be toying with me. I cannot imagine two men have ever been less prepared for a meeting than we are. I suppose we'll just have to improvise and see where that leads us.

"What does this Gary Tomkins look like?" I ask.

"How would I know? Never met the bloke."

I cast my gaze across the pub, and the forty-odd random strangers milling around. Any one of them could be Gary Tomkins.

"How the hell are we supposed to know who he is then?"

"Oh, he said he'll be wearing a Hi-Viz jacket."

"Right. Does he always attend meetings in a Hi-Viz jacket?"

"Dunno, but it's probably some health and safety thing. You know what it's like these days."

On cue, and impossible to miss, a man appears at the bar, sporting a luminous, but filthy, green jacket.

"Here's our man," Joe squawks. "Let's do this."

We get up and amble over to the man we hope is Gary Tomkins. Once we get within ten feet, I already have concerns as Mr Tomkins looks nothing like what I imagine an office-dwelling council official looks like. I don't think it's his size— I'm sure the council don't have a policy on employing the obese. Nor is it his filthy jeans or steel toe-capped boots. It's not even his greasy hair and week-old stubble. For me, the real clincher is the spider web tattoo covering much of his neck.

Undeterred, and seemingly oblivious to my concerns, Joe thrusts out his hand. "Mr Tomkins? I'm Joseph Faulkner, we spoke on the phone. And this is my business partner, Adam Maxwell."

"Alright?" Mr Tomkins replies in a gruff voice. He shakes both our hands but I get the feeling it's not how he usually introduces himself.

"Pint of lager," he then adds. "You're buying the drinks, right?"

"Yes, of course," Joe responds.

Having acquired Mr Tomkin's pint, the three of us return to the table. As we walk, Joe wastes no time in getting his first question in.

"How are you?"

Mr Tomkins glares back at him, as if Joe had asked to examine his prostate.

"What do you care?" he grunts in reply.

"Forget it," Joe wisely concedes.

We sit down and Mr Tomkins promptly necks half his pint in one go. I look at Joe and tap my pocket in the hope he takes the hint.

"Right, yes," he splutters before extracting his list of questions. "So, Mr Tomkins. Firstly, thank you for agreeing to see us this afternoon."

"No skin off my nose, mate. You keep the beers coming and I'm happy."

"We will."

An uncomfortable silence falls on the table as Joe seems unsure which of his questions to ask first. As it happens, I have a few questions of my own, and decide to interject.

"How long have you worked for the council, Mr Tomkins?"

"About twenty years."

"And has that always been in the environmental services department?"

"The what?"

"Environmental services. You know … waste management and the like."

"Yeah, yeah, gotcha. Waste management."

I'm not sure he answered my question, but I press on. "And what exactly is your role in waste management?"

Mr Tomkins turns his attention to Joe.

"Is he taking the piss?" he growls.

Joe shakes his head. "Um, no."

Mr Tomkins returns his glare to me. "Are you taking the piss?"

"Err, no. I just wondered what your role was at the council."

"I drive a fucking bin lorry, don't I."

I look across at Joe. People say it takes more facial muscles to frown than smile. All I know is there are not nearly enough muscles to convey my annoyance, and Joe is trying hard to avoid my glare anyway. God only knows how, but it looks like I now have to fix his balls-up.

"I'm sorry, Mr Tomkins. I think there's been a bit of a mix up."

"Mix up?"

"Yes, I think my colleague here got the wrong end of the stick. We were hoping to meet somebody who works in the council offices."

"And?"

"And … you don't."

"So? What's your point?"

"In a nutshell, the meeting is over."

Mr Tomkins empties his glass. I assume he got the message, right up until he bangs his empty glass on the table.

"I was promised free beer," he growls. "The meeting is over when I say it's over."

Any man willing to endure hours of a tattoo needle piercing his neck is clearly not a man to be messed with. Now what? Do we just sit with this angry bin-man all afternoon until he passes out? He looks the sort of bloke who could easily neck a dozen pints and still do a day's work, so it could be a long afternoon if that's the plan.

Alternatively, we could simply get up and walk away.

I stand up and straighten my jacket. Never have I felt more overdressed.

"Where are you going?" Mr Tomkins grunts.

"The meeting is over. I'm going home."

"Sit the fuck down. Now!"

I sit back and throw another glare at Joe.

"Get me another pint, then," Mr Tomkins adds.

"Now you want me to get up?"

"Yeah and be quick about it."

"Want to give me a hand, Joe?" I ask, getting to my feet.

"He's staying here."

Great.

Joe looks up at me and, clearly not thrilled with the prospect of being left alone with Mr Tomkins, offers a solution of his own.

"Um, how about I just give you some money for beer, Mr Tomkins?"

The angry bin-man ponders Joe's proposal for a few seconds. "How much?"

"Twenty pounds?"

"Forty," Mr Tomkins retorts.

"I've got thirty, but that's it."

"Give it here then."

Joe reluctantly extracts his wallet and hands three ten pound notes over. Without another word, Mr Tomkins snatches the notes, gets up and leaves.

"Another drink is required," I groan. "Same again?"

Joe nods and I head for the bar.

As I wait to be served I take a moment to assess our car crash of a meeting. Thinking about it, perhaps I should have quizzed Joe more thoroughly on the details before agreeing to meet. I've only ever had two reasons to contact the local council: the first time to order a new wheelie bin, and the second to complain about an old fridge someone dumped on our driveway. In both instances, it was a painstaking process involving forms, numerous calls to different departments, and saintly levels of patience. That considered, the fact Joe managed to orchestrate a meeting with a council official within a few hours should have set my alarm bells ringing.

This is the inherent problem with Joe and I—we both act on impulse and rarely pause to consider if we're heading towards yet another clusterfuck of our own making.

I return to the table with our consolation pints.

"That went well," I remark, handing Joe his drink. "If you discount the psychopathic bin-man and thirty quid loss."

"I tried," he mumbles.

"I know. Guess it was too good to be true."

Joe looks at me with the same rueful expression I've born too many times myself. "Sorry, mate."

"Don't worry about it. It's just a setback."

"Yeah, just a setback. I'm going to have stern words with my bloody client though."

"What exactly did he tell you about Mr Tomkins?"

"Not much, just that he knew a bloke who worked for the council."

"Technically, he wasn't wrong."

It would be easy to rib Joe for the rest of the afternoon. However, I know all too well how it feels to be on the receiving end of ridicule for a genuine mistake, so I won't mention it again unless he pleads poverty when it's his round.

"What time you gotta be back?" he asks.

"About six. Daisy's going to be late tonight."

"She's probably having an affair with her boss," he jests. "It always starts with working late."

"Thanks mate. I hadn't considered that until now."

"You're welcome. I'll be here for you when she ditches you."

Not wishing to dwell on Joe's ridiculous theory, and with several hours to kill, I suggest we play pool. Perhaps aimlessly whacking coloured balls around will provide some development inspiration for our business idea. Or not.

We grab our drinks and head through to the bar where the pool table is situated. It seems we weren't the first to have the idea as two women, in their late twenties, are already in the middle of a game. Both have similarly styled, shoulder-length brown hair, and both look like they don't want to be interrupted.

"Shall we wait," Joe whispers.

"Guess so."

We take a seat at a table about ten feet away and watch on. The two women appear to be harbouring some anger issues, judging by the way they strike each ball as if it's a cheating partner's testicle. With no finesse and little skill, very few balls are potted. Inevitably, one shot is hit with such force the cue ball leaves the table and rolls across the floor; coming to a rest at Joe's feet.

The guilty player then approaches and offers a half-smile. For the first time I notice both women are wearing near identical clothes; jeans and a black fleece jacket with a company logo embroidered on the breast.

"Sorry about that," she says. "We're just working off some steam."

I immediately spot a familiar look on Joe's face: a saccharin smile and his haven't-had-sex-in-years eyes.

"No worries," he replies, handing her the cue ball. "Having a bad day?"

Oh, Christ. Here we go.

Despite being knocked-back by virtually every woman he's tried to chat up, Joe never misses an opportunity to add to the tally.

"Could say that," the woman replies. "We were made redundant an hour ago."

"Shit. Sorry."

"When life gives you lemons," she says with a shrug. "Just add vodka."

The woman turns to leave but Joe is nothing if not persistent.

"Can I make a donation to your vodka fund?"

It's not the worst line he's ever used. The woman actually stops for a moment and looks him up and down.

"Yeah, alright," she says. "And my friend will have one too. Vodka and coke."

Joe doesn't even stop to ask if I'd like a drink and scurries off to the bar, leaving me with two women I now feel compelled to chat with.

"Sorry to hear about your job," I offer by way of conversation.

"Thanks," she replies.

Just as I expect her to return to the pool table, she steps towards me. "I'm Lauren by the way, and that's my friend, Sandy."

"Oh, like in Grease," I chuckle, turning to Sandy. "Have you ever left a guy stranded at the drive-in?"

"Twat," she mumbles under her breath.

Seems I've been branded a fool. I decide not to share that witticism with Sandy.

"Excuse her," Lauren adds. "A lifetime of hearing bad *Grease* jokes will do that to a girl."

"Right, of course. Sorry."

I offer Sandy an apologetic smile.

"Are you guys waiting for the pool table?" Lauren asks.

"Yeah."

"We're in for the afternoon … drowning our sorrows."

"Oh, fair enough. We'll leave you in peace then."

"We could play doubles, if you like?"

Before I can make a decision, good or bad, Joe reappears and makes it for me.

"We'd love to."

It seems we are playing pool after all; with two random strangers, one of which clearly doesn't like me. On the plus side, at least it'll keep me away from the fruit machines. I don't argue.

"You guys have names?" Lauren asks.

"I'm Joseph and this is my business associate, Adam," Joe replies, handing over the drinks to Lauren.

Business associate?

I'm no expert in body language but I don't think Lauren sees Joe as her type. While nowhere near as pretty as Daisy, she's not an unattractive woman, and certainly out of Joe's league. Perhaps he'll have more luck defrosting sulky Sandy.

Pleasantries exchanged, Joe racks up the first game and breaks. Four balls go down before he misses a shot. Lauren takes her turn and misses the simplest of shots. This pattern is repeated for the duration of the five minute game.

"It'd be fairer if we split the teams," Lauren suggests to me. "I'll pair up with you, and Joe can partner Sandy."

"Err, sure."

I look across the table where Joe, sensing he's on a hiding to nothing with Lauren, has already realigned his sights on Sandy. I probably should have warned him not to make Grease-based jokes but I guess he'll discover that himself in due course.

We start another game with our new partners, and being the

gentlemen we are, let them take the first shots. They're nothing if not consistent. Joe and I clear a few balls each before Lauren and Sandy continue with their hit-and-hope strategy. By the time Joe sinks the black ball on his fourth visit to the table, it's clear we might as well be playing on our own.

More drinks are acquired and another frame set up.

And then another, and another.

As the drinks flow and the balls become increasingly reluctant to head in the direction she hoped, Lauren finally decides she might benefit from some hands-on tuition. With cue in hand, she leans across the table and asks me to stand behind her in order to adjust her bridge into the correct position. I duly oblige while trying to ignore her pert backside being pressed into my groin. My tuition is clearly useful though, and Lauren requests further assistance with every shot for the remainder of the game.

By the time we rack up the seventh frame, and order possibly the ninth round of drinks, it would be fair to say we're all moderately pissed; quite an achievement considering it's only four o'clock in the afternoon.

Then, after a lengthy visit to the toilets, Lauren and Sandy return with a proposition.

"Do you fancy coming back to our place for a smoke?"

"We don't smoke," I reply. "You know cigarettes cost, like, thirty quid a packet now … or something like that?"

"I'm not talking about cigarettes," Lauren giggles. "I've got some excellent weed."

Before I can answer, Joe pulls me aside.

"I think I'm in there with Sandy," he whispers.

"Good for you."

"So?"

"So what?"

"Will you come back to their place with me?" he pleads.

"You know I've never smoked weed and don't really see the appeal."

"Come on, mate. If you don't agree to come back I think they'll change their minds. And you don't have to smoke anything—just hang around for an hour so I can get better acquainted with Sandy."

"I'm not sure."

"It's an hour or so. You said Daisy was going to be late so you'll still be back home before her."

He looks at me expectantly. I can't even remember the last

time Joe had an offer like this so can I really deny him now?

"Alright, one hour. And I'm not smoking anything."

"Nice one, mate," he grins, slapping me on the back. "I really appreciate it."

Plans fixed, the four of us leave the Wheelwright Arms.

I tell myself it's just an hour of making small talk. Where's the harm in that?

7.

It turns out that up until they were made redundant today, Lauren and Sandy worked and lived together. Now they just live together in a third-floor flat on the outskirts of the town centre.

With Joe panting like an asthmatic bulldog, we traipse up three flights of stairs to the front door.

"This is us," Lauren declares, opening the door to flat twenty-eight.

She steps inside with Sandy close behind. As we wait for the girls to kick their shoes off, the scent of curdled milk bursts past them and greets us on the landing. Perhaps premature, but I suspect the convenient location is all the flat has going for it.

Joe takes the lead and we follow the girls through the hallway and into the lounge.

"Excuse the mess," Lauren says, almost apologetically. "We weren't expecting guests."

Her use of the word mess is interesting. I'd have gone for carnage, devastation, or utter filth myself. Much like a teenager's bedroom, the space is littered with fast food packaging, discarded clothes, and an entire dinner service of used crockery. I swap glances with Joe, his arm now draped across Sandy's shoulder. Inexplicably, he doesn't appear too concerned the lack of good housekeeping might also extend to her personal hygiene. I guess a starving man will dine from the dirtiest of bowls, and Joe is a starving man in every sense.

Our hosts set about unearthing two sofas—both buried beneath landfill—and invite us to sit. Joe immediately takes a seat next to Sandy on one sofa, leaving me with no option but to sit next to Lauren.

"Oh, drinks," she suddenly announces before I sit down. "I think we've got some beers in the fridge."

While Lauren heads off to the kitchen, and I dread to think what state that's in, Sandy plugs her phone into a speaker and swipes the screen in search of suitable background music. I reluctantly take a seat on the sofa while making a mental note to burn my suit when I get home.

Lauren then pops her head around the door. "Do you want your beer in a glass?"

"God, no," I blurt. "I mean … no, thank you."

She disappears again, seemingly oblivious to any offence.

The cleanliness of the glassware in the Red Lion is bad enough and I don't think my immune system could handle a new strain of glass-bound bacteria.

As Sandy finally selects some inappropriate music, Lauren returns clutching two cans of tramp-strength lager and a bottle of vodka. Using her foot, she clears a space on the coffee table and places the drinks down. A transparent bag is then plucked from the back pocket of her jeans.

"This should get the party started," she declares, waving the bag in the air.

Party? Nobody mentioned a party.

I glare across at Joe but he's hopelessly devoted to Sandy's tits and doesn't notice.

"Shift up," Lauren orders, flopping down right next to me, despite ample space at the other end of the sofa.

Like the filling in an idiot sandwich, I find myself pressed up against the arm of the sofa with Lauren squashed against me on the other side. A bad feeling rises from the pit of my stomach. I'm not sure if the cause is Lauren's proximity or the combination of lager and Red Leicester. Temporary relief is delivered when she leans forward and clears another space on the coffee table. The contents of the polythene bag are mixed with tobacco and efficiently rolled into four joints.

One of those joints is then handed to me.

"Here you go," Lauren chirps. "It's some seriously good stuff."

"Honestly, I'm good, thank you. But you go for it … don't mind me."

She eyes me for a second and then a smile breaks.

"Ahh, I get it," she says in a sultry voice. "Weed gives you whisky dick, does it?"

"Err, gives me what?" I splutter.

"Whisky dick—trouble getting a boner."

"I … um."

"Don't worry," she coos. "I'm flattered. Why don't we grab our drinks and head to my room?"

Let's not.

My gaze shifts towards Joe. For some inexplicable reason he's now rubbing his hand up and down Sandy's thigh as she stares vacantly into space. There will be no support coming. Perhaps now would be a good time to make my exit but, then again, Joe would never forgive me if I break up his tryst before he hits first base.

"You know what, Lauren?" I announce. "Maybe I will try some weed after all."

It has to be the lesser of the two evils on offer.

"Fair enough," she replies with a shrug.

Lauren then leans over and passes two of the joints to Sandy; offering the poor girl temporary respite from Joe's busy hands.

A cigarette lighter is ignited. Sandy holds the flame to her joint first and takes a long drag before puffing a plume of blue smoke towards the ceiling. Joe, not needing much encouragement, quickly follows suit.

Lauren then lights the third joint. After a single drag, she holds it towards me. "All yours."

My experience of narcotics doesn't extend beyond alcohol and a year of smoking Marlboro Lights back in the mid-noughties. Not only have I never smoked weed, I know virtually nothing about the effects either, beyond the fact it's supposed to make you happy.

Surely I can cope with being happy?

I look towards Sandy and Joe, who are both now lying back on the sofa and smiling. They certainly look happy and relaxed.

"Come on, handsome," Lauren beams. "Unless of course there's something else you'd rather do?"

A spot of hoovering appeals but I don't think that's what she has in mind. Therefore, it comes down to a binary decision: smoke the joint or risk being dragged to her lair?

Sod it.

Tentatively I grasp the joint between my forefinger and thumb. Lauren then proceeds to light her own as I watch the thin line of smoke snake up from the tip of what is now my joint. The smell alone is pungent, like damp leaves burning on a bonfire.

Go on—it'll just make you happy.

I can sense three sets of eyes staring at me in expectation. No words of encouragement are forthcoming but the weight of stares is enough to push me over the line. I bring the joint to my lips and take a cautious drag.

Seconds pass and I exhale. Besides a peculiar, herby taste in my mouth I don't feel any different—possibly because I'm fairly pissed.

I risk another, deeper drag.

Nothing.

I look across the room and, for possibly the first time all afternoon, Sandy is smiling; her hand resting on Joe's thigh as they puff away.

"What do you think?" Lauren asks, pulling my attention away from the happy couple.

"Yeah, it's good stuff," I lie.

Underwhelming would have been a better description but I don't wish to be impolite. Content the effects won't be able to fight their way through the lager fog in my head, I smoke on.

Something of a melancholy atmosphere descends as the four of us sit back and take turns puffing smoke towards the ceiling. Despite sucking the life out of the joint, I don't feel anything other than relaxed. Perhaps that's the limit of its effects. It does beg the question: why smoke an illegal substance when the same state of relaxation can be achieved with a perfectly legal cup of cocoa, or by listening to the shipping forecast on Radio Four?

By the time I stub the joint out in an already overflowing ashtray, Lauren has another lined up. Assuming I've already experienced all it has to offer, I thank her and light up my second-ever joint.

Six drags in and something changes. No, not something—everything.

It begins with the sound of a heartbeat, thumping away in my chest. The more I try to block it out the louder it throbs, and with that volume, increasing detail. It's as if I can hear the valves open and close, and the blood sloshing through my arteries.

In an attempt to distract myself I focus on an Amy Winehouse track playing in the background. It's a song I've heard a thousand times and I know every note and every word of the lyrics—or, at least I did. Now though, all I can hear are a cacophony of sounds akin to the gates of hell scraping back and forth on rusty hinges. Sound, it seems, now hurts.

As my concern mounts, I try to seek assurance in the faces seated around me. Surely if this sensory nightmare is happening to everyone I'll be okay.

It's not assurance I find, but confusion.

Joe and Sandy, or two shapes I assume to be Joe and Sandy, are now sponge-like formations with no definition. I know they're there but I simply cannot focus on their features. I turn to Lauren and, for a moment, thank God, I can see her face. That same God then delivers a celestial wedgie as Lauren speaks.

"Are … you … okay?"

That was the question, I'm sure, but every word is drawn out like a record played at the wrong speed. I try to speak but my bottom jaw has other ideas and refuses to move. It's all I can do to stare at Lauren, wide-eyed and panicky. She responds with laughter.

"You're ... fucked," she sniggers, although the words arrive in a slow plod. "Think ... I ... overdid ... the ... weed ... in ... that ... second ... joint."

From somewhere in my fuddled mind a conclusion arrives. This is bad. So very bad.

Lulled into a false sense of security, it appears I've imbibed mind-altering levels of whatever Lauren put in that second joint. I know this, but what I do about it is another matter; particularly as reality and function now appear to be operating in concept alone.

A can of something—lager I suppose—is placed in my hand. I don't know who put it there, but it feels like I should drink it. Pouting like a teenage girl taking a selfie, I press the cold can to my lips and gulp; no thought to the consequences of drinking super strength lager while already out of my mind.

I empty the can and flop back on the sofa. As every sense approaches meltdown, I enter a bizarre world somewhere between a kid's cartoon and a Balearic nightclub. The lights blur and the music throbs and the room spins. Even by my standards, I have to concede this was a catastrophically bad idea.

I close my eyes tight and try to will away the horror. Maybe it's a safety valve, but my brain decides we've had more than enough excitement for one night, and enters shut-down mode.

My final memory is of an arm around my shoulder, and a warm sensation flowering from my crotch.

Checkout.

8.

"Adam! Adam!"

Daisy sounds a lot like Joe.

"Mate. Wake up."

Daisy never calls me mate. Something isn't right.

I open my eyes and quickly close them again—probably a bad dream.

"For fuck's sake. Get up."

Several times in the past I've woken up and, for a few seconds, believed the dream I was experiencing to be real. However, I've never woken up to the lingering stench of a dream before. Either my brain hasn't quite finished rebooting or I'm somewhere other than the fragrant surroundings of my bedroom.

I open my eyes again. I'm definitely not in my bedroom and Joe is definitely not my fiancée—unless something very bad happened before I went to sleep.

"Where …?"

"Don't you remember?"

"No."

"Lauren and Sandy? This is their place."

I let my eyes drift beyond Joe's shoulder but the gloomy scene doesn't trigger any memories.

"Who?" I croak.

"The girls we played pool with, in the pub. You obviously don't remember having rampant sex with Lauren?"

Joe's shocking revelation shifts me from a semi-conscious slumber to wide awake in a nanosecond.

"I, eh … what?"

As Joe shakes his head, I scrape my mind for any recollection of something I'm sure I'd remember. Nothing comes my way, other than several tuts and a contemptuous glare.

"I'm kidding," he finally admits before sniggering to himself. "You passed out before the party got going."

"Jesus Christ," I gasp in relief. "Don't do that to me."

"Woke you up though, didn't it?"

It did that, but I really wish it hadn't. I attempt to sit up and regret it in an instant.

"What time is it?" I croak.

"Just gone seven."

Thank Christ I'm only an hour late for dinner. If I hurry, I

51

can still make it home before Daisy goes into meltdown mode. Now I have the motivation, I just need the strength to move. I gingerly turn and haul my legs off the sofa.

"Christ, I feel awful."

"You smell awful," he snorts. "You know you pissed yourself, right?"

I risk a glance at my groin and see no evidence. The smell emanating from my crotch, though, is both rancid and damming.

"Did I?"

"Yeah, just before you passed out, or was it while you were passed out? Can't be sure as I was pretty wasted myself."

At the moment, piss-stained trousers are not my greatest concern. I blink a few times and study Joe's chubby face. Nothing particularly untoward, apart from the fact it's bathed in muted blue light. I turn to the source—a window with a thin blue curtain draped across.

Seven o'clock on a January evening. That's not right.

"Why is it light outside?"

"Do you want me to explain the earth's rotation?"

"Eh?"

"It's morning, idiot."

"What? You said it had just gone seven."

"Yeah, seven in the morning."

"As in the day after yesterday?"

"That's how it works."

"As in, we went to the pub and met those girls yesterday?"

"You're getting the hang of this."

Clarification obtained, my addled brain processes the ramifications. None of them are good.

"Daisy is going to lose her shit."

"Just tell her you crashed at my place," Joe replies dismissively. "It'll be fine."

I pat the pockets of my crumpled jacket and locate my phone. The only thing worse than finding half-a-dozen angry messages from Daisy would be a blank screen.

"Great," I groan.

"What's up?"

"The battery is dead."

"I did warn you about the iPhone battery, mate," he helpfully adds. "I've had wanks last longer."

I slip the phone back into my pocket. "I am in so much trouble."

"You'd better get going then," he suggests, before

apparently pondering his own situation. "Actually, it might be a good idea if I make a move too."

"Why?"

"I might have puked in the bath at some point in the night."

As my eyes adjust to the tepid light, the shit-hole of a room reveals itself.

"I doubt they'll notice."

Like thieves in the night, we slip out of the flat before my theory is tested.

We escape the block of flats into a frigidly cold morning with dawn still reluctant to break. If only hypothermia was all I had to worry about.

We stomp a safe distance from ground zero, by which point my hangover has acquired a resentful edge.

"Daisy is going to have my bollocks for breakfast, thanks to you."

"Why is it my fault?" Joe groans in reply.

"If you hadn't dragged me into the pub for that pointless meeting, I wouldn't be in this mess."

"Bullshit. You could have left any time you wanted. Don't blame me, mate."

"And the weed?" I spit, ignoring his defence. "You made me smoke it."

"What?"

"You pressurised me."

"And how did I do that exactly?"

"You looked at me with … that look."

With a shake of the head, he digs his hands deeper into his jacket pockets. "You know how lame that sounds, right?"

It does, and I know deep down there's only one person to blame. Another situation has spiralled out of control due to my poor judgement. Still, I need to vent.

"What the fuck am I going to tell her?"

"I told you—just say we had a few beers at my place and you fell asleep on the sofa."

"Several problems with that," I snap. "Firstly, I was supposed to be home before Daisy, so why didn't I leave your house early evening?"

"As I said, you fell asleep on the sofa."

"Right. So, I fell asleep at some point in the afternoon with your parents sat beside me, watching Countdown?"

"Erm, yeah."

"I know your parents aren't exactly enthralling company but

53

that's a stretch. One of them would have woken me up, or you, come to think of it. Does it seem plausible all three of you left me snoozing on the sofa all night?"

"Well, when you put it like that, no."

With the one and only excuse undermined at the first attempt, we continue to trudge silently through the town centre. There's almost a post-apocalyptic feel with the absence of human life and darkened shop windows. I can't remember the last time I was out and about at this early hour and vow never to do it again.

As my appointment with oblivion looms ever closer, I conclude my time would be better served thinking about what to tell Daisy. Every paving slab we cover signifies another lost fraction of a second; time I should be using to formulate the mother of all excuses. And just when I think things can't get any worse, Joe begins whistling a tuneless rendition of *Yesterday*. It does little to help either my pounding head or anxiety levels.

"Do you have to do that?" I grumble.

"It helps me think."

We turn a corner and he suddenly stops.

"Hold up," he orders. "I think I've got something."

"If it's anything to do with alien abduction, I don't want to hear it."

"Better than that, mate—tell her you've been in hospital all night."

His self-satisfied expression is that of a six-year-old who finally found Wally.

"And what exactly was I doing in hospital all night? A spot of midwifery?"

"Now you're being a dick," he chides. "Think about it: what was the weather like yesterday."

I sense we're about to stroll up a blind alley but I humour him.

"It was freezing and it snowed for a while."

"Exactly. So, you tell Daisy you were working at a customer's house when you slipped and knocked yourself out. They called an ambulance and you were rushed off to the hospital."

"Right."

"And because you were unconscious, you couldn't call home. Just tell her they kept you in overnight."

I admire Joe's creativity. However, he has woefully underestimated Daisy's almost forensic ability to dissect my bullshit. Even an idiot like me can spot the obvious flaws.

"Why was I cleaning windows in a suit?"

"Bugger. I hadn't thought of that."

"And then there's Alan. How the hell was I cleaning windows when he was parked on the driveway, with all my gear inside?"

"Alright, I get it," he groans. "It needs a polish."

"A polish? As explanations go, it thoroughly sucks."

We press on in silence, and the lack of whistling suggests Joe is no longer willing to contribute. However, it dawns on me that perhaps not every part of his suggestion sucks. Clearly I can't say I was at work but being in hospital all night is a pretty watertight alibi.

"You know, you could just tell her the truth," Joe suddenly suggests.

"Are you insane?" I gasp. "I can't tell her I willingly went back to some random girl's flat and got so wasted on drugs I passed out."

"Why not? It's not as though you did anything with what's-her-name, is it?"

Only a man with Joe's inexperience of the opposite sex would make such a suggestion.

"Let me tell you about the time Daisy asked my opinion on a new dress. You know what I said? It made her arse look odd … sort of square."

"And did it?"

"Yes, but do you think she thanked me for being honest?"

He shrugs.

"She didn't speak to me for two days. Two fucking days … just because I was honest enough to say her arse resembled a loaf of bread. If I tell her the truth about my whereabouts last night, I'll be a pensioner before she speaks to me again, and that's assuming I make it to pension age."

"Can't help you then, mate. I'm out of ideas."

"Great."

We reach the end of a street lined with Victorian terraced houses; time to go our separate ways. Joe wishes me luck although I doubt he means it. I watch him waddle away before I shuffle off in the opposite direction. Even if I drag my heels, I have less than ten minutes to come up with something plausible to tell Daisy. The only consolation, if there is one, is that I should arrive home with only minutes to spare before she leaves for work. Hopefully, that'll prove insufficient time for my explanation to be probed in any detail, and I'll have the rest of the day to fill in the gaps while she's at work.

A flawless plan if only I can concoct that initial explanation.

I return to Joe's idea of saying I was in hospital. That part works, if coupled with a plausible reason for being in a suit, and a situation where I might be knocked unconscious while wearing said suit.

As I wait to cross the road, a shiny, nearly new van pulls up to the junction and the driver waves me across. I wave back and, while admiring his vehicle, note the company name emblazoned on the side: *Banks Carpentry Services.*

Something connects in my head and an epiphany arrives.

After yesterday's disaster, perhaps fate is keen to make amends. The name on the van might just have provided an explanation for the suit, and that in itself opens up some possibilities for the overnight stay in hospital I never had.

With only minutes to spare, I run through the list of possibilities until I arrive at one that ties in with my reason for wearing a suit, and feels vaguely believable. I use the final hundred yards of pavement to fine tune the finished explanation.

By the time I put the key in the front door, I'm sure I've got every base covered; or at least the bases Daisy will aim to destroy before she has to leave.

I kick my shoes off, adopt my best puppy-eyed face, and head straight to the kitchen.

"Honey, I'm so sorry. I've had an absolute nightmare."

Daisy is leant with her back to the sink, casually flicking a finger across the screen of her iPad. She stops, looks at me, and puffs a resigned sigh.

"Come on then. Let's hear it."

This is a good start. No apoplectic outburst.

"It's a long story."

"It usually is. You've got five minutes to tell it."

"Okay. You're probably wondering why I'm wearing a suit."

"It did cross my mind."

"As you know, Alan has been playing up recently, and I thought maybe it's time to invest in a new van. You keep telling me to replace him, don't you?"

She nods.

"So, I made an appointment with a loan advisor at the bank yesterday afternoon. I wore a suit to make a good impression."

No reaction. I press on.

"Anyway, you know how cold it was, and I stupidly decided to walk into town. I was frozen to the bone by the time I arrived at the bank and I started feeling faint. Probably something to do with my blood pressure."

Her expression is now one of mild curiosity but there's no obvious concern for my wellbeing.

"As I waited for the loan advisor I started getting cold sweats and my vision blurred. Then, when she finally called me into her office, I tried to walk and … and I fainted."

"You fainted?"

"Out like a light, honey. The next thing I know, I'm lying in bed at the hospital. They reckon my head must have struck the floor so hard it caused a concussion."

"Concussion?" she parrots.

"Yeah. I was spark out for hours, apparently."

"And nobody from the hospital thought to contact your next of kin?"

Fortunately, I was expecting this question. One reason I never carry a wallet is because I've lost so many in the past, and when you lose a wallet, you lose every form of identification in one fell swoop. Unless I need something specific, I now only carry around my debit card.

"I didn't have anything on me apart from my debit card, which only has my initials and surname. I guess they assumed I'd be okay and wouldn't be there long enough to warrant the police tracking you down."

Despite Daisy's lack of concern, I don't detect any obvious signs of disbelief. Remarkably, it looks like I might have pulled this one off.

"Did you wet yourself?" she suddenly asks, somewhat out of the blue.

"I, um, might have done, in the hospital."

"You stink."

"Yeah, I'd better take a shower."

Before I scuttle off to the safety of the bathroom, I chance my arm with a final glance in Daisy's direction. If they awarded Oscars for appearing forlorn and sincere, I'm sure my parting expression would secure a nomination, at least.

I make three steps.

"Oh, Adam," Daisy beckons. "Before you go, can I just show you something I found on Facebook? It's so funny."

I turn and offer a feeble smile. "Course you can, honey."

She shuffles over to me, but not close enough to enjoy the

full aroma of my trousers.

"Now where is it?" she says to herself, while flicking a finger across the screen.

Seconds pass and, just as I'm about to suggest waiting until tonight, she stops.

"Ah, here it is."

She holds up the iPad so I can see whatever tickled her.

I was expecting a video of a cat playing the piano, or a toddler smearing its podgy face with ice cream. There's no video—just a photo. And there's no cat or ice cream-splattered toddler.

I wouldn't necessarily call the photo funny either.

"Hilarious, eh?" Daisy remarks.

I gulp and turn to her. "I can explain."

She bites her bottom lip and draws three heavy breaths through her nostrils.

"What I find hilarious, Adam," she continues, steeling herself. "Is that someone who looks *exactly* like you, was photographed last night with some floozy draped around him, and clearly pissed out of his tiny mind. Obviously it can't be you—that would be silly because you were in hospital, apparently unconscious."

Despite the overwhelming desire not to, I glance at the photo again. I have no recollection of it being taken so I can only assume it happened when I was out for the count. There's no denying it looks bad, though.

"It's not how it looks, honey."

A well-worn line which, as excuses go, has probably never worked. It doesn't work on Daisy either as she ignores my feeble protest.

"That's the thing about posting photos on Facebook, Adam, and in particular, this photo, is they are usually shared by all and sundry. And as luck would have it, a friend of a friend also shared it, before it was sent to me."

"Honestly … it really … nothing happened, I swear."

There is no response as she turns and carefully places the iPad down on the kitchen side. More deep breaths are inhaled when she suddenly spins on her heels. Before I even see it coming, an open palm slaps across my cheek.

"Fuck! That hurt!"

"Good," she spits. "Because I want your last memory of me to be a painful one."

My mouth falls open. "What?"

"I can just about put up with your constant cock-ups, but I won't stand for lying and I sure as hell won't stand for cheating."

"But …"

"Save it," she fumes. "I've had enough. It's over."

9.

As a rule, I don't tend to heed advice from fortune cookies. I do, however, recall one profound statement offered on a recent trip to the Oriental Kitchen: never lie to the ones you love. You know life has reached rock bottom when your biggest regret is not following the advice of a tasteless oriental snack.

To make matters worse, if that's even possible, Joe was also right—I should have told Daisy the truth.

Organised as ever, her bags are already packed and lined up beside the bed.

"I swear to you, honey, nothing happened. I got drunk, smoked some weed, and passed out."

She ignores me and pulls a coat from the now empty wardrobe.

"I only went back to their flat as a favour for Joe, and ..."

She spins around. "Fuck off," she screams. "Just fuck off."

Her outburst was perhaps a bung, holding back a tide of emotions; pent up since last night. Her bottom lip trembles as she fights to keep control.

There are lots of reasons why people shed tears: joy, sorrow, regret, relief. In Daisy's case, I suspect her tears are now rage fuelled. Whatever the reason, it breaks my heart to see her cry. A bitter irony, but I've never wanted to hold her in my arms more than this precise moment. Even I know that wouldn't end well.

"You ... stupid ... stupid ... bastard," she sobs; each word delivered between a shallow breath.

"You don't have to tell me, honey. I know I am, but not so stupid I'd ever cheat on you."

Beyond the snorts and sniffles, she doesn't offer a word in reply. As silent seconds tick by, my mind steadfastly refuses to deliver a worthwhile defence—not that there is one.

Daisy swallows hard and, with her composure returning, wipes a tear from her cheek with the back of her hand. More deep breaths are sucked through pursed lips as she pulls herself together; her pride won't allow her to be a victim any longer.

She glares at me. Her usually radiant skin is pale and taut, and her blue eyes cold.

"You've ruined everything," she says, breathlessly. "And the sad thing is: you don't even realise what you've lost."

"I do. Honestly, I do," I plead.

"Trust me, Adam—you don't."

She slips her coat on and squeezes her eyes shut. For a few seconds, the beautiful woman who is no longer my fiancée just stands there motionless, biting her bottom lip.

The silence is horrendous. I have to say something, anything, just to buy some time if nothing else.

"Would you like some toast before you go?"

Daisy opens her eyes and her mouth follows suit. "Are you kidding … what?"

"I, um, don't want you to leave on an empty stomach. Breakfast is the most important meal of the day … isn't that what you say?"

She plucks a tissue from her handbag and dabs her eyes. The silence returns and just as I consider my next move, Daisy answers my question.

"No, I don't want toast," she replies, flatly. "Do you know what I did want, though?"

Don't say Coco Pops. Don't say Coco Pops.

I shake my head.

"The very least I wanted was an apology, and for you to take some responsibility for once in your damn life. But I bet that never even crossed your mind, did it?"

Fuck.

"God, I am sorry, honey, I really am. I didn't think."

A snort escapes as she buttons her coat. "No, and that's always been your problem."

"I'll change. I promise."

She shakes her head. "It's too late. You're a liability, Adam, and I can't afford to have a liability in my life."

I'm losing her, but my mind is so scrambled I can't find the right words to pull her back. I resort to the only remaining hope.

"For the love of God, please don't go. I'm begging you."

"I'll ask Dad to collect my things later."

"Please ..."

"Goodbye, Adam."

Without a second glance in my direction, Daisy grabs her handbag and walks out of the bedroom. Her footsteps fade away before the click of the door latch echoes down the hallway.

She's gone.

Every fibre of my being wants to race after her but I know it's pointless. Once Daisy has made her mind up about something, there's no going back.

I slump down on the edge of the bed and stare at the

wardrobe; the doors open and the contents now consigned to various bags and suitcases. We've had arguments before, and Daisy might have half-heartedly threatened to leave on a couple of occasions, but this is a first. It's also, I fear, a last.

As I continue to stare at the empty wardrobe, a cruel thought taunts: this is the death knell of the best relationship I ever had. No, that's not right. It's the death knell of the best anything I ever had.

What have I done?

For some reason my mind turns to a wildlife documentary I watched last week about Harp Seals. Twelve days after birth the mother stops feeding her pups and sods off to mate again; leaving the poor mites stranded on an ice shelf until they're old enough to fend for themselves. Maybe it's the helplessness I saw in their eyes which now resonates. My Daisy has gone and I already feel every bit as lost and bewildered as those seal pups.

What do I do?

Crying feels appropriate but the raw grief, for the moment at least, is trapped beneath thick layers of shock, regret and self-loathing. So, rather than cry, I sit and sip on a bitter cocktail of my own making.

Fool.

Time passes, although I'm not sure how much. Nothing changes. The wardrobe remains empty while my mind remains cluttered with conflicting thoughts. I should go and find Daisy. No, I should give her time to cool down. I should climb into bed and hide from my stupidity. No, I should go to work and keep myself busy. I should take a shower. Yes, I should take a shower.

I reluctantly clamber to my feet and stumble through to the bathroom. Staring in the mirror above the sink, I conclude my breath might actually smell worse than my trousers, and I look a total mess.

You are a total mess.

As if trying to protect itself, my mind goes into safe mode like a corrupted computer. I have no specific recall but sometime later I emerge from the bathroom having brushed my teeth and showered. Continuing on autopilot, I get dressed and head into the kitchen to make a coffee.

After putting my phone on charge, I sit at the small bistro table by the window and try to gather my thoughts.

To anyone looking on it would appear a fairly typical morning in Adam Maxwell's life. They would be wrong. I've read enough articles in enough dog-eared lifestyle magazines—

the kind you find in every doctor's waiting room—to know what's going on. If those articles are to be believed, I might have entered the first stage of a break up—denial.

Then again, I might not.

I consider myself an optimist and, rather than wallow in self-pity, I'd rather assume there is a solution to every problem I create. Am I being positive, or am I in denial about being in denial? How would I even know as surely you'd deny your own denial about the original denial? It's a paradox even the greatest minds would struggle to comprehend. What hope do I have?

An acute throbbing in my head offers a timely reminder why I don't think as much as I should.

I take my final sip of coffee and get up. With some trepidation I cross the kitchen and switch my still-charging phone on. Slowly the screen flashes into life before a series of chimes ping out. Six text messages; all from last night, and all from Daisy.

Unread, I delete them. I think it's already obvious how badly I've screwed things up, and there is nothing to be gained by inviting additional guilt to my door.

It's not denial. It's self-protection.

I leave the phone on charge, neck a couple of pain killers and pour another coffee. Before I take my first sip, the doorbell rings.

I trudge down the hallway and open the door, expecting to find our grumpy postman in need of a signature. The man I open the door to is not grumpy; more like enraged.

"I knew you'd balls it up eventually," he snarls. "You're a fucking moron."

Eddie—Daisy's Pitbull of a father—barges past me. I close the door and prepare myself for the inevitable verbal assault.

I turn around, half-expecting a punch in the face. I'm relieved to find Eddie stood just beyond punching range. He glares at me for a moment; his disdain verging on hatred. Despite being a reputable businessman, Eddie has the look of a stocky, shaven-headed nightclub bouncer, and the aggressive demeanour to match.

"What the bloody hell were you thinking?" he barks.

Very little, as usual.

"I swear to you, Eddie," I plead. "Nothing happened. I got wasted on weed and passed out … that's all."

"I couldn't give a rat's arse what you get up to, but when you hurt my girl …"

63

"I didn't mean to hurt her," I blurt.

"Yeah, well, you did. And now you've fucked up the best thing in your sorry life."

With that, Eddie turns and heads towards the bedroom. He takes three steps before pausing.

"You know what?" he says, over his shoulder. "I've always thought you were okay. A bit of a dickhead, but okay. There's one thing I can't stomach though, and that's liars, and neither can Daisy."

He ambles off to the bedroom before I make another stupid decision and try arguing with him. He reappears, carrying two suitcases.

"I'll get the rest of her stuff when I've organised a van. Probably best you're not here."

I nod.

"I'll text you tomorrow."

I open the door and he walks straight past me. Apparently, there's nothing left to be said.

As I watch Eddie head down the stairs, I sense something else leaving with him. By the time I close the door I'm almost certain denial snuck out with him; probably because the faint hope I held—that Daisy might come back home later—is now gone.

I thump my fists against the door. "You stupid, stupid, twatting, twat!"

It appears denial only intended to stay a short while, and stage two of the break up process is now here.

Hello anger.

10.

Nelson Mandela spent twenty-seven years in prison but, according to those who knew him, he never gave up hope.

Daisy walked out on me forty-nine hours and seventeen minutes ago. I'm already close to giving up hope.

Saturday morning and I should be having breakfast with my fiancée. I'm not. I'm lying in bed, staring at the various cracks in the ceiling, none of which are as wide as the cracks now forming in my life.

In some respects, I have moved on, though. Anger left by Thursday evening and stage three arrived—bargaining. I'm not particularly good with anger anyway. It's not a constructive emotion and there are only so many inanimate objects you can kick, punch, and swear at before you realise the futility. Alan now has two more dents in his bodywork that weren't there a few days ago.

With anger out of the way, I awoke yesterday morning in a determined mood. Whatever it took, I was going to convince Daisy I was worthy of a second chance. I say second chance, but I think my previous chances now run into double figures. Nevertheless, I had to try, and I did—more than a dozen text and voicemail messages went unanswered.

With frustration mounting, I decided to make a grand gesture. At seven-thirty last night I turned up unannounced at the home of the couple who were almost my in-laws. It proved a valuable lesson—you can't bargain with someone who doesn't want a deal under any circumstances, and you certainly can't bargain with Eddie when he's brandishing a meat cleaver.

His final words—growled as he handed over Daisy's engagement ring—still echo in my head: *she doesn't want you in her life.*

It's probably a record, and not an achievement I'm proud of, but I think I've already entered stage four— depression.

Up until I awoke an hour ago, I always thought depression was a just a handy label for the self-obsessed and feeble minded. I remember reading about a Premier League footballer who claimed he was suffering from depression—just grow a pair, I thought. How could a young, talented, multi-millionaire, with everything going for him, be depressed?

What I realise now, is that depression isn't about what

you've got, but what's missing. There are millions of people in this world who are far, far worse off than I am. I might not have the fame and fortune of a footballer but I'm also not living in poverty or, God-forbid, suffering some awful disease. My life is markedly better than millions of others, but does that matter? Not one jot because at some point during the night, a black hole formed in my mind—a hole so deep and so vast it has consumed me. And now, every time I grasp for a positive thought, it slips through my fingers and gets sucked in to that bastard hole.

I cannot find reason or strength to even get out of bed. Depression, it seems, is real.

My phone rings.

Snapping out of my malaise, I snatch it from the bedside table. In that briefest of seconds, before I see the screen, I have hope.

Please, please let it be Daisy.

My heart sinks. I jab the screen.

"What do you want, Joe?"

"Just seeing if you've calmed down yet."

Joe called by yesterday to show me some spreadsheet he'd devised for the venture which will never happen. I told him about Daisy, and then told him to fuck off, on the basis I hold him partly responsible for the situation which sparked her departure. He claims he was in the toilet when the incriminating photo was taken, which I find hard to believe.

"No, I haven't calmed down."

"Come on, mate. There's no point wallowing in self-pity. You've got to get out there and …"

"Save it," I snap. "I swear, if you tell me to get back on the horse, or there's plenty more fish in the sea, I'll swing for you."

"Fair enough, but I was going to suggest maybe you'd like to come and watch the footy in the pub."

"No."

"Why not? It'll take your mind off things."

"Still no."

"But …"

I hang up.

Within seconds of slapping my phone back on the bedside table, guilt arrives to compound my dark mood. Joe might be misguided, but maybe he has a point about taking my mind off things. As tempting as it currently seems, I can't just wallow in my own filth and depressive thoughts all day.

Stage five, I know, is acceptance. I feel a million miles away from accepting Daisy is no longer part of my life, but like somebody, whose name escapes me, once said: *every journey begins with a single step.*

I call Joe back.

"Who's playing?"

"Stoke and West Ham."

"Christ," I groan. "Just when I thought I'd hit rock bottom."

"We could always watch the weeds grow in the car park, if you'd prefer?"

"Tempting, but I prefer to be bored in the warm. I'll see you in the Red Lion in an hour."

I end the call and crawl back under the duvet, not quite ready to leave its sanctuary. I grab Daisy's pillow and hug it tight to my chest. The lingering scent of her perfume is still strong enough to drag me into the black hole. I go willingly and, for the first time in years, tears well. At no point do I recall reading about this stage—the stage where I sob uncontrollably into a pillow.

The tears offer a temporary release but they fail to fix the dull ache in the pit of my stomach. I say ache, but it's tinged with an emptiness unlike any physical pain I've ever felt. Perhaps that's how it's supposed to be; a constant nagging reminder that Daisy is no longer part of my life. I know there will be moments when I forget—moments where I want to ask how her day is going, or arrange a night out, or just laugh about something stupid that happened at work. For a second, I'll think all those things are possible, until the dull ache reminds me they're all gone, along with the thousand other things we'll never do together.

I have no idea which stage I'm currently now at. Depression, acceptance—it doesn't matter. Maybe they're one and the same thing. Acceptance is depressing and accepting depression is … well, depressing. Wherever I am, though, I fear it's going to be the longest and cruellest of stages.

"Come on then, you bastards," I mumble to myself. "Let's get on with this."

I put Daisy's pillow back in its place and draw several deep breaths. With leaden limbs, I clamber from the bed and head to the bathroom.

A shower, clean clothes and a strong coffee prove a boon, and I leave the flat feeling a fraction better than abysmal. That feeling lasts about five minutes; up to the point a text arrives from Eddie, confirming he'll be coming around tomorrow at one o'clock with a van. He makes no effort to underplay the threat if I'm there. Clearly Daisy will be with him, and they'll spend a couple of hours stripping the flat of every last reminder she ever lived there.

While I have no intention of being home when he arrives, Eddie's threat carries little weight. His text alone summoned more pain than a punch ever could. Now, beyond all refutable doubt, I know Daisy is leaving for good.

As that thought sinks in, I stop for a moment and suck in a lungful of cold air. A tiny seed of consolation sprouts in the back of my mind—this has to be better than a long, drawn out process. The pain is inevitable, but like removing a sticking plaster, surely it's better for the pain to be served with one sharp tug than a slow, agonising pull? Now, I just need to keep that thought from being swallowed by the black hole. If I don't, I know I'll turn around and head back to my bed, and Daisy's pillow.

Mercifully, Mother Nature intervenes and the heavens open, forcing my hand. Five minutes to get home, or I can complete the final few hundred yards to the pub. I slip my phone back in my pocket and sprint toward the Red Lion, icy rain lashing my face as if the black hole is punishing my defiance.

I burst through the door into the bar and, for one glorious moment, the burning pain in my chest drowns out the dull ache in my stomach. It doesn't last.

"Adam. Pint?"

I nod at Vince while scanning the faces of the dozen-or-so punters milling around the bar—none of which are Joe.

My pint arrives and I throw some loose change across the bar. I don't even have the energy to complain about the short measure.

"You alright, mate?"

Joe pitches up beside me; his hair a damp, windswept ginger nest.

"What's the opposite of alright?" I ask.

"Err, not alright, I guess."

"That's what I am then. Not alright."

He shuffles awkwardly on the spot, perhaps unsure what to say in the circumstances.

"Everything will be okay, mate," he cheerfully declares. "Let me get you a chaser."

"Thanks for the sage words. Ever considered a career in counselling?"

"Are you being sarcastic?"

"Very."

In fairness, discussing affairs of the heart is not comfortable ground for either of us.

Joe orders a pint plus a couple of whisky chasers and, once furnished with drinks, we take a table by the TV. It's not even twelve o'clock yet and I'm about to take my first drink of the day. For one brief moment I start plotting my excuse for Daisy, but the dull ache quickly reminds me she won't be waiting at home to hear any excuse I concoct.

The first sip of lager is unusually bitter.

"Is it definitely over then?" Joe asks, subtle as ever.

I can't bring myself to answer so just nod.

"I don't know what to say, mate."

"Nothing to say," I sigh. "And to be honest, I'd rather not talk about it."

"Fair enough. Fancy putting a bet on the match to liven things up a little?"

Before I can answer, my phone chimes to signify the arrival of another text. Eddie again, seeking confirmation I received his first text and I won't be home tomorrow afternoon. I send him a single word reply and switch the phone off. The only person in the world I want to hear from clearly doesn't want to talk to me and I can't stomach any more messages from Eddie.

Really, all I want is to quietly drink myself into oblivion. I know I'll regret it tomorrow but for now it seems the only way to escape this torture.

By the time the match starts at twelve, we're already into our second round of drinks.

Forty-five minutes of mind-numbing football ensue; the only highlights being two further rounds of drinks. Four pints and four whisky chasers within seventy minutes—if I keep it up I should be wankered enough by mid-afternoon to slip into a coma for at least fourteen hours.

The half-time whistle blows.

"Games that kick-off at lunchtime are always shit," Joe groans.

"And yet, here we are."

"I'm going for a piss. Let's hope the second half is better."

I watch him waddle away and neck my chaser. With no football or Joe to distract my thoughts, a realisation arrives. Never mind the match, without Daisy in my life, it's impossible to see how anything will ever be better.

A lump dances in my throat. Knowing this is neither the

time or place to break down in tears, I swallow hard.

I return my attention to the screen in the hope it'll keep my mind occupied until Joe returns with his mindless conversation. In a bid to fill the space around the adverts, they're repeating a pre-match interview with Stoke's new twenty-million-pound signing, Santiago Otero—an Argentinian striker signed from some Italian club I've never heard of. In broken English, Santiago confesses his love for the Premier League and how it's a dream come true signing for Stoke City.

"Bullshit," I mumble to myself.

"What is?" Joe asks, returning to his seat.

"Him," I huff. "He claims it's a dream come true signing for bloody Stoke."

"Maybe he's an avid collector of pottery."

"Or maybe he's just another fucking mercenary."

Even I can hear the aggression in my own voice. I fear that aggression has little to do with Santiago Otero and a lot to do with my darkening mood. Anger, it seems, just popped out for a sandwich and has returned.

Another round of drinks are acquired just before the second half kicks-off.

For forty-five minutes, I stare blindly at the screen and gulp down alcohol. Sensing my broodiness, Joe wisely decides against conversation and only passes comment when another sitter is missed or the referee makes a blindingly obvious blunder.

The game ends goalless, only serving to confirm what a waste of life the last few hours have been.

"That was possibly the worst game of football I've ever seen," Joe remarks.

"You surprised?" I scoff. "Just another in a long line of disappointments."

"Not really, mate. Last night's game was pretty decent."

"I wasn't talking about football."

"Oh."

As I return to my sulky silence, I can feel my emotions shifting like sand on a windswept beach. No doubt fuelled by nine pints and nine whisky chasers, those emotions switch places with increasing frenzy, all laced with an undercurrent of anger. I stare at the table as resentment, regret and bitterness whip back and forth.

"Tell you what," Joe chirps. "Why don't we play some pool and then head into town? Tiffany's opens early on a Saturday so we could pop in there for a few hours. That'll take your mind off things."

Tiffany's was once a backstreet pub that employed a couple of ropey strippers to get their kit off twice a week. For some unknown reason it proved a popular attraction, and the landlord eventually converted the failing pub into a low-rent version of a lap-dancing club.

"What do you reckon then?" Joe presses.

"I'm not in the mood."

I get up before he can attempt to change my mind.

"Where are you going?"

"To play the fruit machine," I snap back. "It doesn't make dumb suggestions."

I stomp over to the nearest fruit machine and load it with pound coins. With little thought or strategy, I thump the buttons and watch the reels spin over and over. To an accompaniment of flashing lights and electronic melodies, I slip into a drunken haze and find some comfort in the simple task of repeatedly pressing buttons.

Three pounds down and Joe sidles up to me.

"Are you pissed off with me?"

His presence piques irritation so I ignore him and continue thumping the buttons. Another pound disappears before Joe tries again.

"Don't be a dick, mate. If you've got a problem, tell me."

I spin around. "Yes, I've got a problem," I bark. "You!"

Dragging me away from my mindlessness is not wise as my hackles spike.

"What have I done?" he whines.

"Where do you want me to start? If it hadn't been for your stupid business idea I'd now be at home with Daisy."

"It's not my fault she saw that picture. I told you not to lie."

"If you hadn't insisted we went back with those bloody women I wouldn't have needed to lie."

"Nobody forced you, like nobody forced you to smoke weed either."

Faced with a fact I'm ill-equipped to counter, I resort to the de facto method of ending any argument.

"Just fuck off, Joe."

He mumbles something I don't catch. I return to my button thumping but from the corner of my eye I can see Joe has not heeded my advice.

"Yeah, I'll fuck off," he snipes. "And then you really will be on your own."

"Go on then."

"Actually, no. I'm not going anywhere, so you fuck off."

"No, you fuck off. I said it first."

"Jesus. No wonder Daisy left—you can be a childish twat sometimes."

A valve pops and the pent up anger mixes with the nine pints and the nine whiskies. It proves a volatile combination—my mind decides it's had enough and promptly disengages. What happens next feels like an out-of-body experience.

Without thought or reason, I throw a feeble punch. I haven't thrown a punch since school, and that lack of practice is telling as my fist glances harmlessly off Joe's cheek. However, the momentum throws my balance and I stumble forwards, my legs splaying uncontrollably like those of a new-born giraffe. I doubt I'd have been able to arrest my fall if I was sober but in my drunken state, I have no chance.

I sprawl headlong across the floor. Although the alcohol was a contributory factor to my fall, it also proves an effective anaesthetic as my forehead meets a table leg with a dull thud. Time appears to stop for a second, until raucous laughter explodes around the bar.

I sit up, and immediately wish I hadn't.

My position offers a view of a dozen heckling faces, and Joe. While the dozen faces are clearly amused by my embarrassment, Joe's face paints a very different picture. He takes two steps towards me and I presume he's about to offer me a hand up.

"That's it," he spits. "We're done."

I clamber to my feet while trying to ignore the braying bystanders who are clearly overdue some half-decent entertainment.

My mouth opens but no words come. In all the years I've known Joe, I've never seen such disgust in his eyes.

Just say sorry.

The braying and the shame overwhelm me. My mind disconnects from my mouth and I scarper from the pub.

No more than a hundred yards of sodden pavement are covered before the cold air does its job; dragging my inebriated state from drunk to paralytic. In that moment, Adam Maxwell ceases to exist and a shame-ridden carcass of a man stumbles onwards.

His coma … my coma … can't come quickly enough.

11.

My first thought upon waking: is there a word?
Horrendous? Not strong enough? *Appalling?* Lacks impact. *Dreadful?* Doesn't come close.

I conclude there is no word in my vocabulary capable of capturing the full extent of this horrendously appalling dreadfulness. As I slowly come around, a succession of fragmented memories arrive like a line of militant dwarfs— queueing patiently to take their turn head-butting me in the nuts.

The only way to escape the fuck-awful mire is to go back to sleep.

I close my eyes and endure long minutes seesawing between physical and mental pain. My bladder is fit to burst, but simply turning my head a fraction induces a skull-cracking ache followed by ripples of nausea.

There cannot be a word. Surely no human could have ever felt this utterly awful and lived to tell.

I think I'd like to die now and, as luck would have it, I'm pretty sure my bladder will explode any minute. However, I doubt it'll have the necessary force to finish me off, and drowning in my own piss isn't a particularly dignified way to go.

The Grim Reaper will have to pop back later. I'm in no fit state to die just yet anyway.

Beyond the fact I absolutely have to take a piss, I know there won't be any respite until I've consumed painkillers and several gallons of water.

Slowly, cautiously, I crawl from my pit. It pains every bit as much as I feared but I eventually make it to the bathroom. I can't even stand up, though, and have to sit on the loo to relieve myself. As I sit and wonder why I thought it was a good idea to get so wasted, I stare up at the clock on the wall. I have no recollection what time I got back from the pub yesterday but it's now eight in the morning. Plenty of sleep but it's not enough, though.

After a difficult trip to the kitchen to consume water and painkillers, I return to bed and set my alarm clock to go off in three hours—sufficient time to clear the worst of the hangover, and get out of the flat before Eddie and Daisy arrive.

Somehow I manage to doze for a couple of hours, but when my mind decides I need to relive a depressing montage of the last few days' events, I admit defeat and get up. The physical pain may have eased but the mental pain has simply filled the void.

After a shower, I make a token effort to tidy up a little. It seems a futile gesture, but if Daisy finds the flat in a mess, it'll only serve to confirm she made the right decision. Surprisingly, a bit of light housework proves a welcome distraction from the tortuous thoughts. It doesn't help the hangover much, but the combination of strong coffee and painkillers keep the worst at bay.

By half eleven the flat is tidy and I feel vaguely human. I consider calling Joe and asking him if he fancies lunch in the cafe but I don't think I can face him. We've fallen out more times than I care to remember, but it's usually over something silly and we've always patched up our differences within a day or two. A lingering pang of guilt confirms just how badly I've screwed up this time. I'm actually too ashamed to speak to him just yet so perhaps I should allow a few days for him to cool off before I wave the olive branch.

As I consider where I can spend a few hours, a rumble in my stomach offers a suggestion. It's not even noon yet so if I get my skates on, I'm sure Mum can stretch her legendary Sunday roast to one extra serving. To coin a phrase I've never really understood; I think it might be just what the doctor ordered.

I grab my jacket from the bedroom floor and pat the pockets to ensure my keys and phone are where I left them. With both present and correct, I take a wistful gaze around the room. This was Daisy's sanctuary and she chose everything from the shabby chic furniture through to the pastel coloured curtains and bed linen. I don't know precisely what she'll remove, but I try to capture the final image of *our* bedroom. When I return, the final traces of Daisy will be gone and it'll be *my* bedroom alone.

I close the door and pause while I toy with the idea of staying until Daisy arrives. The urge to see her is almost overwhelming but Eddie's threat is enough to quickly extinguish that urge. With a sackful of regrets and resentment slung over my shoulder, I leave.

I'm greeted outside by a cloudless blue sky which helps to lift my spirits a fraction. Alan's temperamental behaviour quickly dampens them.

"I don't need this, Alan. Not today."

If my troublesome van was human, I suspect he'd have signed a *do not resuscitate* order, such is his apparent desire to remain comatose.

Eventually, and reluctantly, he coughs into life.

Despite neither of us having much appetite for life, we make our way across town towards my parents' home. In the cruellest of twists a tune plays over the radio: Ellie Goulding's version of *Your Song*. It was one of three contenders for our first dance. It probably wasn't my top choice but I guess that doesn't matter one iota now as the dull ache reminds me there won't be a first dance, nor a wedding for that matter.

I switch the radio off.

In order to banish the tune from my mind, I focus on Alan's symphony of mechanical complaints for the remainder of the journey.

Knowing my parents don't like Alan dripping oil on their driveway, I park on a verge and walk the forty yards to their house. My mind is so pre-occupied with thoughts of Daisy, I barely notice the Porsche parked behind Dad's Volvo.

I let myself in and I'm greeted by the wonderful aroma of roast beef and the sound of laughter. Hoping they haven't already served up, I kick my shoes off and dart through the door into the kitchen.

I find Mum stood at the hob and Dad seated at the table alongside my sister, Kate, and her twat of a husband, Ethan.

Ohh, for Christ's sake.

All four heads turn in my direction. Not one of them is baring even a hint of a smile, and no greeting is offered. I detect something is amiss here.

"And a good morning to you too," I mumble sarcastically.

Mum turns to me and wipes her hands on a towel.

"What are you doing here, Adam?" she asks, her tone cold.

"Sorry, do I need a reason to visit my parents?"

"I'll ask again. What are you doing here, because you certainly weren't invited?"

I stare at her, incredulous. "What's going on here?"

"I assume you haven't listened to the messages I left on your phone?"

Patently she's referring to the phone I switched off yesterday lunchtime and haven't turned back on.

"Err, no. My battery died and I couldn't find my charger. Why were you trying to get hold of me?"

"You don't remember?"

I shrug my shoulders which only serves to heighten Mum's irritation.

"I don't believe you, Adam. I really don't," she yells, waving a towel towards the door. "Get out, before I lose my temper."

"Hold on. At least tell me what I've done first."

Sensing Mum is close to losing it, Kate decides to intervene. "I think it might be best for you to go, Adam."

I glare across at my sister with her honey-blonde locks and designer makeup, and Ethan with his immaculate dark hair and chiselled features. They look every bit the stereotypically perfect, middle-aged couple from a clothing catalogue—all white teeth and Botox.

"Who the hell asked you, Kate?" I retort.

Ethan—the gallant husband he considers himself—decides to stick his oar in. "There's no need for that tone, Adam. Apologise to your sister."

Much like the moment before I punched Joe, self-control and forethought both abandon me.

"Piss off, Ethan," I spit. "This is none of your business."

I turn back to my mother. "Well? What have I done?"

I've pushed Mum to the brink many times, but I've never seen her cry before. To see my own mother sobbing over something I've allegedly done, does little to buoy my already funereal mood.

Mercifully, Dad, as head of the house, decides he's had enough and it's time to intervene.

He steps across the kitchen and places a hand on my back. "I think we all need to cool off a little. Come with me, son."

Speechless and ignorant, I let Dad guide me back through the hallway and into the lounge. He closes the door and ushers me to take a seat on the sofa. As he settles into his armchair, I let my eyes drift around a room which has barely changed in decades; the same floral-print curtains and pelmets, the same mahogany veneered furniture, and the same lace doilies on the coffee table. The ever-present scent of Pledge furniture polish completes the homage to suburban conservatism.

"You really don't remember, do you, son?"

"Not a clue, Dad."

"My bowls tournament yesterday. Ring any bells?"

Oh, shitting, shitting hell!

I slap my palms against my forehead. "I'm so sorry, Dad."

"Never mind. It's not the end of the world."

"It is," I whine. "I let you down."

"No. You let your mother down because you broke a

promise. And I'm sorry to say this, but it's happened once too often now."

Mum can scream and shout at me all she likes, but Dad can force his point home by simply changing the tone of his voice. It's devastatingly effective and my shame deepens. I really didn't want to tell my parents about Daisy but there's no other option now it seems.

"I honestly didn't mean to forget, Dad, but something terrible happened during the week and my mind has been all over the place ever since."

"Terrible?"

Usually, my definition of terrible covers everything from losing my keys to inadvertently putting my underpants on inside out. The slight hint of incredulity in Dad's voice suggests I might have stretched the definition of terrible once too often.

"Daisy has left me," I sniff.

"Oh dear. Is it … permanent?"

"Yeah, I think so. She's due at the flat in about an hour with Eddie to collect all her things."

Dad sits back in his armchair and puffs his cheeks. I know what he's going to ask next, and it doesn't take long for the question to come.

"What happened?"

"A misunderstanding."

"I thought that's what you'd say. People don't tend to break up over a misunderstanding though, son."

"She thinks I was unfaithful."

"And were you?"

I glare at him defiantly. "No. I wasn't. But thanks for thinking I might."

"You've done some pretty foolish things in the past. You can't blame me for asking."

He's right, and I can't.

Dad, ever the pragmatist, then decides to address the practicalities of our separation rather than my emotional turmoil.

"What are you going to do about the flat?"

"Eh?"

"The rent and all the other bills."

Unsurprisingly, I haven't given any thought to the financial implications of Daisy's departure.

"Can you afford to keep it on your own?" Dad adds.

"I could, if I can get by without eating ever again."

We both know what the other man is thinking, and it's a

prospect we'd both rather avoid. Returning to live with my parents would, I think, be delivering the final shove over the edge of sanity. As for Mum, I think she'd probably join me on that rapid descent into madness.

"You have a spare bedroom don't you? You could get a lodger," Dad ventures, a little too enthusiastically. "You know, just to maintain your independence."

Nice recovery.

It's not the worst suggestion in the world. Our spare bedroom has only ever been used as a storeroom for the excessive amounts of miscellaneous crap Daisy brought with her when we first moved in. I'm guessing most of that will be gone by the time I return home. And while living with a complete stranger doesn't hold much appeal, neither does living under my mother's comprehensive list of house rules, or residing in my teenage bedroom once again.

"I guess I could."

"There you go," he chirps. "That's one problem sorted."

Dad smiles across at me before a more solemn expression arrives. "Now, we just need to deal with your mother."

"I think I'll leave her to calm down for now. I'll pop back later."

Like a Jedi mind trick, the simple arching of his eyebrows tells me that's not an option.

"Tell her about Daisy and I'm sure she'll look upon it differently."

"I can't, not with Ken and Barbie watching on."

"Who?"

"Doesn't matter. Besides, she'll just give me grief for screwing up rather than sympathy."

"Don't be so quick to assume, son. Your mother was very fond of Daisy and, you never know, perhaps she might even have a word with her to see if there's any way to salvage the situation."

I take a moment to reflect on Dad's advice. It's certainly true that Mum got on better with Daisy than any of my other girlfriends, but would she even fight my corner, let alone stand any chance of changing Daisy's mind?

"Do you really think she'd do that?"

"She might, if you go back in the kitchen, apologise, and explain."

"Can't you ask her to come in here, please? I really don't want to air my dirty laundry in front of Kate and Ethan."

"Fine. I'll go and get her," he replies with a shake of the head.

"Thanks, Dad."

He gets up and shuffles towards the door.

"Oh, Dad."

"Yes."

"How did you get on, with your bowls match?"

"I won. I'm in the final."

"Nice one. I promise I'll be there for that."

We swap smiles—mine apologetic, his dubious.

"Thank you. Give me a minute."

Closing the lounge door behind him, he heads off to placate my mother and, hopefully, bring her to my rescue. I'm not optimistic but considering I've already resigned myself to losing Daisy, I'm prepared to grasp even the prickliest of straws.

Anxious seconds pass until I hear hushed voices in the hallway. I can't hear what's being said, but judging by the general tone, Dad is trying to be the diplomat while my mother is trying not to be exasperated. Dad is succeeding. Mum isn't.

I do, however, catch Mum's final word.

"Fine," she huffs.

The lounge door opens and my parents enter. Dad retakes his seat in the armchair but Mum decides to stand, her arms folded. Her expression and body language don't bode well.

The uncomfortable silence is split by Dad's throat clearing. It also serves as a prompt—humble pie is about to be served.

"Sorry, Mum," I mumble like a sulky teenager.

"For what?" she replies curtly.

"For being a selfish brat," I sigh. "I know you've heard it a million times but I really am sorry, and I shouldn't have spoken to you like that. For what it's worth, I feel bloody awful about missing Dad's match and there's nothing you can say that would make me feel any worse."

Mum's stern expression relaxes a little as she takes a seat next to me on the sofa.

"Your father told me about Daisy."

I nod, and await the inquest into what I did wrong.

"I need your word, Adam, that you weren't unfaithful."

I turn and look my mother straight in the eye. "I swear, Mum. I would never do that to her."

She eyes me, searching for the now familiar signs of deceit.

"Okay, I believe you, but whatever you've done this time, clearly it's gone too far."

"I know."

She lets out a resigned sigh. "I'll give her a call tomorrow once the dust has settled. I can't promise anything, but I'll at least see if there's any hope."

I lean over and kiss her on the cheek. "Thank you."

"But," she adds. "There are two conditions."

The urge to groan is almost too much. "Name them," I chirp through gritted teeth.

"Firstly, I want you to apologise to Kate and Ethan for your tone."

"Ughh. Do I have to?"

"No, you don't, in the same way I don't have to call Daisy."

"Okay, point made and understood. I'll speak to them in a minute."

"And the second condition: I want you to promise me you'll get some help."

"Help? For what?"

Her eyes flick towards Dad. I don't know if there was any collaboration on this second condition, but I'm guessing not, judging by my mother's furtive glances.

"Listen, Adam. We think …"

Dad clears his throat again.

"Sorry. I think … maybe you should try speaking to a therapist."

"A therapist? Why?"

"Because they might be able to help you get to grips with your decision making."

I'm not sure whether to be flattered my mother cares enough, or incensed she thinks a grown man is incapable of making his own decisions. I decide to hedge my bets.

"It's an interesting idea Mum, but I don't think you can get therapy for making crappy decisions."

"You can. I've read about it."

"You've read about it? Where?"

"On the interweb."

"You mean the Internet?"

"Yes, that. Anyway, I found this treatment called CBT."

"Cognitive behavioural therapy."

"Oh, you've heard of it?" she replies with no effort to hide her surprise.

"I'm not a complete moron, Mum. Joe used to suffer from anxiety and had CBT therapy for a while."

"Really? Did it work?"

"I think so. I'll ask him when he's talking to me again."

She rolls her eyes and presses on.

"I don't know if it'll help but I do know one potential benefit it might bring."

"What?"

"It'll prove to Daisy you're willing to try and change your ways. She does love you, Adam, but even you have to admit, you make yourself hard to love sometimes what with all your constant … calamities."

Half-an-hour ago, I'd have laughed at anyone suggesting I should see a therapist, but Mum has packaged the idea up in Daisy-coloured wrapping paper, knowing I'd find it impossible to reject.

"Alright, Mum. I'll look into it."

"Promise?"

"I promise."

"Good. Now, I suppose you'd like some lunch?"

Lunch, I want. Apologising to Kate and Ethan, I don't.

Truth be told, both are of little consequence now the light at the end of my tunnel has been restored. That light might be dim, but it's better than the pitch black void I've been staring into for the last few days.

Hope, it seems, has been restored. For now.

12.

I could never be a politician.

How anyone can remain civil when their career involves a constant barrage of questions, most set to trip them up, is beyond me. I reckon I'd only last a few days before telling a reporter or constituent to go fuck themselves.

However, I managed to maintain my composure for three whole hours at lunch yesterday and, despite Ethan's best efforts to get under my skin, I sat there smiling and never swore once. I even managed to maintain my smile when Eddie texted to say they'd finished and I could return to my much emptier flat.

However, on the journey home Alan was treated to a Tourette's-grade tirade as I unleashed my pent-up rage towards Ethan's twatishness and Eddie's mocking text message.

My mood did not improve when I stepped through the front door of the flat.

I spent a few minutes touring the rooms and running a mental inventory of missing items. As I slumped down on the sofa it occurred to me the most important item removed wasn't even material—the very soul of our little home was now gone.

If it hadn't been for my lingering hangover, and Mum's terms and conditions still ringing in my ears, I'd have almost certainly spent the evening getting reacquainted with Jack Daniels. Instead, I went to bed at nine o'clock and fell into a fitful sleep clutching Daisy's pillow; grateful one piece of her still remained.

That early night proved worthwhile, though, and I actually got up at seven o'clock this morning, feeling vaguely human again. Not great, or remotely positive, but just about human. It's a start.

Showered, and with a coffee in hand, I grab my laptop and take a seat in the kitchen. As the laptop boots up, I wrestle with a dilemma: if I take Dad's advice and find a lodger, what happens to said lodger if Daisy can be persuaded to return? Can I simply kick them out without notice? It would be just my luck for Daisy to say she's coming back, only to change her mind upon discovering she'd be living with a third wheel.

Then again, the rent is due at the end of next week and I can't cover it.

What to do?

Once the laptop finally wakes up, I drum my fingers on the table. For once, I invest all of thirty seconds trying to think logically about the best way forward. I suppose, even if I place an advert for a lodger, it'll be at least a week before they'd actually move in, by which point I'll know if a chat with my mother has made any difference to Daisy. However, if I wait until that conversation takes place and it proves futile, I'll be two or three days closer to rent due day.

Man, just do something.

Before the inevitable indecision kicks in, I open a web browser and search for a suitable website to advertise my shitty spare bedroom. With no real idea what I'm doing, I randomly click links until I land on a page where I can post an advert. After diligently inputting all the required information, I reach the final section where I'm required to add a description of the room. I sit back and inwardly groan. It's a room for Christ's sake— floor, walls, ceiling … what else is there to say? I suppose it has a window with curtains, a radiator, and carpet. Oh, and a door, and a light. It seems strange they require me to list the obvious but I do it anyway.

I click the button to submit the form.

My click prompts a sense of accomplishment; I've started the day on a constructive footing. The dull ache then reminds me why I need a lodger and the positivity ebbs away. Still, this exercise has shown I can keep the dull ache at bay for short periods by distracting myself.

I must keep busy.

As luck would have it, I'm running low on my homemade window-cleaning solution. Measuring and mixing a new batch should keep me occupied for another twenty minutes. I finish my coffee and pad through to the storage cupboard in the hallway where I store the ingredients.

The solution, created eighteen months ago, started life as a vinaigrette salad dressing. Daisy's parents were coming over for lunch and I was tasked with one job: to purchase salad dressing. Obviously I forgot and, at the very last minute, decided I could create my own while Daisy was in the shower. She would never know I failed my one-and-only contribution to lunch.

So, I googled a recipe and adapted it based upon the limited ingredients we had in the flat. Time was also against me and, feeling rushed, I might have inadvertently misread the specific quantities of each ingredient. The finished product certainly looked, and even smelt, like a vinaigrette salad dressing. Alas, it tasted like an aborted experiment in Scottish wine making, and rendered the salad inedible.

We went out for lunch.

When Daisy and I returned to the flat two hours later, I was ordered to clear up the kitchen as penance for ruining lunch. It was while drying-up the glass salad bowl I noticed something—the bottom, where my hideous dressing had pooled, was crystal clear, while the rest of the bowl looked almost opaque by comparison.

Always looking for ways to make my life easier, I salvaged the remains of the dressing from a jar in the bin and applied it to the inside of the kitchen window. Not only did it instantly remove the greasy film from the glass but it did so without leaving any streaks or smears. Even Daisy was impressed and, after I hashed together another batch, she calculated the cost to be seventy-percent less than the off-the-shelf cleaner I'd been using.

To this day, that solution remains the only hallmark of success in my life—ironic considering it only exists due to another of my cock-ups.

I measure, pour and then mix the ingredients together in a large tub and then transfer the solution into a plastic keg my dad once used for home-brewing bitter. The keg is then returned to the storage cupboard where I can use the little tap on the front to fill up my squeezy bottle each morning before I leave.

Another job done.

With little else to fill my time, I do something I haven't done in over two years—I leave the flat for work before nine o'clock. Having lost almost two days' work last week due to hangovers, and the minor inconvenience of my fiancée leaving, I really need to put in a shift today. If the weather holds out, I should be able to get through a dozen houses before it gets dark.

I arrive at the first house at nine on the dot and for four straight hours I work like a dog. With seven houses done, I take a few minutes to sit and binge on a family pack of Twiglets. It also gives me an opportunity to check my phone. One thing I learnt very early in this job is to never check a phone while stood at the top of a ladder. To avoid such temptation I always leave my phone in the glove box.

I have one voicemail and one text message.

The voicemail is from my mother; possibly with news about Daisy. Even if the text message was from Camelot and hinted at a major lottery win, I'd still have checked my mother's message first. I jab at the screen and listen.

The message is short but tantalisingly sweet—Mum is having lunch with Daisy tomorrow.

My mind begins to process the potentially positive reasons Daisy would agree to meeting Mum for lunch. Then, just as quickly, the potential negative reasons. I spend five minutes swinging back and forth between optimism and pessimism. I conclude any further thought on the matter is futile, particularly as the growing swarm of butterflies in my stomach threaten to eject the recently consumed Twiglets. I'll know one way or another tomorrow afternoon and until then, I need to remain distracted.

I click on the message icon in the hope it achieves that aim. It's not from Camelot, but somebody responding to my advert, asking if they can view the room at five-thirty today. Surprised to have received an enquiry so quickly, I reply to confirm it's fine and put the phone back in the glove box. On the whole, my short break has been worthwhile.

I crack on with house eight.

My record for windows cleaned in one day is seventy-two. By the time dusk arrives, I'm up to ninety-one. I'm filthy, cold, and absolutely knackered, but I can't deny the cathartic effect of a hard day's graft. Compared to how I felt at my lowest point last week, I'll take aching limbs over an aching heart any day.

I strap the ladder to Alan's roof before falling into the driver's seat.

"Not a bad shift today, my old mate."

Perhaps not wishing to dampen my spirits, Alan starts on the first turn of the key. We head back to the flat as dusk eases towards darkness.

It's nearly five o'clock by the time I pull into the driveway. It's not something I had cause to consider before now, but the fact I always arrived home from work before Daisy is now a blessing. At least I'm used to walking in to a dark, empty flat but I'm sure the dull ache will remind me I won't be cooking for two tonight. I guess, over time, these little routines will lose their Daisy-factor as new routines are forged. So many to face in the coming weeks and months, unless of course …

I stop myself and focus on the impending visit of my first potential lodger.

After a quick search under the sink, I locate four scented candles Daisy either forgot about or didn't want. I'm not sure the scent of wild orchid and ylang ylang are particularly masculine but I guess it's preferable to the current scent of unwashed socks and stale farts. I light all four candles and strategically place one in each room; all the while wondering what the fuck a ylang ylang is.

None-the-wiser, I run the hoover around and tidy the kitchen.

With five minutes to spare, I stand in the doorway to the spare bedroom and complete a final check—not that there's much to actually check. Thinking about it, perhaps I should have furnished the room with at least a second-hand bed and wardrobe. In its current state of absolute emptiness, it doesn't exactly shout practical living.

Bollocks.

Too late now I guess.

The doorbell rings.

I trudge down the stairs and across the hallway. Time to put on a brave face and play the part of genial landlord, which should be quite a challenge considering I'm really a no-idea-what-I'm-doing kind of landlord. By the time I've swung the door open, it dawns on me I should have perhaps changed out of my grubby work clothes.

It matters not, as any concerns about my own attire are quickly forgotten as I cast my eye over the prospective lodger.

"Adam Maxwell?"

I nod, and stare open mouthed at the odd figure stood on my doorstep.

The guy is short—about five foot two—and dressed head to toe in black. It's not so much his height or clothing that throws me, but his hairless, egg-like head and piercing eyes which are closer to turquoise than blue.

"Uh, yeah … sorry," I splutter. "Come in."

I can't put my finger on it but there is something deeply disconcerting about the man. His expression is completely unreadable: no smile, no frown, no nothing. Perhaps if I'd thought about it, I wouldn't have invited him in but I find myself stepping backwards into the hallway.

He follows me in and it occurs to me I don't even know his name.

"You'll have to excuse me. I didn't catch your name."

He looks up at me with eyes cold enough to summon a chill.

"I never told you my name," he replies flatly. "I am Mungo Thunk."

13.

I have many faults, but poor hearing isn't one of them. However, I still feel compelled to ask the weird man to confirm his equally weird name.

"Mungo Thunk?" I parrot.

"Yes."

"That's an … unusual name."

"If you say so."

That topic of conversation closed, I shuffle nervously on the spot; suddenly conscious Mr Thunk is not quite what I was looking for in a lodger.

"Is there a problem, Mr Maxwell?" he asks. "You appear uncomfortable."

I replay his question in my head. His voice lacks even the slightest hint of an accent or intonation; almost robotic.

"No … um, I'm fine."

I really don't know what to say to him. With nothing else better to offer, I refer to Joe's list of questions composed for the angry bin-man.

"Um, how are you doing?"

"Is my wellbeing of consequence to you?"

"I … eh? Not really, if I'm honest."

"Then why ask?"

It's a good question. "I don't know. It's just polite, I suppose."

He tilts his head a fraction. "Do you think it is polite to ask a question if you have no interest in the answer?"

I'm not sure whether I find his question profound or dumb. Either way, it's a little unsettling I'm giving it any thought at all.

"Now you come to mention it, I suppose not."

"In which case, shall we address the purpose of my visit?"

I'm about to turn and head back up the stairs when an obvious thought strikes—if he likes the room, I'll actually have to live with this guy. He's not popping up for coffee or to enjoy the scent of ylang ylang; we could be potentially sharing the same space every single day for months, or even years.

And he's clearly a nutjob.

Shit.

I need to nip this in the bud.

"Sorry, before we look at the room, can I just check

something?"

"You may."

"Do you have a job? Sorry to ask but unless you're in full-time employment …"

"I will pay six months' rent in advance."

"Oh. That's very generous, but you didn't answer my question."

"You only need to establish my employment status to determine if I can afford the agreed rent. Seeing as I am offering to pay in advance, your question is no longer relevant."

A fair point. There must be another loophole I can use to wriggle out of this.

"What is it you do for a living?"

My money would be on undertaker, or aspiring serial killer. It doesn't really matter because somehow I'm hoping to use his employment as a reason why he can't have the room. I'll say we have incompatible hours, or some other flaky reason why his job would make it difficult living together.

"My vocation is complex but in simple terms, my speciality is therapy."

"Ahh, that's a shame … wait. Did you say therapy?"

"Yes."

"What sort of therapy?"

"I deal with behavioural issues."

For a few seconds I stand open mouthed until a thought arrives. This can't be a coincidence after my chat with Mum yesterday.

"Did my mother send you?"

"Why would your mother send me?"

"Because only yesterday she was nagging me to see a therapist."

"Inconsequential as I do not know your mother."

He could be lying, or he could be telling the truth—his expressionless face doesn't offer any clues either way. He doesn't strike me as the lying kind, though, so I give him the benefit of the doubt.

"Fair enough. Obviously it's just a coincidence."

"Indeed. May I see the room now?"

"Yeah … sure."

Fresh out of excuses, I beckon him to follow me up the stairs. Chances are he'll hate the room anyway. And if he doesn't, and I can look beyond the fact he might be a serial killer, the prospect of free, on-tap therapy might not necessarily exclude him from my very short shortlist of potential lodgers.

I open the front door and decide I'll reserve any further judgement until he's seen the room. Perhaps he's just a naturally reserved type of bloke and he'll relax a little when he gets to know me.

"What is that odour?" he asks as we step through the front door.

"Candles. Orchids and ylang ylang, I think."

"It is most unpleasant."

"Not as unpleasant as the smell it's masking," I chuckle.

He doesn't laugh. He doesn't even break a smile.

"The room is through here," I quickly add, moving the conversation along.

I open the door to the spare bedroom and switch the light on. I have to concede it looked more homely with the light off.

"Well, this is it."

Without waiting for an invite, he shuffles into the centre of the room and slowly turns to survey the small space.

"There is no furniture," he remarks, stating the obvious.

"No … I … um, wanted to see if the new lodger had their own stuff."

Ignoring me, he steps over to the window and feels the curtains.

"Is this material fire retardant?"

"No idea, but probably."

"Were you aware there was a fourteen percent increase in household fires last year?"

"Um, no. I wasn't."

"Do you have smoke detectors?"

"Yes, we have two," I reply confidently. Probably best not to mention I removed the batteries as my cooking sets them off on an almost daily basis.

"Anyway," I add, changing the subject. "Let me show you the rest of the flat."

"That is not necessary," he replies.

Thank God; he hates the room enough.

"I will move in tomorrow."

What?

Despite the fact this guy has been here barely ten minutes, my mouth has already bobbed open more times than a gum-chewing goldfish.

"I'm sorry?"

"Do you have a problem with your hearing, Mr Maxwell?"

he adds. "Shall I repeat myself?"

"What? No, you just took me by surprise."

"Tomorrow then? I do have other rooms to view if you are not in agreement."

This feels far too rushed. If I let him move in tomorrow, and Daisy does change her mind, I'm stuffed. Free therapy or not, I've found my excuse.

"Truth is, Mr ... Thunk, I'm waiting on confirmation my fiancée won't be moving back in. I won't know for sure until tomorrow afternoon. And besides, the room is empty so I'd need to find some furniture."

"You can call me tomorrow afternoon to confirm, and I will arrange for the necessary furniture to be delivered, at my expense."

This guy has an answer for everything.

"I ... err ... I suppose."

"That is settled then."

Before I can argue, he delves into his coat pocket and withdraws a thick envelope.

"Six months' rent, in cash," he says, handing me the envelope.

I tentatively take it and open the flap—over two thousand pounds in crisp, fifty-pound notes are a good enough reason to park my concerns.

"But what if ...?"

"If your fiancée returns," he interjects, as if he'd read my mind. "You can refund my rent and I will find alternative accommodation."

He holds out a hand.

"Do we have a deal, Mr Maxwell?"

I should really think about this.

I shake a hand colder than his eyes and as smooth as his bald dome.

"Deal and, seeing as we're going to be flatmates, call me Adam."

"And you may call me Mungo."

"Right. Thanks ... Mungo."

His name is going to take some getting used to, as is he, to be frank.

As he makes his way towards the door, he hands me a business card. The only information it contains is his name and a phone number.

"If you call me tomorrow at two-thirty with confirmation, I

will be here by three o'clock to oversee the furniture delivery."

"Will do. And can I ask you a question before you go?"

"You may."

"This behavioural therapy you do—would you be able to help me with that?"

"You require therapy?"

"Apparently so."

"What is it you are looking to change about your behaviour?"

"Basically, I keep fucking things up."

For the first time since he arrived, his expression changes, and not in a good way.

"You need to be more specific," he scowls.

"You know, making bad decisions."

As I relay the recent events, and the many examples of my poor decision making, his expression defaults back to unreadable.

"I see," he says, as I conclude my explanation. "I can help if you are able to answer one question."

"Shoot."

"Shoot?"

"I mean, what's the question?"

He takes two steps forward and stares straight up at me. "During which month do people typically sleep the least?"

"Um, I'm not sure. I suppose the summer months, when it's hot at night, or maybe in December when there's lots of parties and late nights."

He continues to stare up at me until, barely perceptible, the edge of his mouth curls upwards a mere fraction.

"February," he declares.

"What?"

"That hearing issue again. I said February."

"Why February?"

"Because it has the least amount of nights so therefore people sleep less. The answer is obvious if you thoroughly analyse the question."

My turn to scowl. "Great. A trick question."

"No. It was a simple question with an obvious answer. You chose to over-complicate it; or more precisely, your mind did."

"Whatever," I sigh. "Have I passed then? Will you help me?"

He offers a nod so slight it might not even have been a nod.

"Goodbye, Adam Maxwell. Until tomorrow."

He breezes out of the room and a second later, I hear the front door open and close.

What. The. Fuck.

I remain rooted to the spot, trying to decipher what just happened. Did he just analyse me? And more importantly, did I just agree to him moving in?

In no time at all, something akin to buyer's remorse arrives. With barely any thought at all, I have just agreed to share my home with a pint-sized weirdo I know absolutely nothing about, and invited him to nose around the inside of my head while he's at it. Even by my impulsive standards, I may have been a tad rash.

But, I do have an envelope full of cash, and I can now tell Mum I'm talking to a therapist, which she'll hopefully relay to Daisy.

Maybe my rash decision was the right one, for once.

I stash the envelope in a drawer in the kitchen and call Mum.

She answers without a greeting. "You took your time."

"I've had a long day at work, Mum."

"And I'm guessing you want to know how my call with Daisy went?"

"Please."

"Have you done anything about speaking to a therapist?"

"Actually, I have. I'm seeing him tomorrow afternoon."

It's not really a lie, I suppose. I will be speaking to Mungo tomorrow afternoon and he is a therapist.

"Really?" she replies, clearly not convinced.

"I can give you his name and number if you'd like to check."

"No," she huffs. "I'll give you the benefit of the doubt. Let's just hope he can help."

"I'm sure he can, but seeing as I kept my promise, are you going to tell me what Daisy said?"

The brief pause is not a good sign. Neither is the resigned sigh she puffs before answering.

"I need to be honest with you, Adam. You've really hurt that girl and I'm not hopeful she'll change her mind."

"I didn't do anything, Mum," I plead.

"Reading between the lines, your latest indiscretion was the final straw. There's only so much anyone can take, Adam—God, I of all people know that."

"You've got to try, Mum, please. Tell her I'm trying to sort myself out."

"I'll do my best but don't get your hopes up."

Hope is about all that's kept me going for the last few days. I'm not about to abandon it just yet.

"What time are you seeing her?"

"Twelve. She has to be back at work by one so I'll let you know as soon as I get home."

"Thank you, and I do appreciate it, Mum."

She ends the call.

The fate of my relationship with Daisy now rests solely in my mother's hands and the helplessness smarts. However, there is another relationship I can try to salvage myself. I compose a grovelling text to Joe and ask him if he wants to watch the football in the Red Lion tomorrow evening.

As there's nothing more I can do other than wait, I turn my attention to dinner. The options are limited so I toast a couple of slices of stale bread and empty a tin of baked beans into a saucepan. There is no more tragic a meal than beans on toast, but beggars can't be choosers.

I eat dinner in front of the TV, all the while keeping an eye on my phone for a reply from Joe. This has got to be a new low.

Mercifully, a two-word reply arrives as I shovel the final forkful of beans into my mouth: *Yeah, sure.*

Even such a short text is enough to confirm Joe has forgiven me. If he was still angry, he'd have either ignored my text altogether, or replied with a very different two-word answer. That's the thing about Joe and I—we don't tend to dwell on an argument; even when that argument involves a punch apparently. We apologise, call each other a twat, shake hands and everything goes back to normal. I wish it were so simple with the women in my life.

With nothing else better to do, I take a shower and watch an action movie which keeps me occupied for a few hours. In reality, I know I'm simply trying to avoid thinking about tomorrow, and the million ways it could turn sour. Despite the temptation, I keep away from the booze cupboard in the kitchen and eventually head to bed at ten.

As I switch the bedside lamp off, the darkness brings out the demons. No matter what I try to think of, my mind torments me with a single question: will I be in this bed alone tomorrow night or, as I fear, will I be lying here waiting for Mungo to murder me?

Sleep can't come soon enough.

14.

It was a particularly bad nightmare.

I awoke in a cold sweat, almost convinced the hideous scene, conjured by my own mind, was real. Christ alone knows why, but my mind thought I'd like to witness a reality where both Mungo and Daisy moved into the flat, and then enjoyed noisy sex together in the spare bedroom on a nightly basis. And for some inexplicable reason all I did was lie there inert, listening to Daisy's squealing and Mungo's monotone commentary.

If I didn't need therapy before, I sure as hell do now.

Even though there's still an hour remaining before I have to get up, there's no way I'm going back to sleep and risking that torment again. I get up and head straight to the bathroom.

After a shower and two bowls of Coco Pops with water, in lieu of the milk I didn't buy, I leave the flat before nine o'clock again. If I learnt anything yesterday, it's that throwing myself into work is a partial antidote to the dull ache. However, knowing my fate will be sealed in a little under three hours does nothing to quell my nerves.

Must keep busy.

My first task of the day is clearing ice from Alan's windscreen. It's so cold my cheeks sting within seconds, but the clear blue sky is, in my head at least, a positive sign. Alan is feeling less positive, though, and five frustrating minutes are wasted trying to wake him up.

Surrounded by a fog of my own frozen breath, we eventually set off for the first house of the day.

If window cleaning were an Olympic sport, I'd have nailed a gold medal before lunch. Such endeavour has an unexpected side-effect as, for the first time, I consider just how many windows I can clean, and therefore how much extra money I can make, if I really apply myself. Lazy has always been an easy place to work but the pay isn't great. Lesson learnt perhaps.

I calculated Mum should return home by about one-thirty, and I deliberately didn't wear a watch today as I knew I'd glance at it every five minutes. By luck or good judgement I take a break minutes before my estimated D-day. I sit in Alan with my phone resting against the steering wheel and stare at the clock while willing the minutes to pass. Even if I'd had the foresight to pack something for lunch, there is no way I could keep anything down.

One-thirty comes and goes.

The slight tremble in my jaw builds into a chatter—possibly due to the cold but more likely nerves.

One thirty-five.

I can't stand sitting still and extract myself from Alan. The pacing up and down helps to stave off the cold but does little to settle my nerves.

One-forty.

Nerves edge towards irritation and it takes some effort to not kick a plastic gnome on the driveway.

One forty-five.

Concerned I'm wearing a trench in the tarmac, I return to Alan and turn the radio on.

Long seconds tick by as I become increasingly convinced the phone will never ring, until it does. I swipe the screen with a trembling finger.

"Mum," I gasp. "Thank God."

"Adam … are you okay? You sound out of breath."

"I'm fine, I'm fine," I pant breathlessly. "How did it go?"

"Are you sure? Your Uncle Stephen suffered from asthma so it does run in the family."

If it were possible, I'd reach down the phone line and rip the words from my mother's mouth.

"For crying out loud, Mum. Please, just tell me."

"Alright, calm down, young man. There's no need for that tone."

If she doesn't tell me within the next five seconds, I swear I'm going to boot that fucking gnome halfway down the street.

"Sorry, but please, just put me out of my misery."

"Not over the telephone."

"What?"

"I'm not going to discuss it over the telephone, Adam."

"Why the hell did you ring me then?"

"I won't tell you again, young man."

"Sorry, sorry, but I just want to know if my relationship is over or not, Mum. Can you not understand why I might be a little testy?"

"And I will tell you … tomorrow."

"Eh? Why can't you tell me now? Why tomorrow?"

"Because it's complicated and I'd rather talk to you in person. You can come over for dinner and we'll discuss it like grown-ups."

Patronising cow.

I draw a few heavy breaths to calm myself down.

"Can you not at least give me a clue what was said?"

"No, because I know what you're like. Do you remember your twelfth birthday?"

"What the …"

"You kept nagging us about your present because you couldn't wait. You went on and on for weeks and I foolishly gave you a clue. That, as I discovered, was a mistake and you kept asking for more clues right up until the day before your birthday."

"It's hardly the same thing, Mum."

"You need to learn some patience, Adam, and that sometimes parents know best."

"Mum, please."

"I'll see you tomorrow at six. Don't be late."

She hangs up.

"Fuck! Fuck! Fuck!"

The phone is thrown back into the glove box and I grip the steering wheel until my knuckles turn white.

It takes several minutes for my anger to subside, and for any clarity of thought to arrive. And when it does finally arrive, much to my surprise that clarity is carrying a small parcel of hope—why would Mum want to talk over dinner if Daisy flatly stated there was no hope of us getting back together? A no is a no, and it's not like Mum to serve a shit sandwich with a side order of sympathy; it's not her style. My mother has never been the type to avoid hard truths, particularly when it comes to me.

Something must have been said, other than a flat-out no.

The merest hint of a smile creeps across my face. It does feel good to lose the frown, even for a few seconds.

Another thought then gate-crashes my happy party and quickly kills the atmosphere. What do I tell Mungo?

After recent events, even the biggest idiot would realise the folly of more lies. While I still don't know if there's a future for Daisy and I, there is a slither of hope, but that doesn't necessarily mean she'll be moving back in tomorrow. She might not even want to move back in at all, and perhaps that's the complication Mum referred to. The same waiting room magazines which offered advice on coping with a breakup also featured articles about saving a relationship. I seem to recall space was mentioned a lot, and perhaps that's what Daisy needs right now—a little time and a little space.

I retrieve my phone from the glove box, along with Mungo's business card. I jab the screen a dozen times and he answers almost immediately.

"This is Mungo Thunk."

For a second I'm not sure if it's a recorded voicemail message, such is his mechanical tone.

"Hello … Mungo?"

"Did I not adequately clarify my name, Adam Maxwell?"

"What? Yes you … doesn't matter. Can you talk?"

"Clearly I can."

Christ, this guy is hard work.

"Right, well, I wanted to update you on the situation with the room."

"Go ahead."

I tell him everything I know about the situation with Daisy, which isn't much. Mungo then delivers his cold assessment.

"If your fiancée decides to return, it is unlikely she will do so immediately as there will be much to organise. During that period of organisation, I will seek alternative accommodation while assisting in your treatment."

"So, you still want to move in?"

"As agreed."

"And you're still willing to help fix my … issues?"

"Again, as agreed."

This makes no sense. Not only am I dicking him around but he's also prepared to offer free treatment while being dicked.

"I must say, Mungo, you're being very … what's the word …?"

"Pragmatic."

"Yeah, that's it. My dad is pragmatic. It's a good quality."

"It is who I am, Adam Maxwell."

"And just to be clear, you're totally cool about moving out, if needs be?"

"Why would my body temperature have any bearing on the decision?"

Frustrated at his literal interpretation, a hand slaps across my forehead.

"No, Mungo. I meant you'd be happy to move out if Daisy comes back?"

"Not happy. Indifferent."

"Uh, okay. Shall I meet you at the flat then, at three o'clock?"

"Yes."

The line goes dead. He's clearly not one for long goodbyes.

I return the phone to the glove box as the tension in my body eases a fraction.

The call to Mungo went better than expected but I'm still no clearer on the motive for his accommodating attitude.

I give it some thought but quickly conclude it doesn't matter.

Maybe my lack of concern is because the situation with Daisy is all encompassing, or perhaps it's because I have an envelope stuffed full of Mungo's cash. And, if push literally comes to shove, I'm about nine inches taller and several stone heavier, so physically evicting him shouldn't be too difficult.

No need to think about it any further. I'm sure I've got every base covered.

With half hour spare before I need to make my way home, I have just enough time to squeeze in a ground floor flat and its four windows.

I arrive home at ten to three and head straight to the bathroom for a quick, and much-needed, shower.

Bang on cue, the doorbell rings just as I'm pulling on my socks. I scuttle down the stairs and open the door to my new lodger.

"Alright, Mungo?"

"You wish to know if I am alright?"

I should have learnt from yesterday. "Honestly, I couldn't give a toss if you're alright or not, so let me try again—hello, Mungo."

"You are learning. Hello, Adam Maxwell."

"Thanks, and can you please stop using my full name?"

"You prefer Mr Maxwell?"

"No, just Adam."

"Very well. I will call you Adam."

"See, we both changed our behaviour," I remark with a grin. It isn't reciprocated.

Our painstaking greeting out of the way, my attention turns to the large black suitcase next to him.

"Do you want me to take that up for you?"

"No."

"Are you sure? It looks heavy."

"You do not have to ask the same question twice. It is highly unlikely I would have changed my mind in such a brief period of time."

"Fair enough. Come on up."

For such a small man, he handles the suitcase with surprising ease. Less of a surprise is his attire which consists of black everything: coat, jacket, shirt, trousers and shoes.

I follow him into the bedroom and hand over a set of keys.

"Sometimes the main door downstairs doesn't close properly and you won't need it, but there's a key for it anyway. What time is your furniture arriving?"

He glances at his watch. "Twenty-seven minutes."

"Great. Do you want a tea or coffee? I'm out of milk, though, so you'll have to take it black."

"I do not drink tea or coffee. Do you have bottled water?"

I've never met anyone who doesn't drink tea or coffee. His weirdness has just hit new heights.

"Um, afraid not. How about tap water?"

His eyes narrow a fraction. "All tap water contains some level of faecal coliform."

"What's that when it's at home?"

"In simple terms, human excrement."

I try not to think of the water-drenched Coco Pops I had for breakfast.

"Shit," I murmur.

"Yes. I believe that is the colloquial term."

"Thanks for that Mungo. Remind me to get some milk later."

"Pasteurised cow's milk contains …"

"Stop right there," I interject. "I don't want to know. And for the record, I don't want to know what's in a pork pie, a saveloy, black pudding, or anything else. Understood?"

"Understood."

"Good. Now, shall I show you around?"

He nods and I give him a guided tour, pointing out the obvious as we tour the lounge, bathroom and, finally, the kitchen.

"Do you want me to show you how to use the oven and the microwave?"

"Notwithstanding the fact they both look highly unsanitary, I have no need for such appliances."

"So, how are you going to cook anything?"

"I consume only raw fruit, vegetables, and pulses."

"Christ. I'd best get in the bathroom before you in the mornings."

"Why?"

"Do I really need to explain?"

The doorbell rings before I have to. Mungo checks his watch again and disappears down the stairs to open the door, clearly quite at home already. I check the kitchen clock and note it's three-thirty so it must be his furniture—impressively punctual considering I can't even get a pizza delivered within twenty minutes of the promised time.

I decide to keep out of the way and put the kettle on, but not before lifting the lid to check a rogue turd hasn't slipped in.

Once I've made myself a coffee, I sit at the table and listen to the voices from the hallway. I can hear Mungo offering curt advice to the delivery men, who don't appear to appreciate his input.

"Just let us do our job, mate," one of them says gruffly.

"My advice is not welcome?"

"No, it ain't."

After ten minutes of grunting and groaning, the front door slams shut and Mungo enters the kitchen.

"The furniture has been delivered."

"I gathered. Let's see what you've got then."

I follow him through to the bedroom. Besides a single bed, the room now houses a solid-looking oak wardrobe with matching chest of drawers and bedside table. I assumed he'd order cheap flat-pack furniture but clearly my new lodger has expensive taste.

"Shit, Mungo. This stuff must have cost a fortune."

"You have clearly not heard the familiar adage: *buy cheap, buy twice.*"

"Well, no."

He looks me up and down, examining my ripped jeans and faded hoodie.

"I would recommend you bear it in mind for future purchases."

Having slated my clothes, he lifts the suitcase onto the bed and opens it up.

"You've certainly got a thing for black, Mungo."

It's quite the understatement considering the entire contents of the suitcase are black.

"It is practical."

"That's one word for it. I'll leave you to unpack."

I retire to the lounge and, with a couple of hours spare until I'm due to meet Joe, switch the TV on. After the physical and emotional exertions of the last few days, it'll be good to simply slouch on the sofa and watch some mindless crap; assuming Mungo stays in his room.

He does … for fifteen minutes.

"I require your assistance," he remarks, while stood in the doorway.

"What's up?"

"I must acquire provisions. Where is the nearest retail outlet?"

"There's a Tesco Express a few streets away. Can you get some milk while you're there?"

"I will acquire milk if you provide substantive directions."

I reluctantly clamber to my feet and grab a scrap of paper and a pen. After scrawling a rough map, I hand it over.

"Just call me if you get lost. Now, if you don't mind, *Pointless* is about to start."

He takes the less-than-subtle hint and shuffles off.

An entire hour passes and, just as I'm about to leave for the Red Lion, Mungo returns, laden with carrier bags.

"I didn't realise you were doing a weekly shop."

"I have acquired adequate provisions, and milk, as you requested."

"Nice one. I'll clear a cupboard in the kitchen for you."

"Not necessary. I will store my provisions in the bedroom."

Odd, but perhaps he thinks I'm going to steal his loose-leaf spinach.

"Suit yourself. Anyway, I'm off to the pub."

"I require three minutes."

"Three minutes? For what?"

"To prepare myself."

"Again, for what?"

"To attend the public house with you."

I stare at him, open mouthed. I have absolutely no recollection of inviting him and I'm slightly miffed he assumes he can just tag along.

"No offence, Mungo, but I don't think it's really your scene. If you think my microwave is unsanitary, you're not going to like the Red Lion much."

"My attendance is necessary."

"Why?"

"In order to observe you."

"Alright," I sigh. "I'm going to play along. Why do you need to observe me?"

"To determine the root of your behavioural issue. I can only diagnose your specific disorder by observing how you function in different environments."

"It's a pub, Mungo. The only function you're likely to observe is me getting mildly pissed and watching another shit football match."

"Do you require my therapy or not?"

"Well, yeah, but …"

"It is not a matter for negotiation," he interrupts. "If you wish to remedy your disorder I must follow a set procedure and that involves observation."

The only benefit of letting him tag along is it's likely to be a one-off as most people vow never to return to the Red Lion after their first visit.

"Okay, Mungo—you win. But I should warn you, it's a bit of a shit-hole."

"A shit-hole? Are you implying the public house is comparable to an anus?"

"Pretty much."

Unperturbed, he disappears and returns precisely three minutes later.

"I am now ready to leave."

That makes one of us.

I have a feeling I've just tipped over the edge of another bad decision.

15.

Despite my best efforts at small talk as we wander through the dark streets, Mungo is clearly a man of few words. He enquires what I do for a living and follows up with a few related, but concise, questions before returning to his silent self.

I've never been more glad to step through the door of the Red Lion.

I scan the bar and spot Joe playing the fruit machine.

"Right, Mungo, I'm just going to grab my mate. Stay here and do not talk to anyone."

He nods and I wander over to Joe. In true blokey fashion, there is no warm embrace to signify the end of our quarrel and no appetite to discuss the reasons behind it.

"Alright?" he grunts upon seeing me.

"Yeah. You?"

"Not bad."

"We cool?"

"Yeah. Pint?"

Joe then presses a button to collect his winnings. As coins clatter from the machine, I decide I need to pre-warn him about Mungo.

"Listen, mate. Things have changed a bit over the last few days and I've had to take in a lodger."

"No luck with Daisy then?"

"Not yet, but it's a work in progress. Anyway, the thing is, this lodger of mine is also a behavioural therapist and he's offered to help me deal with ... you know ... my problem."

"Bloody hell," he chuckles. "They can treat stupidity now?"

"Very funny, but yes, he reckons he can help. The only trouble is, he insisted on coming along tonight to observe me."

"That sounds a bit creepy."

"You don't know the half of it. He's the short bloke, stood over there."

Joe's gaze follows my nod towards the bar.

"Your lodger is a Bond villain?"

"That's him. And just to warn you, he's a bit ... blunt, and well, odd."

"You gonna introduce me then?"

"You'll regret asking, but sure."

Joe follows me over to the bar and I do the introductions.

"Mungo, this is my best mate, Joe."

Joe holds out his hand. "Alright, mate?"

Mungo looks him up and down before focusing his attention on Joe's hand.

"The deposits beneath your fingernails suggest poor personal hygiene. And are you enquiring about my general …?"

I step in. "Um, let's just leave the introductions there. Who wants a drink? Mungo?"

"Bottled water. No glass."

"You don't want a proper drink?"

"What is a proper drink?"

"One that contains alcohol."

"Why would I purposely imbibe a toxin?"

"Err, forget it—bottled water it is. Pint I assume, Joe?"

Joe lets his unshaken hand fall to his side and nods. In an attempt to escape the awkward scene, I approach the bar.

"What's his problem?" Joe whispers as he sidles up to me.

"I did warn you. Don't fuck this up for me, though. Just grit your teeth and try to ignore him."

With drinks acquired, I usher Mungo towards a table as far away from the bar as possible. As we sit, he then plucks a straw from the inside of his jacket and drops it into the bottle of water.

"Bit old for straws ain't you, mate?" Joe jokes.

Mungo turns to him. "The overall standards of hygiene in this establishment are verging on criminally negligent. I do not wish to place the neck of this bottle anywhere near my mouth."

I look at Joe. "He has a point."

For the next hour we sit in near silence and watch the highlights of the weekend's football on the TV. Just to make me feel even more uncomfortable, every now and then Mungo produces a small notepad and scribbles something down.

"Who's round is it?" Joe asks, waving an empty pint glass in the air.

We both know it's Mungo's and stare at him in expectation.

"You wish me to acquire more beverages?" he asks.

"Please," I reply. "Two pints of lager."

Expressionless as usual, he gets up and shuffles off to the bar; thankfully without further judgement on our choice of drink.

"Jesus Christ, mate," Joe groans. "Only you would use a therapist suffering a mental illness himself."

"What are you on about?"

"Did you ever meet my cousin, David?"

"Don't think so. Why?"

"He suffers from something called Asperger Syndrome. Basically, he can digest and recall huge amounts of data like we remember a pin number, but he has real problems with his social skills. I took him to the corner shop once and he asked Mr Singh if he wore his turban in the bath."

"Really?"

"Yeah."

"And did he?"

"I'll never know because he kicked us out," he replies wistfully. "But I reckon that Mungo fella has Asperger's too. They don't have a social filter and just say stuff without considering if it's offensive."

"Can't say I've ever heard of the condition but I doubt Mungo has it. Surely you can't get a licence to work as a therapist if you've got some loose wires yourself?"

"Probably not, but did you check if your bloke is licenced?"

Ohh.

Joe doesn't need me to answer—my expression is answer enough.

"You didn't ask, did you?"

"Er, I didn't think to."

"Twat."

On cue, Mungo returns with our drinks.

"The man at the bar is unhappy," he remarks.

"What man?"

"I never asked his name. He appeared to be under the misguided impression I was admiring his partner's breasts."

"And were you?"

"Certainly not. I was trying to establish if one was larger than the other."

"I'm not even going to ask why, but what did this man look like, Mungo?"

"Shaven head, leathery complexion, and in need of urgent dental work."

"Oh, shit," Joe groans. "Angry Pete."

Angry Pete is the pub's resident psychopath, and the breasts Mungo inspected presumably belonged to his wife, Sharon.

"Oi, fuckers, is he with you?"

We spin around to find Angry Pete marching towards our table. This is not good. Pete does not respond well to reasoned discussion and usually resolves disputes via the medium of extreme violence.

Joe and I remain rooted in our seats while Mungo stands and

watches Pete approach. If he's at all concerned, it's not reflected in his face.

"Alright, Pete?" I whimper as he comes to a stop a few feet away.

"No, I fuckin' ain't," he growls. "This little tosser was leering at my wife's tits."

"That is incorrect," Mungo replies. "I was in the process of calculating the approximate volume of each breast for the purposes of comparison."

Angry Pete is not the brightest star in the sky and, for a second, appears confused as he tries to decipher Mungo's response to his claim.

It's no great surprise when he concludes Mungo's motive is irrelevant.

"I couldn't give a fuck why you were staring at 'em, but you're gonna step outside, and I'm gonna teach you a lesson."

Mungo shakes his head. "I do not wish to step outside, Angry Pete, and I suspect your poor use of English would make you a most unsuitable tutor."

Up until this point, I had no reason to think Mungo was a complete imbecile, but taunting a man a foot taller, and with barely any fuse worth lighting, is beyond stupid.

I need to intervene, but I'd rather not collect my teeth from the floor on the way out.

"Suit yourself," Pete continues. "I'll fuck you up here and now then."

With that, he throws a punch directly towards Mungo's head. As I watch on, I fear my therapy is about to be terminated before it even really began.

Mungo, though, has other ideas.

With his palm open, his hand shoots up and meets Pete's oncoming fist. Now, I'm no expert in physics, but I'd have been pretty certain the force of Pete's fist would easily bypass Mungo's hand.

It doesn't.

Almost as if he'd punched a Blue Whale's snout, Pete's fist comes to an immediate stop with a dull slap. Mungo remains completely expressionless. Pete, on the other hand, does not. His face contorts in pain, and the muscles in his neck spasm like taut rope, as he tries to extract his fist from Mungo's now-closed hand.

"Fuckin' let go," Pete bellows. "You're crushin' my hand."

"Apologise," Mungo says flatly.

"Fuck you!"

I stare across at Joe and then back at Pete. Still unwilling to apologise, his pride eventually gives way to pained yelps as he falls to his knees.

"Please," he begs.

"Apologise."

"Alright, I'm sorry."

Mungo releases Pete's fist and offers some advice. "I would recommend seeking immediate medical attention. Advise the doctor you have likely sustained multiple bone fractures and ligament damage."

Pete's broken hand droops at the end of his arm like a stringed mitten.

"Fuckin' bastard," he whimpers before getting to his feet. He then stumbles back to the bar, and his wife's disproportionately-sized breasts.

Mungo, apparently nonplussed by the event, sits down and sips at his straw.

"Oh my God!" Joe suddenly booms. "That was bloody amazing. How do you do that?"

"An explanation would be beyond your comprehension," Mungo replies.

"Oh, come on," Joe begs. "Is it some kind of ninja martial art thing?"

"I am not willing to discuss the subject any further."

Conversation closed, a more pressing matter comes to the fore, and I raise my concern.

"I think we should go somewhere else. Angry Pete is too stupid to let it go and I'd bet he's gone off to muster his equally stupid mates."

"Good point," Joe agrees. "Let's go to Tiffany's."

If the Red Lion isn't Mungo's cup of tea, a seedy strip joint certainly won't be. I'm really not in the mood but if it means losing him, perhaps it's a price worth paying for a few quiet pints.

"Hey, Mungo. I don't think Tiffany's is really your scene so why don't you head back to the flat?"

"What is Tiffany's?"

"A strip joint. You know, a bar where women take their clothes off."

"Why?"

"Because ... what?"

"Why do they take their clothes off?" he repeats.

"So we can see their tits," Joe suggests.

"That is your reason for visiting such an establishment," Mungo replies. "It does not answer my question."

I have to concede I've never given the matter any thought. Why would I?

"I suppose it's just a job and they do it to pay the bills, same as the rest of us."

Mungo takes another sip of water before announcing his decision.

"I will attend."

"Really?"

"There is still much to observe."

"Fine," I groan. "Let's get going then, before Angry Pete comes back."

We slip out of the fire door and scuttle away as fast as Mungo's little legs will allow. I suspect we won't be returning to the Red Lion for a while.

It's a ten-minute walk to Tiffany's and while Joe and I chat about the usual blokey nonsense, Mungo remains silent. The notebook doesn't make an appearance but every now and then I catch his stare, ever observing.

By the time we step through the door of Tiffany's I feel like a lab rat.

Being a Tuesday, the place is fairly quiet with barely a dozen men enjoying the delights of three bored-looking strippers who take turns to hop onto the small stage and unenthusiastically remove their attire. When they're not stripping, the girls float amongst the customers with a pint glass, in which you're expected to deposit money for the show. If you dare deposit anything less than a pound, a scowl is returned until you dig deeper into your pockets.

Beyond the bar and the stage sit four booths which resemble toilet cubicles, where you can enjoy a four-minute private dance for a tenner. The drinks might be cheap in Tiffany's but, as well as depositing money into a glass every ten minutes, you're also constantly badgered into having a private dance. It's not a cheap night out.

We head straight for the bar and I get the first round in.

"Before you get any ideas, Joe," I warn. "I'm only staying for a few. I've got a lot on tomorrow and I don't want a raging hangover."

"Yeah, yeah. Whatever," he replies dismissively, his attention already on a blonde girl waving her bra around on the stage.

"She looks a bit like Daisy," he remarks.

I shoot him a look to let him know my ex-fiancée is not a topic for conversation, and certainly not in that context.

We stand silent for a minute and watch the blonde girl go through her routine.

"Why do you watch females remove their clothing?" Mungo suddenly asks.

"Eh? Err, because they're attractive, I guess. And men like looking at naked women."

"Why?"

"What do you mean: why? Men just like looking at naked women—it's in our genes, unless you're gay, or Catholic ... too much guilt I'd imagine."

"And what emotion does looking at naked females invoke?"

"For fucks sake, Mungo ... what do you think? They're sexy so I guess it invokes lust."

"You'd like to have sexual intercourse with them?"

I almost choke on a mouthful of flat lager.

"I would," Joe intervenes. "Definitely.

Once I've wiped lager from my chin, I ponder Mungo's question.

"I suppose I might like to have sex with them, yes; if it wasn't for Daisy."

"And are patrons permitted to have sexual intercourse with these females?"

"Shit, no," I splutter. "You've got more chance of a shag from Joe than any girl in here."

Mungo extracts another straw from his jacket pocket and slips it into the bottle of water.

"Do you enjoy eating in restaurants?" he then asks.

"Yeah, sometimes."

"Would you order a meal in a restaurant and simply stare at it?"

"Of course not. Why would I?"

"That is precisely what you are doing in this establishment. You pay money to watch females undress, but you are not permitted to fulfil your base instincts. If you are hungry, you must eat, and if you are sexually aroused, you desire intercourse. That is correct?"

"I guess so. And your point is?"

Before Mungo can answer, the blonde girl, having finished her spot on the stage, saunters over with a pint glass in hand.

Mercifully, she has at least put her underwear back on…

"Alright, gents," she chirps. "How are we this evening?"

There's something quite disconcerting about holding a conversation with a stranger when that stranger is wearing just lacy underwear and stiletto heels.

"Good, ta," I reply timidly.

"I'm Scarlet," she adds, as if any of us really care.

Joe and I delve into our pockets for change while Mungo continues sucking at his straw. Scarlet scowls and holds her glass towards him.

"Pay up then, sweetheart. We don't strip for free."

Mungo returns his bottle of water to the bar and assesses Scarlet's demand.

"I did not witness your performance."

A smile creeps across her face. "Ahh, in that case, you need a private dance, sweetheart."

"What is a private dance?"

A tiny part of me wants to warn Mungo of what comes next, but a significantly larger part is happy to see how this unfolds. I watch on as Scarlet edges up to Mungo and explains.

"A private dance means we go into one of the booths over there. You sit down then I dance for you … and undress."

"And what do I derive from this arrangement?"

"You get to see me up close and personal."

"Am I able to ask questions, for research purposes?"

"You can do whatever you like, sweetheart, as long as you don't touch the goods."

"I have no desire to touch any goods."

"Right," she frowns. "It's a tenner then."

Mungo pulls out his wallet and hands over a ten pound note which Scarlet stuffs into her bra.

"Come this way," she beckons.

Joe and I watch on as the oddest of couples wander across the bar and disappear into a booth.

"He's a dark horse," Joe remarks. "I wouldn't have thought lap dancing was his thing."

"No, but then again, I have no idea what floats Mungo's boat."

For twenty minutes we sit and sip lager while the other two girls take turns to strip on the stage. I watch on, but no longer with any real appetite.

Whether it was his intention or not, Mungo's words sit heavy. I don't look at the girls' naked bodies but I do look at their faces. Someone's daughter, or sister, or mother even; just trying to scratch a living. Look beyond the painted smile and there's nothing remotely sexy about it. If anything, the experience only summons the dull ache as I think back to the times Daisy would waltz naked from the bathroom to our bedroom. So beautiful.

"He's been in there a bloody long time," Joe mumbles.

Considering a private dance is usually over within five minutes, it's a valid point.

"Well, I hope he isn't much longer as I've had enough for tonight."

"I reckon he's done his ninja thing again."

"You honestly think he's crushing her hand in there?"

"No," he sniggers. "But I reckon her hand is crushing something."

At the exact same moment I shake my head, the booth door opens. Mungo steps out and Scarlet follows behind. She leans over and plants a kiss on his bald dome and, with that, Mungo turns and shuffles over to join us.

"You were in there a long time," I comment.

"It was most enlightening."

"I bet," Joe sniggers. "What did you get up to?"

"I asked questions. She answered them. That is all."

"For twenty minutes?" I add.

"It was the amount of time I required to conduct preliminary research."

"Research into what?"

"The female mind."

My own mind takes a trip back to Joe's comment about Mungo's behavioural issues and his credentials.

"Wait a minute. Surely you've had female patients before?"

"No."

"No? Not one?"

"Is repeating the same question a habit? The answer will not change."

"Are you even a therapist?"

"I never said I was."

"Yes you did."

"No. I said my vocation is complex but, in simple terms, my speciality is behavioural therapy."

"If you're not a therapist, what the hell are you then?"

He looks up at me and his turquoise eyes widen.

"I am what you are missing, Adam Maxwell."

113

16.

Before I have a chance to digest his bizarre statement, Mungo is already heading for the exit.

I turn to Joe. "Did you hear what he just said?"

"Sorry, mate. I was too busy staring at Bianca's tits."

"Good for you—I'm off. Are you coming?"

His gaze returns to the stage and Bianca's jiggling bosoms.

"Nah. I'll give you a buzz tomorrow."

Trying to extract Joe from Tiffany's is like trying to extract actual fish from a chip-shop fishcake—futile. I leave him to it and hurry out of the door to find Mungo waiting on the pavement.

"Is your unhygienic friend not departing too?" he asks.

"No, and besides, we need to have a little chat on our own, don't you think?"

"You have questions?"

"Yes I do. Plenty. And you have the time it takes to walk home to answer them."

"Your tone suggests a consequence if those questions are not answered."

"Right again, and the consequence will be your eviction from my flat."

We walk on under dark skies, Mungo seemingly unperturbed by my threat.

"What did you mean in there, about you being what I'm missing?"

"Your life is in chaos. I am what you need to resolve that chaos."

I can't deny he's right about the state of my life at the moment but who is he to judge?

"Hold on a minute," I bark. "I've known you for a little over twenty-four hours and, unless you've forgotten, you're my lodger. My life isn't perfect but I'm not the one renting a room in a crappy flat."

"It is a necessity rather than a choice."

"Why? Have you been struck off the therapist's register or something?"

"I have already clarified I am not a therapist, at least not in any way you would understand."

"What are you then? Because, at the moment, I'm thinking

you're some kind of socially-retarded nutjob, while Joe thinks you've got Asperger's Syndrome."

"You are both incorrect in your assumptions."

"So who are you then, and what makes you think you can help me?"

We cover twenty yards of pavement before I get a response, and it's not an answer to my question.

"Do you admit you have a problem with your decision-making process?"

"Duh, yeah," I reply mockingly. "And to be honest with you Mungo, the only reason I let you move in was because I thought I'd get some free therapy."

"That much I gathered. But does it matter who I am, as long as I can help you address your problem?"

"Maybe not, but I don't know the first thing about you, or what qualifies you to even offer help?"

"I can explain and you will understand."

"Go on then—I'm listening."

We turn a corner and walk a few dozen steps while I wait for Mungo's explanation. It comes in a one word answer.

"Logic."

"Logic?"

"Do you not understand the definition of the word?"

"No, I know what logic means, but what does it have to do with my issues, or you, for that matter?"

"Logic is your problem, or, if you wish to apply a more colloquial term, common sense."

"I don't get it."

"It is simple. Depending on the circumstance, people make decisions based on three primary drivers: emotion, impulse, and logic. These drivers are not always used exclusively but in combination with one or both of the other drivers. Does that make sense?"

"I think so."

"For example, if I were to throw a ball at you, the decision to catch it is primarily impulsive. However, in your subconscious mind, emotion also comes into play as you do not wish to drop the ball and look foolish. Equally, if you drop the ball, you will have to retrieve it from the floor which involves additional effort you would rather avoid, so there is also some degree of logic involved. Do you follow?"

"Sort of."

"In short, every decision and every reaction requires your

drivers to be balanced correctly, otherwise the decision, or reaction, will be flawed. The best example of this is when a person is angry or upset. Emotion clouds their judgement and logic is lost from the decision-making process."

"So, a crime of passion would be a decision made without logic?"

"Correct. A wife might stab her adulterous husband in a fit of rage with eighty percent of that decision driven by emotion and twenty percent impulse. Clearly there is no logic involved, as the long term consequences for both parties are dire."

"Okay, I get it, but how's it relevant to me?"

"My initial observations conclude you are making certain decisions without applying logic. Put simply: you have lost the capacity to apply common sense and that is why you continue to make ill-judged decisions."

"Lost? Is it even possible to lose common sense?"

"In a way, yes. The human mind is fragile and consequently has evolved numerous self-protection mechanisms. Your mind has inadvertently suppressed your capacity for logical thought in order to protect itself."

"Protect itself from what exactly?"

"Typically it would be a trauma of some kind, usually experienced during childhood."

"That can't be right. I never had any trauma as a kid, unless you count that one time I heard my parents having sex. I guess that was fairly traumatic."

"The trigger is of no relevance. The solution is all that matters."

Mungo clearly has nothing further to add and falls silent.

We continue onwards and, with his analysis fresh in my mind, I think back to last week and the decision which destroyed my relationship. Why did I agree to go back to that flat? In hindsight, it was beyond stupid but, now I look at it, I went because I felt sorry for Joe and didn't want to ruin his chances with Sandy. As it proved, it was an ill-judged decision based upon emotion. There was no logic or common sense involved, that's for sure.

My introspection continues as we cover more pavement. I think back to dozens of other catastrophic decisions I've made and apply Mungo's theory to all of them. It's a damning experience. In every case I cocked-up because I made a decision impulsively or emotionally. Every single one of those decisions would have been different if I'd bothered to shine a little logic on them.

By the time we turn into my street, I have no doubt Mungo has correctly diagnosed my problem, but the cure is still a mystery.

"Alright, Mungo, I concede you have a point about the way I make decisions. What can I do about it, though?"

"With my assistance you will be able to regain your ability to think logically."

"How?"

"It will not be easy as there is no simple solution. You will need to embark upon a journey of self-discovery and I will be your navigator."

"And you're qualified to be my navigator are you?"

We reach the edge of the driveway outside the flat and Mungo stops.

"I concede some degree of faith is required on your part, but think of me as the living embodiment of your common sense."

"Right," I scoff. "So, you're like some kind of logic doctor are you?"

"No. I *am* logic, and your first step on our journey is to consider that statement."

He turns and makes his way down the driveway as I stand and mull his words. Now he's mentioned it, everything about Mungo is logical: from the way he speaks and acts, through to his monotone clothes and clinically sensible diet. It's almost as if he's some kind of method actor, trying to be the very personification of a purely logical character. It's bloody odd, but perhaps that's the way he delivers treatment; by being the very thing he's trying to teach.

Without a doubt his approach is unorthodox but, then again, it's not as though I have a list of conventional therapists waiting in the wings to help. The more I think about it, the more it does make sense and, more importantly, I can see how it might work.

I scuttle after Mungo and catch him as he's opening the front door.

"Okay. I'm in."

"You are definitely outside."

"What? No, I meant I'm in with your journey of whatever it was."

"Self-discovery."

"That's it. Whatever it takes, I'm willing to give it a go."

A thought belatedly arrives.

"Err, this is free, right?"

"In the sense I do not require payment, yes."

I'm tempted to ask why he's offering his help for free but why look a gift horse in the mouth. I'm sure he has his reasons and, even if this fails in the long term, at least it shows some short-term willing to Daisy.

"That's very kind of you, Mungo. When do we start?"

"We already have."

He pulls the key from the lock and shuffles into the hallway. Keen to understand what the hell he means I scurry after him, and catch up just before he disappears into his bedroom.

"What do you mean we've already started?"

"Although your reluctance was obvious, you allowed me to observe you this evening. And that is how we shall continue—with ongoing observation and coaching."

My eyes narrow. "Define ongoing observation?"

"It is necessary for me to observe every aspect of your day-to-day interactions. There is no pattern to your behaviour and, therefore, I must be present to identify and correct illogical decisions as they occur."

"Really? You want to observe me whenever I take a shit?"

"How often have you made life-changing decisions while defecating?"

"Well, never, apart from that one time, but I'd rather not talk about it."

"You have your answer then. As you appear capable of functioning on a basic level within your own home, I have no need to observe the minutia of your life here."

"That's a relief but, if you're going to observe my day-to-day interaction, does that mean you're going to follow me around?"

"Yes."

"What, everywhere?"

"Yes."

"But …"

"There is no scope for negotiation. If you wish to find logical thought, you must live with logical thought."

"I am, quite bloody literally," I groan. "But I'm going to dinner at my parent's house tomorrow. Surely you don't need to be there?"

"I cannot fix what I cannot see."

Great. As well as my mother sitting in judgement, I now have to tolerate Mungo as well. And that's before I've even come up with a reason for him being there.

"What am I supposed to tell my parents?"

"The truth. I believe there is an adage about honesty being the best policy."

"You've never met my mother."

"That is correct."

"So, I tell them you're helping me, like a therapist?"

"Yes."

On reflection, it's actually not such a terrible idea. Whatever Mum intends to reveal about her chat with Daisy, the fact I'll have my therapist in tow will go some way to proving I'm making an effort.

"Okay. You can come along."

"You must inform your mother about my dietary requirements."

"And they are?"

"I will consume only organic vegetables. Either raw or lightly steamed."

"What about pudding? Mum makes a killer spotted dick."

"Fruit. Again, organic."

"You don't like spotted dick?"

"It contains suet: a saturated fat derived from the kidneys of cattle and sheep."

"Christ, you're a complete buzzkill, Mungo."

"Is that an insult?"

"Doesn't matter."

"In which case, I believe it is customary to wish you goodnight."

With that, he steps into his bedroom and closes the door.

"Yeah," I puff, staring at the now shut door. "Night, Mungo."

It's not even nine o'clock yet but maybe he wants some quiet time to indulge in logic-based porn. I'm not sure such a genre exists, but the thought of watching a passionless couple mechanically, and silently, copulate for ninety seconds doesn't do it for me. Perhaps my dad, but not me.

A cold shudder follows me to the lounge.

I send Mum a text to confirm I'll be bringing a plus-one tomorrow, and she'll get the chance to meet my therapist, which I'm sure she'll be pleased about. She's unlikely to be so pleased about his dietary requirements but it can't be that hard to steam a few stalks of broccoli.

Message sent, I make myself comfortable and turn the TV on.

120

The few pints I've drunk do little to enhance the experience. I flick through the channels but, with my mind elsewhere, I pay little attention. With the distraction of Mungo out of the way, my thoughts drift to the earlier telephone conversation with my mother. It only serves to agitate. Why did she have to be so bloody-minded? Would it have killed her to at least thrown me a bone of hope? In some twisted way, I'm actually looking forward to introducing her to Mungo. They're cut from a similar cloth, and she'll finally get to see what it's like dealing with an inflexible autocrat.

One thing is for sure though: whatever she tells me, it'll finally draw a line under this whole sorry saga with Daisy. Whether my name is above or below that line remains to be seen.

17.

Is it another bad dream?

I roll over and open my eyes to near darkness. It's not the darkness that feels unreal, but the whining sound beyond my bedroom door.

It sounds a lot like a hoover.

I grab my phone and check the time—half-six. Who the fuck is hoovering at this time of the morning?

It's a rhetorical question because unless the housework fairies have pitched up in the night, it can only be one person—Mungo.

I clamber out of bed and throw on my dressing gown. Leaving the cosy confines of a warm bed on a January morning is always a shock to the system but, even so, it feels especially chilly this morning.

I open the bedroom door.

The whining appears to be emanating from the lounge so I shuffle through the hallway and stand in the doorway.

"What the hell?"

Both windows are wide open and, in his full black ensemble, Mungo is attacking the sofa with the nozzle end of the hoover pipe. He turns and, upon seeing me, switches the hoover off.

"I believe I am now obliged to bid you a good morning."

"Mungo, no good morning ever began at half-bloody-six. What are you doing?"

"Is an explanation really necessary? I would have thought it obvious what I am doing."

I squeeze my eyes shut and open them in the hope this really is a bad dream. It isn't.

"Let me rephrase my question: why are you hoovering at half-bloody-six in the morning?"

"I am attempting to improve the cleanliness of your home, but of greater significance is the fact you are already learning, Adam Maxwell."

Lord, give me strength.

"Will you please stop using my full name, and how am I learning anything by walking into a noisy fridge?"

"You now know that in order to obtain the correct answer, you must first ask the correct question."

"It's too early for this shit," I mumble. "I need coffee."

"Coffee contains high levels of caffeine which …"

"Mungo," I interrupt. "Don't. Just don't."

He switches the hoover back on. I close the door and make my way to the kitchen.

Unsurprisingly, there isn't a pot of coffee on the go. I put the kettle on and shovel three heaped teaspoons of granules into a mug along with two heaped teaspoons of sugar. With my supplies dwindling, I suppose I should be grateful Mungo only drinks water. Daisy and I used to do the weekly shop together and I can't face doing it alone—not yet, anyway.

Much to my horror, the Coco Pop levels are also dangerously low. I eke out just enough for a single bowl, thankful I at least have milk this morning.

I sit and resentfully munch at my too early cereal while waiting for the kettle to boil; all the while serenaded by the whine of the hoover.

Fifteen minutes later—having consumed a bowl of Coco Pops and a mug of coffee—the hoover is still going. I'll give Mungo credit for doing a thorough job but I hope to God he doesn't start every morning with the same regime.

I get up from the table and trudge over to the sink. I carefully place my bowl and mug on top of the already prodigious stack of unwashed crockery at the precise moment the hoover falls silent. I take a moment to tell myself the washing up can wait and turn around to find Mungo stood in the doorway.

"All done?" I ask.

"For now."

"Great. I can take a shower in peace. Have you closed the windows?"

He doesn't answer but his gaze shifts towards the sink behind me.

"Most unsatisfactory," he remarks.

"What is?"

"The amount of crockery and utensils in the sink."

"I'll do it tonight," I reply with a shrug.

"Why not do it now?"

"Frankly, I can't be arsed."

"And will your motivation be greater after you have completed your day at work?"

"It's washing up, Mungo. Nobody is ever motivated to wash up so it doesn't really matter when I do it. However, feel free to grab a scourer if it bothers you."

Unfortunately, he declines my invitation and remains stood in the doorway.

"It does matter," he eventually retorts.

"Why?"

"The task itself is unimportant, but the principle is worthy of your regard."

"Go on," I groan. "What principle?"

"Responsibility. You are avoiding the task because you do not wish to take ownership of it. You are aware nobody else will take the responsibility?"

The dull ache chips in and agrees with Mungo's assessment. For the first few weeks after we moved in together, Daisy relentlessly nagged me about washing up but, in the end, she realised doing it herself was less effort. From that moment onwards, I took for granted there would always a plentiful supply of clean crockery and cutlery.

No more.

"You must accept ownership, and therefore responsibility, of every facet of your life," Mungo adds. "The sooner you do that, the sooner you'll be able to efficiently process both tasks and decisions."

"Right," I scoff. "Doing the washing up will help me make better decisions will it?"

"In itself, no, but procrastination and evasion of responsibility will not serve you well; either when dealing with tasks or making decisions."

I'm about to press that theory when he abruptly turns and walks away. Seconds later, I hear his bedroom door close.

My first instinct is to ignore his advice, and I take six steps towards the door, intent on leaving the washing up where it is. I would have made it too, if it hadn't been for Mungo's last sentence sitting like an invisible brick wall across the kitchen, barring my exit. I stop dead and wait for the wall to shift. It doesn't, perhaps because the foundations of the imaginary wall are forged from a single word—responsibility. It was the very same word Daisy used just before she walked out.

I've never got on with responsibility. It's not my fault, though, and I blame society. Whenever anything goes wrong, someone, anyone, has to accept responsibility so we can all take to social media and hurl vitriolic abuse at the hapless patsy. An unforeseen by-product of blame culture is that we, as individuals, simply don't want to shoulder responsibility any more. If we're fat, it's the fault of fast food outlets for tempting us with chicken nuggets. If we binge-drink, it's the fault of the supermarkets for selling cheap booze. And then there's the litigious element to all this responsibility—blame for anything and everything has to lie somewhere, just so lawyers can aim their compensation cannons accurately.

In my view, responsibility is best avoided because it carries with it the burden of blame.

Yet, now I think about it, I've spent much of my adult life avoiding responsibility, but still managed to attract considerable amounts of blame. How does that work?

I ponder that question while I wash up.

Without really thinking about it, I complete the washing up, then dry up and put everything away. A glance at the kitchen clock tells me the task took barely five minutes. I'd like to be annoyed with Mungo for being right but I can't deny his words nudged my thinking in a different direction. It'll take a damn sight more than a new-found enthusiasm for washing up to convince Daisy I'm making an effort, but perhaps there is something in Mungo's psychobabble that will prove to her I am capable of change.

We'll see.

Somewhat delayed, I head to the bathroom and stink it out before Mungo has the chance. After a shave and a long shower, I emerge to find my flatmate outside the door.

"Are you ready?" he asks.

"Ready for what?"

"Work."

"What? You want to watch me clean windows? How is that going to help with my treatment?"

"I have already told you I must observe. Do you have a problem with your short-term memory too?"

"No, but … oh, whatever. Anyway, it's not even eight o'clock yet so you might as well go eat some more pulses. And if you want the bathroom, I'd give it ten minutes if I were you."

"Why?"

"Because," I reply with a grin. "It smells a bit ripe in there."

"It is of no consequence," he replies. "I conducted my ablutions while you were still in bed and, as you are self-employed, why can you not commence work before eight o'clock?"

I try to mask my disappointment that he doesn't need the bathroom.

"It's too early."

"Too early for what?"

"Me."

"What do you intend to do now then?"

"Watch a bit of TV, I guess."

"Is that a constructive use of your time?"

"Probably not."

"Time is finite, Adam Maxwell; a fact you should consider when you waste it on idle pursuits."

"It's an hour, Mungo. It really doesn't matter."

He breathes a slight sigh and closes his eyes a fraction longer than a blink. Perhaps he is capable of displaying emotion, albeit exasperation.

Just when I think he's about to relent and I can go watch TV, he throws me a question.

"What value would you place on an hour with your former partner?"

"Um … I'd pay anything."

"And would you pay the same price to stare at a brick wall for an hour?"

"Of course not. What's your point?"

"Time spent with your former partner would be gratifying but time spent staring at a brick wall would not. Therefore, the same measurement of time can only be improved if you fill it with gratifying or constructive activities."

I stare at him blankly.

"Would watching television for the next hour be either gratifying or constructive?"

"It's slim pickings this time of the morning, so probably not."

"Then it is not a good use of your time. Work, however, most certainly is."

One thing I've already learnt about Mungo is that he uses silence to end a discussion in the same way Angry Pete uses his fists—with brutal efficiency. But unlike Angry Pete, Mungo possesses an uncanny knack of knowing how to succinctly conclude his point so it resonates—drop the closing argument and then shut the fuck up so I feel compelled to give it some thought or deliver a response. Either way, his point penetrates my thick skull.

"Alright," I concede, puffing my cheeks. "I'll get my coat."

"A sensible decision."

"For a change."

"Indeed."

Once I've donned my coat and trainers, I scuttle down to the driveway and retrieve my cleaning solution bottle from Alan. Mungo, now sporting a black coat, joins me on the driveway as I close Alan's rear doors. Despite the teeth-chattering cold, my lodger appears content to stand, watch, and wait; apparently impervious to the cold.

"Give me a sec. I've just got to refill my spray bottle."

He returns a nod and I scoot back inside.

I return a minute later and find Mungo exactly where I left him.

"You could have waited in Alan."

"Alan?"

"My van. We call him Alan."

"Why?"

"Why not?"

I await his analysis but he remains silent. I unlock the driver's door and clamber in. Unfortunately, Alan doesn't have such luxuries as functioning central locking so I have to manually unlock the passenger's door from inside.

Mungo opens the door but, rather than get in, he stares at the stained, threadbare upholstery.

"It's a work van, Mungo," I remark. "Sorry if it doesn't meet your hygiene standards."

"I will return within two minutes."

He closes the door and disappears before I can argue. With little else to do, I count seconds in my head to test his claim. He returns before I reach one minute-fifty, and opens the door.

"What the fuck?"

"The seat is unsanitary so this suit is required. It is disposable."

His black attire is covered with a polythene suit similar to those worn by forensic detectives; albeit Mungo has, unsurprisingly, gone for the black option.

"Why do you even own such a thing?"

"I considered it a necessary precaution upon establishing your injurious hygiene standards."

"Good grief, Mungo. Have you got OCD?"

"Expectation of basic hygiene is neither obsessive, or a disorder. It is a pity so few people, yourself included, understand that."

For some unknown reason, my mind chooses to consider how his attitude impacts his sex life—assuming he's ever had sex, which, based upon his Vulcan-like demeanour, I very much doubt. I can only imagine his poor girlfriend lying naked on the bed while Mungo stands over her, wire brush and bottle of disinfectant in hand. Who knows, though—perhaps some people consider that foreplay.

I turn the ignition key. Alan, true to form, fails to start.

"Come on, Alan," I plead, turning the key again.

"Why are you offering encouragement to an inanimate object?" Mungo asks.

"It's just something I do."

"It will not make any difference to the outcome. I suspect the vehicle requires maintenance rather than verbal encouragement."

"Thank you, Captain Obvious," I snap back. "Just be quiet for a minute and let me deal with this my way."

I turn the key again. Alan, perhaps taking my side, decides to start. I shoot Mungo a *told you so* look which provokes no reaction.

We set off on the short journey to my first house of the day—Alan spluttering away, Mungo silent. After barely two minutes, we pull up at the end of a long queue of traffic waiting for the lights to change.

"Bloody traffic," I grumble. "I knew it was a bad idea leaving the flat so early."

"It was not a bad decision."

"Wasn't it? Rather than being on the sofa, I'm sat in traffic so how is it not a bad decision?"

"If there were no traffic, would it have been a bad decision?"

"Well, no, of course not."

"Then the decision was not bad. You cannot control the levels of traffic, but the logic behind starting your working day earlier is sound. Even if the journey is delayed, you will still have more time to conduct your business."

On cue, the lights change and the procession trundles forward. I manage to sneak through on amber and we arrive at our destination a minute later. I glance at the dashboard clock: the delay added roughly four minutes to the journey.

"Do you ever get bored of being right, Mungo?"

He doesn't answer.

The first house of the day isn't actually a house but a squat little bungalow with an equally squat little resident. I ring the bell and wait for Mrs Bakewell to shuffle along the hall.

The door opens and the elderly widow greets me with a warm smile.

"Good morning, dear," she beams. "Cup of tea?"

"That would be lovely, thanks."

"And your friend?" she adds, her smile cooling as she glances beyond my shoulder.

I turn around to find Mungo stood a few feet behind me. Dressed in his black polythene boiler suit and with no hint of friendliness in his face, I have to concede he has a certain bored mortician vibe going on.

"Sorry, Mrs Bakewell. This is Mungo and he's ... err ... my new apprentice."

A barely believable lie but safer than allowing Mungo to explain his presence.

"Would you like a cup of tea, Mungo?" Mrs Bakewell asks.

I glare at Mungo in the hope he understands how little I want him to answer the elderly woman's question in his usual brusque manner.

"No. Thank you," he replies.

I breathe easy, Mrs Bakewell confirms she'll bring my tea out once the kettle boils, and closes the door.

"So, you are capable of the occasional pleasantry then?"

"It is not logical to offend your customers so I employ social etiquette when the situation demands it."

"But not with me?"

"The least of your concerns should be a perceived lack of pleasantries on my part."

He makes a valid point.

"Shall we get on with it then?"

"It?"

"Yeah, cleaning windows."

"I am here to observe. I cannot participate unless I receive formal training and the necessary liability insurances are in force."

True to his word, Mungo spends the next four hours doing little else other than watching as I work my arse off. As we scoot from house to house in Alan, no questions are asked and my attempts at small talk are quickly thwarted with single word replies. In fact, it's only when I stop to eat a bag of crisps does he finally show any interest in anything.

"What is the solution you apply to the window panes?"

"It's my own secret concoction. Works a treat and it's much cheaper than off-the-shelf cleaning products. Oh, and you'll be pleased to know it's completely organic—no chemicals."

"What does it contain?"

"If I tell you that, Mungo, I'll have to kill you."

"Why would that be necessary?"

"To stop you from telling anyone else."

"A patent is usually more practical than murder."

If it were possible, I'm sure my eyes would roll through a full rotation.

"It's just a saying, Mungo. If you're that interested, I'll show you when we get back to the flat."

"And my life would not be at risk if you divulge that information?"

"No. Although I might administer a swift kick to the nuts if you continue taking everything I say so literally."

"That would be a highly inadvisable course of action."

Considering how he dealt with Angry Pete, he might be right. I decide not to press the matter and get back to work.

After another four hours of toil, in which I clean the windows of seven properties, another record-breaking day comes to an end. Despite my exertions, Mungo continues to stand idly by while I load the ladder onto Alan's roof.

"Alright there, Mungo?" I snipe. "It must have really taken it out of you; standing there all day doing the sum total of fuck all."

"Your assumption is incorrect. I have been observing."

"Tell you what, tomorrow, why don't you do the window cleaning and I'll do the observing?"

"Would that benefit you?"

I give Mungo a taste of his own medicine by not answering. As irritating as it's been having him observe me all day, at least I've had something else to think about other than my impending dinner with destiny. But, as I drive back to the flat, thoughts buzz and butterflies dance.

By the time I pull onto the driveway I'm a bundle of nerves, and no amount of spotted dick is going to help.

18.

The first song I can truly remember is *The One and Only* by Chesney Hawkes. I must have been about six or seven when it came out and, at the time, it was hard to ignore it. Radio stations played it relentlessly which, in the days before digital downloads, propelled it to number one in the charts where it remained for five long weeks. I can even recall the video, and the fresh-faced Chesney looking like a guy with the world at his feet.

Obviously he didn't know it at the time, but *The One and Only* proved to be the beginning and end of his chart career. That song must now be an albatross to poor Chesney; a tortuous reminder of what might have been.

As I stand in the shower, I'm minded of that song; not because of the lyrics or any sentimental attachment, but because one day I might look back on this evening with the same wistful lament as Chesney Hawkes does for his one-hit-wonder. Within a few hours, I'll know if I have a future with Daisy, or not. Either way, I suspect this evening will prove to be a watershed moment in my life.

As for Chesney, at least he won't be cleaning windows tomorrow—to the best of my knowledge.

I get dressed and knock on the door to Mungo's bedroom.

"Are you ready?"

The door swings open.

"Yes."

"Good, but before we go, I want to set a few ground rules."

"Such as?"

"Firstly, try to be at least vaguely human. I can put up with your weirdness but my parents will just assume you're rude."

"Understood."

"Secondly, please don't analyse everything I do or say in front of my parents. Save it until we've left."

He nods.

"And thirdly, do not side with my mother on any subject. Trust me, she'll encourage you, but don't—under any circumstances. Once you validate her complaint, I'll never hear the last of it."

"What if her complaint is valid?"

"Even more reason not to agree with her. Just smile and nod."

I'm about to confirm he understands the significance of my third point when I reflect upon it.

"Wait … you can smile, can't you?"

"Of course."

"But you never do?"

"That might be remedied if you occasionally said something amusing."

To prove his point, the merest hint of a smile forms on his face. In truth, it's not a look that suits him. For most people a smile brightens their face, but for Mungo it conjures up visions of Humpty Dumpty; post-lobotomy.

"Yeah, perhaps best if you keep the smiles to a minimum."

His expressionless face returns, much to my relief.

"Come on then, let's go."

"Are we travelling in your work vehicle?"

"Have you got a car?"

"No."

"Then yes, we're going in my work vehicle."

"I require another disposable suit. Wait one minute."

Despite my exasperation, I've more to worry about than Mungo's aversion to filthy seats. I slump against the wall and try to quell my nerves. Never have I been so anxious about visiting my parents, and there have been plenty of reasons in the past where I had good reason to be.

Mungo returns from his bedroom, sporting another polythene boiler suit.

"You're not going to wear that all evening are you?"

"No."

"Good. Let's try again, shall we?"

We leave the flat to dark skies and drizzle.

Mungo refrains from questioning my motivational techniques as I encourage Alan to start. However, it doesn't stop him staring at me, his glare deepening with every failed attempt.

"Come on, Alan," I scold." Start, you bastard."

My stress levels ease a fraction as Alan responds in his usual raspy, spluttering way.

We set off and, within a few hundred yards, run straight into the rush hour traffic on the main road across town. For once, I'd factored potential delays into our departure time, but I still hoped to avoid spending any longer than necessary locked in a confined space with Mungo.

We come to a standstill. With nothing else better to do, I make an attempt at conversation.

"Seeing as you've got a ringside seat to my life, tell me a bit about yourself, Mungo."

"No."

"What do you mean, no?" I huff with mild incredulity.

"If you require the dictionary definition, it is a word used to give a negative response."

"You know that's not what I meant. Why aren't you willing to tell me anything about yourself?"

"Because it would not benefit your treatment."

I turn to him. "You won't tell me anything? Where you're from, family, hobbies?"

"No."

"Well that's just fucking weird."

"Why is it weird?"

"Because, for some inexplicable reason, we now share a flat, Mungo. And most people are generally happy to share a little of their life with someone they live with."

"I am not most people."

"That much we can agree on."

For five minutes we edge slowly through the traffic without another word spoken. I've already decided it's better to suffer my anxiety in silence than to seek distraction from Mungo. It is then, with some surprise, he resurrects our conversation.

"Whilst I am unwilling to discuss my life, I am prepared to discuss *you*."

"Me?"

"Yes and my observations thus far."

"Okay. This should be interesting."

"It was most enlightening to witness you engage with your customers today."

"Really? Why?"

"It is your strength. You possess above average interpersonal skills."

"Bloody hell, Mungo—is that a compliment?"

"Take it as you wish."

It's the first positive thing he's said about me, but coming from somebody with all the interpersonal skills of a sulky teenager, I'll take it with a pinch of salt.

"As flattering as your feedback is, I'm not sure it has any bearing on the root problem."

"But it does."

"How?"

"You will discover that in time, Adam Maxwell."

"I wish you'd quit with all the Yoda bullshit, Mungo. If you've got something to say, just say it. Don't give half answers and then leave me hanging."

He doesn't reply. Frustrated, I slam the gearstick into first and rev the engine. Alan isn't impressed and promptly stalls as I lift the clutch pedal.

On the third attempt to start my troublesome van, and with horns blazing from all directions, Alan reluctantly cooperates and we trundle onwards to the turning where I can escape the queueing traffic.

A mad dash through the side streets and we arrive at Rosemary Gardens a few minutes before six.

"Your driving style is most erratic," Mungo remarks, unzipping his polythene suit.

"Not sure if you'd noticed, Mungo, but everything about my life is pretty erratic."

He opens the passenger door without responding. After a long minute waiting, while he extracts himself from the polythene suit, we're ready to meet destiny.

"Don't forget my three rules," I stress as we wander up the driveway to the front door.

"Your rules have been duly noted, Adam Maxwell."

"And for the love of God, call my parents Mr and Mrs Maxwell. Don't use their full names—understood?"

He nods as I open the front door and announce our arrival.

"Mum? Dad? We're here."

"In the kitchen," Mum hollers back.

I kick my trainers off. Mungo unlaces his polished leather shoes before meticulously positioning them against the skirting board. Unsurprisingly, his socks are black.

As I glance at my oddball lodger, I can't help but wonder how the hell I got to this point.

"This way," I sigh.

Mungo follows me down the hallway and into the kitchen where Mum is sat at the table; overdressed for a casual family dinner, and almost certainly not for my benefit. Unlike the first time I set eyes on Mungo, Mum appears unfazed by either his diminutive stature or the fact his head resembles a cue ball.

I inwardly cringe when she stands and virtually curtsies.

"Good evening, darling," she coos in my direction before turning to Mungo. "And you must be Doctor …?"

"Mungo."

"It's an honour to have you here, Doctor Mungo."

He picks up on my slight shake of the head and doesn't correct her. I have no idea if Mungo is a qualified doctor but if my mother wants to make that assumption, it's best just to let her.

"Thank you, Mrs Maxwell."

"Can I get you a drink?"

"Do you have bottled water?"

Crap. I should have mentioned that.

"We have filtered water."

"That will suffice."

Without asking if I'd like a drink, Mum plucks a glass from the table and scuttles across to the fridge. She fills the glass with water from a transparent plastic jug and returns, handing it to Mungo.

"Thank you."

"Please, take a seat."

In unison, we all sit down at the table.

Although we've managed to get through the first few minutes without incident, I kind of feel like I'm an unwitting participant in an unlikely, and poorly cast, sitcom. Any second now, I fear John Cleese will burst through the door and offer a passing impression of my father.

Talking of which.

"Where's Dad?"

Mum ignores me and turns to Mungo. "I have to apologise on behalf of my husband. He's been feeling a little off colour this afternoon and thought it best to retire early."

"He's pissed and gone to bed." I confirm.

"He's unwell, darling," she replies through gritted teeth.

This isn't unusual. If Dad has nothing better to do, and he usually doesn't, he'll happily spend an hour or two browsing the aisles of the local wine merchant before returning home to sample his purchases. While we're all used to it, the fact I've just outed Dad in front of my mother's esteemed guest doesn't sit well. My mother has always had ideas above her station. I recall her arguing with Dad when he took up bowls because the local golf club attracted a better class of member.

"I'll just pop upstairs and see if he's okay. You two alright for a minute?" I ask, aiming the question towards Mungo rather than my mother.

He nods. I don't wait for Mum's answer and leave them to it. Maybe she'll have more luck getting small talk out of Mungo than I have.

On the landing, I avoid glancing towards my old bedroom, just in case it tries to lure me back.

"It's just me, Dad?" I call, knocking on the door my parents' bedroom. "You awake?"

I don't wait for him to answer and ease the door open to a dimly lit room.

Decked in striped pyjamas, I find the old man propped up in bed with a magazine open on his lap.

"Bloody hell, Dad. You look awful."

"Alright, son," he rasps. "I don't feel too chipper either."

Clearly Mum was telling the truth on this occasion as he looks quite sober. Frail and sickly, but sober.

I pad over and take a seat on the edge of the bed.

"What's the matter?" I ask.

"Oh, I don't know," he puffs, trying his best to appear stoic. "Just old age I guess."

"That's suitably vague."

"Alright. Specifically, I feel like crap. That better?"

"Anyone ever tell you, you're not a great patient?"

"Your mother, many times."

We swap smiles before he adopts a more sombre expression.

"Talking of your mother, has she told you yet?"

"Why I've been summoned? No, not yet."

Despite the fact he must know, Dad wouldn't dare steal my mother's thunder by even hinting. Such is the dynamic of our family, we both know the score when it comes to Mum, and Dad moves the conversation on.

"So, did you bring your shrink along?"

"He's downstairs. Mum put on her best frock."

"I know, son. We don't dine with doctors very often so just indulge her this once."

"I will. Are you sure you're going to be okay?"

"Don't you worry about me," he says, patting my arm. "I'll be right as rain in a few days, but pop up and say goodbye before you go, though."

"Sure."

"Go on. You'd better get back down there before she gets the photo albums out."

He chuckles to himself which prompts a spluttering cough. I hand him a glass of water from the bedside table.

"Seriously, Dad. You're okay?"

He takes a sip of water and waves his hand towards the door. "I'm fine. Get out of here."

I do as I'm told and head back down the stairs.

Before I even step through the kitchen door, I can hear Mum talking enthusiastically at, rather than to, Mungo. As I re-join them at the table, Mum concludes her diatribe.

"And they honeymooned in the Maldives. It looked idyllic in the photos, didn't it, Adam?"

"You're not boring Mungo with a synopsis of Kate's wedding, are you?"

"Actually," she snipes, her wistful tone no more. "I was explaining to Doctor Mungo how you're both so … different."

I look across at Mungo but there's no clue to what he's thinking. In his shoes, or black socks to be precise, I'd be thinking about getting the fuck away from my mother.

"Anyway, Mum, can we talk about why I'm here?"

"We will, after dinner."

"But, Mum …"

"Patience, Adam. I'm sure Doctor Mungo is hungry so we'll eat first."

Mungo doesn't look particularly ravenous but then again, Mungo doesn't look particularly anything. Unfortunately, and because I instructed him to, he simply nods and smiles, affirming my mother's assumption.

"I understand you're vegan, Doctor Mungo," she says, getting up from the table.

Another nod, and a smile so slight it could just as easily be a stifled burp.

"I've prepared a selection of lightly steamed root vegetables. I hope that's okay with you?"

"Thank you," he replies.

"And what have we got?" I ask.

"Oh, I thought it would be nice to have something different for a change," she casually replies, while arranging plates on the kitchen side. "So tonight we're going to try vegan cuisine."

"What?"

"We're all having steamed root vegetables."

I glare at Mungo. I can't be sure but I'd swear his thin smile is approaching a smirk.

"And just to add a little extra flavour," she adds. "I prepared a vegan jus."

"Extra flavour? Vegetable gravy?"

"No, Adam. A vegan jus."

"Great," I puff. "Steamed turnip soaked in boiled cabbage water. I can barely wait."

Ignoring my sarcasm, Mum serves up, and three plates of anaemic gruel are duly delivered to the table. Seemingly proud of her culinary abomination, she orders us to tuck in and we duly oblige; one enthusiastically, the other reluctant. As I suspected, it proves so bland I can taste the cutlery.

To compensate for the lack of usually enthusiastic feedback on her cooking, Mum fills the silence by interrogating Mungo.

"So, how are you getting on with my son?" she asks. "Any progress?"

"It is very early in the process," Mungo replies in his trademark flat tone. "But some progress has been made."

"Do you think you'll be able to help him deal with his issues?"

"Yes, given time and cooperation."

"I do hope he is being cooperative."

"His cooperation is satisfactory."

"Err … excuse me," I declare. "I am here, you know."

Mum stabs a chunk of swede with her fork and, ignoring my protest, continues her conversation with Mungo.

"The thing is, Dr Mungo, Adam is approaching a pivotal time in his life. Now, more than ever, he needs to grow up and start taking his responsibilities seriously."

"I concur," Mungo replies.

To call time on the conversation, I drop my fork so it clatters on the plate.

"Right, that's enough," I snap. "Do you know how rude it is to talk about someone when they're actually sat next to you?"

"Now, now, Adam," she replies in her most patronising tone. "Don't make a scene in front of our guest."

Even as a child, humiliation was my mother's weapon of choice when dealing with my insubordination. I've lost count how many times, as a teenager, I was told to stop showing off. This only ever happened when I was in the company of my mates and it always ended with their ribbing and my cheeks flushing pink.

But Mungo is no mate and I'm no longer thirteen.

"Mum, I couldn't give a shit about making a scene. In fact, I've had enough of this charade—just tell me what the fuck Daisy said."

"Language, young man."

"Are you going to tell me?"

"Not until you've calmed down. You're embarrassing Doctor Mungo."

"Are you kidding? Look at him … go on."

With her own cheeks now flushed pink, Mum finds a weak smile and glances at Mungo. She finds a picture of aloof indifference.

"Does he look embarrassed?" I add.

Rather than answer my question, Mum chooses to apologise on my behalf.

"I'm so sorry for my son's behaviour," she gushes. "What must you think of us?"

"That's it," I bark, getting to my feet. "We're going. Come on Mungo."

This is not what I planned, but my patience was already at an all-time low before we left the flat.

"Adam! Sit down this minute," Mum yells, having apparently got past her concern for Mungo's embarrassment.

I continue to stand in defiance. "Are you going to tell me what Daisy said?"

"When I'm good and ready."

"Yep, that's about bloody right," I scoff. "Everything has to be on your terms, doesn't it?"

"I beg your pardon."

"You're only happy when you're in control. I'd say you were getting some perverse pleasure from this."

Her cheeks continue to redden but I doubt it's embarrassment.

"Excuse me, young man. I thought I was doing you a favour."

"A favour? Firstly, you imposed conditions before you agreed to call Daisy, and now you won't tell me what she said."

"You always were impatient," she huffs.

"It has nothing to do with patience. We're talking about my life, Mum, not some titbit of gossip you picked up in the post office queue."

"I know full well how important it is, Adam, which is why I asked you to come over."

"Well, just tell me then."

"Sit down."

"Are you going to tell me?"

"I said, sit down."

"Tell me and I'll sit down."

"Oh, do grow up," she snaps, tossing her fork down. "You're making a complete show of yourself."

We reach a stand-off with neither willing to concede defeat.

Mungo, having witnessed enough, decides to intervene.

"This situation is not constructive," he remarks. "You are both letting emotion cloud rational thought."

I can't put my finger on why but there's an inescapable authority to Mungo's dry, impassive tone. Like scolded children, I glance at Mum and she glances back.

"Sorry," we both murmur in unison.

"An apology is not necessary," he replies. "A solution, however, most certainly is."

"I just want to know what Daisy said," I mumble.

Mum exhales a long breath.

"Fine. Sit down."

I flop back on the chair.

"The reason Daisy moved out, and decided she can't be with you is …"

She appears to search for the right words.

"Adam, Daisy is pregnant."

19.

I don't know whether it's just my mind or the male mind in general, but there are two stock reactions to news of impending fatherhood. The first, and least sensible, is to confirm you're actually the father. The second reaction, and one I choose, is simply to repeat the word as if you have no understanding of its meaning.

"Pregnant?"

"Yes, Adam. Daisy is pregnant."

"Is it …?"

"Don't you dare."

Beyond the stock reaction, I don't know what to think, let alone what to say. Me? A father? The implications are so broad, so complex, so life-changing; I can't even pin down a starting point for my thoughts.

Long seconds tick by as I stare at my plate, dumbstruck.

"You had no clue?" Mum asks, in an unusually soft tone.

I look up from the plate and the face looking back at me is that of a very different mother.

I shake my head. Shamefully, I should have had at least an inkling—there were plenty of signs, thinking back.

"Do you now understand why I couldn't tell you over the phone?"

I nod, although I'm not entirely sure I understand much of anything at the moment.

"Please. Say something," Mum urges.

Despite Mungo's sage advice, there is no logical thought involved in my response.

"I need to see her."

"And you will, but not yet."

"Why?"

"Because, she's not ready."

If there is a point beyond not understanding, I'm there. Noting my confusion, the woman who can't be my mother reaches across the table and grasps my hand.

"She's a very confused girl. What she needs right now is a little time and space to think things through."

Thoughts of those waiting room magazines flash through my mind. Why are time and space the recommended antidotes to every relationship problem? To me, it sounds like a handy way

141

to avoid tough decisions because time is eternal and space infinite—in short, it's an indeterminate period of hell for the poor sap on the waiting end of the deal.

"I need to see her," I repeat.

She gives my hand a gentle squeeze. "Look at me."

I shift my gaze.

"You need to tread carefully here and, more than ever, you have to think things through. If you go steaming in before she's had a chance to properly come to terms with this, I fear you'll push her away … and towards a decision you'll have to deal with for the rest of your life."

"What decision?"

The answer punches its way through my fuddled mind before Mum's lips even move.

"An abortion?" I gasp. "No, she wouldn't do that."

"Under any other circumstances, no, she wouldn't. But … how can I put this?"

I'd almost forgotten Mungo until he intervenes to answer my mother's question.

"You are currently ill-equipped for the responsibility of parenthood."

"Says who?"

"I do, and clearly both your mother and former partner are of the same opinion."

"Yeah, well, you're all wrong," I protest, with admittedly scant conviction.

"Are we?" Mungo replies. "And I would urge you to think before answering."

Never have I wanted Dad at my side more than now—at least the battle would be even. But, despite his absence, I know he'd tell me to heed Mungo's counsel and think carefully. Well-intentioned advice perhaps, but clear thought is not my forte, especially as I'm still reeling from a bombshell of life-changing magnitude. Chances are, nothing good will come of my thinking.

And yet, maybe I've inadvertently stumbled across the root issue here. My thinking is irrelevant; it's Daisy's thinking that matters now.

How is she feeling at this very moment? In itself a stupid question, because how can she feel anything other than terrified when facing such a decision? How do you even approach that decision; to end a life that hasn't even started? Fuck, I can't even make up my mind when faced with a choice of Pot Noodle.

But the hardest part of viewing the situation from Daisy's

perspective, is her need for time and space. Am I so irresponsible I can't even be trusted to offer an opinion? Clearly I am, to the point she'd rather carry the burden alone. That hurts on many levels, with a seam of shame running through them all.

"I can't let her deal with this alone," I murmur, as much to myself as to Mungo or my mother.

"No, you can't," Mum replies. "But you can't go wading in either. There's a good reason she told me rather than you."

"Is there?"

"Yes, there is. She knows you, and how you'd likely react."

"What's that supposed to mean?"

Despite my obvious agitation, I can tell Mum is making a concerted effort to keep a calm head. It isn't like her.

"Okay," she sighs. "Tell me: how would you have reacted if she told you herself?"

My initial instinct is to just say I don't know, but deep down I really do—I would have reacted without thinking and said something crass or inappropriate, like suggesting *Spartacus* or *Princess Leah* as possible names for our firstborn. Now though, given time to properly consider my reaction, I know the right answer.

"I would have asked what *she* wants."

Mum's eyebrows arch. "Really? You'd have said exactly that?"

"Probably not."

"There you go then."

"Fair enough, but you spoke to her, Mum, what can I do?"

She takes a sip of water and considers my question.

"Reading between the lines, I think what Daisy wants … no, what Daisy needs … is support and reassurance. She's currently facing a decision I wouldn't want to make: either bring up a child alone, or have a termination."

"She wouldn't be alone," I protest. "I'd be there for her."

"Like you were that evening you smoked drugs and passed out in some trollop's flat?"

I can't honestly say if Lauren was a trollop, but the rest of Mum's question is excruciatingly valid.

"Or the time you went on that all-night stag party barely a few hours after Daisy had her appendix removed?"

"I, um …"

"Or maybe that evening at her works party where you got drunk and offended every one of her colleagues?"

"Well, err …"

143

It seems Daisy's chat with my mother included a comprehensive run down of my greatest crimes. Mercifully it stops at three.

"I'm sorry to say this, young man, but you have a lousy track record of being there for that girl. You can hardly blame her for excluding you now."

Since his earlier intervention, Mungo has kept quiet—I doubt affairs of the heart are really his thing. I can still sense him observing me, though, and I glance in his direction. I should have known better than to expect anything other than a blank look in return. I'm on my own here, in every sense.

"You're right, Mum," I huff. "And I can't blame her, but I can't just sit back and do nothing."

"Just try to be patient for the minute. I'll talk to Daisy again."

"And say what?"

"That she should talk to you."

"But you said she didn't want to talk to me."

"She doesn't, but maybe if you have something constructive to say rather than just shooting your mouth off without thinking, she might be willing to listen."

With that, she turns to Mungo. "Can you help him with that, Doctor Mungo?"

"I can."

"Good," she replies, turning to face me. "So, we have a plan?"

As I nod, a question of my own springs to mind.

"Don't take this the wrong way, Mum, but why are you being so … understanding?"

True to form, I perhaps didn't think my question through, or consider the veiled insult within.

"Meaning I'm not usually?"

"No, I … um …"

"This is my grandchild we're talking about here. Did you honestly think I was going to stand back and watch that poor girl make the wrong decision?"

"No, and I didn't mean to suggest you don't care."

"Forget it," she says flatly. "I think you've got more important bridges to build."

"Right, yes. Sorry."

The only one of us to finish our meal is Mungo. Even if we'd been ravenous, I doubt either Mum or I had the stomach to finish a whole plate of steamed root vegetables. Nevertheless,

Mum seems pleased Mungo cleared his plate.

Much to my disappointment, dessert turns out to be organic fruit cocktail rather than spotted dick. A reflective hush descends on the kitchen as we eat and, with every mouthful, the urge to call Daisy grows stronger. But, despite my phone burning in my pocket, I know Mum is right—this is a one-shot deal, and it would be reckless wasting that one opportunity until I have something worth saying.

We finish dessert and, despite Mum's best efforts to spark after-dinner small talk, there's clearly little conversation to be had from either her esteemed guest, or her son. To his credit, though, Mungo insists on helping to tidy up the kitchen; a task I'm sure he'll fulfil with silent efficiency. I make my excuses and head back upstairs to say goodbye to Dad.

I knock on the bedroom door and enter. The scene is virtually unchanged.

"How was dinner?" Dad croaks.

"Eventful, but you knew it would be."

"Indeed. Not really the way any man wants to learn he's going to be a father."

I retake my position on the edge of the bed. "I should have known, Dad. How can a bloke not notice his own fiancée is pregnant?"

"Because, on the whole, men are hopeless when it comes to noticing what's under our own noses."

"Glad it's not just me. I could have done with you down there."

"From what your mum told me, son, I think she has your best interests at heart."

"I know, but that doesn't stop me feeling completely helpless."

"I wish I could say something to change that but you've got to play this one by the book. There are no second chances this time."

"I know, and my therapist has agreed to help. I just want to talk to Daisy and let her know having the baby wouldn't be a mistake."

Dad carefully removes his glasses and looks me straight in the eye. "You sure of that?"

My face adopts an involuntary scowl. "What do you mean?"

"Trust me when I say this, but the initial joy of learning you're going to be a father soon fades. What comes after is cold realisation you're responsible for another human. It's not like buying a new shirt, son—you can't take it back if you change your mind."

This is not the support I was either expecting, or hoping for.

"Are you saying Daisy should have a termination?"

"Not at all. I'm saying you need to look at the bigger picture. Parenthood is both a blessing and a curse."

"A curse? You're saying Kate and I are a curse?"

It could be argued one of us comes close.

"Inasmuch that from the moment you were born, and until the moment I fall off my perch, I'll never stop worrying about you both. Look, I know you love Daisy but that love comes nothing close to what you'll feel for that child. And with that love comes a lifetime of responsibility and worry."

"Jesus, you make it sound like the worst job ever."

"I don't mean to, and that's why I said parenthood was also a blessing—you need to accept both, because one day that child will fill your heart with joy, and the next day they'll rip it out and stamp all over it. That's the reality of parenthood."

"Well, that's brutally candid," I mumble in reply.

"And you need a good dose of that when you talk to Daisy, as promises and petrol station flowers won't cut it this time. You need to show her you've thoroughly considered the implications of parenthood otherwise you'll just be spouting platitudes. Time to prove you're a grown up, son."

It's funny, but I can almost hear Mungo offering the same advice in my head, albeit heavily abbreviated and devoid of emotion.

"You're right," I sigh. "Thank you."

Never one to overplay his point, Dad replies with a slight nod and puts his glasses back on.

"Good magazine?"

"Christ knows," he grunts. "I think it's about time I paid a visit to the opticians. I'm struggling to read it."

"Do you want me to read it for you?" I chuckle. "Like a bedtime story?"

He snorts a half-laugh. "The circle of life," he says wistfully.

"Eh?"

"Don't you remember I used to read you bedtime stories? You wouldn't go to sleep without one."

I remember many things about my childhood but I don't recall Dad ever sitting at the end of my bed and reading stories. But clearly Dad does and I don't wish to spoil a memory he's obviously fond of.

"Right, yeah. Happy days."

My lie is met with a yawn.

"I'll let you get some rest, Dad. Are you going to be okay for the bowls final on Saturday?"

"You remembered," he replies, trying to hide his surprise.

"Of course, and I'll be there, although I'm not sure you will."

"I'll be fine. There's nothing that a few days of rest won't sort out, so you'd better be there."

I give him a hug and leave him squinting at his magazine.

Back in the kitchen I'm greeted by a surreal scene. Mum is washing up while Mungo is in the process of polishing a glass to within an inch of its life. I can only assume Mum felt uncomfortable with the silence and switched the radio on; a slow jazz tune providing a soundtrack to their new-found domestic bliss.

"Is he okay up there?" Mum calls over her shoulder.

"I think so. I left him reading a magazine."

She turns around and peels off her bright-yellow marigold gloves.

"I suspect he's been overdoing the wine sampling of late. He'll be fine in a few days."

"That's what he said."

A thin smile is the only assurance returned. "Anyway," she chirps, putting Dad's health to one side. "Doctor Mungo has been helping with the drying up."

Oblivious to the mention of his name, Mungo diligently continues to polish the same glass.

"So I see," I reply. "And he's nothing if not thorough."

With a dozen items still resting on the draining board, I fear we'll be here until midnight at his current work rate. His overly-fastidious technique isn't lost on my mother either.

"Please, Doctor Mungo, just leave the rest and I'll do it later. I already feel awful allowing a guest to dry up."

"Very well," he replies, handing her the tea towel.

It feels an appropriate time to make our exit.

"Anyway, Mum, I think we're going to make tracks now. Mungo and I have a lot to talk about."

I step across the floor and plant a kiss on her cheek. "Thank you for … you know."

"I'll ring Daisy later, but I want your word you'll work with Doctor Mungo so you've got something sensible to say to her."

"You've got it, and thanks again … honestly."

She returns a kiss and then takes a step towards Mungo. Barely detectable, but his eyes widen a fraction when it occurs my mother might say goodbye with a show of affection. I can't imagine Mungo is the kissy huggy type. Much to his relief, Mum holds out her hand and Mungo gratefully shakes it.

"Thank you for the nutritionally balanced meal, Mrs Maxwell."

"You're most welcome and please, call me Carol."

"Very well. Goodbye, Carol Maxwell."

Jesus wept.

20.

Whilst I have no recollection of my dad reading bedtime stories, I do recall how much time he spent in the garden shed. To call it a garden shed might suggest it was a communal facility, but it was very much Dad's domain and admission was strictly forbidden. Whenever I asked what he did in there, he'd tap the side of his nose and tell me it was a secret only dads were allowed to know. Once I reached my teenage years I stopped asking and assumed he was up to the same thing I was in the secrecy of my bedroom. I didn't dwell on that too long.

I'm minded of Dad's shed as I stand in the shower at ungodly o'clock. Upon our return to the flat last night, Mungo retired to his bedroom under the pretence of devising an action plan for my supposed treatment. Quite what he's gleaned in only three days is beyond me, but I need something to offer Daisy, and Mungo is my best hope. So, while I watched TV on the sofa, Mungo locked himself away with strict instructions not to be disturbed,

I wish he'd paid me the same courtesy this morning, rather than commencing his cleaning regime at half-six again. I also wish I'd remembered to pick up some Coco Pops on the way home last night.

I finish my shower, get dressed and wander into the kitchen. As I scour the cupboards in search of anything other than Daisy's forgotten but tasteless muesli, Mungo appears in the doorway.

"Your cleaning solution: where do you store the ingredients?"

"In the hallway cupboard. Why?"

"I wish to examine them."

"Again, why?"

"I will discuss the reason when you return from work."

"You're not coming then?"

"There is no need."

"What are you going to do all day then?"

"Research."

If I wasn't still half-asleep I might be inclined to delve deeper but I'm suffering from too much morning and not enough coffee.

"Fine, whatever."

He shuffles off and I continue my search for a cereal which doesn't resemble the sweepings of a hamster cage. It proves unsuccessful but I do find five out-of-date digestive biscuits. Dunked in coffee they taste okay and certainly better than muesli. One thing is clear though: I can't put off a trip to the supermarket much longer.

Whilst Mungo might be hiding in his room, his words from yesterday morning are still pottering around my mind. After no more than maybe ten minutes of procrastination, I resist the urge to watch TV and decide I should leave for work.

I rap on his door. "Mungo. I'm off."

Silent seconds pass before it swings open.

"Is there a reason you are confirming your departure?"

"Err, no. Just being polite I guess."

"It would be polite not to interrupt me, as I requested."

He shuts the door.

"Shit," I mumble to myself. "And I thought I wasn't a morning person."

I skulk off, slamming the front door behind me. Halfway down the stairs, my phone rings.

Considering the unsociable hour I'm tempted to ignore it but curiosity gets the better of me. Plucking the phone from my pocket I'm glad curiosity won.

"Morning, Mum."

"I'm in a bit of a hurry," she replies in lieu of a greeting. "I spoke to Daisy last night and she's aware you know about the pregnancy."

"And?"

"She's agreed to meet you tomorrow."

My internal reaction to this news takes me by surprise. Rather than the warm embrace of relief, anxiety arrives and promptly punches me in the gut.

"Really?" I gulp, my mouth unexpectedly dry. "Where and when?"

"Some coffee shop opposite her office, at one o'clock. She said you'd know it."

"I do. Did she say anything else?"

"Beyond asking how you reacted to the news, not a lot. She seemed a bit down if I'm honest."

"Right. What did you tell her?"

"That you were getting help and doing everything you could to change your ways."

"And do you think she believed you?"

"I really couldn't say, Adam."

Detecting a spikiness to Mum's tone I conclude she probably is in a hurry. I thank her and end the call.

A minute passes as I stand motionless, staring at the chequerboard tiles covering the communal hallway floor. A quick glance at my watch does little to remedy the inertia. Twenty-nine hours to demonstrate how I'm getting my shit together—something I've summarily failed to do for almost thirty-three years.

Perhaps if I throw myself into work, inspiration will arrive. I step beyond the front door and my resolve is instantly tested by the biting cold and doleful sky overhead. On days like this I really dislike my job.

From quarter past eight to one o'clock, I work harder than I've ever worked before. Every window is mercilessly buffed while I ponder what I'm going to tell Daisy. As Dad rightly suggested, I need to offer more than just words this time—I need to offer hope.

With that in mind, I run through a list of possible gestures which might prove I'm ready to face the responsibility of parenthood. Most of them are ridiculous, except the most obvious. If I am to be a provider the first thing I surely need to provide is a home, and one more practical and less dilapidated than my current one.

Alas, that plan has a major stain no amount of buffing can remove; a stain of my own naive, short-sighted thinking.

Most of my customers pay with cash and, somewhere along the line, I decided it would be far more tax efficient if I only declared enough income to appear solvent. The rest I frittered away without either the tax man or Daisy ever knowing I earned it.

I thought it was a foolproof scheme and, in my mind at least, justified. If big corporations can get away with paying fuck all tax, why shouldn't I? However, I've now made a rod for my own back, because my on-paper earnings aren't anywhere near enough to secure a better flat suitable for a newborn baby. As for buying a place, my income wouldn't stretch to a mortgage on a second-hand caravan, let alone something built from bricks and mortar.

In the race to persuade Daisy I'm capable of at least providing a suitable home, I've not so much fallen at the first hurdle—I've actually shot myself in the leg before even reaching the bloody hurdle. Maybe Dad was right and I should consider if

I'm even worthy of the same label.

My work rate for the rest of the afternoon is sloth-like and resentment filled. I shouldn't even be cleaning windows. I should be shopping for prams, and cots, and whatever else babies need. I should be painting the spare room blue, or pink, or yellow. I should be ignoring the instructions whilst trying to construct a self-assembly high chair.

I should be with Daisy.

At the first sign of fading light I make excuses to myself and pack up; my positivity sinking below the horizon alongside the watery sun.

If I didn't fancy a solo trip to the supermarket this morning, I sure as hell don't now. I find a compromise and stop by a convenience store on the way home, where I can at least pick up some basic provisions. As I wander the aisles, I pass a chiller stocked with a range of microwave meals. I open the door and scan the boxes, each adorned with an enticing picture of either lasagne, cottage pie, lamb casserole, or chicken risotto—a stark contrast, I'm sure, to the sloppy mush within. I grab one of each and throw them in the basket.

Shopping acquired, and paid for with undeclared cash, I trundle home.

I arrive to find the flat in darkness, apart from a thin strip of light leaking below Mungo's bedroom door. Unsure if he wants to remain undisturbed, I scoot straight past and into the kitchen. I'm halfway through emptying the second bag of shopping when I hear a door open and close. I turn to find Mungo in his now familiar position, stood in the doorway.

"You can come in here you know. There's not a quarantine in place."

"There should be," he replies, without a hint of humour in his voice.

Ignoring his insult, I continue unpacking.

"Had a good day?" I ask, without really thinking.

It's a question asked out of habit, and the same question I always asked Daisy when we convened in the kitchen after work. Looking back, neither of us really cared for it. She was usually too tired to offer a proper answer and I wasn't really interested anyway, truth be told.

Mungo, it seems, is.

"If by good you mean constructive, then yes."

"Oh, tell me more?"

"Once you have unpacked your provisions we can discuss

my findings in the lounge."

I'm about to suggest he tells me whilst I unpack but he walks away before I get the chance. His parting expression, or lack of one, offers nothing to hang my hopes upon. He could hold the answer to all my woes, or he could suggest I'm beyond help and it'd be best for all concerned if I throw myself off a bridge—there's no telling until I'm told.

I finish putting the groceries away and, with a can of beer in hand, wander through to the lounge. It would have been of little surprise to find Mungo stood in front of a flip chart, but he's perched on the sofa with a black folder on his lap.

"I'm guessing you didn't want one?" I remark, holding the can of beer in the air.

"You guessed correctly. Sit down."

"Yes, sir," I reply, saluting.

I flop down on the sofa as Mungo opens his folder to reveal a page of hand-written notes. The ensuing silence summons a sudden and unexpected nervousness.

"Cause and effect," he suddenly announces."

"What about it?"

"Lack of common sense is the cause of your problems."

"No shit. I could have told you that."

"But the effect is your self-esteem; which has suffered due to your lack of common sense."

"Oh," is all I can think of to say in reply.

"Do you understand?"

It's not as if I haven't heard the term before, but I've never had any reason to consider what self-esteem really is.

"You might need to spell it out for me, Mungo."

"In short, self-esteem is the opinion one has of oneself. In your case, that opinion is particularly low."

I adopt a gormless expression and stare back at him.

"Is that … bad?"

"Your low self-esteem has an adverse effect on every facet of your daily life. In my opinion, the reason you shirk responsibility is because you are afraid of making wrong decisions, which …"

"Hold on," I interject. "Is this about the washing up again?"

"No. Your laziness is merely a symptom of the broader problem."

I slump back on the sofa and take a moment to process Mungo's words. I don't get very far before he continues his character assassination.

"When you are faced with a significant decision, you subconsciously doubt yourself. Your lack of common sense means you form conclusions based primarily on your emotions. Those emotions are tainted by negativity and therefore more likely to produce a negative outcome."

"You're saying I make idiotic decisions because, deep down, I think of myself as a bit of an idiot?"

"That statement, in itself, validates my diagnosis."

"Right."

I don't know if I should be mortified or relieved. To be told you have any kind of mental illness can't be good, but surely it's better than blundering through life with a problem to which there might be a solution.

"Can it be fixed?"

"It can."

"How?"

"By focusing on the positive aspects of your life."

"Yeah, right," I scoff. "Good luck finding any."

"Again, that statement validates my diagnosis."

I stare at the can of beer on the coffee table. Now feels like an appropriate time to empty the can, along with a dozen more, but this doesn't feel like a problem I can drown with alcohol. More to the point, I'm not sure how Mungo's findings help with the more pressing issue of talking to Daisy.

"This doesn't help, Mungo. In fact, it makes matters worse."

"In what way?"

"In a Daisy kind of way. I'm supposed to convince her I'm parent material, yet you're telling me I've got mental health issues. It's not exactly something you want to pass on to your kids, is it?"

"It is not a hereditary condition."

"That's not what I mean. Daisy already thinks I'm a liability and you've just confirmed it. If I tell her, she won't want me anywhere near this baby, assuming there even is a baby."

My own words stir the dull ache.

"In which case, do not present her with problems—present her with solutions."

"Brilliant," I huff. "So we're back to square one because I don't have any bloody solutions."

Mungo turns his attention to the page of notes before fixing his gaze back on me.

"I do," he declares.

"Go on then—I'm all ears."

"Your business. It is a positive aspect of your life?"

"It's the least shitty end of a particularly shitty stick."

"I do not understand your analogy."

"It's positive if you compare it to the rest of my crappy life I guess."

"Understood, although I do not concur with your negative assessment. You have a profitable business with low overheads, minimal liabilities, and a loyal customer base."

"And a fucked van. Don't forget Alan."

"Quite, although I would include your vehicle in the list of liabilities."

I don't argue, and then feel guilty for not defending Alan.

"Anyway, as much as I appreciate the analysis, there's one major problem with my business you've overlooked."

"And that is?"

"Me."

"Explain."

With my own analysis still painfully fresh in my mind, I explain to Mungo how I've been syphoning cash from the business, and the implications of my short-sighted tax evasion strategy.

"You see the problem?"

"I do, but it is a problem I had already identified, albeit from another angle."

"What angle?"

"Essentially, your customers are paying for your time in the same way they pay a gardener to cut grass, or a mechanic to service a car."

"Yeah, I get it."

"Unless you are willing or able to hire additional staff, your income is capped by the amount of hours available to work in any given week."

"And my competition. There are three other window cleaners in town and we all have our own agreed patch."

"Indeed. Therefore, the problem you have is one of selling a commodity that is, by definition, limited—time."

I stare at the can of beer again and sense my resistance weakening. This is beginning to feel like groundhog day in the Red Lion with Joe about to unveil another of his terrible business ideas.

"Are you going somewhere with this, Mungo, or just reminding me why my business sucks?"

My question is met with a fractional upward curl of his lip. I wouldn't call it a smile as such.

"Your business cannot grow by simply cleaning more windows. However, it can grow if you mass produce and retail a product to clean windows."

If it was his intention to declare a eureka moment, it doesn't arrive with a fanfare; more a bewildered scratch of the head.

"My cleaning solution?"

"Precisely."

"Let me get this straight: you're saying my fucked up attempt at a salad dressing is the solution to all my problems?"

"Ironically, yes. However, you do not have multiple problems. You have one problem, low self-esteem, which has created multiple issues in your life."

"I still don't get how the cleaning solution fixes anything."

He glances at the page of notes again.

"Let us imagine you are able to develop a commercially successful business by selling your cleaning solution. Such a venture would utilise your strengths whilst boosting your self-esteem. A by-product would be financial security which in turn would deliver stability to your life."

My thoughts return to Joe and the plethora of dubious business ideas we've concocted together. This couldn't be more different. Overlooking the fact it's such a ridiculously obvious idea I should have spotted it myself, there's one other, arguably more critical, reason to credit Mungo.

"This will tick a lot of boxes when I talk to Daisy, too."

"It is a factor I had considered. The conversation with the lap dancer helped me understand the needs of the female."

"Um, okay. And you really think I can build a business with the cleaning solution?"

"On a small scale initially, yes. Your product is effective despite containing only natural components. My research suggests there is a growing demand for environmentally responsible products."

"There are other products out there, you know, that are environmentally friendly?"

"That, I do know. However, they are also considerably more expensive than chemical-based cleaners. By acquiring the ingredients of your solution in bulk, you will be able to undercut the retail price of your competitors by as much as fifty percent, and still retain a gross profit margin of ninety-eight pence per litre."

"Err, in simple terms."

"You can sell for half the price and still make approximately one pound profit on every litre."

A familiar feeling of nervous excitement surfaces. And seeing as the idea was suggested by Mungo, rather than Joe, it isn't tainted with the usual blind optimism and naive hope. Could this really be my path to success, both in business and with Daisy?

"You're a bloody genius, Mungo. I could kiss you."

"That would be most unwelcome."

"Okay, I'll save the kiss for now. How do we get started?"

He lifts his page of notes to reveal a bound document almost as thick as the tenancy agreement Daisy and I signed before moving in to the flat.

"This is your business plan," he replies, handing it over.

I take a quick flick through the pages of graphs, tables, and lists.

"Christ, Mungo. You did all this in a day?"

"No. Five hours and eleven minutes, to be precise. Your local library is a most useful resource."

"I'm impressed."

"Let us see if you are equally impressed once you digest the content."

I'd be lying if I said the prospect of spending the evening crunching data with Mungo appealed. But before I know it, two hours pass, and I'm furnished with a virtually foolproof system to set up and operate my new venture.

With remnants of molten brain dripping from my ears, I flop back on the sofa.

"There is one variable I was unable to calculate," Mungo adds.

I do my best to sound enthusiastic. "Really? What's that?"

"You."

"Me?"

"Yes. The whole point of this exercise is to bolster your self-esteem. If you do not fully embrace this strategy, the business will not succeed, and your self-esteem will suffer further. I can only provide the tools and only you can utilise them."

This sounds like advice I should really follow. Perhaps if, just for once, Mungo conveyed the seriousness in his voice, it might have carried more weight.

"Trust me, Mungo," I reply dismissively. "I've got it covered."

There's no reaction. He stands up and, just as I expect him to shuffle off, he glares down at me.

"Do not underestimate the gravity of your situation, Adam Maxwell. Time is already running out."

21.

I'm stood in a nondescript room with a row of wooden chairs lined up against a magnolia wall. A waiting room of some kind, maybe?

I might be puzzled as to my whereabouts but a greater issue soon grapples my attention. I sense movement below my feet and look down, only to find the vinyl-clad floor slowly rising upwards. With panic mounting I look for a means of escape but there are no windows and no door. Inch by inch, the floor continues to rise and the ceiling creeps steadily nearer. I stoop, then crouch, then squat, until the space between the floor and ceiling is no more than the height of the chairs. The ceiling presses down on the backs of the chairs, and still the floor continues to rise. Simultaneously, each chair cracks, then splinters, and eventually collapses into kindling. With only inches remaining, I've no option other than to lie on my back and stare hopelessly at the ceiling as it edges closer, and closer, and closer.

I don't so much as wake up, but endure a frenzied escape from sleep. It's my second nightmare this week and far worse than the last.

Breathing hard, I sit up and wait for the pounding in my chest to ease. What the fuck was that all about?

I grab my phone from the bedside table and groan at the time: two minutes to six. Usually, I wouldn't think twice about going back to sleep but not this morning. There was something particularly unnerving about that nightmare, and whatever it was, it's filtered into my waking world. There's no way I want to encourage it any further. Sleep can do one.

I get up and put my dressing gown on. As I tie the cord I hear the sound of a door opening and closing from the hallway. My worst fears are confirmed when I hear another door open and close two seconds later.

"Bloody hell."

I scoot into the hallway and thump the bathroom door.

"Mungo, let me in. I really need a piss."

"Wait," comes the muffled reply.

I jig up and down, trying not to think of running taps or babbling brooks. Unfortunately, my mind doesn't play ball and won't allow me to think of anything else.

"Come on, Mungo. I'm busting."

The door opens.

I stand open mouthed, somewhat taken aback.

"What?" Mungo snaps.

"You're naked."

"I was about to commence my ablutions. Why would I be clothed?"

"You might have wrapped a towel around your waist before opening the door."

"Why?"

"Because I've just woken up from one nightmare. The last thing I want to see is your pasty junk."

Much like when you feel compelled to check if paint really is wet, I fight the urge not to let my gaze fall south.

"I assume you are referring to my genitalia?"

"Actually, shall we leave the conversation there?"

He stands aside and, avoiding further eye contact, I dash towards the toilet. There is nothing more disconcerting than trying to empty your bladder with a naked man stood silently behind you.

"I hope you're not still observing."

He doesn't answer and I finish up. I don't attempt to reengage the conversation on my way out.

Trying to shake the image of a naked Mungo from my mind, I head into the kitchen and put the kettle on. The Coco Pops call me from the cupboard but I can't face breakfast. If my horrific nightmare wasn't enough to leave me queasy, in a little over seven hours I'm due to sit down with Daisy. Granted, I've now got Mungo's flawless business plan and a bucketful of good intentions, but I don't know if it'll be enough to convince her I'm capable of change.

I guess it'll have to be.

While I wait for Mungo to emerge from the bathroom I make a coffee and drink it at the kitchen table. I had every intention of sleeping in until late-morning so I'd avoid half a day of fretting. That plan has already been thwarted but I know I'll drive myself crazy if I sit around doing nothing. I guess there's no time like the present to start implementing Mungo's business plan. I fetch said plan from the lounge, along with the laptop, and return to the kitchen.

While the laptop boots up, I study the first part of the plan— a daunting to-do list containing a series of tasks I need to complete before I can even think of selling my first bottle of cleaning solution.

I decide to break myself in gently and send an email to Joe. I'll need a basic website so customers can order the yet-unnamed cleaning solution plus I'll need labels and business cards designed. Joe might possibly be the world's worst designer but he won't have a backlog of work to clear before he can make a start.

I write a short email to Joe, outlining what I'm up to and what I need, and send it.

There's a certain satisfaction in ticking one task off my list so while I'm in the zone, I send emails to the potential suppliers Mungo identified.

I glance up at the clock and I'm pleased to see I've spent fifteen minutes doing something constructive. I guess that's the beauty of modern technology—the ability to work whenever and wherever you like. How the hell anyone ran a business before the invention of email is beyond me.

I'm about to compile a list of potential names when Mungo appears in the doorway—thankfully fully clothed.

"I have completed my ablutions," he says.

"I'll have a shower later. I'm trying to come up with a name for the solution."

"In which case I shall commence with my cleaning programme."

He closes the door and I return to my laptop.

The irony of compiling a list of names isn't lost on me. But, rather than contemplating inappropriate baby names, I have to create a list of potential names for the cleaning solution, and I need to improve on my first two efforts: *WindowBang* and *Come Shine With Me*.

I'm not sure if it's my lack of imagination, or the impending meeting with Daisy, but my mind won't play nicely. Minutes tick by as I stare at a virtually blank screen. Every time I try to focus on the list my mind drifts off in another direction; ultimately to a daydream where Daisy and I live happily ever after. At the centre of that daydream is the wedding that will never be. Although I constantly complained about the planning, there's no doubt it would have been an amazing day.

Sadly, a daydream is all it'll ever be. I'll never stand at the altar and watch in love-struck awe as my fiancée glides up the aisle. I'll never get to lift her veil and stare into those blue eyes. And I'll never get to vow: I take thee, Daisy Crystal Wallace, to be my lawfully wedded wife.

Just saying the name 'Crystal' prompts a chuckle. Daisy hates her middle name and I used to tease her about it mercilessly. Every time we visited Starbucks, I'd always quote the names Adam and Crystal, just to see Daisy's face when they called our order. Admittedly, the joke wore thin pretty quickly, but it was our thing.

The dull ache reminds me I should get back to my list. Surprisingly, it also offers a spark of inspiration.

Crystal Clear? Too vague. *Crystal Cleaner*? Too generic. *Crystalene*? That's not bad.

I say it over and over in my head and every time it sounds more like a proper brand name. I open a web browser and google it; half-expecting the name to be already in use. After checking ten pages of results, I don't find any cleaning products called Crystalene.

Decision made—my cleaning solution will now be called Crystalene. I only hope when I tell Daisy she takes it as a compliment rather than a piss take. Then again, that's the least of my worries.

I ping another email to Joe confirming the name.

Having made sound progress, and with little else to do until I hear back from Joe and the suppliers, I shut the laptop down. Judging by the whine of the hoover, Mungo is busy with his cleaning regime and if I'm to remain sane, I guess I should make myself busy too.

After a shower and another coffee, I head off to work. Three hours of swinging from a ladder has to be preferable to three hours of swinging between wistful daydreaming and gut-churning apprehension.

As it turns out, it is—just.

I arrive back at the flat a little after eleven o'clock and return to the kitchen to check my emails before getting ready. Two of the four suppliers have replied, confirming their prices and stock availability. I just need two more and I'll have everything I need to produce almost a hundred gallons of Crystalene. There's also a reply from Joe.

It isn't quite the reply I was expecting.

"Shit," I mutter to myself.

"Problem?"

I almost jump out of my skin.

"For Christ's sake, Mungo," I gasp. "Don't creep up on me like that."

"How would you like me to announce my arrival? Should I

sound a bugle?"

I almost choke at his sarcasm.

"You're getting the hang of this sarcasm lark, aren't you?"

"We all have to open ourselves to new ways of thinking. I am no exception."

"Well, you might want to work on the delivery before you consider a career as a stand-up comedian."

"That is not a career I wish to pursue."

"I'm sure Michael McIntyre will be relieved. Anyway, I've got an issue with Joe."

Rather than offer a reply, he stares at the vacant chair next to me.

"You can sit down, you know."

After a brief pause he does, with obvious reluctance.

"The area in which foodstuffs are prepared and consumed are prone to high levels of bacteria."

"What doesn't kill you, Mungo."

"Kill me?"

"Forget it. Can we talk about this email from Joe?"

He nods and I read it out to him.

"You see my problem, Mungo? He's kind of assumed we'll run the business together."

"Why would he make such an assumption?"

"Because we've always talked about running a business together. Unfortunately, talk is all it's ever amounted to, but he's obviously got the wrong end of the stick."

"Tell him then."

If only it were that easy.

"He does have some skills I could use. Maybe I could offer him a small share in the business."

"No."

"That's your response? No?"

"Correct."

"Do you understand the concept of discussion? You know, people talk things through, and weigh up the pros and cons?"

"There is nothing to discuss. Involving your friend will severely undermine the primary purpose of this venture."

"But ..."

"Think," he orders.

Being told to think is like being told to walk—perfectly simple until you focus your attention on it. Then, it all turns to shit.

"What am I supposed to think about?"

"It is not what you think about, but how you think. Suppress your urge to think emotionally."

"Be you then?"

"If that helps you to remove the emotion from your thought process, then yes. I have no emotional connection to your friend which is why I can see the logic in not involving him in your venture."

I sit back and ponder the Joe problem as if I were Mungo. It doesn't take long to see the obvious issues if I get Joe involved but it doesn't make me feel any better about excluding him.

"I get your point, Mungo. Joe is a liability, but he's also my friend so it's not as black and white as you see it."

"Let me frame the question another way. What is more important—your friendship or the opportunity to be a parent?"

Put like that, it's an awful question, but there's only one answer.

"A parent," I mumble.

"You have your answer then. If he is a true friend, he will understand the reasons behind your decision."

Whichever way you cut it, Mungo is right. There is too much at stake to risk buggering it up, even if it's at the cost of my friendship.

"I'm not sure I like thinking logically. Joe isn't going to be happy."

"You cannot please everyone, so I would advise you stop trying. You must focus on doing what is best for Adam Maxwell."

I exhale a deep sigh. "I know, and you're right. Thank you."

"Your gratitude is unnecessary but acknowledged."

With that, he gets up and heads back to his bedroom; probably to soak his trousers in bleach.

A glance at the clock agitates the already lively swarm of butterflies in my stomach. I steel myself and traipse off to the bathroom for a shave and a shower.

Once I'm squeaky clean and smelling as good as I'm ever likely to, the next task is deciding what to wear. I need to make an effort but not so much it looks like I'm trying too hard. My smartest pair of jeans, a black shirt and a casual jacket just about strike the right balance. I take a glance in the mirror and wish myself luck.

Despite the fact I'll probably receive a veiled insult, I knock on Mungo's door on the way out.

I'm greeted with his usual curt manner. "Yes?"

"I'm off to meet Daisy. Wish me luck?"

"Luck is merely a social construct. Wishing for it will have no bearing on the outcome of the meeting."

"Right, well, wish me …"

"If it comforts you, I shall impart some advice: be the master of your thoughts; not a slave to your emotions."

With a slight nod as his farewell, he shuts the door.

"Thanks, Mungo," I sigh.

With precious little time for a plan-B, never have I been so nervous about Alan starting. A few words of gentle encouragement and my worst fears are put to bed as he kicks into life. We set off, trailing a cloud of silvery-blue exhaust fumes in our wake.

Daisy's office is on the outskirts of the town centre and no more than a ten-minute drive. It takes half that time to find a parking space but a glance at my watch tells me I'm still ahead of schedule as I lock Alan's door. Quite why I bother, I don't know. Anyone stupid or patient enough to steal my temperamental old van probably deserves it.

At five to one I step through the door of the coffee shop. After a quick scan to confirm Daisy hasn't arrived, I join the short queue and shuffle nervously on the spot. On any other day, the scent of ground coffee beans and freshly baked cinnamon buns would have me salivating at the counter, but today the rich aromas just stoke my queasiness.

I grab a bottle of mineral water from the cooler and wait for the suited guy in front of me to be served his ridiculously-named coffee. As I watch him trying to find sufficient change in his pockets, I feel a gentle tap on my shoulder. I spin around.

"Hiya," Daisy chirps.

"Oh, um, hi," I splutter back.

This is it.

22.

In all the time we were together, Daisy and I never spent more than twenty-four hours apart. It's been eight days since I last saw her, and all I want to do is scoop her up in my arms. I have to remind myself we're no longer a couple so rather than offer a hug, I stupidly hold out my hand.

"You want a handshake? Seriously, Adam?"

"Um, no. Sorry."

She leans forward and pecks me on the cheek. Just to feel the touch of her lips and the sweetness of her perfume is enough to spark a savage longing.

I draw a deep breath, hoping to find some composure.

"What can I get you?" I squeak.

"Just a cup of green tea, please. Shall I grab us a table?"

"Sure."

I watch her meander past the sprawl of occupied tables towards the far end of the room. As much as I'd rather she was still by my side, at least I've got an extra minute to gather my thoughts.

The young woman behind the counter greets me with a tired smile and feigned enthusiasm. I place Daisy's order and it's dealt with in a silent but efficient manner. Drinks acquired, I make my way across the room and take a seat opposite the love of my life. We swap niceties as if we were casual business acquaintances.

"So, how have you been?" Daisy asks.

Wretched. Heartbroken, miserable, and wretched.

"I'm okay, I guess. You?"

"Not great, to be honest."

I don't really know what to say to that. I offer a feeble smile and move the conversation on.

"I guess we should … um, talk about the elephant in the room."

"The elephant in the room?" she repeats, frowning. "Is that how you see this?"

Nice one, dickhead.

"No, God, no. That's not what I meant."

Daisy rolls her eyes and tuts under her breath. Neither are indicators I've made a positive start so I need to get back on track.

"Look, I'm sorry," I plead. "The next hour is going to be the most important of my life and I'm just a little nervous."

Her expression softens a little although I wouldn't go as far as saying it's friendly.

"Fair enough," she sighs. "But this isn't exactly easy for me either."

"I know. I know."

My words hang in an uncomfortable and worryingly long silence.

I spent most of the morning planning what I was going to say. In my head, I'd hatched a series of perfectly articulate statements to demonstrate how seriously I was taking the situation. Sitting here now, every one of those statements has decided there's somewhere else it would rather be.

"I've decided to keep the baby," Daisy suddenly blurts. "So, whatever you're thinking, that's not up for discussion."

Is it possible to look pleasantly shocked? My face gives it a go.

"You are? But Mum said you were thinking about …"

"I was, but deep down I knew I couldn't go through with it, even if I really thought it was for the best."

"For definite?"

"Yes. I've talked it through with my parents and we've come up with a plan."

I fear any plan with Eddie's involvement isn't likely to feature me.

"Can I ask what that plan is?"

"If you're interested," she shrugs. "Basically, my parents are going to give me the money they'd set aside for the wedding so I can buy a flat. I've also had a chat with my boss and, after I've completed maternity leave, he's agreed I can work from home three days a week."

It's taken just eight days for me to be written out of her life, it seems.

"And where exactly do I fit in? This is my child too."

"We'll have to work something out. Maybe you can pop over one afternoon a week."

"One afternoon a week?" I huff. "That's the sum total of my involvement?"

"If it were up to my dad, you wouldn't have any involvement. He thinks one afternoon is more than you deserve."

My nerves are elbowed aside by irritation. Who the hell does Eddie think he is, telling me when I can see my own child?

"Tell Eddie he can go fuck …"

I stop myself mid-sentence. This is precisely the kind of emotional thinking Mungo warned me about barely an hour ago. A sip of water provides a suitable time-out to recall my agitation.

"That seems unfair," I say in a level voice. "I'd like to be part of his or her life too, and not just for a few hours a week."

Daisy takes a sip of green tea and her nose wrinkles because she doesn't actually like green tea. I guess she's decided to abstain from caffeine for the baby's sake.

"Well?"

"It's not that easy," she sighs.

"Why not?"

"Two reasons. Firstly, you do remember how we got into this situation don't you?"

"We had sex. That's generally how babies are made isn't it?"

"Not the pregnancy, dummy. The break-up."

"Oh, yes. That."

"That indeed. I don't think I'll ever be able to forgive you for cheating, Adam, and Dad certainly won't."

A fight kicks off in my head: Mungo's advice versus agitation, with frustration also keen to get involved. I take a few seconds to let the fracas play out and thankfully, Mungo's advice claims victory … just.

I look Daisy straight in the eye. "I did not cheat on you. I swear on our baby's life."

It would be so easy to continue pleading my innocence but I remain silent and hold her gaze.

"Maybe you didn't," she eventually concedes. "But you still spent the night at some random girl's flat and you still got wasted on weed."

"I know, and I was an idiot."

"And that's the problem, Adam. It was just the last in a long line of idiotic scrapes you've got yourself into. It's one thing hurting me and letting me down, but I can't afford you acting like that with our child. I just can't."

"Well, I'm working on a solution which I won't bore you with now. What was the second reason I'm being rationed time?"

Her eyes dart left and right, avoiding mine. Whatever the answer, she clearly isn't comfortable discussing it.

"Daisy?"

"Alright, it's Dad. He will only give me the money for the

flat on one condition."

"Go on."

"That you aren't part of my life, least not in any significant way."

"What have I ever done to him? If you're prepared to believe I didn't cheat, why can't he?"

"It's not just that. He's willing to help fund a home for me and the baby, but not you. He's convinced you'll screw things up and we'll end up having the flat repossessed."

"So, it comes down to money?"

"A bit, I suppose."

"A bit? I'd say it features quite heavily in his motives."

"Do you blame him for being protective? When was the last time you made anything close to an astute financial decision?"

Ohh. Did not plan for this question.

"Um, there's Alan."

"Alan?"

"You told me to get rid of him six months ago. By keeping him, I've saved six months of payments on a new van."

"And how many times have I had to rescue you after Alan broke down?"

"Five or six. Seven at most."

"And how much have you paid to keep him on the road in the last six months, including all the times he's returned home on the back of a recovery truck?"

"Err, five hundred … ish."

"Not such a great example, is it, Adam?"

"Probably not."

"And that's why Dad is so concerned. You're a nightmare with money … actually, you're just a nightmare, and he only wants the best for me and the baby. You can't blame him for thinking the way he does, can you?"

She's right, I can't. Even with months of preparation, the best barrister in the land would struggle to defend my past so there's no point in me even trying.

It seems we've reached an impasse. We both sit back and stare beyond one another with Daisy perhaps close to concluding our time is up. I might have convinced her I didn't cheat but that's pretty incidental in the grander scale of my fuck ups. In that sense, I've got nothing to offer.

I desperately need to show her I'm trying to change. I desperately need to find my inner-Mungo.

One final throw of the dice.

"Can I ask you a question?"

"Go on," she replies, wearily.

"Do you still love me?"

"Does it matter?"

"Yes, it does. Tell me you don't love me, even just a tiny bit, and I'll walk away now. And I'll agree to whatever access terms you and your dad want."

Seconds tick by as she stares into her cup. This is a high risk strategy and I can only hope I've read her right.

"I can't just turn my feelings off," she finally admits. "But love isn't enough, Adam."

"No, it's not. But it's enough for me to work with."

"Meaning?"

"Meaning I have something to aim for. What if I can come up with the money for the deposit? All twenty thousand of it."

If Mungo were here I'm certain he'd slap me around the face for making such an offer. It is, without argument, short of any logical reasoning.

"Yeah, right," she snorts. "Are you going to blow a week's wages on lottery tickets again?"

"That was a one-off experiment, and no, I'm not."

"How then?"

Perhaps now would be the ideal time to take Dad's advice. Actions do speak louder than words so there's no point in making promises about how I'm going to get the money. I just need to get the money.

"Don't worry about that."

"Every time you've ever told me not to worry about something, I've regretted it. Please tell me you're not going to do something stupid, or illegal, or both."

"It's perfectly legitimate, I promise."

"What is it then?"

"Just let me worry about that. All I'm asking for is a chance to prove I can support you and the baby. I know I don't deserve any more chances but this is different—I know what's at stake this time."

"This isn't just about money, Adam."

"I know that, but it would be a start. At the very least it'll prove to Eddie I'm not the complete idiot he thinks I am."

Her attention returns to the cup. Whatever she's thinking, her face doesn't give anything away.

"Look, Daisy. All I'm asking is that you don't completely shut me out. I'm genuinely making an effort to sort myself out and if everything goes to plan, I will be able to help pay for a nice home. And, in time, I will prove I'm not a complete liability."

The slight nod and raised eyebrows are as good a reaction as I could have hoped for.

"Your mum tells me you're seeing a therapist again," she says, moving swiftly on from my declaration.

"That's right, and he's really helping me ... hold on ... what do you mean, *again*?"

"I don't know," she shrugs. "Your mum said you saw a therapist as a child but she didn't give me any details. It was just a throwaway comment."

Did I ever see a therapist? I have no recollection whatsoever but it can't have been that significant as surely I'd remember something about it. If I had to guess, it was probably because I was a serial bed-wetter. If that was the reason, it worked. Well, on the whole.

"Anyway, I've had a diagnosis and I'm slowly getting to grips with the way I process decisions."

Her head snaps up. "Diagnosis?"

Shit. I shouldn't have used that word.

"Don't worry," I chuckle, trying to make light of it. "That sounds worse than it is and I'm not suffering from some major psychosis. It's all to do with self-esteem and basing my decisions upon logic rather than emotion. Early days but it's already sinking in."

"I hope so, Adam, for your sake. You can't go on living your life the way you have."

"I know."

With the heavy part of our conversation out of the way, all I want to do is talk about the baby. I want to be excited. I want us to be excited. Looking at Daisy, though, it's clearly not mutual. Of everything I regret, stealing the joy from what should be such an exciting time summons the sharpest pang. Just the look in her eyes is enough to know I've let her down more than ever before.

"I am sorry, you know."

"You always are, Adam," she sighs.

Harsh, but fair.

If I've learnt anything from our time together, it's knowing when to quit a conversation with Daisy—her tone tells me now is that time. I've achieved as much as I could hope considering the circumstances, and I think it would be best to walk away with the consolation prize on this occasion.

"I better get off," I say, trying to appear positive. "Lots to do."

She nudges her cup away and starts buttoning her coat.

"Can I see you again?" I venture. "Maybe next week?"

"I don't know. I'll think about it."

Don't push your luck.

"Fair enough. It was just to have a chat, you know, about the baby."

"We'll see."

We both stand and make our way to the door.

Once we're outside, I resist the urge to offer a handshake and risk a peck on the cheek.

"Thank you for seeing me. I know I don't deserve it."

"Enough with the self-deprecation, eh. It's not an attractive trait."

She touches me on the arm and, with a parting half-smile, turns to walk away. After a brief pause, she glances back over her shoulder.

"Good luck finding that twenty grand."

My former fiancée then walks away.

As I wander back to Alan, I replay Daisy's final words over and over again, trying to decipher the tone. Not sarcastic but not sincere. Not positive but not damning. However, it's not so much her tone that bothers me—it's why I even made such a ridiculous offer. What was I thinking? It doesn't take much introspection to find the answer—Eddie. I let his interference get under my skin and, once again, emotions guided my reaction. Knowing I shouldn't think that way and stopping myself are still a long way from being the same process. It's going to take more than a few days with Mungo to change the habit of a lifetime.

If there's any saving grace, it's that Daisy probably took my offer with an entire cellar of salt. She's heard enough of my promises, and witnessed enough subsequent failures, to keep her hopes in check.

And that is one of the reasons why Daisy isn't now returning home with me.

If ever there was a time to break the cycle, this is it.

23.

One difficult conversation down. One to go.

I pull onto the driveway and extract my phone to find a missed call from Joe. This is one of those problems that will only get worse the longer I let it fester so I might as well bite the bullet now. I call him straight back.

"Alright, Joe?"

"Yeah. You busy?"

"Not really. I've just got back from seeing Daisy."

"Are you still trying to wheedle your way back into her good books?"

"It's a bit more complicated than that. Actually, it's a lot more complicated than that."

"Want to discuss it over a few pints? We can chat about this new business too."

I could murder a pint and just as I'm about to confirm a venue where we're unlikely to meet Angry Pete, I pause.

"Actually, mate, can you pop over to my place?"

"What's wrong with the pub?"

"Nothing. I'd just rather keep a clear head."

"Fair enough. I'll be over shortly."

I end the call and make my way up to the flat. The second the latch clicks on the front door, Mungo appears in the hallway.

"Productive meeting?" he asks.

"I wouldn't go that far but it wasn't a complete disaster either."

"One might argue an improvement over the last meeting with your former partner."

"Thanks for reminding me."

"As I have told you before, your gratitude is unnecessary."

"That was sarcasm, not gratitude."

I wait for his reply but nothing comes.

"Actually, Mungo, I've got some good news and some bad news."

Still nothing.

"The good news is that Joe is coming over shortly."

"I would have assumed that to be the bad news."

"Afraid not," I reply, coyly. "The bad news is: I told Daisy I'd be able to raise twenty thousand pounds for a deposit on a flat, for her and the baby."

"That is not bad news. That is bad judgement on your part."

"I know. It just came out."

Besides the slightest crease in his forehead, there's no indication of his feelings towards my latest blunder. I do wonder how bad things have to be before Mungo really loses his shit.

"I might have got a little annoyed with the way her dad is trying to cut me out of the baby's life."

"And you thought an unrealistic offer of financial support would help?"

"Well, no, but I had to say something."

"No, you did not. You should have stopped and considered the implications."

Of course, he's absolutely right, but that doesn't help put the genie back in the bottle.

"I will rework the financial forecast," he adds.

"Eh?"

"Seeing as you have put yourself in this position, I must calculate how you might fulfil your obligation."

"Are you serious? Do you think I might be able to raise that kind of money with the new business?"

"I have no idea."

"Oh."

"I can only calculate what is required to raise the funds. The application of my revised strategy is down to you."

"Again, in English?"

"I will revise the instructions but you must do the work."

"I'll do whatever it takes."

He shuffles across the hallway to his bedroom door. "We will reconvene in two hours. Ensure your friend has vacated the premises by that point."

"But, I was going to go …"

The door is shut firmly in my face. It looks like I won't be going to the pub later.

I wander into the kitchen and make myself a cup of strong coffee while I wait for the laptop to boot up. Hopefully the last two suppliers will have answered my emails from earlier and I can start on the next task on the list—finding somewhere to mix, bottle, and store hundreds of litres of cleaning solution. The flat is a non-starter as it's too small and I don't want to spend half my life lugging heavy containers of liquid up and down the stairs. However, there's no way I want to tie myself into a commercial lease, even if I could afford the rent, which I can't.

In the hope of prompting a solution, I get up and pace the

kitchen. Five fruitless minutes later, I try staring out of the window.

"Idiot," I mumble to myself.

A potential solution, as it transpires, was right under my nose in the form of a dilapidated garage belonging to my landlord, George. Positioned at the end of the driveway but hidden behind a set of weathered wooden gates, it's a sorry looking structure, but it could be a perfect short-term home for my new venture.

I scurry across to my laptop and send an email to George. Job done, I then check my inbox and find replies from the final two suppliers. Both deliver the news I hoped for, and with it, two more pieces of the production jigsaw fall into place. All I need now is a supplier for the plastic bottles, and hopefully a positive response from George about the garage.

I'm about to check the business plan for the next item on my task list when the doorbell rings. The clock tells me it'll almost certainly be Joe, and it's time to dash his hopes of a business partnership. While I was desperately looking forward to seeing Daisy earlier, I can't say I'm relishing my chat with Joe to the same degree.

I wander through the hallway and open the front door.

"What's the deal with the pub then?" Joe asks, wandering straight past me without a greeting. "Are you on the wagon or something?"

"Go through to the lounge and I'll explain. Do you want a coffee?"

"Nah, you're alright."

I follow Joe through to the lounge and we both flop down at opposite ends of the sofa.

"Where's that weird Mungo bloke?" he asks in a voice too loud.

"Keep it down," I hiss. "He's in his room."

"How's it going then? Is your unlicensed quack helping?"

"It's going okay, actually."

It's unlikely Joe really cares one jot. When he was seeing a therapist for anxiety, we had an unwritten rule never to discuss it. In fact, our relationship forbids us to discuss anything even slightly touchy-feely, so I move the conversation on to more important matters.

"Anyway, forget Mungo. There's something I need to tell you."

"Oh, Jesus," he groans. "I knew this day would come."

"What day?"

"You, coming out. Let me guess—Mungo is really your lover."

"Don't be a dick."

"I'm not. He's moved into your spare bedroom and you're spending an awful lot of time with him. All the signs are there, mate."

"I'm not gay and, even if I were, Mungo wouldn't be my type."

"Who would be your type then?"

"I don't know. Maybe someone like … wait. Why are we even discussing this?"

"Because you're coming out."

Joe has aptly demonstrated why we rarely discuss serious subjects. If I don't get straight to the point, we'll only continue on this ridiculous path.

"Daisy is pregnant."

"Shit," he gasps. "Sorry, mate."

"Sorry?"

"Yeah. It can't be easy, knowing another bloke has knocked your bird up. Is that why she left you?"

"What? No, the baby is mine."

"You sure?"

"Yes."

Joe scratches his stubbly chin, and for a moment looks lost in his thoughts.

"Are you going to congratulate me then?" I ask.

"Err, yeah. Nice one, mate."

"Gee, don't go overboard with the enthusiasm."

"I don't know what else to say," he mumbles. "This changes everything, doesn't it?"

I've seen the same look in his eyes before, but not in a long, long time. We were kids, and I'd just told Joe my parents had booked our summer holiday the same week as his eleventh birthday party. He tried to pretend he didn't care but the moist eyes and scratchy voice suggested otherwise. I found out a few months later that only three kids turned up; cousins invited by his mum to make up the woeful numbers.

"Things change, mate, but that doesn't mean we can't still go to the pub and talk crap for hours on end."

"Yeah, but not as often."

Suddenly his face brightens a touch. "But at least we'll be working together, eh?"

Inadvertently, Joe has just made the next part of our conversation ten times harder.

"Yeah, about that."

"Don't tell me you've changed your mind? It's a great idea."

"No, I haven't. It's just that …well, the thing is …"

When you've known someone as long as we've known each other, a reaction is often more telling than words. This, apparently, is one such time.

"Say it then," he snaps.

"Mate, I need to think about the baby and this is too important …"

"You don't want me involved, do you?"

"Well, I do … in a way. I want you to design a website and all the other stuff."

"But you don't want me as a partner?"

I'm suddenly an eleven-year-old kid again. I react accordingly by shifting the blame elsewhere.

"Mungo told me I had to do it on my own," I bleat.

"And you just went with it? Just tell him to fuck off and mind his own business."

"It was his idea, and …"

"And what?" he blasts. "You just do what he tells you?"

"It's not like that."

"Sounds exactly like that. You're his bitch."

His accusation trips a switch in my head. I tried to be nice, and to explain why he can't be involved, but now I'm just annoyed.

"I'm nobody's bitch," I spit. "I'm doing this on my own because I can't have you fucking things up for me like you usually do. Not this time."

A second after the words pass my lips, I regret them. Not just because I've twisted the knife in Joe's back, but because I've done exactly what Mungo told me not to—act on emotion.

Joe gets to his feet and glares down at me.

"Suit-your-fucking-self then. I know when I'm not wanted "

He makes for the door.

"Joe, wait. I'm sorry."

"Go screw yourself, and that poisonous dwarf."

I'm still scrambling to my feet when the front door slams shut. In frustration, I launch a forgotten scatter cushion across the room and it silently strikes the far wall before flopping to the floor. Turning to the window, I catch the final seconds of Joe lumbering up the street before he disappears from view.

"Not a productive meeting, I assume?"

I spin around and Mungo is stood just inside the door.

"I was going to complain about the raised voices," he adds. "But that now appears a moot point."

"Joe is totally pissed off with me."

"Because of the facts, or the way those facts were served?"

"Both, but mainly because I pretty-much accused him of being a liability."

"That is ironic."

"In what way?"

"Your former partner considers you a liability, does she not?"

Rather than quashing my irritation, Mungo's observation only stokes it further.

"That's not the point. You told me to ditch Joe so you're partly to blame for this."

"No, you are solely to blame, Adam Maxwell. You said, and I quote: '*I can't have you fucking things up like you usually do.*'"

As amusing as it is to hear Mungo swear, hearing my words coldly replayed in his clinical tone, only heightens my remorse.

"I didn't mean it. I was annoyed."

"You were emotional."

"I'm not a bloody robot, Mungo. It's all well and good you telling me to think logically but that's easier said than done."

"Clearly it is, but given the opportunity to have that conversation again, would you approach it differently?"

"Of course. I should have explained I need to provide for the baby, and I should have told him about my self-esteem issues."

"Then you are learning. I never claimed the process would be easy, but recognising your mistakes will hold you in good stead the next time such a situation arises."

"Great," I mumble. "And in the meantime, what am I supposed to do about Joe?"

"He will calm down and, when he does, perhaps he might realise the need to control his own emotions."

He's right. He's always bloody right; to the point it's almost irritating.

"I hope so. I was counting on Joe to do that design work over the weekend."

"You cannot afford for the venture to stall because of loyalty to your friend. If he is unwilling to assist, you must find an alternative designer."

"I know. I'll pop round there tomorrow and apologise. I'm

sure he'll be fine."

I'm not sure at all but I need to try. Apologising to Joe is becoming a habit, and it's yet another hard landing on the seesaw which has become my life of late.

"I am sure he will be fine," Mungo replies, although I can't tell if he's being sincere. "How are you progressing with the tasks I set you?"

"Really well, as it goes. I just need to find a company to provide the bottles. Oh, and possibly a designer."

"Do you require my assistance?"

"It's all under control, thanks."

"In which case, I shall return to my task."

With Mungo back in his room, I ponder how I'm going to spend the rest of the afternoon. I could squeeze in a few hours of window cleaning but the schizophrenic weather keeps switching from sunshine to heavy showers. With little appetite for a soaking, I return to the kitchen and the laptop.

After half an hour of online research, I manage to stretch my knowledge of plastic bottles from nothing to something. Once I know what I'm looking for, I reap the benefits of globalisation and locate a company who can supply Chinese-made plastic bottles for what seems like a ridiculously low price. Not wishing for a repeat of the British Airways fiasco, I check the company out and establish they're legit. The only downside is that I have to place a minimum order of a thousand units. Fingers crossed George lets me use the garage otherwise I'll be up to my neck in boxes.

With no savings to call upon, this entire venture will have to be funded with my credit card. As I'm about to enter the card details on the website, I stop for a second and stare at the kitchen drawer—the one containing Mungo's rent money.

I vowed I wouldn't touch that money, as without it, I'm in deep shit when it comes to making the rent. Then again, the interest rates charged on my credit card are the equivalent of financial sodomy. By the time I pay for all the supplies I need, I'll be over a grand in debt and still be paying off the interest by the time my unborn child is old enough to legally drink with me.

Rent money or credit card?

With my finger hovering over the keyboard and my eyes fixed on the drawer, I'm torn. This is just the kind of decision I've screwed up in the past but knowing that doesn't make it any easier. If anything, it only adds to the pressure and muddles my thoughts.

"Think logically," I murmur to myself.

I take a moment to clear my mind and weigh up the pros and cons of each option. After five minutes of wrestling with my own indecision, I finally reach a conclusion. However, before I commit I want to get Mungo's view. If my decision turns sour, at least I can lay some of the blame on my lodger.

I scurry through to the hall and knock on his door.

"Yes?"

"Can I ask your advice on something?"

"You may."

I explain my dilemma.

"Have you reached a conclusion?" he asks.

"I have, but I wanted to run it past you first."

"There is no need."

"Why not?"

"The decision you have reached is immaterial in that I cannot tell you if it is right or wrong."

"Terrific," I groan. "But what if I make the wrong call?"

"If you reached the decision in the correct way, as I instructed, that is as much as you can do."

In the seconds I've been stood at Mungo's door, self-doubt has crept up behind me and I can feel it about to whisper in my ear.

"Trust yourself, Adam Maxwell," he adds. "The decision will likely be right if you unequivocally decide it is right. Make it, and commit to it."

It's of no great surprise when he shuts the door in my face. I have to admit his rudeness is now edging towards endearing; like my dear-departed old granddad who hated everyone and trusted no one. He was a cantankerous old git but, beneath his gruff exterior, he had a good heart—right up until it wasn't, and he suffered a terminal cardiac arrest whilst ranting at a politician on TV. It was the way he'd have wanted to go.

I slope back to the kitchen and sit down at the table.

"Fuck you, self-doubt," I snap.

I pay for my order with the credit card.

I allow myself a moment of self-congratulation for actually making the decision. Whether it's the right one remains to be seen.

24.

2007 was the best year ever, unless you were the manager of the England football team or enjoyed smoking in pubs. For Adam Maxwell, though, it was a year spent being unashamedly young, single and foolish. I was twenty-two years of age, and had a decent job working for a firm of estate agents; a firm who appeared remarkably relaxed about my woeful A-level results or lack of experience. I started that job in March and they fired me in November.

Nevertheless, for eight months I wore sharp suits, drove a company car, and earned more than a twenty-two year old idiot should. Still living at home, I had a handsome disposable income and duly spunked it every month, without fail. Life was a series of parties, nightclubs, work jollies and girls—lots of girls. The sun was shining and I was making hay, particularly on Friday nights after work when we'd hit the town and party hard until the early hours of the morning.

As I sat in the lounge last night, I thought about those days and how my Friday nights had changed: the sharp suit replaced with jogging pants and a sweatshirt, the champagne with cocoa, and the stream of girls with a Netflix box set. And rather than staying up till the early hours, I was in bed by eleven o'clock.

My exuberant lifestyle might only have been a decade ago but it feels like an eternity this Saturday morning. Today, my diary includes such highlights as grovelling to my best mate, clearing junk from a garage, and watching my dad play bowls. Somehow, without even realising, I've become prematurely middle-aged.

On the plus side, Mungo allowed me to lie-in until eight o'clock before commencing his cleaning regime. Quite what he finds to clean every morning is beyond me but it keeps him happy. Actually, *occupied* would be a better word—he's not really the happy type.

"What are your plans for the day?" he asks as I tuck into a bowl of Coco Pops in the kitchen.

"My landlord has said I can use the garage so I need to clear it out. I've also got to see Joe at some point, and if I'm not at the leisure centre at two o'clock, my mother will have my testicles for earrings."

Cogs appear to turn as he digests my schedule.

"Before you say it, Mungo, I didn't mean literally. I think even she'd draw the line at wearing her son's bollocks as earrings."

"Indeed. Why are you required to be at the leisure centre at two o'clock?"

"My dad is playing in a bowls tournament. He's in the final."

"I will attend with you."

"If you like. I should warn you, though, besides any football match involving Stoke City, bowls is the most tedious sport I've ever had the misfortune to watch."

"I will draw my own conclusions."

"In the meantime, I don't suppose you fancy helping me clear the garage?"

"No."

"Thanks. Much appreciated."

"I detect sarcasm."

"And I detect a lazy git not willing to help out a mate."

Based on previous conversations with Mungo, this is typically the point where he walks off, or slams a door in my face. On this occasion, however, he gurns an expression resembling mild surprise.

"A mate?" he echoes.

"Well, yeah. I guess we're kind of mates now."

"Assuming it is used as a noun," he declares. "Mate is an informal description of a friend or companion. Do you consider me a friend or companion?"

"Err, I guess, until you started making this weird."

Ignoring my jibe, he puffs out his chest. "Adam Maxwell, I formally accept your friendship."

It's a particularly unfriendly acceptance with no hint of a smile or sentiment.

"Are you taking the piss?"

"No. I am being most sincere."

To prove just how sincere he is, he shakes my hand, and promptly walks away without another word.

It's telling that I respond by simply rolling my eyes and putting the kettle on. After six days of Mungo, his weird behaviour isn't as unsettling as it once was, although this is a new development. I wouldn't be surprised if he's gone off to create friendship certificates and lapel badges.

For now though, it looks like I'll be clearing the garage without the assistance of my new-found friend. I make a coffee, put my trainers on, and head downstairs.

George was good enough to drop the garage keys off last night, with a promise he wouldn't charge any extra rent for six months on condition I cleared the garage of the unspecified junk inside. I'll probably need to take a trip to the council tip but it's a small price to pay for six months of free storage.

Emerging on to the driveway, I'm pleased to find the weather is also feeling friendly this morning with no sign of rain. I place my coffee mug on a window ledge and approach the two six-foot-high wooden gates which stand between the driveway and the garage. After a minute or two of pushing, pulling, and kicking, the gates finally open. Even just looking at it, I can tell the rusty garage door will prove a sterner test.

I turn the key in the lock and tug at the handle. It doesn't budge. Several harder tugs are administered but the door refuses to give. Conscious I'm on a tight schedule, I quickly dispense with subtlety and aim repeated kicks at the bottom of the door; taking a moment in between each kick to tug the handle. On the tenth kick it gives in and creaks open.

"Uh, for fucks sake."

I seem to recall George once rented the flats out as bedsits, and when he decided it was too much hassle he must have moved all the furniture into the garage. It seems I've agreed to clear six single beds with mattresses, four armchairs, a tumble dryer, three flat-pack wardrobes, a coffee table, and a dozen boxes of miscellaneous crap from the kitchen. I probably should have clarified what was in the garage before agreeing the deal.

My motivation ebbing away, I stand and stare at the packed interior of the garage.

Two weeks ago, I'm sure I'd have dealt with this problem in one of two ways: I'd have either piled everything in the garden and thrown a match at it, or shut the garage door and hoped the problem would somehow solve itself. I take a moment to consider both options. The child in me quite fancies the idea of a thirty-foot bonfire but I don't think George would be too impressed. As for doing nothing, that only shifts the problem in a different direction.

No, my only option is the sensible, but back-breaking one. With negligible levels of enthusiasm, I make a start.

It takes nearly two hours to clear just half the garage. Two hours of colourful language, sweat, and spider webs.

It's nearly eleven o'clock by the time I offload the final piece of flattened wardrobe at the council tip. There's just enough time for an overly-officious dick in a Hi-Viz jacket to complain about my haphazard tossing before I set off to Joe's house.

As I pootle through the streets I replay our conversation from yesterday. I can't help but wonder if this is the beginning of the end of our friendship—I know it happens. People change, and although I've made scores of friends over the years, through school, college, and work, they've all subsequently re-categorised themselves as old acquaintances. You might befriend one another on Facebook, or share a few words if you bump into one another in the supermarket, but to all intents and purposes you're not the same people anymore. Maybe this is now the time for Joe and I to drift off in different directions. I don't know how I feel about that, but it's certainly not positive.

Joe's house, or more precisely, Joe's parents' house, is in a cul-de-sac not too dissimilar to Rosemary Gardens. The drier weather has encouraged several residents to venture outside, and cars are being washed and lawns tidied. I abandon Alan on a grass verge and, with more apprehension than I anticipated, wander up the driveway of number sixteen.

Opening the front door, Joe doesn't appear pleased to see me.

"What do you want?" he growls.

"Are you going to let me in?"

"Why? I thought you said all you needed to say yesterday."

"Come on, mate. I need to explain."

"Whatever," he huffs, walking away but leaving the door open.

Taking it as an invite, I follow him through the hallway and into the kitchen at the back of the house.

"Are your folks in?" I ask, hoping small talk will defuse his apparent wrath.

"Nah. Gone shopping," he mumbles before sitting down at a large oak table.

It would be no exaggeration to say several hundred trees gave their lives to create Mr and Mrs Faulkner's recently-fitted kitchen. I guess they were going for a rustic look, but they've overdone it, and their kitchen now has the ambiance of a shed.

I join Joe at the table. Time is not on my side so I get straight to the point.

"I'm sorry, mate. I didn't mean what I said."

"Then why say it?"

"Do I really need to answer that? I opened my mouth

without thinking, okay?"

"Seems your therapist is as crap as I thought."

"I know you don't like him and, to be fair, there's not a lot to like, but I've got to stick with him because Daisy won't let me be part of the baby's life if I don't get my shit together."

His frown eases as he leans back in his chair.

"That's harsh."

"It is, and that's why I need to get this business off the ground. I need money, and I need it yesterday."

"What do you need money for? I could lend it to you."

"You can lend me twenty grand?"

"Shit, no," he coughs. "I thought you meant, like, fifty quid."

"I wish. Daisy's old man has reallocated our wedding budget so she can put down a deposit on a flat. I might have inadvertently suggested I could come up with the cash instead, you know, to show I'm a responsible parent."

"You dickhead."

"Agreed, but can you now see why this business is so important to me? This is my one and only chance, mate. If I blow it, the best I can look forward to is seeing my kid for a few hours a week."

Joe isn't a big thinker but, judging by his silence, something is going on in his head.

"Do you really think I'd fuck it up for you?" he eventually murmurs.

"I, um …"

"Cos' I probably would," he adds. "Not intentionally, but we're both as bad as each other when it comes to fucking things up."

"I said I didn't mean it."

"No, you were right," he sighs. "Look at me. Thirty-three years of age and still living at home with my parents. No girlfriend, no proper job, and my only mate …"

As his voice trails off, his head slumps forward.

"Your only mate what?" I ask.

"Don't suppose it matters now, but when you started seeing Daisy, I was gutted."

"Why?"

"I doubt you wanna know."

"Try me."

"Cos' I was jealous."

I can honestly say I didn't see this coming.

"Oh, I see. I'm not sure what to say, mate. I mean, I didn't even know you had those kind of feelings for me."

"Jesus," he groans. "I wasn't jealous of Daisy, you knob. I was jealous you had a girlfriend."

"Ahh, right. Thank God for that."

"And while we're being honest, I'm jealous you're having a kid. That's why I stormed out yesterday … I was just pissed off. You always seem to get the lucky breaks, even after you've screwed up."

It's rare I'm ever lost for words with Joe but this is one such occasion. We've already strayed way beyond our agreed boundaries of conversation and this territory is both uncharted and uncomfortable.

"I don't know what to say, mate. I never really considered myself lucky, and I certainly didn't think I had anything worth being jealous of."

"Seriously? You had a fit girlfriend, a half-decent business, and your own place. And now you've got a baby on the way, and this new business looks like it could be a winner. What the hell have I got?"

His question is posed with an aggressive tone, but there's an unexpected hint of sadness buried just beneath the surface, matched by his eyes. The man now looking back at me isn't a version of Joe I've met before.

"I'll tell you what I've got," he glumly answers for me. "Nothing and no one."

Faced with a rare moment of poignancy in our friendship, my heart says I should relent and offer Joe a share in the new business. My head says I should remind him he does own an enviable collection of vintage porn mags, and therefore does have something I covet. Neither feels an appropriate response.

"Is there anything I can do?"

"Not unless you've got the phone number of a supermodel with a thing for chubby gingers."

I'm relieved to hear his attempt at humour, as half-hearted as it is.

"Sadly not. But on the bright side, at least you don't have to spend the afternoon watching a bunch of geriatrics playing bowls."

"Are any of them fit?"

"Yeah, that's nasty."

"Any port in a storm mate, and I've been at sea a bloody long time."

I wish I had more to offer Joe besides banter, but I don't. I also don't have time to continue our conversation over a few pints, as much as I suspect he'd like to. The best I can offer is a compromise.

"Why don't we meet up later? A few beers, maybe an hour or two in Tiffany's?"

"Can't do tonight. I'm busy," he replies.

"Oh, right. Doing what?"

"What you asked me to."

"Eh?"

"The website and design work."

"But I thought ..."

"If you're going to fuck this up, it won't be on my account. And besides, I need the work, even if it is at mates rates."

With Joe's moment of soul bearing now put to bed, and unlikely to ever be discussed again, I offer the only acceptable method of physical contact permitted between blokes, and slap him on the arm.

"Cheers, mate. I do appreciate it."

"No worries, but promise me one thing."

"Name it."

"If this thing takes off, you'll hire me as your marketing director."

"Alright, you're on."

"Oh, and one other thing."

"Go on," I reply hesitantly.

"You're definitely not *my* type."

25.

Joe's confession plays on my mind for the entire journey back to the flat. I've been wallowing in so much self-pity of late, nobody else's feelings have really crossed my mind, least of all Joe's. I suppose it cuts both ways as he hardly offered a shoulder to cry on when Daisy left, but if you can't talk through the serious problems in life with your best friend, what's the point of having one? Perhaps it's time for us both to grow up a bit—we're not teenagers any more, despite our best efforts to act as such.

I vow to have a proper, grown-up chat with Joe later. Well, I'll attempt to, but for now I need to get my arse in gear.

After a quick shower and a change of clothes, I rap on Mungo's door.

"Are you ready? We need to get going."

He opens the door and I'm surprised to see he isn't sporting one of his polythene boiler suits.

"You know we're going in Alan, right?"

"I recommend we walk. I have checked the distance and it should take no more than twenty-four minutes."

I glance at my watch. We have time but I'm not sure I have the motivation.

"I'd rather drive, Mungo."

"There are numerous health benefits to walking."

"But …"

"We will walk."

He shuffles past me and opens the front door. A glance back in my direction and I get the impression this is non-negotiable.

"Fine," I huff. "But if we're late, you can explain to my mother."

Fortunately, the weather is still vaguely pleasant as we stroll through streets lined with tatty houses and tattier cars. We clear the first half mile in silence, until I decide to take advantage of our new relationship status.

"Seeing as we're friends now, Mungo, are you going to tell me a bit more about yourself?"

"Such as?"

"Anything would be a start. I know literally nothing about you."

"If you ask a specific question, I will provide an answer."

"Okay. What's your favourite movie?"

"I do not watch movies."

"Alright. Your favourite band or artist?"

"I do not listen to contemporary music."

I'm about to ask what his favourite meal is, but I can already guess.

"Forget favourite things then. Where did you live before moving in with me?"

"My prior life is complicated and I cannot provide specific answers."

"Can't or won't?"

"Both."

I guess there are many reasons why a person might not wish to discuss their past; some justified, some not. For all I know, Mungo might have suffered a terrible tragedy and he's moved here to forget. But equally, he might have just been released from prison after committing some heinous crime.

"Tell me something, Mungo: did you end up in my spare room because something bad happened to you?"

"Define *bad*?"

"Did something happen in your life, you know, like a personal tragedy?"

"No."

"Okay. Did you do something that harmed someone?"

"Directly, no. Indirectly, yes."

I stop dead in my tracks. "Whoa! Hold up a minute."

"Is there a problem?"

"You can't answer a question like that and expect me to just let it pass. This thing you did … was it illegal?"

"No."

I breathe a little easier knowing I'm not inadvertently providing a bail hostel. We continue on but my curiosity is now piqued.

"If you don't mind talking about it, how did you indirectly harm someone?"

"My presence in an individual's life caused them extreme emotional distress and I never got the opportunity to put matters right."

"Can I ask who that individual was?"

"You can ask but I will not tell you."

"Was it a partner, or a family member?"

"I will not tell you."

Despite his lack of emotion, clearly this is not a topic of

conversation Mungo wishes to pursue any further. At least I know a little more about him than I did when we left the flat, so I'll take that for now.

Fifteen minutes later we reach the outskirts of the town and the street scene changes from tatty houses to tatty shops; all of which look like they're barely clinging on to solvency. Even if we fancied a chat, which one of us clearly doesn't, the steady stream of vehicles zooming past would make it difficult to be heard.

We turn a corner and the leisure centre comes into view. I check my watch.

"We'd better hurry. It starts in five minutes."

We dash the final hundred yards and enter the reception area. A large sign just inside the door points us in the direction of the main hall where the bowls final is apparently taking place.

"This way," I beckon to Mungo, and head off through a set of double doors.

After taking two wrong turns, we eventually crash through another set of double doors into the main hall. We're greeted by the low hum of conversation from the gathered crowd and more obvious hum of sweaty socks—the signature scent of every sports hall and gym.

Two thirds of the floor space has been taken up by the temporary bowls green in all its immaculately flat greenness. Running parallel to the green are stepped rows of seats, housing a surprisingly large number of spectators. One thing is immediately obvious: if an asteroid were to hit the leisure centre and wipe out the occupants, sales of Werther's Originals and travel blankets would plummet overnight.

I scan the sea of grey and white heads looking for my mother. Fortunately, or otherwise, she spots me first and waves down from the fourth row of seats in the nearest block.

We head up the steps towards my still-waving mother. While I'm relieved I actually made it this time, and Mum has saved a couple of seats, my relief is short lived when I reach the row and discover the empty seats are next to Ethan.

There's no way I'm sitting next to him for an entire bowls match.

"Please, after you, Mungo."

Without argument, Mungo shuffles along and takes the seat next to my brother-in-law. I plonk myself down on the end seat and reluctantly lean forward to offer introductions.

"Mungo, this is my sister, Kate," I mumble, waving an

errant hand in my sister's direction as she returns a saccharin smile towards Mungo. "And this is her husband, Ethan."

Ethan holds out a hand which Mungo briefly inspects before shaking.

"Nice to meet you," Ethan chirps. "I understand you're helping Adam with his ... problem. How's it going?"

The word *problem* is delivered with a pinch of sarcasm and a smirk. I'm about to answer his question with some choice words when Mungo scrunches his nose and frowns up at Ethan.

"You are suffering from acute halitosis," Mungo comments in his usual flat tone.

"I beg your pardon," Ethan splutters.

"Halitosis: bad breath caused by a build-up of bacteria."

"Yes, I know what it is, thank you," Ethan snorts, his face reddening.

"I would recommend a medicated mouthwash and regular flossing."

"My dental hygiene routine is beyond reproach, I'll have you know."

"Your fetid breath suggests otherwise," Mungo replies.

"Are you always so rude?"

Mungo turns to me. "You would be better placed to answer that question."

"Yes, Ethan, he is, but he's also honest and very good at his job. Maybe he could help with your *problem* too?"

If God were to strike me down at this precise moment, I'd go with a mile-wide grin on my face. He doesn't, but a sudden ripple of applause from the crones surrounding us drags my attention to the green. My dad and his opponent have entered the hall—Dad sporting a red polo shirt and his opponent a blue one. I thought, because it's the final, they might enter to walk-on music, like they do in boxing and darts, but this is bowls so the two men just shake hands as the applause peters out.

Quiet anticipation fills the air—ideal for a nap in any other circumstances.

"Do you know the rules?" I whisper to Mungo.

"I studied them this morning."

I understand the basics; a small white ball called a jack is rolled to the end of the green, and then the two players take turns rolling their four larger balls towards it. Whoever has the most balls nearest the jack wins the game, or *end,* as I believe it's called. This is repeated until at least ten percent of the audience pass away from boredom or natural causes.

Dad rolls the jack and the game begins.

Ten minutes in and a tin of sherbet lemons are passed down the line from my mother. Mungo declines so I take two and pass them back. Those two boiled sweets prove to be the highlight of the first half hour. On the plus side, Dad is apparently winning by two points.

I close my eyes for a moment and listen to the pattern of sounds: near silence punctuated by the occasional cough, the murmurings of the crowd as the bowl closes in on its target, the clacking of the bowls against each other, and then the gentle applause. This hypnotic soundtrack is repeated over and over until I drift into a relaxed state just about on the awake side of sleep.

As the crowd applaud, I await the start of the next cycle and the near silence. Just as it begins, I'm dragged from my malaise by a communal gasp followed by a particularly animated rumble of conversation. Something is afoot it seems.

I open my eyes and squint. Where a bowls match should be taking place, five men decked in blazers and beige trousers are huddled together in a circle at the far end of the green, staring at something on the floor. One of them then turns and frantically beckons towards the corner of the hall. I turn to my right to find all three members of my family on their feet; hands clamped across their mouths.

"Mungo, what's going on?"

"The man in the red shirt collapsed."

"Christ, Dad."

While my family might be content to stand and watch the drama unfold, I am not. I dart down the stairs and sprint across the green towards the huddle of men which now includes two St John's Ambulance first-aiders.

"What's happened?" I blurt to nobody in particular as I reach the huddle.

One of the men turns. "He just collapsed. They're trying to resuscitate him now."

I barge my way into the huddle.

"Who are you?" another grey-haired man asks.

"That's my dad."

"Spectators aren't permitted on the green during a match," he blurts.

"Fuck off."

I kneel down next to Dad. An oxygen mask has been placed over his mouth and a female first-aider has hold of his wrist.

"Is he okay?" I wheeze.

The woman looks across at me. "We don't know. He's got a pulse, although it's weak. My colleague has already called for paramedics and they'll be here any minute."

"Can't you just wake him up?"

"We tried but he's unresponsive. He needs expert medical attention."

I grab his other hand and squeeze it tight in the hope of summoning a reaction. "Dad? Dad ... can you hear me?"

Nothing.

Seconds turn into minutes and all I can do is continue to squeeze Dad's hand and say his name with increasing panic. Never have I felt so utterly helpless. The huddled men stand back and talk in hushed tones while looking grave. Eventually, Mum and Kate arrive on the scene and add hysteria to the mix.

"Dear God, what's happening?" Mum shrieks.

"He's unconscious," I reply.

"I told the stubborn old fool to pull out. He's not been well all week."

I think back to Wednesday evening at Dad's bedside. Looking at him now, his face is just as pale and gaunt.

"He's probably just got ... I dunno ... a virus or something," I stammer, more to reassure myself than anyone else. "He'll be fine once they get him to hospital."

On cue, two paramedics in green uniforms arrive and take over. While one of them sees to Dad, the other ushers us all back.

"Please, just give us some space," he commands.

Once we're all six feet away, the paramedic joins his colleague and they both attend to Dad. I watch on, trying to determine the severity of the situation from their body language. If they move with urgency then the situation is serious. Conversely, if they move slowly, it suggests the situation isn't life threatening. I offer a silent prayer they don't stop altogether as that could only mean one thing.

I suddenly feel an arm brush against mine.

"He's going to be alright, Adam, isn't he?" Kate whimpers.

I turn to my kid sister. The plastic smile has gone and there's an unfamiliar look of vulnerability in her eyes.

"Yeah, he's tough as old boots. I'm sure it's nothing to worry about."

She takes a few seconds to steel herself.

"Yes, of course. You're right," she chirps, suddenly

snapping back to her usual self.

I return my attention to the paramedics just as one of them darts away. I consider approaching the one still knelt by Dad but, by the time I make that decision, the first paramedic returns with a stretcher.

We watch on as the two men carefully transfer Dad's limp body to the stretcher before covering him with a red blanket. They then fix straps across his chest before pulling a lever so the stretcher rises to waist height.

"We're taking him in to St Martin's," one of them says in a tone Mungo would appreciate. "Please inform his next of kin."

They start pushing the stretcher away while Mum and Kate gallop after them. I remain rooted in the same spot and watch the procession disappear through the emergency exit.

"Adam," a voice booms from behind me. "Is he alright?"

I spin around to find Ethan approaching.

"Oh, yeah, he's brilliant," I scoff. "He just fancied a ride in an ambulance."

"There's no need for sarcasm."

"And there's no need for stupid questions. Of course he's not alright."

"Where have they taken him?"

"St Martin's."

"Right, I'd better head over there. I'm sure Kate needs my support."

"Yeah," I mumble. "Off you fuck."

"Sorry?"

"Nothing."

His mouth forms a half-smile, half-sneer and he walks away. He gets within a few yards of the exit when it dawns on me I don't have any way of getting to the hospital other than walking. Do I take a brisk ten minute walk or swallow my pride and beg Ethan for a lift?

I'll walk.

I'm about to set off when I remember Mungo. I should probably tell him what's going on before I disappear so I scoot back across the green and up the steps.

"I've got to go to the hospital, Mungo," I pant. "Will you be okay getting back to the flat?"

"Yes."

I wait a moment for him to ask about Dad but he just blankly stares up at me.

"Thanks for asking how my dad is," I snort.

"Would you like me to offer a hollow platitude?"

"No, but you could at least ask how he is."

"He lost consciousness. That much is obvious."

I'm clearly wasting my time and should be making tracks, but his lack of empathy irks.

"Would it kill you to show some compassion for once?"

He doesn't answer and I don't have time for his bullshit mind games. With a parting frown, I skip back down the stairs and bolt towards the exit.

St Martin's is over a mile away but I complete the journey in nine minutes through a combination of sprinting, jogging, and breathless staggering. I arrive a sweaty mess and, after a heated exchange with the receptionist, barrel onwards towards the accident and emergency department.

More by luck than judgement, I find it, along with Mum, Kate, and Ethan in the waiting area.

"What's going on?" I wheeze.

"The doctor is examining him now," Mum replies tearfully. "He's still unconscious."

I collapse on a chair next to her.

If there is a worse place to spend time than a hospital waiting room, I've yet to experience it. The room lives up to its name as we anxiously sit and wait, surrounded by the sick, injured, and whiney. Conversation is limited and there's not a great deal to distract. All we can do is stare into space and take turns to glance at our watches.

However, one of our party appears more anxious than the others.

"This is ridiculous," Ethan huffs. "What the hell are they doing?"

"Just be patient, please," Kate begs.

"You do remember Tristan and Libby are coming over for dinner at seven?"

"Can't we cancel?"

"Certainly not. It's far too late."

She finds a feeble smile. "Okay. I'm sure it'll be fine."

Ethan folds his arms and mumbles under his breath.

I should be irritated with Kate for not telling Ethan to stick his dinner date up his arse, but I can't say I even recognise her as my sister these days. The feisty tomboy I grew up with is now a model Stepford wife, and a virtual stranger.

We settle back into our anxious silence as the hustle and bustle continues around us.

It's another twenty minutes before a doctor approaches Mum.

"Mrs Maxwell?"

She looks up at a man who looks dead on his feet, and nods. "Yes, that's me."

"I'm Dr Rowe. Would you like to come with me, please?"

We follow the doctor along a corridor away from the waiting room and into an office. He closes the door and flops onto a chair behind an untidy desk.

"Please, take a seat."

With only two chairs available, Mum and Kate sit down. I stand behind Mum while Ethan leans up against the wall and checks his watch again.

I watch as the doctor opens a folder and studies a page of notes. I'd guess he must be a similar age to me, but the dark circles around his eyes and flecks of grey in his stubble make him look a decade older.

"Right," he coughs, looking up at Mum. "At this moment, we're not entirely sure what the problem is with your husband. He's still unconscious but stable, so we're sending him for a scan and running a few other tests. Hopefully, we'll get to the bottom of it once the results come back."

"But, he'll be okay?" Kate squeaks.

"I'm afraid it's too early to make that call but he's in the right place. Let's just see what we're dealing with first."

"Where is he now?" Mum asks. "Can we see him?"

"We've moved him to the intensive care unit and you should be able to see him once he's back from the scan. Give us an hour or so."

With a smile that, I guess, is supposed to offer reassurance, Dr Rowe closes the folder.

"There's a more comfortable waiting room at the ICU. I'll take you there now."

As we return to the corridor and follow the doctor, I trail a few feet behind, held back by the millstone of dread I'm suddenly dragging along. What I wouldn't give to be Mungo about now, and feel nothing. Emotions are all well and good when they're positive, but I have a horrible feeling we're heading to a place where positive emotions are in short supply.

26.

Comfortable: a well-worn pair of pants, or when a football team wins by a four goal margin. It isn't, however, a word I'd use to describe the intensive care waiting room. In fairness, it's not so much the utilitarian furniture or the cheerless beige walls that make it an uncomfortable place to be, but the reason we're there.

There is no comfort to be found in waiting for news which, quite literally, could mean life or death for my dad.

The only small mercy is that Ethan left after twenty minutes, and Kate's reaction was one of relief as much as irritation. Rather than the support he was supposed to offer, he seemed far more concerned about telling his guests they'd have to get their Pinot Grigio and polite conversation elsewhere this evening. Prick.

Another check of the watch and over an hour spent. Strained doesn't even come close to describing the atmosphere.

We've all made attempts at appearing positive, and we've all nodded and swapped thin smiles in reply. I don't think I even believed my own words, let alone those delivered so unconvincingly by Kate: *Dad's a fighter, he's in good hands, it could be nothing*—we all know we're still here because something is seriously wrong. They don't usually commit patients to intensive care for a gippy stomach.

Just as we pass the ninety minute mark the door finally opens and Dr Rowe bustles in.

"I'm so sorry to keep you waiting," he remarks, as if the protracted waiting time is our primary concern.

"I have some news."

He leans against the wall in a manner inappropriately casual for the situation.

"Mr Maxwell has suffered an ischaemic stroke."

The three of us, still seated on a lumpy sofa, look up at him. The first word might as well have been in Welsh, but the second word needs no explanation.

"A stroke?" Kate clarifies.

"Yes, and I'm afraid to say it was severe."

"It was definitely a stroke?" I ask.

Perhaps not the most sensible of questions. What was I expecting: the doctor to hurry away and interrogate his colleagues because I questioned their diagnosis?

"Um, sorry," I splutter. "I mean, isn't it obvious when someone is suffering from a stroke? I've seen the adverts on TV about the warning signs."

"Usually, yes, but not always. And if the stroke is severe enough, as it was in your father's case, the victim can become unconscious in a matter of seconds."

That's twice he's used the word *severe* and in my experience, no type of severe anything is good.

"So how is he now?"

"My colleagues are administering treatment in the ICU but he remains unresponsive."

"Unresponsive?" Kate parrots, as if repeating the doctor's words make them any less unpalatable.

"Put simply, he's in a coma."

A simple four-letter word but it prompts an audible gasp from my mother.

"Oh, dear God," she gulps. "He'll be okay won't he?"

Perhaps unsure if the question was aimed at him or some imaginary deity, the doctor pauses before answering.

"I wish I could give you some assurance, Mrs Maxwell, but with a stroke of this magnitude there's really no telling. The human brain is an incredibly complex organ and we can't say for sure how much damage the stroke caused and therefore, when, or if, he'll gain consciousness."

There's a question that surely has to be asked but my mouth is so dry I can't choke the words out. Kate just about manages it.

"He's not ... he's going to pull through, isn't he?"

"The next twenty-four hours are crucial and we'll have a better picture tomorrow. In the meantime, you should hope for the best, but it might also be prudent to prepare for the worst."

The phrase trips from the doctor's mouth with ease. So easy to say, but digesting it is anything but.

"What do you mean by *the worst*?"

"Your father is a seriously ill man, Mr Maxwell. I don't want to leave this room without you understanding he might not recover."

The doctor has clearly been trained to say what we don't want to hear without actually saying the word.

"He could die?" I gulp.

"His condition is serious enough for that outcome to be a possibility."

Just fucking say it, man.

Rather than pressing the subject, I stare at my feet.

"Do you have any questions?" the doctor asks.

"Can we see him?" Mum replies.

I really don't want to see my dad in a coma but the decision is removed from me as the doctor beckons us from the waiting room. Before I know it, we're stepping through a door to my version of hell. Surrounded by all manner of monitoring devices lies my dear old dad with a ventilator tube rammed in his mouth like a petrol pump nozzle. I don't think anything could have prepared me for such a sight, nor my sister judging by her stifled sobs.

Mum puts an arm around Kate and glances across at me. I'm used to seeing a certain look in her eyes—usually disappointment or despair—but not on this occasion. It's a look so unfamiliar I don't know how to react other than to return a blank stare. Her eyes close and when she opens them again, she's already turning towards the awful vision of my comatose father. Whatever reaction she was hoping for, clearly I failed to provide it.

With her arm still around her shoulder, Mum slowly guides Kate over to the edge of the bed, and the two plastic chairs that have probably borne witness to more trauma than any plastic chairs deserve. Why I find the presence of only two chairs symbolic, I don't know, but as my mother and sister position themselves close to Dad's side, I remain rooted to the spot between the door and the end of the bed—in every sense apart from my family.

I watch on as Mum takes her husband's limp hand and clutches it tightly. He might be her husband but I don't recognise the grey, lifeless body as my dad. He's not the man who ran beside me as I first learnt to ride a bike. He's not the man who used to bark encouragement from the edge of windswept football pitches every weekend. And he's not the man who sat beside me and kept smiling throughout countless driving lessons.

I want that man back. No part of me wants to stand here a second longer and watch the life slowly drain from this impostor.

"I'm sorry," I croak. "I can't do this."

A form of autopilot engages and before I know it, long stretches of corridor are behind me and I'm stood outside the hospital entrance.

It feels an appropriate time to stop and think but thinking is the last thing I want to do because I know what's lurking in the back of my mind. Common sense will tell me to turn around and head back to my Dad's bedside. Common sense will tell me that my mother and sister need me. Common sense will tell me I should remain positive until all hope is gone.

I know all the good reasons not to walk away yet that's exactly what I do, because snapping at my heels is an almost primordial sense of fear. Running away is the only option. I'd say it's unlike any fear I've ever felt but that wouldn't be entirely true. Almost like déjà vu, I know I've felt it before but the *when* and *why* are out of reach. All I know is I must escape it.

My strides grow longer until walking becomes jogging, and jogging becomes sprinting. Oblivious to my surroundings, I run and run until my lungs burn and my leg muscles scream in submission. Even then I don't stop. Gasping, I stagger onwards; never questioning what I'm running from, or why, but knowing I daren't turn around, even for a second.

I have never been so relieved to return home. Sanctuary, of sorts.

I crash through the front door and make straight for the kitchen. Collapsing on a chair by the window, I close my eyes and wait for my breathing to settle. Still petrified, I focus on the ticking of the clock and try to match the passing seconds to my breathing. Quite how or when I learnt the technique, I don't know, but it gradually slows my racing heart.

"I must apologise."

Mungo's voice startles me and my heart rate peaks again. I open my eyes to find him seated on the other chair, a few feet away.

"Fuck's sake, Mungo," I gasp. "Don't creep up on me like that."

"I must apologise," he repeats.

"For what?"

"My earlier lack of empathy. It does not come naturally to me."

For a moment, I'm taken aback by his admission, but the stark reality of what I've just run away from is far more pressing.

"How is your father?"

"Not good," I murmur. "Really not good."

"Specifically?"

"He's in a coma and they don't know if he'll recover."

Unlike Dr Rowe, Mungo doesn't mince his words. "He might die?"

"Yes," I reply in barely a whisper.

"If that is a possibility, why are you here?"

A question I'd rather not answer. I'm scared witless, and it's easier to be a coward than face my fear.

"Because …"

Just say it.

"I …"

You can't run from this.

"It's … I'm fucking terrified of losing my dad."

Mungo fixes me with an empty stare. I can't imagine what's going on behind those turquoise eyes, but whatever it is, his face isn't telling.

"Say something then?" I blurt. "Go on, tell me I'm a coward?"

The only sign Mungo hasn't slipped into his own coma is an occasional blink.

"Well?"

"I am thinking," he finally replies.

"What's there to think about?"

After a brief pause, I receive an instruction rather than an answer.

"You must return to the hospital," he orders.

"I can't."

"Why not?"

"It's just too much. I can't bear seeing him like that."

"You are doing it again."

"Doing what?"

"Letting emotion, specifically fear, cloud your judgement."

"But I can't ignore it. I just can't."

"Fear is not real, Adam Maxwell—it is simply the product of your own thoughts. Danger, however, is real, but there is no danger at the hospital therefore your fear is irrational."

"Are you shitting me?" I snap. "My dad might die so I'd say my fear is very bloody rational."

"You say *might* because you do not know if your father will die. Correct?"

"No, obviously not."

"Therefore your fear is a manifestation of your own negative thoughts. It is similar to those who have a fear of flying inasmuch as their fear is based upon what *might* happen to the aircraft. You share the same irrational thoughts, but the reality is that aircraft rarely crash, and eighty-eight percent of stroke victims survive beyond thirty days."

For all I know, Mungo might have plucked that number out of the air but I can't deny it does offer some comfort.

"You are not afraid your father might die. You are afraid of fear itself," he adds. "And that is why you must return to the hospital. You must challenge that fear, not run from it."

It seems odd he should use the word *run* considering I've just been chased home by the spectre of fear. Nevertheless, a lot of what he says makes sense.

I take a moment to pull myself together, by which point the unadulterated shame of my behaviour arrives. Not only did I abandon my dad, but I now realise the look Mum gave me was almost certainly one of dread. However scared I might have been, and I still am, Mum and Kate must have felt it too. Running away from my sick father, whilst simultaneously abandoning my mother and sister, is a new low in my catalogue of terrible decisions.

"Jesus, I'm pathetic," I groan. "I need to get back to the hospital."

I'm about to thank Mungo but I know how he'll react so I offer a nod.

"You would like me to come with you?" he asks.

The phrasing of his question is strange, in that it sounds more like a declaration. He's right, though.

"Would you mind?"

"I would not."

With my legs still reeling from their earlier exertion, I insist we drive back to the hospital.

"I'll give you a minute," I remark, getting up from the table.

"For what?"

"To put on one of your silly plastic boiler suits."

"No need. I will not wear one on this occasion."

"Oh, dare I ask why?"

"I must practise what I preach, Adam Maxwell. Although your passenger seat is, frankly disgusting, perhaps my concerns are as irrational as your fear."

"Bloody hell, Mungo. Are you sure?"

"No, but one has to lead by example."

I make a break for the front door before he changes his mind. I only hope I don't change my mind before we make it back to the hospital.

27.

Once Alan is safely abandoned in the hospital car park, we make our way towards the entrance. I would be lying if I said the fear isn't still lurking in the back of my mind but Mungo's quirky behaviour provides a welcome distraction.

"You know there are hand-sanitiser dispensers all over the hospital, right?"

"All of which will be covered in bacteria," he replies, pulling a latex glove over his left hand.

"Where did you even get those?"

"I have a supply in my room."

"Of course you do."

As much as Mungo's behaviour is a distraction from my growing dread, his presence alone offers a surprising level of reassurance. If ever there were a time I needed his logical thinking and calm demeanour, this is it. I only wish those traits weren't packaged in such an odd-looking individual.

We make our way through the maze of corridors towards the intensive care unit. The dryness returns to my mouth and I subconsciously slow my pace to the point Mungo's short strides propel him ahead of me. The distance between us reaches six feet before he stops and turns around.

"Why are you walking so slowly?" he asks.

"I'm trying, Mungo, I really am, but this isn't easy."

"It is one foot in front of another. I fail to understand the difficulty."

"Not the walking itself. It's where we're walking to."

"We are simply visiting your father. That is all you have to concern yourself with."

He turns around and continues on his way. A deep breath and I scurry up alongside him.

"You're good at this, you know?" I blurt, just to talk about anything other than the reason we're here.

"Good at what?"

"The whole psychology thing. I've got to be honest: I doubt I'd be here if it wasn't for what you said back at the flat."

"I am simply redressing the balance," he remarks, perhaps even more matter-of-factly than usual.

"Eh? What do you mean by that?"

"It matters not."

Any desire to press him further is immediately quashed as we turn the corner and reach the main doors to the intensive care unit.

The urge to run returns with a vengeance. Sensing my apprehension, Mungo opens one of the doors and looks up at me.

"Challenge the fear, Adam Maxwell. Go. Now."

For once in my life, not thinking is the right thing to do and I step through the door. Somehow, my legs keep moving and before I know it, I'm at the door to Dad's room. A second or two to draw breath and I enter.

The scene is as grim as I remember it, and not helped by the look of abject scorn on my mother's face.

"Where the hell have you been?" she hisses.

I'm about to offer a grovelling apology when her expression changes.

"Oh, err, Dr Mungo," she splutters. "I didn't realise you were here."

Mungo nods at my mother and shuffles over to the end of the bed. An awkward moment ensues as he stares at my inanimate father.

"I'm sorry, Mum," I blurt, breaking the silence. "I shouldn't have run off like that. I, erm, just lost it for a while."

"No," she replies sternly. "You shouldn't have."

I wasn't expecting Mungo to join us at Dad's bedside, but his presence at least prevents Mum from delivering the bollocking I probably deserve. With my error of judgement forgotten, for now at least, the next challenge is avoiding a repeat performance. Even with Mungo's advice fresh in my mind, it takes epic levels of focus to keep a full-blown panic attack at bay. No part of me wants to be in this room and whatever fear I left at the door, I can sense it creeping back in.

I need a distraction. Something, anything, just to take my mind elsewhere.

Mercifully, my vertically-challenged friend again comes to the rescue when he addresses my mother.

"When did you last consume fluids?"

"Err, I'm not sure," Mum replies. "I had a cup of tea at lunchtime, I think. Why do you ask?"

"The pallor of your skin suggests dehydration."

"Oh dear, really?"

"Yes, and you, Kate Maxwell? When did you last consume fluids?"

My sister looks across at Mum, as if querying why Mungo is

even here, let alone asking her banal questions.

"Answer the doctor," Mum urges.

"I'm not sure," Kate huffs. "Hours ago, I guess."

"I believe the hospital provides rudimentary catering facilities. Adam Maxwell will escort you there so you can both rehydrate."

"I suppose I am a bit thirsty," Mum concedes. "But what about …"

"I will wait with Mr Maxwell. If there is any change in his condition, I will find you."

As I've learnt, the emotionless authority in Mungo's voice renders objection almost futile. Accordingly, Mum gets to her feet.

"We'll only be ten minutes or so," she says. "And you'll come and find us if anything changes?"

"I will."

Kate begrudgingly follows suit, while I don't need any encouragement to lead them out of the room.

The short walk to the cafeteria is unsurprisingly sombre and not a word is spoken until we join the queue at the counter.

"I'll get the drinks," I offer as a conciliatory gesture. "Tea?"

They both mumble a vaguely affirmative response and head off to find an empty table.

The queue moves quickly and I'm served within a few minutes. Three small stainless-steel teapots, together with the accompanying cups and saucers, are stacked on a tray. I add a handful of sugar sachets and three tiny milk pots with, if experience tells, impenetrable lids.

I pay and make my way across the cafeteria to find Kate alone at the table.

"Where's Mum?"

"Toilet."

I take a seat and decant the cups, saucers, and teapots. Waiting duties complete, I pour a cup of tea and sit back in my chair. Kate, seated opposite, is staring impassively at the empty cup in front of her.

"You alright?"

Her reply comes in a single huffed breath and a slight shake of the head.

"What's the matter?" I scoff. "Worried about your dinner guests going hungry?"

I immediately realise that, considering the circumstances, my comment was inappropriate. In my defence, our relationship has deteriorated to such a degree that every conversation we have is strained, and usually littered with barbed comments or veiled insults. If we didn't snipe at one another, we'd never talk at all.

Finally, she lifts her head and glares at me.

"I couldn't care less about them."

"Your husband clearly does, though. Nice of him to hang around."

"What … like your shrink? What the hell is he even doing here?"

"Don't compare Mungo to your arsehole of a husband. At least he's here now, trying to help, unlike bloody Ethan."

The expected retort doesn't come. Instead, Kate returns her gaze to the empty cup. I sip my tea and bask in the glow of victory, although that glow very quickly turns to guilt. What am I doing? This is not the time for petty point scoring.

"Listen," I sigh. "I'm sorry. I shouldn't have said that."

"Why are you sorry?" she mumbles without looking at me. "It's the truth. Ethan isn't here, and he never is when I need him."

Interesting—it appears there's trouble in paradise. The urge to seize upon my sister's confession is almost irresistible and just as my lips part to deliver a sarcastic reply, the advice of a small man looms large in my head. I swallow my glee and, with nothing constructive to say, decide tea is a more civilised option. I sit forward and reach for the small teapot in front of Kate.

I pour the tea and nudge the cup and saucer an inch closer towards her.

"Drink that. You'll feel better."

"Don't, Adam."

"Don't what?"

She continues to stare at the cup.

"Don't be nice to me," she croaks.

Unsure quite how to react, I sit back in my seat. Only then does Kate slowly raise her head and look towards me, and the reason for keeping her head bowed becomes obvious. Her eyes are puffy and red, her mascara blotchy, and her cheeks tear stained.

"You're not alright, are you?" I remark, stating the obvious. She shakes her head.

I've given her tea but the sympathy element isn't so easy and I'm all out of platitudes. Maybe some of Mungo's wisdom will help.

"Did you know eighty-eight percent of stroke victims survive beyond thirty days?"

"No, I didn't."

She plucks a napkin from a holder on the table and dabs her eyes.

"It's true. Mungo told me."

"That's reassuring," she replies, her expression brightening momentarily. "Would you like to know another statistic?"

"Err, sure."

"Forty-two percent of marriages end in divorce."

"Oh. Very … interesting."

I hope my reply didn't sound as sarcastic as it did in my head.

"Is there a reason why I'd want to know that?" I add.

Almost in an instant, the sister I once knew vanishes and Ethan's wife returns.

"Forget it. Just ignore me," she says flatly. "Mum will be back any minute and I don't want her to see me in such a state. Tell her I'm just popping outside for a few minutes."

She snatches her designer handbag, gets to her feet, and strides away.

With my mother and sister elsewhere, there's little else to do but sit and sip tea in silent reflection. That reflection is stoked when I spot a smiley couple pushing a pram towards the main exit; no doubt heading home with their freshly minted offspring. Will that be Daisy and I in eight months' time? Or is it seven months? I really should know when my own child is due and the fact I don't is telling. It isn't fair, but then again, I sense fairness abandoned me a while back.

Before I get the chance to drown in self-pity, Mum returns.

"How are you doing?" I ask.

"I've felt better."

I pour her a cup of tea as she flops onto the chair Kate abandoned a few minutes earlier. I've never seen her look so drained, so tired, and that in itself is remarkable considering what I've put her through over the years.

"I'm sure a nice cup of tea will help," I say, unconvincingly. "As Mungo said, you're probably a bit dehydrated."

With an unsteady hand she picks up her cup and sips away while fixing a vacant stare on nothing in particular. I attempt small talk but it soon becomes clear Mum's mind is elsewhere; back in a room along the corridor, I suspect.

It's with some relief Kate returns after a few minutes. I

presumed she ran off to reapply her tear-stained makeup but, as she glances at me, there's no longer any trace of makeup on her face. I can't recall the last time I saw my sister without her mask of Estée Lauder products. She now looks like the sister I once knew.

"We should be getting back," she suggests. "Are you ready, Mum?"

Without a word Mum snaps back to reality, empties her cup, and wearily clambers to her feet. I puff a resigned sigh and stand.

Our brief period of respite over and, with much reluctance on my part, we leave the cafeteria and slowly saunter back through the corridors towards the intensive care unit. Maybe because we're all lost in our own thoughts, or perhaps because we're too terrified of skirting close to a subject we can't yet contemplate, there's little in the way of conversation.

All too soon the doors of dread come into view. Happy to be outside for even a few extra seconds, I open one of the doors and let Mum and Kate enter first. Another deep breath and I follow them in. I quickly wish I hadn't.

The calm we left barely fifteen minutes ago has been replaced with frenzy as medical staff bustle urgently up and down the corridor. Taken aback by what is clearly some kind of emergency situation, the three of us stop dead. It's only when we pause do I realise most of the staff are gravitating around Dad's room at the far end of the corridor.

I'm not the only one to notice.

"There's something wrong," Kate gasps.

Taking the lead, I barge past my sister and sprint towards Dad's room. I get within a few feet and Mungo suddenly steps through the door, just as it's slammed shut.

"What's going on?" I pant. "Why have they shut the door?"

I make a move towards the door but Mungo stands his ground, blocking my way.

"You cannot go in there."

Although there are glass partitions either side of the door, the blinds have been drawn. However, whilst I can't see what's going on, I can certainly hear the cacophony of digital alarms wailing, and the frantic voices of the medical staff.

"Mungo, let me past," I growl. "Or so help me God."

"You cannot go in there because there is nothing you can do."

"About what? Will you tell me what the fuck is going on in there?"

"It is your father."
"What about him?"
"I brought him back."

28.

Mungo's reply achieved one thing. I'm no longer trying to force my way past him.

"What do you mean, you brought him back?"

Before he can answer, Mum and Kate arrive on the scene and both of them anxiously repeat my question.

"I don't know what's going on," I wail. "And Mungo won't let me in to find out."

"I would recommend you all remain calm," Mungo advises. "Mr Maxwell is no longer in a coma, however, the medical staff need to assess his condition."

"He's awake?" Mum gulps. "Please tell me he's awake?"

"He was approaching consciousness when I was asked to leave the room," Mungo replies.

"Is he ... okay?"

"I am not in a position to answer that question."

Conveniently, the door to Dad's room suddenly opens and a dumpy female nurse appears. Whilst I can't see much of what's going on behind her, at least the frantic voices and screaming alarms are now silent.

"Mr Maxwell's family, I presume?" she asks, closing the door behind her.

We nod in unison.

"I'm Nurse Gallagher. Would you like to come with me?"

"Can you tell us what's going on?" Kate pleads.

"I will. Just follow me please."

There is no second invite and Nurse Gallagher heads back down the corridor. Mum and Kate scurry after her but I want a quick word with Mungo before we join them.

"You can tell me what you meant now, about bringing Dad back."

"There is nothing to tell."

"Come off it, Mungo," I scoff. "How exactly did you bring him back?"

"You would not understand."

"Try me?"

"It is complicated. I will explain one day, perhaps."

"Don't fob me off. We leave you alone with him for fifteen minutes and by the time we return, he's regained consciousness. What did you do?"

"Would it not be prudent to join your mother and sister to establish your father's condition?"

I stare down at him. Infuriating, obstinate, and also correct.

"I'm not going to let this go, you know. We'll talk later."

As I turn to walk away he has the final word. "To employ the term popular in youth culture: whatever."

I shake my head and hurry away to catch up with Mum and Kate. I reach them just as the nurse is leading them into a small room with no obvious purpose other than it offers more privacy than the corridor.

"Right," she begins, closing the door. "I know you're all anxious to know how Mr Maxwell is doing, and I can tell you he has regained consciousness, but I can't tell you he's out of the woods just yet. We're still conducting tests and monitoring him."

"But he's definitely awake?" Mum asks.

"He is, although he's fairly confused. It's probably the medication—it's fairly common for patients to awake from a coma in a confused state."

"Can we see him?"

"Soon. If you don't mind returning to the waiting room, I'll fetch you when the doctor gives me the all clear."

Compared to the conversation we had with Dr Rowe earlier, I think we're all content to end the conversation with Nurse Gallagher on a positive note, and we return to the waiting room without complaint.

The one person now conspicuous by his absence is Mungo. Maybe he's decided to take himself and his outlandish statements back to the flat. I intend to pick up our conversation later but, for now, it looks like I've got another anxious wait to contend with.

As it transpires, Nurse Gallagher's definition of 'soon' turns out to be almost an hour; most of which was spent padding up and down while fretting about Dad's condition. To ease my anxiety, I decided to open a web browser on my phone and google the effects of a stroke. I hoped to find heart-warming stories of stroke victims making a full recovery and climbing mountains or swimming the English Channel. I didn't. Littered across the results page were terrifying terms such as 'brain damage', 'paralysis' and 'memory loss'. The results page alone was enough to push my anxiety in the wrong direction and I returned the phone to my pocket without clicking a single link.

As ill-advised as it was, knowing the theoretical effects of Dad's stroke is now irrelevant as we're seconds away from discovering the reality.

Nurse Gallagher leads us back along the well-trodden corridor and partially opens the door to Dad's room. She pokes her head in and checks it's okay for us to enter. I swap a nervous glance with Mum and then Kate.

"We're all good," Nurse Gallagher announces as she pushes the door open.

After my brief but damning online research, my expectations are now well and truly grounded. Call it pessimistic, but I'm reliably informed pessimists are rarely disappointed.

I let Mum and Kate enter first. A quick count to three in my head while I prepare myself, and then I follow them in.

Four steps forward and my legs seize, at the same precise moment my jaw falls open. The scene is not what I expected. Not at all. I can only guess Mum and Kate are equally as stunned as they're also rooted to the spot just in front of me.

Dad breaks from his conversation with Dr Rowe and turns to us.

"Why are you standing there like lemons?" he beams, his voice dry and raspy but otherwise no different from when I spoke to him a few days ago.

Kate is the first to break from her stupor. She rushes across to Dad's side and throws her arms around him. Mum then joins her and Dad swaps his daughter's embrace for one from his wife. Any concerns I had about potential paralysis now appear unfounded as he can clearly move as freely as any pension-age man can.

I, however, am still struggling with movement. I just about manage to take a few steps forward until I reach the end of the bed. My ability to speak, however, is still to catch up with play.

As Mum finally releases him from her embrace, Dad looks across at me and smiles.

"You alright, son? You look like you've seen a ghost."

There's no hope of a reply as I bite down hard on my bottom lip. Then, a slight heave in my chest, and I have to blink hard to stop the tears forming. Rather than suffer the embarrassment of a full-on breakdown, I dash forward and throw my arms around my old dad. Old he may be, but at least he's alive and kicking.

"Sorry, son. Didn't mean to scare you," he whispers in my ear.

"Well, you bloody did," I blubber. "You stupid old git."

When our hug approaches the point of becoming awkward, I

excuse myself under the pretence of needing the loo. I then spend five minutes alone in a cubicle, sobbing uncontrollably. Unlike the tears spilled over Daisy, my tears on this occasion are of unbridled relief. As that relief washes over me, it brings with it a realisation—the time I spent in that bloody waiting room, contemplating life without my dad, was unbearable. Yet here I am, currently facing the risk of being excluded from my own child's life.

I make a promise to myself: there's no damn way I'm going to let that happen.

After splashing cold water on my face, I repeat my promise in the mirror. And for once, I actually believe the weary-looking, unshaven knob-head looking back at me.

"You've got this," I whisper.

I take a final reassuring glance at my reflection and head back to join my family.

As I open the door to Dad's room, I'm met with the sound of laughter. Quite a contrast to the awful symphony of sounds I heard earlier.

"Ah, here he is," Dad remarks in the scratchiest of voices. "We were just talking about you."

"Should I leave again?"

"Don't be daft. Your mum was just telling me how you rushed over to my aid after I collapsed."

"Really?"

I glance across at my mother, expecting to see her usual glare of disapproval at my reckless behaviour. Astonishingly, though, her expression is leaning more towards quiet pride. It's been so long I can't be sure. I'm only glad she appears to have forgotten my earlier excursion from this room.

"Well, I wasn't much help," I add.

"That's not the point, son."

His point, whatever it might have been, is interrupted by a coughing fit. Mum passes him a glass of water and shakes her head.

"The doctor told him he's incredibly lucky," she says, looking across at me. "And he needs to take much better care of himself."

"No more wine then."

"Definitely no more wine."

"I'll be fine," Dad rasps. "Stop fussing."

"Fussing?" Mum frowns. "You have no idea what a living nightmare today has been for us."

"I know, but if it's any consolation, I had a nightmare of my own. In fact, I think that's what brought me back."

"Don't be silly," she says dismissively. "Surely you can't have nightmares if you're in a coma."

"Well, I did, and it scared the bloody life out of me. I was being chased by … I'm not sure what … and the next thing I know, some bald bloke is staring at me. He gave me quite a start."

"Ah, that was probably Dr Mungo. He agreed to watch over you while we nipped out to get a cup of tea."

"Right, well, if you see him again, apologise for me. I might have said a few choice words when I came round."

"I'm sure he'll understand. Anyway, why don't we talk about your new diet plan? It's about time we both started looking after ourselves."

"We're virtually vegetarian now," Kate pipes up. "We've never felt better. I can give you some healthy recipes, Mum."

Dad rolls his eyes and slumps back in his pillow.

With Mum and Kate henpecking Dad, I'm happy just to sit in the background. It doesn't take long before the day's events catch up with me and I try to stifle a yawn. It proves catching as Dad, Kate, and then Mum all follow suit.

"You should all get off," Dad suggests. "It's been a long day."

"I'm not going anywhere," Mum replies. "I'll get a taxi back later but you two should go," she adds, looking across at Kate and I.

Kate looks every bit as exhausted as I do and doesn't put up much resistance.

"Do you mind, Dad?" I ask.

"Don't be silly. To be honest, they've pumped me so full of drugs I'm struggling to keep my eyes open."

"Alright, I'll pop back tomorrow. Try not to have any more nightmares."

"I'll try," he chuckles. "I think this family has had more than our fair share of nightmares, don't you?"

"Right, yeah," I chuckle back, although I'm not sure what he means by that.

With hugs swapped, Kate and I leave what will hopefully no longer be Dad's room when we return tomorrow. As miraculous as his recovery appears, apparently they're going to keep him under observation overnight, just as a precaution. Fingers crossed he'll be on the main ward tomorrow.

We make a dozen steps back along the corridor when Mum calls after us.

"Hold on a moment you two."

We stop and wait as she bustles over.

"I just wanted to thank you both for today. I know it's been tough but I couldn't have got through it without you here. It's times like this you appreciate how much we need one another."

Assuming her gratitude is aimed at Kate, I just shuffle awkwardly on the spot.

"And I mean both of you," she adds, placing her hand on my shoulder.

Mum kisses us both before returning to her husband's bedside. As I watch her walk away, I realise that as much as I feared losing my Dad, she stood to lose the man who had been at her side for more than four decades. I guess that puts her gratitude into perspective.

I find a smile and wander on with someone who used to be my sister by my side.

Whilst there's no conversation as we navigate our way towards the exit, at least there's no sniping either. We eventually pass the now-closed cafeteria and the exit comes into sight.

"How are you getting home?" Kate asks, breaking her vow of silence.

"My van."

"Oh, okay. I was going to ask if you wanted to share a cab."

I really should offer her a lift but while I dally over the decision, she pulls out her phone and calls a cab. As she confirms her booking, I loiter, unsure whether to wait with her or save us both the awkwardness.

She hangs up.

"Um, shouldn't Ethan be picking you up?" I ask.

"Fat chance," she huffs. "He sent me a text to say he was going out for dinner. He's probably gone on to a wine bar by now."

"Seriously? His father-in-law is fighting for his life and your husband thinks it's cool to have a night on the town? He's an even bigger cunt than I thought."

I await the ticking off for dropping the c-bomb but it doesn't come.

"That's my husband for you," she spits. "The selfish shit."

Subconsciously, perhaps, but her veil of middle-class civility slips away. Her tone is bitter, angsty and, coupled with her makeup-free face, she looks and sounds more like the kid

215

sister I grew up with. It's just a glimmer, but I've missed that girl.

"So who's looking after Arabella?"

I know my niece is smarter than the average six-year-old but I can't imagine she's smart enough to be left home alone.

"She's staying at Ethan's parents. And for the record, I call her Bella; not that Ethan approves."

I really want to leave but I get the feeling my sister is long overdue a vent. It doesn't take long to come.

"You've never liked Ethan, have you?" she asks.

"Is it that obvious?"

"Yes."

"I'm not gonna lie to you, sis. I think the bloke is a twat and while we're having this heart-to-heart, I don't even recognise you anymore."

"I don't recognise myself. Actually, some days I bloody hate myself."

"That's harsh."

"It's true. This isn't the life I wanted and I'm certainly not the woman I dreamt I'd become."

"But you've got everything: the big house, nice cars, foreign holidays, a smart daughter in private school."

"Don't get me wrong, Adam, I love my little girl more than anything, but the rest of it … I wouldn't care if it all went tomorrow."

It appears there's more than just a smidgen of trouble in paradise—it sounds more like my sister is far from happy with her lot in life. Ironic really, considering I always thought I was the sibling who'd made all the wrong life choices. And whilst I'm touched, and perhaps a little grateful she's chosen to share just how crappy her life really is, I'm not exactly the ideal person to offer advice.

"You know what," she adds. "I envy you."

"Now I know you're taking the piss," I scoff.

"Honestly, I do. I know things haven't been great recently, but you always seem happy, content."

"That'll be down to my incredibly low standards."

"But at least you're still you, Adam," she continues, ignoring my self-deprecation. "You haven't sold your soul for some vacuous bullshit lifestyle."

I don't feel the self-satisfaction I would have expected. There's no glee in hearing how unhappy my sister is; only pity, and more than a touch of sadness.

"Where's all this coming from, sis? Don't get me wrong, I'm glad we're finally having a conversation without sniping at one another, but we haven't exactly been close since ..."

"Since Ethan," she interjects.

"Well, yeah."

"That man gave me everything I can live without, but not the one thing I really need."

"What's that?"

"Family."

"Family?"

"Tonight, in that room when we were all sat at Dad's bedside after he woke up. For the first time in years, I felt like I was part of a family again."

"But you have your own family now. You, Ethan and Ara ... Bella."

"We're not a family," she sighs. "Ethan and his parents want to turn us into middle-class drones. It was his idea for Bella to have a private education. It was his idea for her to take ballet and piano lessons. She's like her mother, though—wants to play outside and collect bugs in jars, and come home with scraped knees and muddy hands. That's not the daughter Ethan wants."

"So, that comment you made earlier, about divorce statistics, was ..."

"Yep. I haven't said anything yet but today has made me realise what's important. I want my little girl to be who she wants to be, and have people around her who'll support her, not mould her into their version of perfection."

"I'm, um, sorry. I honestly don't know what to say. I always thought your life was, well, perfect."

"Perfectly wank," she sniggers. "And, while I'm spilling my heart out, I can't tell you how much I've missed this too."

"This?"

"Chatting with my big brother, just like we used to."

A horn blares outside. Her cab has arrived and just as I'm about to offer a goodbye, Kate puts her arms around me.

"And just so this entire conversation isn't just about me, I do hope everything works out with Daisy," she says. "We all know you're an idiot, but you're a lovable idiot and she'll come around, I'm sure."

"Gee, thanks," I chuckle. "That was really heartfelt."

"You're welcome, and can I ask a favour?"

"Shoot."

"What I've just told you—keep it to yourself for now. I

don't want Mum and Dad worrying about it."

I nod, and the two people who entered as near strangers leave the hospital almost like the brother and sister they once were. Almost, but not quite. Rebuilding my relationship with Kate is going to require a lot of work, like much of my life at the moment.

Tomorrow, that work continues.

29.

I was so exhausted last night I flopped into bed and fell fast asleep within minutes.

At some point it arrived.

I wouldn't go as far as to say it was a nightmare, but it wasn't exactly a sweet dream either. I can't even recall what happened but I awoke with a gasp and needles of anxiety prickling my chest. I tried going back to sleep, but my mind had other ideas, and I spent twenty restless minutes tossing and turning before giving up.

Six-thirty on a Sunday morning and I'm up before the birds. Unprecedented.

I slope through to the kitchen and make a coffee before taking a seat at the table to work out what I'm supposed to do with myself at such a ridiculous hour. That process takes care of ten minutes.

As I gulp the final dregs of coffee from my cup, an idea occurs. I rinse my cup out and retrieve the hoover from the cupboard in the hallway.

"Wakey wakey, Mungo," I chuckle, and switch the hoover on.

On the odd occasion I've been out and about early, I've driven past joggers and wondered what the hell makes someone don Lycra and pound the pavements at such an ungodly hour. However, after five minutes of vigorous hoovering I have to admit there's something to be said for starting the day with exercise. Giving Mungo a taste of his own medicine does add to the experience, it must be said.

Disappointingly, my flatmate doesn't appear until I'm returning the hoover to the cupboard.

"Sorry, did I wake you?" I grin.

"No."

"Oh."

"Why are you hoovering at this hour of the morning?"

It's a valid question.

"Um, I don't actually know. I just felt restless I guess."

"And how do you feel now?"

"Surprisingly chipper, considering it's virtually the middle of the night."

"Your mind-set is changing."

"Is it? Is it really?"

It doesn't feel like my mind-set is changing—more like I'm part of a stage magician's act and I've been tricked into doing something I'd never usually do. I don't know how, but I wonder if Mungo has somehow planted a subliminal urge to hoover when I'd usually be fast asleep.

Just as I'm about to make a beeline for the Coco Pops cupboard, Mungo instructs me otherwise.

"We must talk. Come this way."

"Really?" I groan.

"Yes. Really."

He leads me through to the lounge and we sit at opposite ends of the sofa.

"Yesterday was a pivotal stage in your treatment," he declares. "How was your father when you left the hospital?"

"Pretty good, thanks for asking, but I get the feeling you already knew that."

"How would I know?"

"I'm not sure, Mungo, but I haven't forgotten what you said last night. Are you going to tell me what that was about?"

"I have said all there is to be said."

"Which was very little, but Dad remembers opening his eyes and the first thing he saw was your face."

"That would be correct. He was most enthusiastic in his use of industrial language."

"He had a nightmare and reckons that's what brought him out of the coma."

"There is your answer then."

I eye him suspiciously but, whatever or whoever dragged Dad out of his coma, I suppose I should just be grateful.

"Now, can we return to the matter in hand?" he adds, clearly unwilling to expand on his cryptic statement.

"Fine."

"Did you sleep well?" he asks.

It's the kind of mindless question people ask out of politeness, but knowing Mungo, I sense he wants an actual answer.

"Err, to a point, yes."

"No nightmares?"

"What makes you think I have nightmares?"

"People who operate on a higher emotional plane tend to experience nightmares, and dreams, more than most."

"Oh, right. Well, I did wake up suddenly. Can't say I'd call it a nightmare though."

"That is good."

"Is it?"

"Yes. And you demonstrated control with your emotions yesterday when you returned to the hospital."

"Eventually."

"That is irrelevant. You challenged your fear and controlled it."

"Do you think I'm making progress then?"

"I do. It only remains to see how far you have progressed."

I'm not convinced. I don't feel any different, and certainly not in control of my haphazard decision making. Mungo has only been in my life for seven days and whilst I'm no expert, surely no therapist can change the habits of a lifetime in just seven days.

"No offence, Mungo, but what exactly have you done to change my thinking?"

"What I needed to."

"Specifically? I mean, aren't we supposed to have sessions where I lie on the sofa and you ask me questions about my childhood and stuff?"

"Why would I do that?"

"I dunno. Isn't that what most therapists do when treating behavioural issues?"

"I am not most therapists."

That's not the first time he's given that response when I've challenged his methods.

"So, how do I know my thinking has changed?"

"What are your plans today?"

I roll my eyes. "Just for once, Mungo, it would be nice if you answered my question rather than replying with one of your own."

"Your plans?"

"Good grief," I huff. "I haven't even thought about it but I'll be seeing Dad at some stage this morning if you want to come?"

"No."

"Suit yourself. Anyway, why do you want to know what I'm doing?"

"To test your progress."

"Test my progress?"

"Must you repeat what I say? It is growing increasingly tedious."

"Sorry. Habit."

"It is an irritating habit but to answer your question, we will convene at three o'clock to discuss how your day went."

"Oh, okay. Is there anything I should be doing, or looking out for?"

"No. Just go about your day as normal."

"That doesn't sound very, you know, scientific."

"My apologies," he replies, getting to his feet. "I did not realise you were an expert on behavioural therapy."

He allows the edge of his mouth to curl towards a smirk, and promptly walks away. With our chat apparently now over, I guess I'll just have to see what the day brings.

Putting my therapy to one side, I sit for a moment and replay his parting words. On a few occasions in recent days Mungo has made comments that don't fit in with his usual cold logical persona. Granted, they've mainly been sarcastic comments, but it does appear there might be an actual personality buried somewhere in that dome-like head of his.

In a strange way, his snippets of humanity remind me of a sci-fi movie I once watched. It was set in a future where everyone had their own robot around the home, like an electronic butler, and the plot focused on a particular robot, whose name I can't remember. Basically, the robot started developing human-like emotions and in the end I think it either murdered its host family or took up amateur dramatics—I can't recall which.

Perhaps Mungo is also capable of change, although I can't imagine us ever falling out of Tiffany's at one in the morning, drunkenly wailing *Wonderwall*. With that surreal thought, I get up and plod back to the kitchen. Despite the early start, it definitely feels like Coco-Pop o'clock.

As I sit and eat, I use the time to reflect on yesterday's events. To call it a soap opera of a day would be an understatement and I don't really know how I got through it. I must have experienced every emotion possible, from abject boredom to heart-wrenching dread, and just about everything in-between. And despite my emotional rollercoaster coming close to derailment a few times, I made it. I actually made it.

Now, with Dad hopefully on the road to recovery, and my relationship with both Mum and Kate in a much better place, I can concentrate on the impending addition to the Maxwell clan. With that in mind, it's time to focus on getting the new business up and running, and convincing Daisy I'm no longer the man she walked out on eleven days ago.

Bolstered by the sugar rush I begin to mentally plan my day, and the ridiculously early start means there's plenty of day to play with. With few other options at this hour, I guess the first task is clearing the rest of the garage. Then I can head over to the hospital and check on Dad before meeting up with Joe to see how he's getting on with the design work. Despite the fact he won't read it for at least four hours, I ping him a text message.

Once I've washed up my cereal bowl, I throw on some old clothes in preparation for more sweaty graft and cobwebs. The local tip doesn't open until nine o'clock but I can move everything out and give the garage a good sweep in the interim. All being well, I'll be done by ten and at the hospital in time for the start of visiting hours at eleven.

I'm just about to head downstairs when Mungo opens his bedroom door.

"Where are you going?" he asks.

"I'm going to finish clearing the garage."

"And when you have completed that task?"

"I'm going to visit Dad in the hospital and then I'm seeing Joe to check how he's getting on with the design work."

"Very well."

"Is that it? Anything else you'd like to know?"

"No, but remember what you've learnt. Emotions are your enemy and logic is your friend."

He closes the door.

Considering how much time he spends alone in his bedroom, I'd love to know what he gets up to in there. Then again, the only man I know who spends more time locked away in a bedroom is Joe, and I have a vague idea what he gets up to having once inadvertently viewed the browser history on his computer. On reflection, it's probably best Mungo's bedroom antics remain a mystery.

I grab my keys and head downstairs.

Seven-thirty on a Sunday morning is a surreal place. Our street is rarely ever quiet but, besides the chorus of chirping birds, there's not a single sound, until the rusty garage door creaks open, that is.

Within two minutes of starting work, it's clear one thing has changed since I started the task yesterday. Perhaps it's down to Mungo's advice, or more likely my Dad's near-death experience, but the little annoyances I experienced yesterday don't seem quite so important. When I pick up a box of tarnished cutlery and the bottom gives way, even the prospect of salvaging a few dozen forks, knives, and spoons from the filthy floor, doesn't result in a tantrum.

I even manage to find a smile for the overly-officious dick at the council tip.

The one happy by-product of not losing my shit every five minutes is that I'm back in the flat by half-nine—thirty minutes ahead of schedule. Who knew that oppressing emotion aided productivity, apart from the Germans, obviously.

After a leisurely shower I take ten minutes to check my email and if anything interesting has been posted on Facebook. It proves to be time less constructively spent and, in the case of Facebook, a pointless waste of life.

Still ahead of schedule, I get ready to leave for the hospital. As I pass Mungo's bedroom door, I consider telling him I'm off but decide against it. For whatever reason, he doesn't want to come and I'm not inclined to waste my time trying to change his mind.

For the third time this morning, Alan starts with minimal fuss. However, as we wind our way through the back streets towards the main road, his usual clunky, rattly, wheezy soundtrack is noticeably louder. I don't like to admit it but I fear my trusty old steed is on his last legs. And, if I'm going to make a success of the new business, I need a van I can rely upon, and preferably without the bodywork of a World War II frigate.

For now, though, Alan is all I can afford. I'll just have to hope the old boy hangs on a few months longer.

With significantly less urgency than yesterday, I park up and make my way to the main entrance. I only intend to stay for an hour or so, not least because the hospital car park is so expensive I'll have to sell a kidney if I stay any longer. Still, I'm in the ideal place to find a buyer I guess.

I wander through the doors at precisely eleven o'clock and head straight to the main reception so I can confirm Dad has been moved to one of the main wards. Unfortunately, I'm not the only one seeking help and there's at least a dozen other people lined up at the desk. Unless I'm prepared to take my chances and physically tour every ward, it looks like I'm in for a wait. I reluctantly join the queue.

A minute later, I'm no longer at the back of that queue as I feel a tap on my shoulder.

I spin around.

Half-a-dozen highly emotive reactions line up and beg to be released. With the aim of keeping them at bay, I pause before opening my mouth.

224

"Daisy, hi," I calmly announce. "What are you doing here?"

"You're still asking stupid questions, I see," she frowns. "What do you think I'm doing here?"

I'm about to launch into a spluttering defence when a voice echoes in my head. Not literally, thank Christ, but by way of a memory.

Emotions are your enemy. Logic is your friend.

"Why is it a stupid question?" I reply impassively. "There are plenty of reasons you could be here, which is why I asked."

Her face flushes pink. "Excuse me?"

I appear to have answered Daisy's question in full Mungo mode.

"Sorry, I didn't mean to sound so blunt," I exclaim. "But I genuinely don't know why you're here."

"To see your dad, of course. I only found out this morning."

"Oh, right. I thought you might be here because of the baby."

Realisation arrives in the form of an apologetic smile. "Sorry, yes. Perhaps I should have said. How is he anyway?"

"Lucky. Yesterday afternoon we were told to plan for the worst."

"That's awful. Why didn't you call me?"

The truth is it didn't even cross my mind to call her but, after taking a second to think, a better response arrives.

"Two reasons. Firstly, because it was really late by the time I got home. And secondly, you ended our relationship so it didn't feel appropriate calling you."

Both my statements are factually correct, yet the second one clearly stung and Daisy launches a defence.

"Just because we're not together, Adam, it doesn't mean I've suddenly stopped caring about your family. How could you possibly think I wouldn't want to know?"

"Like I might have wanted to know you were pregnant with my child?"

I didn't intend to, but my response is delivered with such cold indifference I can almost feel the ice crystals forming on my lips.

"I guess I asked for that," she says flatly.

It feels appropriate to apologise but I suspect that's more from habit than for anything I've done wrong. I opt for silence instead.

"Are you okay?" she asks, changing the subject. "You don't seem yourself."

When people typically ask how you are, they rarely care. It's a throwaway question and requires nothing more in response than a generic 'fine thanks'. However, in this instance I detect Daisy is concerned by my aloof attitude. I wouldn't necessarily call Mungo's strategy flawed, but when you strip away the emotion from a conversation, aloof is all you're left with. I guess, in time, I'll find a balance.

"I'm okay," I sigh. "Yesterday was draining so I guess I'm just tired."

"Is that all it is?"

"That's all it is," I chirp, and the more I think about it, the more I conclude that's probably the reason I'm out of sorts.

It's with some relief we reach the head of the queue before we're forced into more conversation. The receptionist confirms Dad has been moved to one of the main wards and gives me directions.

I head off with Daisy at my side.

Clearly we can't continue in silence so I defer to the unanswered questions I have regarding our baby.

"I meant to ask: when exactly is the baby due?"

"Early July."

"So you're …?"

"Just under three months gone."

I think back to the autumn and try to pinpoint when Daisy might have conceived. I doubt we'll ever know as we rarely went more than a few days without getting busy in the bedroom. It's a thought that brings both lament and, more inappropriately, a stirring in the groin area.

"Are you thinking about us having sex?" Daisy asks.

I look across at her in the hope of gauging the motive behind the question but her expression gives nothing away.

"Maybe," I reply with an awkward grin.

Her reaction is surprisingly positive. "That's one thing I really do miss, if I'm honest."

My gut instinct is to enthusiastically leap upon her confession but this is probably not the time and definitely not the place.

"Yeah, me too, but back to the baby. Aren't you due to have the first scan soon?"

"Next week."

"Oh, really? And were you going to tell me if I hadn't asked?"

"I'm not sure."

"Seriously?" I huff. "You didn't think I might like to attend the first scan?"

"If I thought you might actually turn up, I'd have told you, but history suggests you'd probably let me down … again."

Within the space of three short strides, my irritation dial turns up a notch.

"So am I invited, or not?"

"I haven't decided, Adam. Dad thinks …"

Two more notches.

"Oh, of course," I snap. "I might have known Eddie would have to be consulted."

"He just thinks I shouldn't risk ruining such an important moment."

Another notch.

"And you'd think I'd deliberately ruin our baby's first scan, do you?"

"You would, if you said you'd be there and didn't turn up."

Fifty percent peak irritation.

"So, good old Eddie decided it would be better not to tell me at all, did he?"

"He was thinking of me," she snaps. "Something you seldom did."

Seventy percent peak irritation and our raised voices are now echoing down the corridor. The few people we pass avoid eye contact.

"He was thinking of himself, more like. He's never liked me and now he's using my unborn child to twist the knife."

"Don't be ridiculous."

"Oh, so now I'm ridiculous as well as useless. It's a fucking miracle I can breathe and walk at the same time."

"Grow up."

"Grow up? You're the one who's keeping secrets by not telling me about the scan."

"Come off it, Adam," she barks. "What did you expect after the way you've behaved?"

"That was then. I've changed."

She stops dead and grabs my arm.

"If this is the changed version of Adam, let me tell you something: it's no better than the old version."

She releases my arm, turns around, and starts walking away.

"Give your dad my love," she calls over her shoulder. "And tell him I'll come back another time—when you're not here."

I stand and watch her disappear beyond a set of doors.

In the quietness of the corridor, a chorus of voices begin to heckle a single word: *idiot*.

30.

Five minutes after a less-than-enthusiastic greeting, I'm slumped in a chair at Dad's bedside whilst my parents chat idly about their plans once Dad is discharged. It's all I can do to stare out of a grimy window and conduct a post mortem on my disastrous conversation with Daisy. It's easy to see where I went wrong, but what really irks is I got off to such a good start when she first pitched up.

Mungo was right; emotion certainly was my enemy and I should have kept my mouth shut. It's one thing to drift through life making mistakes in a state of blissful ignorance, but now I understand why those mistakes were made, I have no excuses. Christ, all I had to do was keep my irritation in check and Daisy would be here with me now.

"Earth to Adam," Dad quips. "Is anyone there?"

They say a problem shared is a problem halved, so I explain why I'm sporting a face like a slapped arse. Within seconds of sharing my problem, I conclude the saying is a crock of shit.

"You said what?" Mum barks. "What on earth possessed you?"

"I didn't …"

My parents swap glances and I don't need to complete the sentence as they know what comes next.

"I really thought you'd turned a corner," Mum sighs. "Why didn't you just bite your tongue?"

"Because it's not fair. Who the hell does Eddie think he is, trying to exclude me?"

"He's her father," Dad replies, his voice still carrying a slight rasp. "And if I were in his shoes, I might do the same."

"What?"

"You heard me, son. He's looking out for his girl and quite frankly, I don't blame him."

"Oh, that's just bloody great," I groan. "You're taking his side now, are you?"

"Don't be so childish," Mum interjects. "This has nothing to do with taking sides. If it were Kate, and Ethan had behaved like you have, we'd be telling her the same thing."

The urge to tell them where their son-in-law was last night pulls like a puppy on a leash. I just about bring it to heel. I've already pissed off one woman in my life this morning and I don't want to destroy the goodwill I've rebuilt with Kate.

"You know what, son?" Dad says. "Rather than whining about it, if I were in your shoes I'd divert my energies into bringing Eddie onside. Mark my words—without his respect, you're going to face an uphill struggle."

My parents might be wrong about Ethan but I have to begrudgingly admit they're probably right about Eddie. However, I'm no longer in the mood for humble pie and change the subject.

"Anyway, enough of my problems. How long are they going to keep you in for?"

"Don't know for sure. They're still trying to work out how I came through a stroke like that relatively unscathed. I was chatting to the doctor this morning and he asked me to pick six random numbers."

"Um, why?"

"For the lottery," he chuckles. "Apparently I'm the luckiest man in the country. He said the fact I even came out of the coma was remarkable enough, but not to have suffered any long-term effects is extremely rare, he reckons."

His words are followed by a reflective silence. We all know how close he came to death, and the fact he's still here making terrible jokes is a minor miracle considering where we were eighteen hours ago. That thought shines a little perspective on my row with Daisy and the lingering irritation swaps seats with regret.

I spend an hour at my Dad's bedside, talking a lot but saying nothing. At one point I was tempted to share the news of my new venture but decided against it. They've heard it all before and I don't need the extra pressure of their, admittedly low, expectations.

As I head back to the car park, my phone pings with a message. Joe has finally risen from his pit so I can go and see how he's getting on with the design work. I dread to think what he's thrown together in such a short space of time but I'd rather focus on just about anything other than strokes and hospitals and my ever-deteriorating relationship with Daisy. I send a reply to say I'm on my way.

By the time I ring the doorbell at Joe's house, he's just about managed to get dressed and haul his backside downstairs.

"Bit early, ain't it?" he grunts.

"Mate, it's lunchtime."

"Shit. Must have overslept. I was up till nearly two o'clock."

He beckons me in and I follow him up the stairs to his bedroom, or studio as he prefers to call it these days. Whatever the label, it will always be a place of firsts for me. It was in Joe's bedroom I first laid eyes on a genuine porn magazine. The first time I drank alcohol, in the form of cheap cider. And it was in his stinking bedroom I first heard the album, *Definitely Maybe* by Oasis; still one of my all-time favourites.

"Excuse the mess," he says, plonking himself down at a desk strewn with energy drink cans.

"Sod the mess. You mind if I open a window?"

"Yeah, sorry. I ate a six-pack of mushroom bhajis last night."

Trying to ignore the lingering stench, I tentatively sit on the edge of his bed next to the desk.

"Listen, mate. Before we get stuck in, I need to tell you something."

He spins around in his chair. "Christ. What is it now?"

"It's my old man. He had a stroke yesterday afternoon."

"Fuck, mate. Is he alright?"

It's clear from his shocked expression the concern is genuine. Unlike my mother, who has only ever tolerated him, Dad has always got on well with Joe.

"I don't know how, but yeah, he's okay."

I explain yesterday's events, right up to the point Mungo made his ridiculous claim about bringing Dad out of his coma.

"There's something not right about that bloke," Joe warns. "He gives me the creeps."

"He's alright once you get to know him."

My reply doesn't sound convincing as I can't honestly say I have got to know Mungo.

"And why would he say that, about your dad?" Joe adds. "That's just too weird."

"Thing is, mate, maybe he just *thinks* he's responsible when obviously it was just a coincidence Dad woke up when we weren't there."

"As I said before, he's not the full ticket. Clearly he's got his own issues and you should get rid of him once this business is up-and-running."

Inadvertently, Joe has raised a question I hadn't even considered. What is Mungo's end game? If the business takes off and I manage to get my thinking under control, I'm not sure I'll need either a lodger or a therapist. In that situation, do I just sling him out?

However, I can't yet imagine a future where all is well in my life so there's no point pondering a problem so far down the line.

I answer Joe's question as vaguely as possible. "We'll see."

"Your funeral," he replies with a shrug, and turns back to his computer monitor.

Subject closed, I lean over and watch while he clicks away at a mouse.

"I'll show you the product mock-up first," he says, working his way through a series of sub-folders.

Two more clicks and the fruits of his late night labour fill the screen. I'm almost lost for words.

"Bloody hell," I just about murmur.

"What? Don't you like it?"

"No, it's not that …"

"I knew you'd hate it," he groans. "What a waste of fucking time."

"It's … brilliant. Honestly, I love it."

And I genuinely do. Joe has created a mock-up of a product which wouldn't look out of place on a supermarket shelf.

"Seriously? You're not just saying that?"

"Come off it. When have I ever held back on telling you something you don't want to hear? I think it's amazing."

"Oh, right," he says coyly. "I suppose it's not bad."

He then goes on to show me equally impressive label designs and a website he built while I was snoozing away in bed.

"The website still needs some work as I didn't have any text content, but you can add that yourself."

I continue to stare at the screen in stunned silence.

"Problem?" he asks.

"Not at all, but I've got to be honest: this is way better than I expected. Why is your business struggling if this is the kind of work you do?"

"Wish I knew, mate. I only seem to get the cheapskate clients who want the moon on a stick."

An opportunity suddenly presents itself. Rather than gloss over Joe's observation, as I typically would, perhaps a bit of logical thinking might be worth a try. It surely can't go any worse than this morning's attempt with Daisy.

"Just a thought, mate, but have you ever considered telling them to pay more or piss off?"

"Beggars can't be choosers."

I look at the screen again, at a design which would surely

have cost a small fortune if I'd used a professional design studio.

"I reckon that might be your problem. Your rates are cheap so you attract cheap clients."

"It is what it is, mate," he says dismissively.

"But wouldn't you rather do more of this work rather than designing shitty websites for plumbers and the like?"

"Course I would, but … I dunno, guess I never considered myself good enough."

It appears I'm not the only one with self-esteem issues.

"If I could design work like this, I'd be pitching to businesses with a decent budget like accountants, solicitors, and financial planners. Most of them in the local area haven't updated their image since the seventies."

"No disrespect, mate, but what do you know about it?"

"Err, Daisy works for a firm of accountants, Dad worked for a financial planning company, and I've used a few solicitors in the past for my … indiscretions."

"Oh, yeah. Doesn't really help though."

"Why not?"

"How do I get a foot in the door? Cold calling isn't exactly my thing, because … well … look at the state of me. Would you hire *this*?"

There's no getting past Joe's inherent scruffiness, or lack of self-confidence when it comes to his appearance. He needs another way to get a foot in the door, and maybe I might have a solution.

"You remember when they built those new houses on the old dairy site last year?"

"Think so."

"Well, a few weeks after the new owners moved in, I knocked on doors and asked if they wanted their windows cleaned for free, like a one-off trial. Of the ten people I spoke to, eight took up the offer and seven of them are still customers today. I reckon I must have made close to fourteen hundred quid from those houses so far, and all it cost me was half a day's work doing their first clean for free."

"You're saying I should work for free?"

"Why not? Find a business with the worst logo, design something a bit more up-to-date, and then email it to them. What's the worst thing they'll say?"

"Fuck off?"

"Maybe, but even if they do, you can just adjust the design and send it to the next company. I reckon one of them will bite your hand off."

"And then what?"

"You've got a foot in the door. They'll probably want their website updated, and their stationery, plus you'll have something half-decent to show other potential clients. It's gotta be better than scratching a living with the tight-fisted clients you've currently got."

Rather than instantly dismiss my suggestion, Joe scratches his stubble and stares into space.

"You might be on to something," he eventually admits, albeit with a hint of scepticism in his voice.

"Just give it a go, mate. If you produce something half as good as what you've created for me, they'll love it."

"Yeah, maybe I will."

His reply edges on disinterested but his eyes tell a different story. It's the same look he adopts just before approaching an unsuspecting member of the opposite sex—blind optimism. I only hope he has more success with his design work than his chat-up lines.

"Anyway, I better get going," I say. "Still got loads to do."

"Alright, mate. I'll email all the files over to you. Oh, and is it okay to visit your old man?"

"Of course. I'm sure he'll be glad to see you."

"He might, but your mum won't."

"You might be surprised. I think this whole episode with Dad has changed her perspective a bit."

"Won't hold my breath," he mumbles, getting to his feet.

We part with a customary slap on the arm.

Despite some obstinacy from Alan, I eventually pull out of the cul-de-sac feeling better than I did when I arrived. I have no idea if Joe will take up my advice but that doesn't mean it wasn't sound. I think, on reflection, we surprised one another with our hidden talents, although I reckon I got the better end of the deal.

Nevertheless, my impromptu nugget of marketing wisdom suggests I might not be such a terrible businessman after all. And it was all down to thinking logically.

I arrive back at the flat a little after two o'clock and the moment I close the front door behind me, Mungo's bedroom door swings open.

"You are back," he says.

"No, I'm an optical illusion. The real Adam Maxwell is in the pub."

"Most droll."

"Thank you."

"Shall we discuss how your day has gone thus far?"

"It's not three o'clock yet."

"Does it matter?"

"Guess not."

We wander through to the lounge and take up the same positions on the sofa as this morning. I feel I really should lie down, being this is kind of a therapy session, but I'm certain Mungo's voice would send me to sleep.

"Well?" he asks.

"Okay. The good news is Joe did a cracking job with the design work. I'll show you once we're done but I also managed to help with his business, just by applying a little logical thought."

"I detect there is bad news?"

I spend ten minutes giving him chapter and verse about what happened with Daisy, and the subsequent conversation with my parents. Not once does he interject, or give any physical clues to his thoughts.

"So, neither of my parents blame Eddie," I conclude. "They said they'd probably do the same."

"Tell me again: what did your father say about this man?"

"That I should focus on gaining Eddie's respect."

"That seems a sensible approach. Is Eddie Wallace a reasonable man?"

"He's a hard-arsed businessman with a short fuse, so no, not really."

"A businessman?"

"And you accuse me of repeating myself. Yes, he runs his own engineering company."

"There is your solution then."

I stare at Mungo and await the solution to arrive. It doesn't, and the stare becomes very awkward, very quickly.

"Nope, I'm not seeing it, Mungo."

"Think."

I slump back on the sofa and adopt an expression like a toddler surreptitiously shitting his pants. Mungo, sensing he could be in for a long wait, offers a clue.

"The pertinent fact is Eddie Wallace is a businessman."

"Right."

"And you need to gain his respect."

"Got that."

"So, how would you set about gaining the respect of a man

who runs his own business?"

My mind immediately sets to default and searches for an amusing, if not childish response. I'm about to suggest I invite Eddie to Tiffany's when, like a drunk rhino, the answer crashes in.

"Of course," I trill. "My new business."

Mungo nods and tries a self-satisfied grin, or he could be suffering constipation.

Along with the solution, I also conclude my thinking has been arse about face. Part of the motivation for making the business a success is to tell Eddie he can shove his money up his arse—an emotional response born of male pride. Now I think about it, suggesting I could raise the money was a hollow and, admittedly, reckless gesture. This is about proving to Eddie I'm capable of supporting Daisy and the baby. Do that, and surely his respect will follow?

"Right. So, I gain Eddie's respect by making a success of the new business?

"Correct."

"And how do I do that?"

"It is your business and therefore your problem. We have reached the point in your journey where I can no longer do your thinking for you."

"Thanks a bunch" I gripe. "You're just going to let me screw this up on my own?"

"I would suggest you reflect on that statement. The business model is sound so if it fails, it would likely be because of your negativity."

He gets up and heads for the door.

"Is that it?" I call after him. "Don't you even want to look at Joe's designs?"

He stops and turns around. "Are they of a professional standard?"

"Well, yes. They're brilliant."

"If you have faith in the quality of the designs, there is no need for me to look at them. You must believe in your own judgement."

He continues on his way out of the door.

It takes but a moment for the realisation to arrive. This is it—the responsibility now lies on my shoulders, and my shoulders alone. No more second chances, no more blaming others, no more excuses and, apparently, no more Mungo doing my thinking for me.

Everything now hinges on me, and a business forged from a botched salad dressing. And now I've got the added pressure of proving myself to Eddie.

Somehow, anyhow, I've got to make this work.

31.

Despite heading to bed early, my busy mind had no intention of letting me sleep. A never ending list of tasks scrolled mercilessly while the spirit of self-doubt recited the consequences of my impending failure. Those consequences ranged from living with my parents again, through to my own child disowning their wastrel of a father.

Exhaustion finally took over and sometime in the early hours I fell into a fitful sleep.

Now, at six in the morning, I'm awake again and I know my mind will quickly fill with a fog of daunting thoughts if I lie in bed and let it. The only way to keep those thoughts at bay is to get up and tackle them head on.

I can only imagine this is how a marathon runner must feel when they're jogging through their first mile—if you think too much about what lies ahead of you, it must be tempting to just give up. So, like a marathon runner, I've got to approach this one mile at a time; or maybe even a few hundred feet at a time … crawling on my hands and knees.

I've already decided I'll now start each day with a set routine: coffee, housework, breakfast, shower, and more coffee. Caffeine and exercise have proven to be an effective way to jolt myself into a productive state of mind. Ideally, I'd rather start the routine at seven, rather than six, but with the clock ticking I might as well make the most of the extra hour.

As it transpires, the first four parts of my routine take fifty-five minutes to complete. Then, with some degree of satisfaction, I get to enjoy my second coffee of the day.

With mug in hand I sit at the kitchen table, boot up the laptop, and open Mungo's business plan. The man himself is conspicuous by his absence, which is odd considering he's been a perpetual early riser. Everyone deserves a lie in, I guess.

"Right, Maxwell," I mumble to myself. "Let's do this."

The one benefit of owning the window cleaning round is I've already endured most of the mundane requirements you need to run a business. I can therefore dispense with setting up a bank account, registering with the tax office, and dealing with blood-sucking insurance companies. Nevertheless, the business plan still includes a lengthy list of admin tasks to be completed before I can even think about mixing my first bottle of

Crystalene.

I spend a frustrating hour completing a succession of forms. I'm about to take a break and grab another coffee when Mungo appears.

"Oh, good afternoon," I jest.

"You may wish to invest in a new clock. It is ten past eight in the morning."

"I was being flippant. Nice lie in?" I reply, getting up to switch the kettle on.

He ignores my question and watches on as I prepare another mug of coffee.

"That is coffee, correct?" he says.

"Yep."

"I would like a cup of coffee."

"Yeah, sure … wait … what?"

"I said I would like a cup of coffee."

"I thought that's what you said. When did you start drinking coffee?"

"This morning."

"Easy, Mungo. First you lie in till eight, and now you're drinking coffee. Keep this up and you'll be watching *The Jeremy Kyle Show* by next week."

"I have no idea what that is."

"Trust me—you're better off not knowing."

I grab another mug from the cupboard and ladle in a few teaspoons of coffee.

"I'm guessing milk and sugar would be pushing it?"

"Correct."

"Right. One black coffee coming up."

I await a sign of gratitude which doesn't come. Nevertheless, I've enough to think about without stressing over Mungo's rudeness.

"Have you had a productive morning?" he asks.

"Very."

I pass him the mug of coffee. "Any chance of a *thank you*?"

"I might not like coffee, in which case my gratitude would be premature."

"You're thanking me for making it."

"If it pleases you, thank you."

"You're welcome."

I return to my laptop as Mungo takes his first tentative sip.

Curiosity gets the better of me, and I watch on as he puckers a soured expression which makes his face look like an octogenarian's testicle.

"It is," he hisses. "Quite vile."

"Told you." I snigger. "You should have taken sugar."

"I do not like coffee," he declares.

He gets up, tips it down the sink and deposits the mug in the bowl. With that, he leaves.

"Don't worry," I call after him. "I'll wash up your mug."

His bedroom door slams shut. I shake my head and return to the laptop screen.

The final form is completed and I turn my attention to finding a printer who can create labels from Joe's designs. Thankfully, my online options are plentiful but I choose a local printer so I can pick the labels up in person rather than rely on some hapless delivery company. I ping them an email with the artwork attached and with that, my admin duties are done. Now all that remains is a plan for the day.

I've never really been big on planning; another of my traits Daisy found infuriating, particularly as I was so reluctant to get involved with plans for our own wedding. My mind drifts back to those plans, and the dull ache reminds me what a complete tool I was. Daisy must have felt she was dragging me down the aisle, such was my sulky reluctance to discuss what would have been the happiest day of my life. In essence, I'd won the lottery but chose to whine about the paperwork.

Am I still that whiney idiot? Have I changed? God, I hope so because that guy was a monumental dickhead. That acceptance brings temptation, but texting Daisy with possibly the thousandth apology would be futile. The apology ship has long since sailed.

Must. Look. Forward.

A puff of the cheeks and a gulp of coffee brings me back to the moment.

I open the calendar app on my phone and for the first time ever, properly plan my work day. When I've finished, I take a moment to reflect on my planning and stare at the screen. Seeing the list of tasks sprawling across the entire day summons a mixture of dread and anticipation. By anyone's measure, I've got fuckloads to do. The time for planning is over—time for the doing.

I neck my coffee dregs and wash up the mugs. A glance at the kitchen clock and bang on schedule, I leave the flat.

A monochrome scene greets me outside. Brooding clouds threaten rain, and on any ordinary day I might be tempted to turn around and head for the sofa but that's simply not an option today.

"Morning, Alan."

He doesn't answer but starts on the third turn of the key.

We force our way through the rush hour traffic to the first house of the day and arrive within seven minutes.

I've never had cause to think about it before but life contains a surprising amount of wasted time. Not necessarily the time spent watching shit TV programmes, or getting into pointless arguments on Twitter, but the time wasted on mundane tasks that shouldn't take as long as they do. Arguably, no task is more mundane than cleaning windows but applying a little gusto gets the job done just as well as my previous lethargic approach, but takes half the time.

A simple change, but by the time I slide the ladder back onto Alan's roof at the final house on today's schedule, I've completed my previous work day in just over three hours. I've earned the same amount of money but a happy by-product of my new-found productivity is I've created time ... actual time. I can't help but feel just a little smug.

As much as I'd love to spend that time slumped on the sofa, or in the pub, I've got a lot of miles to cover this afternoon; to collect all the ingredients I need for creating Crystalene in bulk. Four stops and hundreds of gallons of weighty fluids that will test Alan's suspension to its limits. It remains to be seen which one of us complains the most.

I return home and transfer all my window cleaning gear to the now-empty garage. With no time to stop for lunch, I head up to the flat and grab a bag of crisps from the kitchen cupboard. As I scoot back through the hallway, I stop outside Mungo's bedroom and rap on the door.

"Mungo? You in there?"

No reply.

I rap on the door again. "Mungo? I'm heading off to pick up the supplies. I'll see you later."

I loiter outside for a moment but there's no reply. Christ knows where he is, but clearly he's not in his room. I continue on my way downstairs.

Back at the wheel, I make a quick check I've got all the addresses I need, and just as I'm about to set off for the first collection, my phone rings. I could do without a hold up but once I see who's calling, accept the call.

"Alright, sis?"

"Adam, have you got a moment?"

I don't, but there's something in her voice that suggests this is more than just a social call.

"Sure. What's up?"

"Is there any chance I can come over and see you?"

"Err, yeah. When did you have in mind?"

"Soon as possible."

Now I'm concerned. "Wait, there's nothing wrong with Dad, is there?"

"No, no. It's about what we discussed at the hospital."

I've got enough on my plate without listening to my sister's marital woes, but it must have taken a lot for her to call, so I guess I should at least hear her out.

"Okay, sure. I've got a lot on this afternoon but I'll be free by six o'clock. Shall we meet at that pub near your place?"

"Um, that wouldn't … no," she stutters. "Can I come over to your place?"

"No worries. I'll see you here at six then."

"You'll definitely be there, Adam? It's important."

My gut reaction is to tell her to piss off and find another shoulder to cry on if she doesn't trust me. Then again, can I really blame her? It's a typical reaction born from experience, and my long standing reputation for unreliability.

"I promise I'll be there."

She mumbles a forlorn goodbye and hangs up.

Whatever she wants to talk about, it sits pretty low down my list of priorities and by the time I pull onto the motorway, I've all but put Kate out of my mind.

Thirty minutes later I arrive at the first collection address; a nondescript unit on an equally nondescript trading estate. After making a payment at the reception, I return outside where a surly warehouse worker is rolling up the loading bay shutter to reveal a stack of forty, five-gallon containers. Each of those containers is prominently marked with a health and safety sticker confirming the weight is just shy of nineteen kilos. I do some extremely rough maths in my head and calculate Alan is going to hate me as the combined weight of all forty containers will be worryingly close to his maximum payload.

The surly warehouse worker asks for my signature on the collection docket, and promptly fucks off.

"Cheers, mate," I grumble to myself.

I open Alan's rear doors and trudge over to the stack of containers. There really isn't time to think about how little I want to shift forty heavy containers and grab the first one before I do. Within seconds, I realise just how heavy nineteen kilos really is—bastard heavy.

It takes twenty sweaty minutes to load all the containers and, by the time I've finished, it feels like I've been subjected to a military beasting. My wheezing is only silenced by the groans from Alan's suspension as we pull out of the trading estate and start the slow journey home.

Somehow, we make it back to the flat and I reverse as close to the garage as I can. With Alan's rear doors open, I stare at the containers and consider popping up to the flat and asking Mungo to help me unload. I conclude it'll only end in a protracted discussion so it's probably quicker just to get on with it myself, so I do.

The only saving grace is it's a lot quicker to unload than it was to load.

For the remainder of the afternoon I shuttle back and forth between the suppliers and the garage. By the time the last container of the last collection is unloaded, it's dark, cold, and nearly five-thirty. When I finally slam the garage door shut, the sense of accomplishment more than makes up for the sore muscles and accompanying stench of dry sweat.

As I trudge up the stairs, a significant part of me wishes I hadn't agreed to Kate coming over. All I want is a long shower and to spend the evening vegged out on the sofa. Too late to cancel, even if my conscience would let me.

I open the front door to dark silence.

"Mungo," I call out. "I'm back."

The sounds of muffled footsteps break the silence and, just as I switch the hallway light on, Mungo's bedroom door swings open.

Stepping from his room, he sniffs the air. "Your body odour is most offensive."

I do a double-take and stare back at him in near disbelief.

"Whoa!" I blurt. "If we're talking about offensive, there's a bigger elephant in the room than my stinking armpits. What the hell are you wearing?"

"It is a jumper I purchased this afternoon."

"It's … what colour would you call that? Amber? Mustard? Venereal discharge?"

"It is *golden harvest*, according to the label."

"Right. It's, um … striking."

"Yes, it is."

"Are you wearing it for a bet?"

He frowns and changes the subject. "Did you have a productive afternoon?"

"I have to say, Mungo, the whole day has been productive, so far."

"So far?"

"Kate is coming over shortly. She wants to have a chat about something."

"I will be in my room."

He retreats a few steps backward and shuts the door, much to the relief of my retinas. I plod through to the bathroom and enjoy a brief, but much-needed, shower.

As quick as my shower was, there isn't time to stuff some food down my neck before the doorbell rings. Kate is five minutes early.

I buzz her in and stand by the open front door. The clack of heeled shoes echoes ever louder as she makes her way up the stairs. It's a familiar sound, and one I've heard countless times, but the dull ache reminds me it's not Daisy trotting up the stairs this time.

Kate's face appears at the top of the stairs. Even in the gloomy light, the absence of a smile is obvious.

"You alright, sis?"

She nods but doesn't answer.

I return to the kitchen and Kate follows. As I flick the switch on the kettle, I turn around just as my sister steps into the harsh fluorescent light. I'm slightly taken aback by the excessive makeup plastered across her face; even by her standards.

Then I realise why.

"Your face," I gasp.

Instinctively, a hand flicks upwards in an effort to cover the mottled bruise on her cheek.

"How the hell did you do that?"

Rather than answer, she slowly lowers her hand, dropping her head at the same time.

"Kate?"

She looks up, and it's clear she's just about holding it together.

"Kate, what happened?"

Shoulders slump and her lip begins to tremble.

"Ethan," she sobs. "He did it."

244

32.

I'd challenge any man to keep his emotions in check upon hearing what I just heard.

I try. I really try, but the fury and hatred spill out.

"He hit you?" I yell. "I'll kill the fucking …"

"Please, Adam," Kate cries. "I need you to keep calm."

The streaming tears and pleading eyes bring another emotion to the table, and it proves just enough to rein my anger in. I calm myself and step across the kitchen. Seizing the opportunity, Kate throws her arms around me and cries into my shoulder. Before Saturday evening at the hospital, the last time we hugged was as teenagers and I'm not good with crying women, as my single status proves.

Despite the initial awkwardness, I'm aware it's no time for words so I keep my mouth shut while she cries herself dry.

Minutes pass before she finds a breath and pulls away.

"I'm sorry," she whimpers. "I didn't know who else to turn to."

"Don't be stupid. That's what big brothers are for."

I reach across to the side and tear off a few sheets of kitchen roll.

"Here," I say, handing them to Kate. "I don't have much use for tissues these days, I'm afraid."

Finding a weak smile, she takes the sheets and dabs her eyes.

"I think we need a chat, don't you?" I say, gesturing towards the table.

She nods and takes a seat.

Seeing my sister looking so broken only stokes my fury. As much as I want to be her shoulder to cry on, the greater part of me wants to head straight over to their house and kick the shit out of Ethan.

Surely if ever there were a test of not thinking or reacting purely on emotion, this is it.

I ball my hands into fists and squeeze until all eight nails dig into the soft skin of my palms. The pain edges out the anger and I sit down at the table, somewhat reluctantly.

"Okay, tell me what happened."

"You promise to keep your cool?"

She should know my promises are worthless but I offer her

one anyway.

"When I got home on Saturday night, after I left you at the hospital, Ethan was still out. I waited up and he eventually staggered in at three in the morning, pissed out of his mind."

Keep calm, Adam. Keep calm.

"We had a blazing row and words were exchanged. Spiteful, nasty words that have been brewing for months; years really."

"I think you were within your rights."

"Maybe, but it didn't help. I should have gone to bed but then he started using Bella as a pawn to threaten me. I saw red and said I'd ruin him financially if he tried taking my daughter from me."

"And how were you intending to ruin him?"

"That's the thing—I can't. He's a fucking lawyer, and a very good one apparently, so what hope do I have if we divorce? Anyway, he just laughed at me so I kinda lost it for a moment."

"Oh."

"Yes, oh. He went to the loo so I took the chance to round up a few of his beloved golf trophies. He found me just as I was dropping the Captain's Anniversary Vase fifteen feet onto the patio. It's now in about two thousand pieces."

I fight the urge to snigger. "And then what?"

"That's when he punched me."

Any lingering urge to snigger dissipates in an instant.

"I don't know what to say, sis," I reply, trying to stay calm. "What lowlife kind of man punches a woman?"

"A self-obsessed, narcissistic, bully of a man," she replies.

It appears Kate now also shares my decidedly low opinion of her husband.

"But he's also the same man who controls my finances, and he's frozen my access to the joint bank account. In fact, he controls everything now."

"What do you mean?"

"I came back from town just before lunch and he'd changed the locks. There was a suitcase outside the front door with a letter attached saying I was trespassing and, if I didn't leave immediately, he'd call the police and enforce a restraining order."

"No way," I boom. "He can't do that, surely?"

She rests her elbows on the table and takes a second to steel herself.

"He can if I'm unfit to be around Bella," she sniffles. "Because apparently I'm mentally unstable, and the vase throwing incident was just one in a long line of supposed examples he'd catalogued to prove just how unstable I am. He's taken every silly mistake I've made over the last few years and blown them out of all proportion. Honestly, Adam, that list makes me out to be the world's worst mother."

Under any other circumstances, I'd be revelling in the fact I'm no longer the only mentally unstable member of the family. Well, I would if I didn't know my sister is anything but mentally unstable.

"He's even sent a letter to the school threatening them with legal action if they let me anywhere near Bella. I've spoken to the headmistress and she's not prepared to take the risk so I can't even pick my own daughter up from school. He's doing it to punish me and prove who's really in control."

I sit back in my chair. "Fuck. The devious bastard."

"You said it."

"What are you going to do? Surely you should report him to the police for hitting you?"

"Don't you think I've already threatened that? It's his word against mine and who do you think they'll believe: a well-respected lawyer, or an unfit mother with a list of allegations against her? He'll say I did it myself, and then he'll have something else to add to his list."

Not only is it clear just how far from perfect Kate's marriage really is, but her life is now immeasurably more fucked than mine has ever been. It's not an irony I can take any satisfaction from.

"Have you told Mum and Dad?"

"Of course not, and neither can you. They've already got enough to cope with at the moment and the last thing Dad needs is this kind of stress."

"So, what are you going to do?"

Beyond heading over to their house and yelling threats at a locked door until the police arrive, I'm lacking inspiration.

"I don't know, Adam" she replies, her voice close to breaking again. "I really don't."

A voice calls out from the other side of the kitchen. "I do."

We both turn to the door where Mungo is stood, still sporting his nasty yellow jumper.

"Have you been eavesdropping?" I ask.

"Yes. The walls in this flat conduct sound extremely well."

His admission derails my annoyance at his nosiness.

"Well, seeing as you've heard it all, you might as well give us the benefit of your wisdom."

Kate shoots me a look which I detect isn't one of agreement.

"Just hear him out," I say in an attempt to ease her concern. "What have you got to lose?"

"Okay," she sighs. "I'm listening."

Mungo takes a few steps into the kitchen. "I simply need to spend ten minutes in a room with your husband."

"To do what?" I snort. "I mean, that jumper is terrifyingly awful but it's not going to scare Ethan into backing down."

"Very amusing," he replies, although his face doesn't relay any amusement. "Do you want my assistance, or not?"

"Why do you want to meet Ethan?" Kate interjects. "I'm not sure what good it'll do."

"I don't want to meet him," Mungo replies. "It is a necessity to change his mind-set."

I catch a glance from Kate and I know what she's thinking. Coupled with his monotone voice, Mungo's words sound like a threat.

"It's very kind of you to offer, Dr Mungo, but Ethan has a short fuse and I don't want you to get hurt."

"He cannot hurt me," Mungo replies.

"I'll go with him," I offer, mindful of the way Mungo dealt with Angry Pete.

My sister looks at me, and then at Mungo. How desperate must a person be to entrust their future to a hapless window cleaner and a pint-sized oddball?

"I don't know what it'll achieve," she replies. "But if you think it's worth a try."

Very desperate it seems.

"When does he get home?" I ask.

"You can't go over there tonight because I don't want a scene in front of Bella. She'll be at ballet practice tomorrow evening, though, so you can go then."

"What time?"

"One of the other parents picks her up at six-thirty."

I turn to Mungo. "We'll leave here at quarter past six then."

"Very well."

I suspect Kate has questions but, before she can get the first one out, Mungo trots off back to his room.

"Is this a good idea?" she whispers, conscious of Mungo overhearing again. "I mean, it's kind of him to offer but you know what Ethan is like. It's hard to see any way Dr Mungo can influence him."

"I honestly don't know, sis, but unless you've got a shedload of money to hire a decent solicitor, what else can you do?"

Her silence speaks volumes.

Another, more practical, issue suddenly crosses my mind. It's a question I hope already has an answer.

"Have you got somewhere to stay?"

"You remember my best friend from school, Donna? I'm staying with her. She's the only real friend I've got."

"I thought you had loads of friends? All those people you have drinks and dinner with."

"They're not my friends," she hisses. "They're people I put up with to keep Ethan happy."

"Right. How is Donna? I haven't seen her since I was a teenager."

"She's good, although yet another boyfriend dumped her last week. I think she's glad to have the company."

"Is she still podgy?" I ask in a cack-handed attempt to lighten the mood.

"She's not podgy," Kate frowns. "She's just big boned."

Judging by her solemn expression, I think it'll take more than a few gags from me to lighten her mood. Understandable, I guess, seeing as her entire life has been turned upside down. What is it they say: the higher you climb, the greater the fall? I've never really had that far to fall but every bump has hurt. I can't imagine how hard it must be for Kate to be kept apart from her daughter.

Then again, isn't that precisely what my future holds if I don't get my act together?

I reach across the table and grab her hand. "I'll do my best, you know. I promise."

"I know you will, but I'd rather you promise not to get yourself in any trouble."

"Trust me."

"Seriously, Adam. Ethan had a security system installed last year so there are cameras everywhere. If you overstep the mark, it'll just give him more ammunition, if and when this goes to court."

I have no intention of overstepping any mark but I guess I should warn Mungo. I'm no wiser than Kate as to what he's got in mind, but I'm hoping he'll use his logic to pull Ethan's allegations apart. Besides that, I'm not sure what he can do.

"Don't worry. I'm just going to chaperone Mungo so I'll

keep out if it."

Her face adopts the *what the hell am I doing* expression again and she checks her watch.

"I'd better get going," she sighs. "Donna's cooking dinner tonight, bless her."

"Right. Are you going over to see Dad later?"

"I've already been. You have no idea how hard it was putting on a brave face."

"I'd have been more concerned about your actual face. Didn't they notice your bruise?"

"Of course they did but I said it was the result of an errant elbow at Zumba class."

"And they believed you?"

"To be honest, they were more interested in telling me their plans."

"Plans? What plans?"

"They're talking of moving to the coast. When I left, they were poring over maps of West Wittering."

It's news to me, but I guess there's nothing like a near-death experience to bring the future into focus.

"How's Dad doing, anyway?"

"Unbelievably well, considering. Are you going over?"

"I was planning to, once I've had a bite to eat."

"Remember what I said, Adam. You know how protective Dad can be and I don't want him discharging himself and doing something stupid."

"Like father, like son, eh?"

"Exactly," she replies, getting to her feet. "You'll give me a call the minute you get back tomorrow, won't you?"

"Of course, hopefully with some positive news."

She smiles but looks unconvinced.

I see her to the door and, after a long hug, watch her clack back down the stairs. Even when I hear the main door slam shut, I remain standing at the doorway. A strange feeling wells inside of me; a feeling I haven't felt in a long, long time. It seems I've rediscovered my sense of fraternal responsibility and, with it, a desire to make Ethan pay for what he's doing to my kid sister. I can't be sure if my hatred for Ethan is the stronger of the feelings, but I do know I need to step up and be the big brother I once was.

Another day, another challenge.

33.

I slept like a baby. In fact, I can't remember the last time I slept so well but it must have been before Daisy walked out.

Before I visited Dad in hospital yesterday evening, I tried to extract more information from Mungo about his intentions when we visit Ethan later. Apart from repeatedly telling me I should trust him, he gave nothing away. I guess I'll find out in a little over ten hours.

Before that, though, I've got another busy day ahead of me.

I'm just necking my second coffee of the day and preparing to leave when Mungo wanders into the kitchen.

"Second day in a row you've had a lie in," I comment. "Did buyer's remorse keep you awake?"

"Your attempts at humour regarding my jumper are becoming tedious."

"Ooh, sorry," I mockingly jibe. "Did someone get out of the wrong side of bed?"

"And that saying is as ridiculous as you are unfunny. What possible difference can it make what side of the bed one exits from?"

"Now you mention it, I have no idea. Why do people say that?"

"It is a superstition from Roman times. They believed it was bad luck to exit the bed from the left, or the wrong side as they saw it."

"Oh, interesting."

"Not really."

Rather than maintain his usual position in the doorway, Mungo shuffles across to the table and sits down. Once seated, he folds his arms and stares into space.

"You alright, Mungo? You don't seem yourself this morning."

"Myself?" he replies, not even bothering to look at me.

"Yeah. You seem, I don't know, in a bad mood."

"Moods of any kind are nothing more than a heightened emotional state. As you are aware, I prefer to keep my emotions to myself."

"Well, you're not doing a great job this morning. Maybe you should have another stab at coffee, with sugar and milk this time."

He continues to stare into space and just as I'm about to give up and leave, he turns to me.

"I will try coffee, with milk and sugar."

"Seriously?"

"Yes."

I glance up at the clock. Seeing as I've got five minutes to spare I flick the switch on the kettle.

The already hot water reaches boiling point within a minute and I pour out Mungo's coffee, complete with milk and two teaspoons of sugar.

"Here you go."

He takes the mug with both hands and holds it to his mouth. After a brief pause, he takes a sip.

"A vast improvement," he comments.

"And you're not worried about the evils of caffeine, or cow's milk, or sugar for that matter?"

"One cup will not kill me."

It's a U-turn of Westminster proportions but I don't have time to question why.

"You enjoy your coffee then. Some of us have got windows to clean."

He offers a slight nod before returning his lips to the mug.

"Oh, and don't forget we're going to see Ethan later."

Another nod and I leave Mungo sipping his coffee.

My first test of the day comes courtesy of Alan. It takes almost ten minutes to get him started and every one of those minutes compounds my annoyance until I'm on the verge of a full-blown hissy fit. By the time I pull off the drive, I know I've got a decision to make regarding Alan's future. If I can't stay mobile I'm up shit creek—perhaps it might be prudent to invest some of Mungo's rent money on a new van before my current van finally gives up on me.

As if he'd read my thoughts, Alan decides he'd better behave himself, and continues to do so for the rest of the morning.

I return home before noon, having completed eight houses in a new record time. I'd like to put that record down to self-motivation but it's more likely because the plastic bottles are being delivered sometime around one o'clock. If I miss the delivery, I'll have to collect them myself from the depot, and that would involve untold trips I don't have time for.

There's no reply when I open the front door and call Mungo's name. Maybe he got my less-than-subtle hints about the jumper and decided to return it. Considering his odder-than-usual mood this morning, it's probably no bad thing he's gone out.

I make myself a cheese sandwich and eat it at the kitchen table; grateful to be sat on my arse doing nothing for ten minutes. Unfortunately, ten minutes is all I can spare as I've emails to check. I clamber to my feet, retrieve the laptop from the lounge, and boot it up.

The first email is from the printer, confirming I can collect the first batch of labels this afternoon. Another task to add to my list. The rest of my inbox is full of the usual spam, besides an email from Joe. He rarely emails so I'm curious enough to open it up.

I scan the two lines of text and as I do, a smile creeps across my face. It appears my little idea has come off, and a firm of solicitors have asked him in for a meeting having been impressed with the unsolicited logo he sent them. The only negative is the invoice he's attached. I know he won't have charged much for his work but as I'm haemorrhaging cash at the moment, I'm sure Joe won't mind waiting a week or two.

With nothing else better to do while I await my delivery, I open Facebook and scan the drivel posted by people who aren't really my friends. I promised myself I wouldn't but I can't help myself, and click on Daisy's profile. It's a decision I immediately regret when I spot her relationship status has been changed to 'single'.

Idiot!

I slam the laptop lid closed and slump back in the chair.

Why should I be surprised? It's not as though Daisy hasn't made it clear we're over, but seeing her publicly announce the fact is like a kick in the teeth. In a matter of seconds, my motivation ebbs away and the dull ache returns with a vengeance.

One step forward, two steps back.

Any hope of spending my time productively is quashed as I sit and stare at the laptop. Two doors appear in my mind: one leading to the pub and whisky-fuelled obliteration, the other leading to a straight and narrow path. I'm drawn to the first door. Would it really hurt to shed the shackles of responsibility for one afternoon? I snatch my phone and start typing a short message to Joe, asking if he'd like to join me in the Red Lion. Just as my thumb is about to press the send icon, a call arrives.

Irritated at the interruption, I answer curtly. "Yes?"

"Is that Mr Maxwell?"

"Who is this?"

"Derek from Barnes Transport. I'm sat outside the address you gave for your delivery."

"Oh, right. Give me a second and I'll come down."

It seems the pub will have to wait.

I scuttle down the stairs and out the front door to find a truck parked on the kerb. The driver, presumably Derek, clambers from the cab and slopes over.

"I didn't realise I was delivering to a residential address," he grumbles.

"Is that a problem then?"

"Not for me it ain't."

He gestures, I follow, and we make our way to the rear of the truck. After pressing a button to lower the tailgate, the rear shutter is rolled up to reveal a wall of boxes.

"I'm guessing you ain't got a forklift truck handy?" Derek asks.

"Funnily enough, no."

"Good luck then. I'll wait here while you unload."

He then leans up against the tailgate and plucks a packet of cigarettes from his pocket.

"Sorry. How many of these boxes are mine then?" I ask.

"All eighty-four."

"Are you going to help?"

"Sorry, mate. You ain't got a forklift and humping boxes ain't in my job description."

I shake my head, step onto the tailgate, and grab the first box. It weighs practically nothing so I stack two more on top and consider adding a fourth before realising I won't be able to see where I'm going.

Stepping down from the tailgate, I begin the slow walk to the garage. I make a dozen steps before Derek calls out.

"Mate, where you going with those boxes?"

I turn around and glare at him. "I thought I'd take them for a stroll around the park, and maybe catch a movie afterwards."

He glares back, apparently unamused by my sarcasm.

"I'm taking them to the garage," I huff.

"I ain't got time to wait," he barks. "Just unload them onto your driveway."

I curse under my breath and place the three boxes down.

Derek appears quite happy to stand idle and puff away on his cigarette while I shuffle back and forth between the truck and the driveway. Carrying three boxes at a time, I make the journey twenty-eight times until the truck is empty.

"Appreciate your help," I snipe, signing the delivery docket.

"Anytime," he grins before returning to his cab.

I'm left stood in a cloud of diesel fumes as the truck rolls away. Perhaps God is punishing me for almost giving in to temptation earlier, as once I'm rid of the feckless delivery driver, the first spit of rain arrives.

"Bloody marvellous," I groan.

Twenty-eight, more urgent, journeys then ensue as I move the boxes from the driveway to the garage. As I stack the final pile, the heavens open. My relief is temporary when I survey the garage and realise I'll have to rearrange all the boxes and the fluid containers to create some space to do the mixing, bottling, and labelling.

It's a job that saps another hour but at least it keeps me occupied, and the lure of whisky gradually fades. By the time I slam the garage door shut, I've reach a conclusion. Based upon my earlier experience, and much like a plate-spinner, I know I've got to keep moving otherwise my endeavours thus far will end up in shattered pieces at my feet. It seems I can either die of a broken heart, or exhaustion, and the latter is preferable.

I leave thoughts of Daisy on the driveway and head off to the printers.

Seeing the bottle labels on Joe's computer monitor was one thing but seeing them for real is another. As Steve in the print shop shows me an example sheet, containing a dozen self-adhesive, glossy labels, a lump of pride bobs in my throat.

"They look amazing," I comment.

"Whoever designed them did a cracking job," Steve replies. "Printing them was the easy part."

"I'll pass that on to my mate. He came up with the design and he'll appreciate the positive feedback."

"If you don't mind, can you give him my number and ask him to give me a call? We're always getting requests for artwork design and we can handle most of it but sometimes the customers want something beyond our limited design skills."

"Yeah, of course. I'm sure he'd appreciate the work."

Steve takes my payment and I leave with two boxes significantly heavier than those I shifted earlier.

Labels acquired, I've got one final collection to make before I can head home. Whilst I was at the tip the other day, getting rid of the crap from the garage, I spotted a pile of old bathtubs behind one of the dumpsters. And seeing as Dad's old self-brew barrel is far too small to mix the quantities of Crystalene I need, it struck me a bathtub might be a better option. After a ten second conversation with a surly woman at the tip, I leave with a plastic bathtub in the back of Alan, along with an old trestle table I might have accidentally liberated when the surly woman wasn't looking.

Twenty minutes later, I'm stood in the garage, or as it will now be called, my production facility. I now have everything I need to launch my new venture, except for some actual customers, that is. It's a troubling thought. Up to this point, everything has been about the planning and I've conveniently avoided thinking about the execution. Tomorrow, I'll have no choice, and once I've got the first few hundred bottles ready, the real hard work will begin.

Nervous doesn't cover it.

I slam the garage door shut and head back up to the flat.

I'm not met by the usual silence but the sound of muffled voices coming from the lounge. If I'm being burgled, it seems odd they'd come as a duo and sit around chatting on the sofa.

I tentatively open the door.

Although I'm yet to experience it, my shock is akin to a parent walking in on their teenage son, mid-wank.

"What on earth are you doing, Mungo?"

He looks up from the sofa. "Watching television, if it is not obvious."

"But … you don't watch television."

"Up until this morning, I did not drink coffee."

"Oh, right. So when I watch TV, it's not a constructive use of my time. But it's okay for you to watch it?"

He ignores me, turning his attention back to the screen.

"What are you watching, anyway?"

"As far as I can tell, it is some kind of competition," he replies, not moving his eyes. "The challenge is to purchase antiques and sell them at auction for a profit, although neither contestant has apparently grasped that fact."

I watch on as Mungo becomes increasingly agitated during the auction process.

"Foolish man," he spits as a hideous vase sells for half the price it was purchased for. "I knew that item was a poor choice."

I sense Mungo is talking to himself, rather than me, but it's not so much his lack of conversation that concerns me, but his obvious agitation. Despite my best efforts, he hasn't as much as raised his voice since he moved in. Yet, here he is, getting irritated at a TV show.

"Are you okay, Mungo? You seem ... a bit, err, annoyed."

"Do I?"

"Yes, you do."

"It is to be expected. Nothing for you to concern yourself with."

"Sorry, what do you mean, *be expected*?"

My question appears to spike his irritation and he lets out a sigh.

"It is a result of your treatment," he replies dismissively. "As your logic slowly returns, I lose it at the same degree. Therefore, my emotions will become more pronounced."

I'm no doctor but surely that's not how these things work. If people could simply swap their neurosis with a donor, surely Simon Cowell would have offloaded his arrogance and penchant for high-waisted trousers a long time ago.

"You don't mean literally, do you?" I ask, still puzzled. "I mean, that would be impossible."

"Do you mind?" he snaps back. "I am trying to watch the programme."

"Alright, calm down," I reply, raising my hands. "I'll leave you in peace, but whatever this is, I hope you've dealt with it by the time we visit Ethan later."

He nods but doesn't take his eyes off the screen.

I leave him to it and head to the bathroom for a ridiculously long shower.

Mindful I need to keep my plates spinning, I then waste an hour changing the bed linen. I'm fairly sure it was a task Daisy completed in five minutes but to a novice such as myself, it proves an epic challenge. At the fourth attempt I finally get most of the duvet into the cover, only to discover it's the wrong way around and many inches of duvet cover are still homeless. I try again, and come close to taking the whole sorry pile of crumpled fabric into the garden and burning it. Common sense just about prevails. Eventually, I get the damn thing in the right way, and then change the pillowcases, which is a significantly easier task. Job done, I then scoop the dirty linen from the floor and drop it in the wash basket; all but one item—a pillowcase. I scrunch it into a ball and, holding it to my nose, draw a deep breath. Much like the woman herself, the scent of Daisy's perfume has all but left.

I toss it into the wash basket.

With half hour still to kill, and despite not having much of an appetite, I throw a ready-meal into the microwave. As I sit and eat, I become aware there's no longer any sound coming from the lounge. Hopefully Mungo has calmed down and is now readying himself to leave; ideally by changing his jumper.

I finish my excuse for a meal, wash the cutlery and wander into the hallway.

"You nearly ready?" I ask, rapping on Mungo's door.

It's no great surprise he doesn't answer. "I'll wait in the lounge."

I'm tempted to switch the TV on but my mind has turned to Ethan and our impending visit. As I sit on the sofa, I imagine the many ways I'd like to inflict my own version of justice on the arsehole. I still don't know what Mungo has in mind but I hope it involves a pair of blunt scissors and Ethan's genitals.

"I am ready."

I look up and inwardly groan.

"Really, Mungo? Was there a sale on?"

"What do you mean?"

"Was the store offering a huge discount on hideous jumpers, because I can't think of any good reason you'd have bought more than one."

"You do not like *Harvest Green*?"

"Is that what they call it? If I was a farmer and my harvest turned out that shade of green, I'd incinerate the lot."

He frowns. "Are we going, or not?"

"Yes, we are," I reply, getting to my feet. "And I really do hope you've got a plan for Ethan as I want to see that arsehole suffer."

Mungo's frown turns into a twisted smile.

"Trust me, Adam Maxwell. I do."

34.

It's a pity Bella's ballet lessons don't start later as we catch the tail end of the rush hour traffic. Sitting in yet another queue, I jab the buttons on the stereo in the hope of finding something worth listening to. I settle on an old Eminem track called *Stan*. I'm not a huge fan of rap music but I don't mind this particular track.

We continue to edge slowly forwards whilst Eminem raps about a crazed fan, unsurprisingly called Stan, and Dido croons the chorus.

"What is this piece of music?" Mungo asks.

"Not sure I'd call it music, but it's called *Stan*."

He tilts his head slightly, almost like a dog cocking its ear to a distant sound.

"The style is unusual; almost poetic in nature."

"I thought you didn't like contemporary music?"

"This is not without merit. What genre would you call it?"

"Rap."

"Interesting. I would like to hear more rap."

It's the first time Mungo has shown a liking for any music I've played, and I'm surprised rap appeals considering his very particular, if not peculiar, use of the English language. I hope to God he doesn't come home tomorrow sporting a baseball cap and gold chain.

"I'll pull some popular rap tracks from Spotify later. I think you'll find NWA … interesting."

"NWA? Is that an acronym?"

"Yes, it is."

"For?"

"Um, google it."

The bottleneck eases and the procession finally moves beyond first gear.

Ten minutes later we pull up opposite the entrance to a plush cul-de-sac and I kill Alan's engine. I'm grateful for the cover of darkness as it looks like we're casing one of the houses to burgle.

"Why have you parked here?" Mungo asks.

"Because we're a few minutes early. We need to wait until Bella has gone."

Almost on cue, a silver Mercedes saloon glides past us and

turns into the cul-de-sac. Of the five, architect-designed houses, Kate and Ethan's home sits at the head of the cul-de-sac and I watch on as the silver Mercedes pulls onto the vast driveway, coming to a stop next to Ethan's Porsche. The driver beeps the horn and seconds later, the front door opens and the tiny figure of my niece scampers across to her ride.

"Okay, she's off," I say. "You ready?"

I don't wait for a reply and turn the ignition key. Alan coughs and splutters but fails to start so I try again. And again.

After the fifth failed attempt, I give up.

"I think we'll walk. Come on."

I get out and join Mungo on the road. We set off up the cul-de-sac past the huge houses—each a series of sleek lines and whitewashed walls; a statement of wealth rather than a home. Quite why Kate and Ethan were looking to move is beyond me. I can't imagine there are many more rungs on the property ladder beyond their current abode.

The second we step onto the driveway a security light flicks on, dashing my hopes of running a key alongside Ethan's precious Porsche. We approach the imposing front door—a slab of oak the size of a dining room table—and ring the bell. As we wait, I spot the camera above the door and realise I haven't told Mungo about Ethan's security precautions.

"Shit, I forgot to tell you. Apparently there are security cameras everywhere so be careful what you do."

"The cameras are of no concern to me."

Whatever strategy he has in mind, clearly it won't involve anything physical.

We continue to wait. In a house this size, I guess it could be quite a walk to the front door but, with my patience already thin, I press the bell again.

Another five or six seconds pass before I hear the door being unlocked from the inside.

It finally swings open and Ethan, wearing suit trousers and a white shirt, glares at us.

"What the hell are you doing here?" he blasts.

I'd already planned my opening gambit but now I'm here, the urge just to launch myself at Ethan and pummel the bastard is almost irresistible. I take a step forward, my fists clenched. Perhaps sensing my fury, Mungo makes the first move.

"I wish to speak with you, Ethan Montgomery," he says.

"About what?"

"I have a proposition."

"Whatever it is, I'm not interested."

"It would be in your best interests to hear me out. May we come in?"

Mungo stares up at the significantly bigger man and waits for a response.

"I'm not letting him in," Ethan spits, nodding towards me. "He's not house trained."

My fists ball tighter.

"He will behave himself," Mungo replies. "You have my word."

Mungo then holds out his hand. Instinctively, Ethan takes up the offer and the two men shake hands. I don't know what is considered a socially acceptable period for a handshake but after three shakes Mungo continues to hold Ethan's hand. However, rather than pull away, Ethan stares down at Mungo, as if transfixed by his turquoise eyes.

"I'll give you five minutes," Ethan eventually mumbles. "But I'll warn you now: there are security cameras inside the house and if he steps out of line, it'll just make matters worse for his sister."

Ethan ushers Mungo into the house and steps back to let me pass.

"I mean it," he reiterates as I step onto the polished tiles in the hallway. "You so much as raise your voice and I'll call the police."

He closes the door as I survey the vast entrance hall and vaulted ceiling twenty feet above my head.

"We'll do this in the kitchen."

We follow Ethan through the hallway to a kitchen bigger than my entire flat, and probably of greater value judging by the number of gloss-white units and acres of polished granite work surface.

Ethan sits down at a glass table almost as large as the front door. He picks up a glass of red wine and takes a quick sip before sitting back in his chair.

"What's this proposition then?" he asks.

Despite there being seven empty chairs, Mungo sits right next to Ethan. I'd rather keep my distance and pull up a chair the opposite side of the table.

"Your relationship with Kate Montgomery," Mungo replies. "I believe it is no longer tenable?"

"I never said that. If Kate is willing to apologise and improve her behaviour, I see no reason why we can't pick up where we left off."

"Are you fucking kidding me?" I interject. "You hit Kate and expect *her* to apologise?"

"It was nothing," he says, glibly. "I was drunk and she just pressed the wrong buttons."

"Right. So, it'd be okay if I punch you in the face because you're certainly pressing my wrong buttons."

"I knew this was a mistake," he replies, getting to his feet. "I don't know what I was thinking, letting you in. I'd like you to leave. Now."

Mungo doesn't budge and I follow his lead. We reach a silent impasse as Ethan glares down at us.

"I should warn you," he then adds. "There's a camera in here and it records sound too. So, I'll ask you one final time—leave."

"Sit down," Mungo replies.

"Don't tell me what to do in my own home," Ethan barks.

"You have not heard my proposition yet. Trust me: you need to hear it."

Mungo's calm authority appears to do the trick and Ethan begrudgingly retakes his seat.

"If he so much as opens his mouth again, this discussion is over," Ethan says, nodding in my direction.

"He will remain silent," Mungo confirms, fixing me with a stare.

"Get on with it then," Ethan demands, before taking another sip of wine.

"Your behaviour towards your wife is unacceptable."

"My behaviour towards my wife, or anyone else, is none of your damn business."

"It is now—it threatens my plans."

"What are you talking about?"

Mungo pauses for a second, drumming his fingers on the glass surface.

"My plans are none of *your* business but they are being undermined by your behaviour. It is clear there are irreconcilable differences in your marriage and, as I understand it, Kate Montgomery has no desire to continue the relationship."

"Her loss," Ethan shrugs. "But she won't get a penny from me and she'll never see Arabella again."

"I presumed that would be your starting position, which is why I wanted to discuss a proposition. Call it a compromise if you will."

"You can propose what you like, but the law is on my side so I won't be making any compromises."

"Hear me out."

"Whatever."

Mungo clears his throat. "My proposition is simple. You will sign this property over to Kate Montgomery, along with full custody of your daughter and fifty percent of all your assets. You will then pay her forty percent of your net income until your daughter reaches eighteen years of age. I believe that is fair."

Ethan sits back in his chair and starts to chuckle.

"Oh, that's absolutely priceless," he chortles. "Ridiculous, but priceless."

Mungo frowns as Ethan's chuckle develops into full-blown laughter.

"Ha ha … give her a million pound house. As if."

Clearly Mungo isn't used to his advice being greeted with laughter and his frown deepens.

"Honestly," Ethan sniggers. "You're wasting my time. I've ensured she won't get a bean from me, you deluded little man."

Ethan's jeering is the final straw. I ready myself to get up and deliver a long-overdue punch to his smug face.

"Silence!" Mungo suddenly yells.

Ethan's laughter peters out and his grin quickly follows. My own desire to deliver a punch goes the same way, such is my shock at Mungo's uncharacteristic loss of patience. He then reaches across the table and places his hand on Ethan's forearm, almost in an act of reassurance. I'd have expected Ethan to withdraw his arm but, instead, he stares down at Mungo's hand.

"Listen to me, you loathsome excuse for a man," Mungo growls, his usually calm tone noticeably absent. "You *will* accept my proposition."

I'm not sure if I'm more gobsmacked than Ethan, although we both respond to Mungo's outburst with stunned silence. I wait for a reaction which doesn't take long to come as Ethan tries to pull his arm from beneath Mungo's hand. The split second he makes his move, Mungo's fingers wrap around Ethan's forearm.

The two men stare at each other and it's clear from his twitching shoulder Ethan is trying hard to pull his arm away.

"Let go," he yelps, clearly confused how such a slight man can possibly be holding his muscled arm in place. He's not alone.

"Do you accept my proposition?" Mungo asks, his voice

level again.

"Like hell I do. Now, let go."

"Not until you agree."

Ethan looks towards the corner of the kitchen; to a camera fixed on the wall.

"This man is assaulting me," he shouts, for the benefit of the camera. "He's refusing to release my arm and leave."

He then turns back to Mungo. "Whatever trick this is, it won't work," he snarls. "You have no idea who I am or the amount of trouble I can bring to your door."

Mungo leans forward and fixes Ethan with an icy stare. "You can shout at the camera all you like—it is of no consequence. And as for your threat, let me make it clear it is I who will be bringing the trouble if you do not comply with my request."

The dynamic shifts when Ethan realises I am the lesser of his troubles. With Mungo not listening, he tries his negotiating skills on me.

"Tell your psychotic friend to let go of me and I'll let this pass. It's a one-time offer."

I shrug my shoulders. "Can't help you. I'd do as he says if I were you, and we can all get on with our evening."

The cogs whirl as he takes a moment to consider his options.

He eventually turns back to Mungo. "Fine, whatever. I agree to your proposition so let go of my arm and leave."

"I do not believe you."

"Believe what you like but unless you're going to keep hold of my arm all evening, your options are limited."

Ethan's smug expression returns with the realisation he can say whatever he likes knowing there's no threat beyond having his arm held.

Mungo then leans forward, his hand still locked around Ethan's arm. "Your problems will only begin once I leave. If you do not comply, and a formal offer is not with Kate Montgomery within twenty-four hours, there will be grave consequences for you."

"Are you threatening me?" Ethan confirms, again loud enough for the camera to hear.

Mungo thinks for a moment. "Yes. I believe I am."

"And I'm supposed to be scared? You can't touch me, and I won't make the same mistake of letting you into my home again."

"Trust me," Mungo replies. "My presence in your home is

the least of your concerns. It is my presence in your head you should be concerned about."

"What's that supposed to mean?"

"You will find out, later this evening."

Without warning, Mungo then sits back and releases his grasp on Ethan's arm. Like a scalded cat, my pathetic excuse for a brother-in-law scrambles to his feet and pulls his phone from a pocket.

"Get out, now," he yells. "I'm calling the police."

"Call them if you wish, but my work here is done," Mungo replies calmly. "We are leaving."

He gets up and waves a hand in my direction to beckon me along. I guess we are leaving. I slowly stand and glance at Ethan; his expression mirrors my own confusion.

I follow Mungo out of the kitchen and back through the hallway. Despite a cricket score of questions begging for answers, the only sound I emit is the squeaking of my trainers on the polished floor.

We reach the door and Mungo heaves it open. I'm about to follow him out when he spins around and looks straight past me. I turn my head and follow his line of sight to Ethan, stood at the far end of the hallway.

"Sweet dreams, Ethan Montgomery," Mungo calls out.

As his voice echoes around the cavernous hallway, he makes his exit.

With Ethan stood mute, and perhaps perplexed by Mungo's parting words, the temptation to deliver a parting shot of my own proves too much.

"You so much as glance at my sister again, I'll fucking kill you."

I slam the door shut and scurry after Mungo.

We clear the driveway and a dozen yards before the first question finally breaks free.

"What the hell just happened?" I hiss.

"I enacted my plan."

"What plan? You held his arm, made some vague threat, and left."

"As I said, I enacted my plan, but it was no vague threat. He will comply."

He marches on and I'm left scratching my head for the half a minute it takes to reach Alan.

After the aborted attempt earlier, I'm relieved to find Alan in a more accommodating mood and he starts on the third turn of the key. Mungo, however, appears less accommodating.

"What am I supposed to tell Kate?" I ask.

"Tell her Ethan Montgomery will agree to my proposition."

"And if I do that, I'll assume she'll ask the same question I want answered: why would he?"

"You will see."

"That's not an answer."

"It is the only answer I can provide."

I take my frustration out on Alan's gearbox and ram it into second as we pull away from a junction.

"Seeing as you're not prepared to give me a straight answer to that question, at least tell me what came over you back there. You're the one who was supposed to remain calm."

"As I have already told you, my ability for rational thought is no longer what it was."

"Come off it, Mungo. That excuse has more than a hint of bullshit to it."

"It is not an excuse. It is a fact."

"Is it? Just because you lost your cool back there, it doesn't prove anything."

"Did you lose *your* cool?"

"What? Christ knows how, but you know I didn't."

"There you are then. I may have let my emotions dictate my behaviour, but you did not. Before your treatment, you would have acted differently—without thought or common sense—and the result would have been damaging to your sister."

Bullshit excuse or not, I can't argue with his assessment. I had every reason to give Ethan a good kicking, but somehow I ignored the screaming voice in my head and walked away without administering so much as a mild slap. For once, I'm not now wallowing in a pool of my own regret.

As satisfying as it might be not harbouring regrets, the raft of unanswered questions cast a shadow over my achievement.

"What did you mean about getting inside Ethan's head?"

"It is what I do."

"I meant, specifically. And what exactly will he find out later this evening?"

"He will find out the consequences of his actions."

"What consequences?"

"You would not understand."

"I'm not a child, Mungo. Try me."

"All you need to understand is that Ethan Montgomery will agree to my proposition."

266

Exasperated, I try another angle. "Okay, when will he agree to it?"

"Within three to five days. It is impossible to predict precisely when."

"And how …?"

"Enough," he retorts. "Your questions are becoming an irritation. He *will* agree, and there is nothing more to be said on the matter."

True to his word, Mungo remains silent for the rest of the journey home.

If I've learnt anything from my time with Mungo, it's knowing when to leave him be. Whatever ridiculous notion he has about Ethan agreeing to his proposition, there is little I can do to change the outcome one way or another. I guess I've just got to trust Mungo, although I'm not sure Kate will be so accepting of the situation.

Back in the flat, a five minute phone call confirms just how little acceptance she possesses.

"Is that it?" Kate sighs.

"We've just got to trust Mungo."

"There's no way Ethan will just give in like that. It's not in his nature."

"I honestly don't know what else to tell you, sis. Mungo is convinced Ethan will agree to those terms."

"But …"

"Kate, please. I know what's at stake here and, believe you me, I want it resolved just as much as you do. We've just got to give it a few days."

"I want to see my daughter."

I don't need to be in the same room to know Kate is close to shedding tears.

"And you will. Just try and be patient."

"Do I have any other choice?"

I consider the option of returning to the house and jumping up and down on Ethan's face until he relents. As tempting as it is, the consequences wouldn't bode well for Kate, or me.

"Hang in there, Kate, and you'll see Bella soon enough."

My words carry the stench of insincerity because I remain unconvinced myself. I'm not sure which is worse: a plan you don't believe in or no plan at all.

"I hope so, Adam."

Kate ends the call, leaving me under no illusion just how disappointed she is. It's a disappointment I share but I'm as much at Mungo's mercy as she is.

The man himself is back in his bedroom and I'm tempted to have another go at extracting some answers. If it were just his stubbornness to contend with, I'd already be banging on his door, but his change of behaviour is a worry and I can't predict how he'll react if I push too hard.

Maybe I'll try again tomorrow. It's not like I've anything else on my schedule to worry about.

35.

Six-thirty in the morning—wide awake and plans for the day ahead are already formulating in my head. It's amazing what a difference a good night's sleep makes, and I put that down to my hectic day yesterday; a far cry from the lazy days I once enjoyed pre-Mungo.

The only two black clouds spoiling my otherwise positive forecast for the day are both of the female formation.

Helplessness is a rotten feeling and that's precisely how I felt last night because, somehow, Kate's problem has become my problem. They say ignorance is bliss, and I was always quite content being ignorant of anyone else's problems, but I suppose you can't be both ignorant and responsible. Now I've got myself involved, I can't do anything else but see it through.

The other cloud is Daisy's impending scan. Beyond knowing it's this week, I don't even know if it's happening today, tomorrow, or Friday. I've parked my annoyance at not being invited but the fact remains I won't get to see those first images of my unborn child. Neither will I have one of those photos all expectant fathers possess and proudly show to friends who couldn't be less interested.

In hindsight, I should have made it clear to Daisy just how important it is to me, rather than throw a tantrum about Eddie. There's nobody to blame but myself and nothing I can do about it now, other than to put it to the back of my mind.

I shake the negativity from my thoughts, get up, and begin my morning routine.

By the time I sit down for my second coffee, there's still no sign of Mungo. I did, however, notice the contents of the coffee jar have declined significantly since yesterday. If he develops a similar appetite for Coco Pops, stern words will be exchanged.

My plan for the day begins with an executive decision—there will be no window cleaning today but I'll work on Saturday to keep up with the schedule. I've never cleaned windows on a weekend before because Daisy liked us to do the kind of things couples are supposed to do at weekends. At the time I was usually reluctant, especially when our day out involved a shopping centre. How times change: I never thought I'd miss loitering outside the Top Shop changing rooms quite so much.

I wash up my mug and head down to the garage.

Once I've got everything prepared, I start mixing a small batch of Crystalene I can use for samples. My strategy, if you can call it that, is to visit a number of local businesses, ranging from car valets through to hardware stores. I'm hoping they'll either use it or stock it, once I've demonstrated how effective it is and relayed the environmental benefits. If any of them are still dubious, I'll leave a trial bottle in the hope of securing an order once they've given it a try themselves.

Using a calculator for the first time since school, I work out the correct ratios for the four ingredients. The old plastic bathtub proves a blessing, but not before I tip in a litre of fluid, which drains straight through the unplugged hole—hopefully my only mistake of the day.

With the bath a quarter full, I start filling the plastic bottles using a jug liberated from the kitchen. It quickly becomes clear I'll need a more effective process if this venture ever takes off as it's slow going. Once each bottle is full, I give it a wipe, attach the spray nozzle, and put it aside ready for labelling. Another challenge presents itself when I get down to the final inch of fluid in the bath as the jug is too big to scoop up the fluid. After manhandling the bath onto some old cinder blocks, I remove the plug and the dregs drain into the jug. A crude, but effective, solution.

Thirty bottles later, I set up the trestle table I borrowed from the tip and start attaching the labels. I waste half-a-dozen trying to apply each label straight and in the same position on each bottle. It soon becomes clear if I don't improve my label-applying technique with practice, I'll either waste half of them or suffer a nervous breakdown.

Nevertheless, after an hour of cock-ups and cussing, I finally have thirty bottles of Crystalene ready. I grab one from the table, hold it in my hand, and take a few seconds to reflect on what I've achieved.

I've never made anything worthwhile in my life, and never achieved anything of note. And yet, here I am holding a product that people might actually buy. A product as good, if not better, than anything else on the shelves. And the most remarkable thing is: it's my creation. Granted, I wouldn't be holding the bottle if it wasn't for Mungo, and it wouldn't look as nice if it wasn't for Joe, but I created it and I put in the graft, and now I've got something to show for it.

Sadly, it's a moment of pride I have to savour on my

lonesome.

I box up the bottles, transfer them to the back of Alan, and dart back up to the flat. The sound of the TV blaring greets me. I detour to the lounge to find Mungo slumped on the sofa with a mug in hand.

"What are you doing?" I ask.

"Goat herding," he replies, rolling his eyes. "What does it look like I am doing?"

"Alright, no need for sarcasm."

He returns his attention to the screen.

"And are you going to sit on your arse in here all day?"

"Possibly. I am yet to decide."

"Well, you could make yourself useful and pop to the shops. We're low on coffee and milk."

"Maybe later … if I feel like it."

As much as his laziness rankles, I don't have time to argue with him.

"Suit yourself. You're probably not interested but I'm heading out to try and sell the first batch of Crystalene."

"Good luck," he mumbles half-heartedly.

"I thought you didn't believe in luck?"

He shrugs his shoulders and continues watching whatever dirge he's tuned in to. Somewhat prematurely, it seems I've had my first taste of what it's like parenting a teenager.

I deliver a parting tut and head into the bedroom.

Apparently first impressions count so I change into my one-and-only suit; grateful the trousers were machine-washable considering the smell after their last outing. Once I'm suited and booted, I inspect myself in the mirror. The old suit hasn't changed but, as I stare at my reflection, I wonder if the man wearing it has. Although it's only been thirteen days since Daisy left, it feels a lifetime ago and surely the intervening events have left their mark? So much adversity, but as Dad would say: what doesn't break you, makes you. It remains to be seen just how much fragility remains.

"Ready for this, matey?" I murmur at my reflection.

He gives me a thumbs up and we set off for what I pray is a constructive day.

Alan contributes to my positivity by coughing into life with the second turn of the key. I pull away and head towards the first address on my list; using the brief journey time to mentally run through my sales pitch for the hundredth time.

I say sales pitch, but calling it that is a stretch. I tried watching a few online videos to get a basic understanding of how you're supposed to sell but with my woeful attention span and scattered thoughts, I don't think much of it sunk in. How hard can it be, though? People buy shit they don't need all the time, and at least my product does the job it's supposed to do. If an agent convinced Stoke City to part with twenty-million quid for some random Argentinian striker, I shouldn't have too much difficulty convincing my prospects to part with a few quid for something that's actually fit for purpose.

On reflection, perhaps belief in the product is better than any sales pitch.

The first port of call is possibly one of the last remaining hardware shops in the country. I pull into a parking bay opposite and transfer six bottles of Crystalene into my old gym bag, along with a clipboard holding a few dozen order forms I optimistically printed off.

Bradshaw's was founded in 1922, according to the weathered sign above the window, and on first impressions, I don't think much has changed in the intervening years. On the upside, I should be able to speak to Mr Bradshaw himself and, of all the places likely to stock Crystalene, a hardware shop must surely be the most obvious.

I draw a deep breath and spend a few seconds psyching myself up. This is it—time to go to work.

With my still slightly pungent gym bag slung over my shoulder, I cross the street and confidently enter Bradshaw's Hardware. True to its antiquated appearance, a bell rings above my head as I'm engulfed by the scent of my Granddad's garden shed: a nostalgic combination of brass polish, turpentine, and wax candles.

With no staff in sight, I approach the counter and wait; taking the opportunity to cast my eye over the shelves crammed full of products I've never heard of.

A full minute passes before I encounter any signs of life. A white-haired man in overalls appears through an archway and shuffles up behind the counter.

"What can I do for you, young man?"

"Um, can I speak to Mr Bradshaw, please?"

"Which one?"

"The one who pays the bills, I guess."

The old man chuckles. "That'd be me then."

"Oh, great. I'm Adam Maxwell, and …"

"Hold on a moment, sonny. Are you here to sell me

something?"

"Err, I was hoping to."

"Sorry. I'm not interested."

"But you don't even know what I'm selling."

"Doesn't matter. Whatever it is, I guarantee I already stock something that does the same job."

"Yes, but …"

"If there's nothing else, I'm a busy man."

Great. What should have been the easiest pitch on my list has been shot down before I've even told the old man what I'm selling.

"Fair enough, Mr Bradshaw. Thanks for your time."

Thwarted at the first attempt, disappointment follows me back across the shop. Unfortunately, by the time I reach the door a very different emotion has settled in. As I grasp the handle, I try to fight the irritation but it's too strong. Knowing I've nothing left to lose, I can't help myself.

I spin around and stomp back to the counter just as the old man is about to shuffle away.

"Wait just one minute," I snap. "Seeing as you're so damn confident, do you want to put your money where your mouth is?"

"I beg your pardon?" he replies, edging back to the counter.

Despite knowing full well my emotions are now dictating play, it's too late to backtrack.

"You reckon you already stock a product that does the same job as mine—I bet you twenty quid you don't."

He eyes me for a moment and, just as I fear he's about to pull a shotgun from beneath the counter, a wry smile arrives.

"Call it fifty and you're on."

I think back to the sales videos I watched. There definitely wasn't a section on making stupid bets to close a sale. Nevertheless, the emotional floodgates are now open and a torrent of male pride sloshes through.

I hold out my hand. "Fifty quid it is."

Twat.

I pull a bottle of Crystalene from the gym bag and slam it on the counter.

"There you go," I proudly declare. "The most effective and environmentally-friendly window cleaning product on the market."

Mr Bradshaw eyes the bottle for no more than a second or two. "Do you want to pay that fifty quid in cash, or by card?"

"I haven't lost the bet."

"Yes, you have."

He steps from behind the counter and slowly makes his way across the shop floor.

"Come this way," he calls over his shoulder.

I follow him over to the far corner of the shop, and a shelf lined with brightly coloured bottles.

"Take your pick, sonny," he taunts. "I stock at least a dozen window cleaning products; all of them tried and tested, and three of them are environmentally-friendly."

Looking at the range of established products quickly dampens my pride-driven bravado. Not only have I lost any chance of a sale but I also stand to lose fifty quid. My first ever pitch couldn't have gone any worse.

I'm about to concede defeat when the old man reaches for one of the bottles.

"This is our best seller," he says, waving it in my face. "And it's a best seller because it's the best product on the market. So tell me, sonny: why would I bother stocking whatever you're selling?"

I recognise the bottle and struggle to contain my excitement. If this were a game of poker, Mr Bradshaw just pitted his pair of sixes against my full house.

"I'll tell you why, shall I?" I reply confidently. "Because Crystalene is a damn sight cheaper and a damn sight better than that crap."

"And what makes you such an expert?"

"Because, I clean windows for a living," I announce, with little thought to the consequences. "And I used to buy that very product."

His expression changes in a flash. "You're a window cleaner?"

Well done.

Just as I was making inroads I've completely blown my credibility.

"Err, well, yeah," I mumble. "It's just a temporary job while I build this business."

"Right, I see," he says, eyeing me up and down. "You should have told me that when you first walked in."

Now exposed as the fraud I am, I just want to pack up my shame and leave.

"It doesn't matter. I won't waste any more of your time."

I'm just about to skulk away when Mr Bradshaw offers me

some advice.

"Listen, sonny. I've been in this business for more than sixty years, and if I never see another sales rep again, it'll be too soon."

"Okay, understood. I'm leaving."

He lets out a sigh. "You're missing my point."

"There's a point?"

"I don't buy anything from sales reps, but you're not a sales rep—you're a window cleaner."

"I think we've established that."

"And that should have been the first thing you told me."

"Why would you give the time of day to a bloke who cleans windows for a living?"

"Simple. If a sales rep tells me a product is the best they've ever seen, I'll take that as sales spiel. However, if a window cleaner tells me they use a product that cleans windows better than anything else, they've got my attention."

He then hands me the bottle of his best-selling cleaning product.

"You've got my attention. Now, prove I'm wrong."

He leads me back across the shop and opens the door to a gloomy storage room packed high with boxes.

"See that window over there?" he says, pointing to a filthy pane of glass. "Show me how your product is better."

I lose the suit jacket and immediately feel more comfortable; not least because I'm back in my comfort zone.

"Have you got an old cloth?" I ask.

He disappears for a moment and returns with a bright yellow duster. "That do you?"

"Perfect."

I step up to the window, and with Mr Bradshaw watching over my shoulder, apply a squirt of the best-selling cleaner to the right hand side of the window. I then apply a squirt of Crystalene to the left side. Droplets of each cleaner then form, and begin a race to the window ledge.

I turn to face Mr Bradshaw. "Just so you know I'm not cheating, can you wipe the cloth down the right hand side of the pane?"

He does as instructed, running the cloth vertically from top to bottom.

I have to admit the cleaner has done a reasonable job of removing grime from the glass and doubts suddenly creep in.

"Now, do the left side."

275

He turns the cloth over and repeats the motion. If I've screwed up the mixture, this might prove to be an embarrassing waste of time.

The cloth reaches the window ledge and the old man takes a couple of steps back to check the results.

"Well, we have a clear winner," he declares. "In every sense."

36.

If you found a five pound note in the street you'd be pleased, but it wouldn't exactly be life changing. A few hours after you've blown your windfall on a cup of coffee, you'd never think about it again

I walk away from Bradshaw's Hardware having just made five pounds profit but it's five pounds I will never forget.

After seeing it in action, Mr Bradshaw agreed to stock five bottles of Crystalene. That moment was thrilling enough, but once he signed the order form he cleared a space on his shelf and put those five bottles of Crystalene dead centre. I was so choked I couldn't thank him properly, but I think he knew just how grateful I was. So grateful, I decided not to call in the bet he lost.

At this point in my new venture, the money is almost inconsequential. What is of far greater significance is that a man who knows the industry inside out has endorsed my product When I factor in the advice he gave me, that tiny order is priceless in my eyes.

It also taught me a valuable lesson; emotions aren't entirely negative if harnessed correctly. As Mr Bradshaw put it: if you show genuine passion for a product, you don't need a sales pitch. Perhaps I let my emotions get the better of me but only because I believed in my product. I guess I just need to hone that passion, and curb the reckless bets.

I set off for the next address on my list, brimming with confidence.

Half an hour later, that confidence has been severely dented. The owner of a car valeting business suggested I shove a bottle of Crystalene up my arse—sideways, I think he said. If I thought it might have encouraged him to place an order, I'd have given it a go. I never got to try, though, as one of his burly staff frogmarched me from the premises before I could unbuckle my belt.

At the third business, I get to meet Lucas Barnes; the managing director of a commercial window cleaning company.

I heed Mr Bradshaw's advice and tell Lucas I'm in the same business, despite his company being on a completely different scale to mine as they employ thirty staff and clean the windows of offices, schools, and hospitals. After being bored witless for twenty minutes as Lucas regales the history of his company, he eventually agrees to trial Crystalene at a handful of sites, and orders six bottles.

For the next four hours I work my way through the list, with mixed results. Some prospects are genuinely impressed with Crystalene and buy on the spot, and some of them are sceptical but willing to take a trial bottle. Others are just arseholes who treat me like something they've stepped in. It's a steep learning curve but I improve with every pitch and manage to channel my emotions in a positive way—except the one time I didn't. I'm now banned from every branch of Pizza Express.

It's just after three when I pull into a trading estate on the edge of town; the last address of the day. I'm hoping to meet Karen Loxton; the owner of a cleaning supplies company. This could be a lucrative deal if I can persuade her to stock Crystalene, as her company supplies scores of cleaning companies across the area with everything from toilet rolls to floor polish.

Conscious of first impressions, I decide to park Alan on the edge of the estate and walk to the unit. I sling the gym bag over my shoulder and set off.

As I stroll through the estate, I inspect each of the units as I pass, in the hope I might stumble across another potential prospect. A few possibilities emerge and I make a mental note to pop in after I've tried my luck with Karen Loxton. Then I turn the corner, and stop dead.

Two huge industrial units stand before me: the furthest away being Loxton Cleaning Supplies, and the nearer one being Wallace Engineering. It appears my prospect has the misfortune of being neighbours with the man who was all set to be my father-in-law—Eddie Wallace.

It doesn't take long for my positivity to be engulfed by a red mist. I tell myself I should just walk on by and get on with what I'm here to do, but seeing Eddie's name plastered across a huge sign is, in my head at least, fate taunting me. In an instant, my irritation dial turns to maximum as I recount the argument with Daisy last week at the hospital. I couldn't give less of a shit if he's protecting his daughter—Eddie Wallace is the reason I won't get to see the first pictures of my child. That fucker has stolen what should have been one of my most treasured memories, and this is too good an opportunity to tell him that.

The irritation fuses with adrenalin and, before I know it, my legs are propelling me towards the reception of Wallace Engineering.

I barge through the door and storm towards the reception desk where a red-haired, twenty-something woman is just ending a call.

"I want to see Eddie Wallace," I growl. "Now."

"Do you have an appointment?" the receptionist asks, seemingly indifferent to my aggressive tone.

"No, I don't."

"In that case, I'm afraid you'll have to make one and come back another time."

"Like fuck I will."

I make for one of two doors next to the reception desk, without any idea where it leads. It turns out to be a storage cupboard. I retreat and take the next door, with the receptionist yelling something I don't catch.

I'm then faced with a choice: a flight of stairs or another door. It makes sense the offices are on the first floor so I bound up the stairs to find a long corridor with around a dozen doors lined up either side. Just as I come to a standstill, a guy in a suit emerges from one of the doors and heads in my direction.

In lieu of checking every single room to find Eddie's office, the suited man represents a timely shortcut.

"Excuse me, mate," I chirp, trying to mask my anger. "I'm looking for Eddie's office?"

"Last door on the left."

"Thanks."

All that stands between me and my foe is thirty feet of carpeted corridor. Without a second thought to the consequences, I charge on.

Five feet from my destination I hear Eddie's foghorn of a voice, rambling on about a delivery schedule. I stop for a second to listen. Judging by the intermittent periods of silence, I'm guessing he's on the phone to someone which means the receptionist can't have warned him about my visit. The element of surprise is an unexpected bonus.

I grab the handle and push the door open.

If I were on the phone in my office, and an unexpected visitor barged in, my first reaction would be to end the call. Eddie, however, does not. From behind his huge desk, he scowls up at me but continues his conversation. I take three steps towards the desk, intent on venting my rage. It's at that point I spot something on the wall behind Eddie's bald head—a framed photo of a young girl with locks of blonde hair and piercing blue eyes. Even from a distance, I can tell that child is Daisy.

If there were just one photo, perhaps the wind would have remained in my sails, but there are three other framed photos: one of Daisy as a toddler, wearing a lacy pink dress and blowing out candles on a cake, a second of a beaming little girl in school uniform, presumably taken on Daisy's first day of school, and a third of a teenage Daisy holding a certificate of some kind.

Four pictures, charting the childhood of the only woman I've ever truly loved.

As I stare at the photo, my anger ebbing away, a realisation steps across the office and slaps my face. As much as I love Daisy with all my heart, that love can't compare to that of the scowling man on the phone; the photos, proudly displayed behind his desk, are proof of that.

As little as I have in common with Eddie, there is one thing we do share: our love for Daisy Wallace. I, of all people, should understand why he wants to protect her.

A gruff voice interrupts my thoughts.

"What the hell are you doing here?" Eddie snarls, having finished his call.

Here I am again, in a sticky predicament due to my lack of forethought. Have I learnt nothing over the last couple of weeks?

"I, err …"

I return my attention to the photos on the wall, hoping little Daisy can provide inspiration for an answer. She can't.

"I, um … she was beautiful, even then," I mumble in an honest, if not pointless observation.

Eddie gets up from his chair and I prepare myself for a verbal, if not a physical assault. In an unexpected twist, he just stares at me, but not with his usual bulldog-licking-piss-from-a-nettle expression. I wouldn't call it a smile, and definitely not a grin or a smirk, but his lips curl upwards as if he's trying to suppress his pride.

He turns and studies the photo of Daisy in the pink party dress.

"She'll always be this little girl," he says wistfully. "To me, anyway."

Silent seconds pass as Eddie continues to stare at the photo. Then, almost as if a switch had been flicked, the Eddie I know is reactivated.

"So, what are you doing here?"

His tone is less aggressive but I wouldn't call it friendly.

I still don't have an answer. What I do have, though, is a head full of good advice and a mind now free from the all-consuming emotion which brought me here.

Seconds pass before a thin strand of logical thought, prompted by the sweaty stench of my gym bag, provides a possible escape route.

"I, err, was hoping you might do me a favour."

He sits back down and folds his arms.

"And why would I do that? What favours have you ever done for my daughter?"

I think long and hard.

"Truthfully, I've done her no favours."

"Finally," he huffs. "We can agree on something."

"I'm not here to defend my behaviour, Eddie. I can't, although I'll keep telling you I never cheated on Daisy because it's the truth. I'm here because I'm trying to do something good for our baby."

"What are you going to do?" he snorts. "Emigrate?"

Keep calm. Keep calm.

I unzip the gym bag and pull out a bottle of Crystalene.

"No, this is what I'm doing," I reply, placing the bottle on his desk.

He looks at the bottle and then at me. "A bottle of window cleaning solution. So what?"

"It's not just any bottle of window cleaning solution. It's the best window cleaning solution on the market, and it's mine."

I resist the temptation to tell him it's also the salad dressing he consumed last summer.

"What do you mean, it's yours?"

"Open up a web browser," I suggest, pointing to the computer on his desk. "And I'll show you."

Perhaps through no other reason than blind curiosity, he complies.

I give him the address of my new website which he slowly types before thumping the enter button. He then leans forward and studies the monitor; clicking the mouse a couple of times.

Long seconds pass before he passes comment.

"You did this?" he says, with no effort to hide his disbelief.

"I did, with a little help from a couple of friends."

"There's a typo on the contact page. *Address* is spelt wrong."

Bollocks.

"Oh, right. I've not officially launched the website yet and the content needs a tidy up before that happens."

He continues to click away while staring at the monitor.

After a minute or so, he sits back in his chair.

"Have you sold any?" he asks.

"Today's the first day," I reply, pulling the clipboard from my gym bag and presenting it to him. "But I've got seven orders so far."

He takes the clipboard and flicks through the order forms.

"I see you got an order from Bradshaw's."

"Just a small one but I'm hoping it'll sell well and he'll come back for more."

"You know who he is, don't you?"

"Who? Mr Bradshaw?"

"Yes."

"Um, he's the owner of a hardware shop."

"He's a bit more than that. I'd suggest you do some research on the Bradshaw family."

I nod as Eddie continues to inspect my orders.

"I'm almost impressed," he concedes, handing the clipboard back. "But let's face it, you have a track record of screwing up when the chips are stacked in your favour."

"This is different."

"Isn't it always?"

"No, this really is different."

"How?"

I point to the photos on the wall.

"I want my child to be as proud of me as you obviously are of Daisy."

Eddie follows my finger and gazes up at the photos.

"If you're trying to pull on my heart strings, it won't work. Talk is cheap, especially in business."

"So I'm learning, which brings me back to my favour."

"Go on," he sighs.

"How well do you know Karen Loxton?"

"The Karen Loxton who works next door?"

"Yes, that one."

"Pretty well. This estate has a tenants association and we're both on the committee."

"In that case, I was hoping you might introduce me to her."

"Why?"

Judging by the sudden change of expression, I suspect Eddie has made the connection without my answer.

"Ahh, right. She runs a cleaning supplies business. A very successful one too, I might add."

"Exactly. I'm hoping she might consider stocking my

product."

"You do realise she's a major player in the industry, and a hard-arsed businesswoman?"

"I'm aware of that," I lie. "But this product really is the best, and if I'm to make any serious money I need to shift more than a few dozen bottles a day."

Eddie sits back in his chair and drums his fingers together. As I wait for a reply, I'm transported back to my old headmaster's office; waiting anxiously while he formulated a suitable punishment for whatever school rule I'd infringed that week.

"What are your margins?" Eddie suddenly asks.

I relay the figures from Mungo's business plan, without admitting I never calculated them.

"First year projections?"

Again, I know the numbers because Mungo adjusted them only a few days ago.

"Trademarks?"

I tell him I've applied for trademark registration, but fail to mention I only did it because Mungo added it to my admin tasks.

More finger drumming ensues until Eddie suddenly reaches for his mobile phone. He prods the screen a few times and then holds it to his ear.

"Take heed," he growls, glaring at me while he waits for his call to connect. "You fuck this up and you'll wish you had emigrated."

His call is answered before I can offer a defence.

"Oh, hi, Karen," he chirps. "It's Eddie from next door."

They spend a minute swapping pleasantries before Eddie reveals the reason for his call.

"Listen, Karen. I've got a family friend with me, and he's got a cleaning product I think you might be interested in."

Although I've been demoted from Daisy's fiancé to family friend, it's a better description than he might have used twenty minutes ago.

"Put it this way," he then adds. "Old man Bradshaw placed an order."

I don't see the relevance of Mr Bradshaw but it seems to do the trick and Eddie confirms we'll pop by in a few minutes, and ends the call.

"She'll see us now," he confirms, getting to his feet. "Grab your stuff."

I do as I'm told and scuttle after Eddie as he heads down to the reception area.

"I'm popping out for half hour," he says to the receptionist as we pass. She smiles at Eddie but throws me a frosty glare.

A minute later, we're stood in another reception area waiting for Karen Loxton. Knowing the ante has been upped, my nerves jangle, but I don't think Eddie is in the mood for mindless banter so I suffer in silence.

A door then swings open and a middle-aged woman breezes in. Her confident stride and perfectly-tailored business suit are enough for me to determine who she is.

"Lovely to see you, Eddie," she chimes as they swap kisses rather than shake hands.

"Karen, this is Adam Maxwell; the guy I told you about."

Karen offers me her hand rather than a cheek.

"Nice to meet you, Adam. I hear you've sold your product to Mr Bradshaw. Well done."

Why are Eddie and Karen so obsessed with Mr Bradshaw? I feel like the one guy in the pub who fails to understand the punchline of a joke as everyone else falls around laughing. A week or so ago, I might have asked Karen to explain, but with the benefit of forethought I'd rather not be that guy in the pub. Better just to smile and let everyone assume you understand.

"Thanks, Karen. Nice to meet you too."

Introductions over, Karen leads us up to the first floor and an office far grander than Eddie's. Rather than her desk, she leads us over to two leather sofas with a coffee table between them.

"Please, take a seat," Karen says.

I flop down on the end of the nearest sofa. Eddie, to my dismay, takes a seat the other end. I assumed he would simply make the introduction and fuck off, but clearly that assumption was wrong and his presence is far from ideal. It's bad enough I have to conduct my pitch in front of a highly-successful, and slightly intimidating businesswoman, without having Eddie sitting in judgement too.

However, other than getting up and running away, there isn't much I can do about it now. Nevertheless, my mind subconsciously plays out the ramifications of legging it, but quickly concludes it might not be a sensible idea.

"Right," Karen begins, taking a seat opposite me. "I haven't got long so tell me why you're here."

Summoning my vast sales experience, garnered over many, many minutes, I begin.

"Can I start by saying I'm not a salesman, so this might be the worst pitch you've ever heard."

My honesty prompts a chuckle from Karen. A good start.

"To be honest with you, I'm just a humble window cleaner and, up until recently, a pretty lazy one at that. Any opportunity to make my life easier, I grabbed it."

"Go on."

"This is what I've been using to make my life."

I extract a bottle of Crystalene from my bag and place it on the coffee table.

"There's not much I can tell you, other than it cleans glass better than any product I've ever used."

Karen picks up the bottle and examines the label.

"I like the branding," she says. "But why would my customers switch to this from products they've been using for years?"

"I wish I could give you a ton of data but the simple truth is; it's cheaper and better. Cleaning windows isn't rocket science and all anyone wants is a product which makes the job easier. Add in the fact Crystalene is cheaper than the competition, and environmentally-friendly, I can't think of any good reason they wouldn't switch."

Although she doesn't respond to my claims, she does move the conversation on to price. That lasts no more than two minutes before Karen gets to her feet.

"Thanks for popping in, Adam," she says flatly. "Leave your contact details at reception and I'll be in touch."

I slowly stand and accept her handshake. "Err, right. Sure."

My pitch is over, apparently. I reach down to collect the bottle of Crystalene on the table.

"Leave that if you will," she demands.

I don't argue.

Less than seven minutes after I walked into Loxton Cleaning Supplies, I'm back outside the main door with Eddie at my side.

"That was short and sweet," I mumble. "That can't be a good sign."

"You've a lot to learn about Karen Loxton," he scowls. "If she didn't want your product she'd have told you straight and you'd be out on your arse within two minutes."

"Really? You think she'll place an order?"

"Probably."

Eddie then checks his watch. "I've got a meeting to attend."

"Right, Well, thanks for introducing me to Karen.

Genuinely, I'm grateful."

"I didn't do it for you," he sneers. "I did it for my grandchild."

I offer him my hand. "I know, and that's why I'm grateful."

37.

Despite a positive day thus far, a gnawing regret has taken hold by the time I return to Alan. With Eddie in an unusually cooperative mood, I should have grasped the opportunity to ask when the scan was taking place. Perhaps he might have even relented and suggested I come along.

My only hope is that I hear back from Karen Loxton before the scan is due and I can call Eddie under the pretence of giving him an update. I don't want to push my luck but I do need him to understand how important it is for me to be there.

For now though, I've got orders to fulfil so I need to get back to the garage and start producing more bottles of Crystalene.

By the time I pull onto the driveway, little of the late afternoon light remains as the temperature continues a downward slide towards bastardly cold. With no heating in the garage, I'll need a few layers of warm clothing and a flask of hot coffee before I start work.

I make a detour to the flat to deal with both.

As I hop up the stairs, my mind turns to Mungo and what he's been up to all day. By the time I reach the landing, I've already got a pretty good idea as even with the front door shut, I can hear music blaring from the flat.

I unlock the door and head towards the source.

"For crying out loud, Mungo," I yell, entering the lounge. "Turn it down."

"You do not like Vanilla Ice?" he yells back from the sofa.

"No, I don't."

I take matters into my own hands and turn the stereo off.

"I was listening to that," he complains.

"I don't care. I'm pretty sure the neighbours don't want to hear *Ice Ice Baby* at full volume any more than I do."

"Buzzkill," he mumbles under his breath.

It's an ironic insult considering I used the exact same word to describe Mungo not so long ago.

"Did you go to the shops?" I ask.

"I intended to, but then I discovered *that* in your kitchen cupboard."

He points at a half-empty bottle of scotch on the coffee table.

"You've been drinking?"

"Yes, I have."

I stand, speechless. Whilst his behaviour has been odder than usual over the last few days, this is on a whole new level.

"But you don't drink. You said it was poison."

"It is, but the effects are worthwhile compensation. It enhances the music, do you not think?"

"No, Mungo, I don't. There isn't enough whisky in the world to enhance Vanilla Ice."

"I disagree."

"And I don't care. This … whatever it is you're going through, has to stop."

"Why?"

"Because it's starting to piss me off. Look at the state of the place, and I bet we're out of milk and coffee too."

"You would win that bet—there is no milk or coffee."

I don't know what's happened to the insanely sensible, pragmatic version of Mungo who first moved in, but if his behaviour continues on this path I might have to consider evicting him.

"Sort yourself out, will you?" I snap. "I've got work to do."

I change out of my suit and head straight back down to the garage, without a flask of hot coffee.

Under the dim light of a feeble bulb, I set to work mixing, bottling and labelling sixty bottles. Despite the cold, and concerns for Mungo's deteriorating behaviour, the process at least feels worthwhile. This morning, I had no idea if I'd sell a single bottle but I've now got willing customers ready to part with their hard-earned cash. It does feel good.

I'm just about to box up the last batch when my phone rings. I wipe my hands and take the call.

"Hello? Adam?"

"Yes, Mum. It's me."

"Oh, good. Have you got a moment?"

"Yeah, sure. How's Dad?"

"I was hoping you'd have been in to find out for yourself."

"Yeah, sorry. It's been a manic few days but I'll pop over later."

"That's why I'm calling. Your father has had a long day and he's tired, so can you make it tomorrow lunchtime instead, around twelve?"

It's not ideal but I'm not in the mood for an argument.

"No problem. Is he okay?"

"He's doing very well and we're hoping they'll discharge him by the weekend."

"That's great news, Mum. And talking of news, I've got some of my own."

"Please tell me it's not bad news."

"Nope, not this time. It's about a new business I've set up, but I'll tell you more tomorrow."

"Twelve o'clock, right."

"Yes, Mum," I sigh. "Twelve o'clock."

The line falls silent and I'm about to wind the call up when Mum poses a question.

"I don't suppose you've spoken to Kate since the weekend?"

"Actually, I have. You'll be pleased to know we've patched up our differences."

"I know. Kate told me, and it's about time too. Has she said anything to you?"

"Like what?"

"Anything that might explain her mood over the last few days. She's been really withdrawn and every time I ask if Arabella is coming in to see her granddad, all I get is a half-baked excuse."

Her maternal instinct is on the money but I made a promise to Kate, and I have no intention of breaking it.

"Um, I think she said something about a problem with one of the parents at school. It's nothing to worry about, Mum."

"You'd tell me if there was, wouldn't you?"

For once, I don't feel bad lying to my mother. "Of course, but you just focus on helping Dad get better."

I don't know if my words helped, but she says goodbye with a trace of relief in her voice.

After packing up the bottles, I take a walk to the shop for more coffee and milk, and a few other provisions. After such a hectic, eventful day, the stroll proves a much-needed opportunity to get my thoughts in order — a challenge in itself. It's at times like this I wish life had a fast-forward button so I could skip past the crap and enjoy the best parts. Thinking on, a rewind button would be pretty useful too, and I wouldn't say no to a pause button either.

Sadly, I'm stuck in the here and now so I've just got to keep plugging away and hope everything falls into place. Responsibility is bloody exhausting.

I return to the flat, and blissful silence.

After unpacking the shopping, I throw a ready meal in the

microwave and flop down at the table. I use the time to email Joe and tell him about the feedback from the printers. I feel bad we haven't been out for a beer in a while, but I don't have the time or the inclination to struggle through my hectic schedule with a hangover.

Once life settles down, I'll take him out for a well-earned blow out. I only hope it's this side of Christmas.

Dinner smells almost as bad as it looks, but it's food and I'm starving. I slap the plastic tray on the table and set about the anaemic mush.

As I eat, my mind turns to the earlier conversation with Eddie and Karen Loxton, and their strange obsession with Mr Bradshaw. Eddie suggested I conduct some research so I open a web browser on the laptop whilst simultaneously shovelling food down my neck. Maybe I can multi-task after all.

I search for Bradshaw's Hardware and scan the first page of results. I don't know what I'm looking for and the search results don't exactly offer much help. I'm about to click through to the second page when I hear the door to Mungo's room open and close. A moment later, he appears in the doorway looking a forlorn figure.

"Sobered up?" I ask.

"I concede the alcohol may have been an error of judgement," he mumbles.

"Let me guess: you felt amazing for a few hours, and now you feel like utter shit?"

"An accurate appraisal."

He shuffles over to the table and gingerly takes a seat.

"What were you thinking, Mungo?"

"Do you not see the irony in that question? Clearly, I did not think."

"That's what I don't understand. What's got into you?"

"Can we not discuss that now? I sense a migraine developing."

"That's no migraine," I snigger. "All you're sensing is the beginnings of a hangover."

"Possibly. I need a distraction."

"In which case, your timing is perfect."

I nudge the laptop around so he can see the screen.

"I'm trying to research one of the companies you included as a possible prospect in the business plan. It's a shop called Bradshaw's Hardware."

"You have been there?"

"Yep, and he placed an order … eventually."

"That is an admirable achievement."

"Okay, now you're doing it. What is it about this old guy I'm obviously not seeing?"

"Where do you keep your household cleaning products?"

"Why? Are you going to clean up the mess you left in the lounge?"

"Later."

"They're in the cupboard under the sink."

With no further explanation, he gets to his feet and shuffles over to the cupboard. I watch on as he inspects each of the cleaning products before selecting one and returning to the table.

"Do you recognise this product?" he asks, placing a bright orange bottle in front of me.

"Yes. It's a multi-purpose cleaner. One of the most popular, I think."

"Inspect the label and tell me who the manufacturer is."

Still none the wiser, I drop my fork in the tray and grab the bottle.

"It's a company called Barton Bradshaw. And your point is?"

"Bradshaw."

I stare blankly at the bottle and then back at Mungo.

"Nope. I'm not with you."

"Do you have any idea how painstaking you can be at times?"

"Funnily enough, you're not the first person to say that."

"I do not have the patience for this. Find their website."

I google the company and click through to their website. It's typically corporate, and clearly aimed at shareholders rather than consumers.

"What am I supposed to be looking at?"

"Click on the link entitled 'Our History', at the top of the page."

I click the link and read the first few paragraphs of text. A series of pictures then scroll into view; one of which is a face I recognise.

"Ohh."

It appears the old bloke I met this morning is George Bradshaw—the former CEO of Barton Bradshaw PLC.

"I don't get it. Why would the former CEO of a multi-national business be working in a backstreet hardware store?"

"That hardware store has been in the Bradshaw family since

the twenties, and it is where George Bradshaw learnt the trade alongside his father. He worked there for ten years after leaving school, and in the late sixties he partnered with Roger Barton to produce and distribute their own range of cleaning products. That partnership became Barton Bradshaw PLC."

"Thanks for the history lesson but that doesn't answer my question. He must be stinking rich so why is he now working as a glorified sales assistant."

"How would I know?" he shrugs. "But, whatever his reason, it is not financial. His estimated wealth is in excess of four-hundred-million pounds."

"Holy shit," I gasp. "And the cheeky git haggled on the price too."

Mungo's revelation about George Bradshaw explains two things. Firstly, why the old man put me through the wringer and, secondly, why Eddie and Karen Loxton were impressed that I'd secured an order.

"I wish you'd warned me."

"Why?"

"Because if I'd have known I was pitching to the former CEO of a huge company, I might have prepared better."

"Are you saying you were ill-prepared?"

"Err, no, but I might have handled it differently."

"You secured an order, did you not?"

"Well, yeah, but …"

"If I had told you, it would have been an added pressure. You have not responded well to pressure in the past."

"I suppose."

"Think about it—if you had not secured an order, it would have been of little consequence and you would have simply moved on to the next prospect. As it transpires, you did secure an order with a man who is notorious for his dislike of salespeople."

The penny drops.

"You just threw me into the lion's den to see if I've learnt anything?"

"It was a calculated risk, and you proved worthy. That should give you confidence going forward."

I choose not to tell him how close I came to walking away with no order, and fifty quid out of pocket.

"And I hope you have learnt a lesson," he adds. "You should conduct research on every prospect before you visit them."

"Noted."

I'm about to give him an update on the rest of my day when

he yawns and gets to his feet.

"I need sleep."

"God knows why. You've been sat on your arse all day."

"You assume that, but I have been busy."

"Doing what?"

"You will find out within the next forty-eight hours. Goodnight, Adam Maxwell."

He shuffles off before I can question him further.

Notwithstanding yet another cryptic comment, at least his behaviour in the last ten minutes has been more Mungo-like. Although I've got no idea how old he is, I wonder if he's perhaps going through a mid-life crisis. I'm no expert, but his sudden taste for new experiences has all the hallmarks, and I wouldn't be surprised if I come home tomorrow to find he's taken delivery of a Harley Davidson.

With the kitchen silent once more, I finish my excuse for a meal and turn my attention back to George Bradshaw. Now I know what I'm looking for, I return to Google in the hope of determining what makes a wealthy man give up a powerful position as CEO of a multi-national company to run a hardware store.

It doesn't take long to determine George Bradshaw's decision was newsworthy at the time as I unearth several news reports about it. However, the reporters only speculate why he made such a move as the man himself shunned their requests for an interview—perhaps he dislikes reporters as much as he dislikes sales reps. I guess if you're worth four-hundred-million quid, you can afford to do what the hell you like.

However, as intriguing as George Bradshaw's story is, I really should be reworking my schedule for tomorrow now I have a hospital visit to shoehorn in.

Another day, another plate to spin.

I could definitely do with a pause button.

38.

It's just gone eight o'clock in the morning and my early start is about to be rudely interrupted.

As I wipe down the last of Mrs Wingfield's windows, her neighbour yells at me from a bedroom window.

"Young man, are you the window cleaner?"

With one hand still pressed to the glass and a bloody great big ladder next to me, I glare up at the woman.

"No, I'm the postman," I mumble under my breath.

"Sorry?"

"Yes, I'm the window cleaner," I yell back.

"Splendid. I'm just coming down … give me a minute."

She slams the window shut.

In order to cram everything in, I've meticulously planned my day to the very last minute. What I hadn't planned for was being accosted by a random housewife. I check my watch and start packing up.

I'm in the process of strapping the ladder to Alan's roof when the woman appears on the driveway.

"Thank you for waiting," she pants. "I've been meaning to catch up with you."

"No problem. What can I do for you?"

"We need a window cleaner."

"Right."

A few weeks ago I'd have bitten the woman's arm off. Then again, a few weeks ago I wouldn't have been here at eight in the morning. Now, though, the prospect of adding to my already heavy workload is far less appealing. It already feels like I'm currently operating on adrenaline and caffeine alone, and that's not sustainable in the long term.

"I'm already at capacity, I'm afraid."

"Surely you can squeeze me in? I'll make it worth your while."

The woman, easily a decade older than me, then winks.

"I'll, err, take your details and check my schedule later."

I don't hang around to discover what might have been worth my while.

As I work through the next six houses, and prompted by my decision to decline the housewife's custom, my thoughts turn towards the future. At some point I'll need to decide which horse

I'm going to back. If it's the new venture, the window cleaning round will have to go because I can't manage both businesses unless I want to drop dead through either stress or exhaustion. It'll be another part of my life I have to say goodbye to, and if I've learnt anything in the last few weeks, it's that I'm not good at letting go. Christ, I can't even bring myself to part with Alan.

Of all the changes I've implemented of late, I suspect moving on will be the hardest. Necessary, but definitely the hardest.

I finish the last house just after eleven and dash back to the flat for a shower. The plan is to visit Dad, deliver the outstanding Crystalene orders from yesterday, and then visit another dozen local businesses in the hope of securing more orders. By the time I finish, and depending on how many bottles I need to produce, I'm looking at a twelve-hour working day. I fear this will be the norm for a while.

I arrive home to find Mungo slouched on the sofa watching TV.

"Bloody hell, Mungo," I groan. "Is this how you intend to spend every day?"

"Why is it of any concern to you?"

A valid point.

"It's not, I suppose, apart from the mess. You know I wasted twenty minutes tidying up in here this morning whilst you were still in bed."

"Would you like me to thank you?"

"No, I'd like you to be a bit more considerate and start pulling your weight."

"What you would like is of no real consequence."

"It bloody well is," I snap. "This is my home."

"It is of no consequence because I will be vacating your home soon."

Despite his erratic behaviour over the last few days, his announcement still comes as a shock.

"You're leaving? But you've only been here five minutes."

"It is probably closer to thirteen-thousand minutes."

"That's not what I meant and you know it. I thought we were getting on okay and, well, I've kind of got used to you being around."

"Sadly," he says with a wistful sigh. "I have no choice in the matter."

"Can you at least tell me why? Is it because I complained about the mess?"

Somewhere in the conversation, and without realising, the tone of my voice has shifted from irritated to desperate.

"No, it has nothing to do with my declining standards of behaviour. It is time to go because your therapy is almost complete."

"Is it? It doesn't feel complete."

"Which is why I said, *almost,*" he replies, turning his attention back to the TV. "There are a few more matters to attend but then I will be leaving. You are almost ready to continue this journey on your own."

They say there's never a good time to hear bad news but in my case, Mungo couldn't have chosen a worse time to give me his bad news.

"Look, I've got to be at the hospital in twenty minutes and I need a shower. Can we talk about this later?"

"We can talk, but you cannot change what has to be."

I'm about to question what he means when I check my watch again. Time is not on my side. I shake my head and dash off to the bathroom.

The journey to the hospital passes in a blur. I wouldn't go as far as saying I'm in actual shock, but Mungo's revelation has certainly put my head in a spin. Despite his quirks, there is no way I'd have made it through the last couple of weeks without him, and I don't think I'll make it through the next few weeks if he goes.

What is it with life? One moment it's patting you on the back, the next it's kicking you in the nuts. Why can't things just be fine for a while? Is it too much to ask?

I pack up my self-pity and set off on the long traipse towards Dad's ward.

Unsurprisingly, on my arrival, I find Mum at his bedside.

"Oh, good," she chirps. "You made it."

"I said I'd be here at twelve, so here I am."

"You've said a lot of things in the past, young man."

Her comment is delivered with a knowing smile rather than the usual scorn.

"That was then."

"Anyway, now you're here, I need to visit the ladies."

She gets up and scuttles away, leaving Dad and I to it.

If there's any positive at all to spending time in a hospital ward, it's the way it puts your own problems into perspective. Despite suffering a major stroke only five days ago, Dad appears in much better shape than the five other men occupying the nearby beds. Two of them look like they're suffering the consequences of a week-long bender in Magaluf, and one poor bloke can't be far off a visit from the Grim Reaper.

I position a chair so I can't see them.

We chat about nothing in particular for five minutes until Mum returns.

"So, Dad. I hear they might be letting you out before the weekend."

"Fingers crossed. I can't wait to get out of this place."

"And then what? I guess it'll be a few months of recuperation before you're back to full health?"

"Not bloody likely, son. If this scare has taught me anything, it's to make the most of the time we've got left. We're going to do all the things we promised ourselves we'd do, before it's too late."

I pray those ambitions don't extend to membership of the local swingers club.

"Good for you, Dad. Is the house move part of that plan then?"

Rather than answer my question, Dad's eyes flick towards Mum and she answers with a frown. I've seen this routine a thousand times—I've clearly touched on a subject neither parent wishes to discuss with me.

"What have I said?"

"Um, nothing, son," Dad blusters. "We're still talking about the house move and it's just an idea at the moment."

Subject closed.

"Anyway, your mum tells me you've got some news. Let's hear it then."

Both parents sit and listen as I run through the entire story of my new venture. After their initial, and expected scepticism, they slowly become more enthusiastic, and seem particularly interested when I mention Bradshaw's Hardware.

"I knew Maggie Bradshaw," Mum says. "She was a lovely woman, God rest her soul."

"How did you know her?"

"She was on the board of governors at the school and did a lot of work for local charities. Actually, the Bradshaws were like local celebrities, being he was some big-shot businessman and she was on every charity committee going."

"I still pop into the shop now and again," Dad chips in. "Knows his stuff does George."

Apparently I am the only man in town who didn't know the

Bradshaw's back story.

The conversation then moves on as Dad recounts his various purchases from Bradshaw's over the years. I get to hear how he once bought the wrong size set of tungsten-tipped screws, twice, and how he and Mr Bradshaw chuckled about it. Perhaps a mind-numbing topic of conversation but, God, how I savour it after recent events.

Forty minutes feels like an appropriate amount of time. Not too long, but not so short I appear rude. With a promise I'll pop over to my parent's house at the weekend, assuming Dad is discharged, I prepare to say my goodbyes. I give Mum a peck on the cheek and then lean over the bed to give Dad a hug. Just as I straighten up, I catch movement in the corner of my eye as a figure sidles up to the bed.

The scent of a painfully familiar perfume identifies the figure before I even look over.

"Hi, Adam."

My body reacts before my mouth as a swarm of butterflies flutter in my stomach.

"Oh, hi."

The last time I saw Daisy was five days ago, outside this very ward. The way our conversation ended that day does not bode well for this meeting.

"How are you?" she asks, her voice soft.

Without consciously giving them permission, my eyes scan her up and down. She's wearing a pair of loose-fitting trousers and a white blouse beneath her favourite leather jacket. My eyes stop at her waist, and the slight bump at odds with her slender figure.

"I'm okay, thanks," I gulp. "You?"

"Good, thanks."

I hate the faux politeness, and the awkwardness is hideous. I'd rather walk away than endure another second of it, and I certainly don't want to risk a continuation of our argument.

"Well, it's good to see you. I'll leave you all to it."

Mum, unusually quiet up until this point, then pipes up. "Daisy isn't here to see your father."

Confused, I stare blankly at my former fiancée.

"I'm here for the baby's first scan," Daisy confirms.

My immediate thoughts are not positive—she's only dropped by to taunt me, and Eddie is probably waiting outside, ready to twist the knife.

I pause for a few seconds as a mental battle ensues.

Common sense just about scrapes victory—no good will come of letting my thoughts reach my mouth.

"Oh, I … right. I hope it goes well."

My calm words are followed by a moment of silence, punctuated by glances between Daisy and my mother.

"I was thinking," Daisy then says. "You might like to come with me?"

I'm the only one stunned by Daisy's offer, which suggests my presence here was part of a premeditated plan.

Sensing my bewilderment, Mum then confirms my suspicions. "I spoke to Daisy yesterday evening, before I called you."

"That's why you wanted me here at twelve?"

"Precisely."

I turn to Daisy. "Don't get me wrong; I'm ecstatic you've asked me but why all the plotting?"

"Honestly? Because I couldn't be sure you'd turn up. And, you're not going to like this but, I didn't want to prove Dad right."

"Right about what exactly?"

"Long story, short—he told me about your meeting yesterday."

"And?"

"He seemed genuinely impressed with your new business, but you know Dad—it takes a lot to gain his trust. If I'd asked you to attend the scan and you didn't show up, you'd be back to square one with him. I wanted to protect that little bit of goodwill you two have built up."

"So, he doesn't know I'm here, and even if I wasn't, he still wouldn't know."

"Exactly. I'm sorry I couldn't ask you but I'm trying to keep everyone happy and it's not easy."

My initial delight at Daisy's invite is suddenly tinged with guilt. She's been stuck between a protective father and an emotionally-charged ex-fiancé. Now, looking at it objectively, neither of us has made it easy for the woman we both profess to love.

"If anyone should be apologising, it's me. For what it's worth, I do understand why Eddie is so protective. You're his little girl—I get that now."

Daisy smiles and mouths the words, *thank you.* Our eyes lock for a split second—long enough to offer a reminder of what we once were. The dull ache makes a brief but telling return.

"Haven't you two got somewhere more important to be?" Mum interjects.

"Yes, we do," Daisy replies. "And thank you for setting this up, Carol."

Daisy then gives both my parents a hug. Despite having already said my goodbyes, I think my mother deserves more than a peck on the cheek.

"Thank you, Mum" I whisper as I put my arms around her.

"Send my grandchild a kiss from me, won't you?"

"I will."

In that instant I sense a shift in our relationship. Too soon to say what it is, but as I break from our embrace, my mother's smile confirms it.

"Ready then?" Daisy asks.

I've never been more ready for anything. Beaming like a five-year-old on Christmas morning, I wave my parents a goodbye.

The walk from Dad's ward to the maternity unit proves short in terms of distance, and conversation. We know each other well enough for the silence not to be uncomfortable, and we probably both have our own good reasons for the lack of chat. I can't speak for Daisy, but my silence is fuelled by paranoia I'll ruin the moment by saying the wrong thing. To be suddenly stripped of this gift by a few poorly-chosen words would easily outrank every stupid mistake I've ever made.

Silence remains my protection, until we reach our destination and talk becomes a necessity.

"I feel a bit nervous," I confess. "How are you doing?"

"Up until ten minutes ago I thought I'd be here alone, so I feel better now you're here."

"You do? Really?"

"Yes, really. Come on."

On the face of it, it's half-an-hour spent in a featureless room whilst squinting at a black and white screen. However, it would be no exaggeration to say it's half-an-hour in which my entire outlook on life changes. Thirty incredible minutes in a joy-filled bubble; impenetrable to all my current trials and tribulations.

I leave clutching the prized photo of what could be my unborn child—it's hard to tell, if I'm honest. It doesn't matter, though, as I could not feel any prouder.

"It feels kind of real now, doesn't it?" Daisy coos.

"Scarily so."

"How are you feeling?"

Never has one question had so many potential answers. Considering how close I came to missing out on this moment, relieved is the strongest contender. Then again, a succession of other answers are equally valid: terrified, exhilarated, anxious, thrilled, plus a dozen more I can't even process.

"I'm still trying to take it all in, but to answer your question I feel grateful more than anything else."

"Grateful?"

"I'm grateful you let me share the moment. I don't think I really told you how important it was to me."

"No, you didn't," she replies with a slight frown.

For once, I'm being chastised for something I didn't say, rather than something I did say. It's just about preferable.

We continue along the corridor without saying another word, although it's a different silence to that we shared earlier. Quiet contemplation, I guess.

As we pass the cafeteria, Daisy is the first to break the silence. "Do you want to grab a coffee?"

I could sit and think all afternoon, and not come up with anything I'd rather do. Sadly, what I *want* to do and what I *need* to do are not the same thing.

"I'd love to, Daisy, but I've got orders to deliver, potential customers to visit, and …"

She raises her hand towards my mouth. "Adam. Stop."

Nice one, stupid.

This is the moment I've been trying to avoid since Daisy wandered up to Dad's bedside. Patently and predictably, I've said the wrong thing.

I visibly deflate and await the ear-bashing I know Daisy is about to deliver. A few seconds pass as I await my fate but when it finally arrives, it comes in the form of a kiss to my cheek.

"What was that for?" I ask, relieved but puzzled.

"For trying to be what I always wanted you to be," she replies.

"And that is?"

"Responsible."

"You might need to expand on that."

"I know how hard you've been working on this new business, and the fact you put your responsibilities before a coffee with me says a lot."

"It says the coffee in here is bloody awful."

"Shut up," she chuckles. "You know what I mean. Now, go

and do what you need to—we'll have that coffee another time."

"Promise?"

"Yes, I promise."

I may have been weighed down with self-pity when I arrived at the hospital, but I leave feeling ten-feet tall.

Maybe, just maybe, Mungo is right. Perhaps I am ready to go it alone.

39.

As I float back to the hospital car park, I switch my phone back on. It immediately chimes the arrival of two voicemail messages.

The first is from Joe to say he's set up a meeting with the printer and they've already offered him some work. He also concedes he needs to focus on his business too, so the promised beers might have to wait until next weekend. That suits me.

The second message is from Karen Loxton of Loxton Cleaning Supplies. It's short, and her business-like tone gives nothing away but she wants me to call her PA and arrange a meeting. Surely nobody arranges a meeting unless there's something worthwhile to discuss? Well, apart from Joe.

I ring the PA.

My initial optimism is undermined when I'm offered just a fifteen minute slot later this afternoon. However, according to her PA that's how Karen Loxton works. Apparently the narrow window ensures all her meetings are productive because there's no time wasted on pointless chit chat. For a man with little time himself, I can't argue with her logic.

I end the call and head back to the flat to pick up the orders. I'm already forty minutes behind schedule so my deliveries will have to be quick, and God knows how I'll find the time for making any sales calls now I've got to see Karen Loxton. Still, where there's a will.

I'm just about to set off when my phone rings. I consider leaving it when I see Kate's name on the screen but, with Mungo's vague plan for Ethan seemingly no further advanced, she must be at her wit's end. I take the call.

"Hi, Kate."

"Please tell me something positive."

"Nothing to report yet, I'm afraid."

"This is ridiculous," she huffs. "Is that doctor of yours doing anything?"

"Look, I know I'm asking a lot but you've just got to be a little more patient. It's not even been forty-eight hours since we spoke to Ethan and Mungo did say it could take up to three days."

"I'm not concerned about the time, Adam. I'm concerned that nothing is happening."

"I'm sure Mungo is working on his plan."

"Are you? Really?"

An image of Mungo floats into my mind. An image where he's slumped on the sofa watching TV, which is pretty-much all he's been doing for the last few days.

"Tell you what: if we don't hear anything back by tomorrow evening, let's agree to meet up again and see if we can come up with an alternative plan. What do you think?"

The line goes quiet. I think I've inadvertently answered Kate's question.

"We'll see. I'll give it until Saturday and then I'll have to look at another option."

"Another option? I didn't think you had any."

"I don't. By option, I mean my last resort."

"And that is?"

"I can't tell you."

"Why not?"

"Because I don't want anyone else being dragged into it."

Speaking from personal experience, last resorts are only ever sought once you've exhausted the sensible and the safe. I've got a horrible feeling Kate's last resort is neither.

"Promise me you're not going to do anything stupid, Kate."

"Call me when you've got some news. And please, keep pressing Dr Mungo—I'm getting desperate."

She ends the call without my requested promise.

Just when I think I've got all my plates nicely spinning, one starts to wobble. Notwithstanding his impending departure, it now looks like I've no choice but to pester Mungo for some answers when I get back. He'd better bloody-well be doing something, because the last thing Mum and Dad need is Kate grasping the baton of reckless decisions just as I'm trying to let it go.

I glance at the clock on Alan's dashboard and curse at the time.

Not wishing to waste another minute, I dash back and forth across town as fast as Alan's fragile engine will allow. My time is further wasted when each of the five customers asks for a delivery note. I have to improvise with some bullshit excuse about the printers letting me down, rather than admitting I have no idea what a delivery note is. Yet another lesson learnt and yet another piece of pointless admin I could do without.

I arrive at the trading estate with three minutes to spare and abandon Alan in the same spot as yesterday. Striding as quickly as I can without breaking into a sweat, I hurry through the estate and arrive at Loxton Cleaning Supplies seconds before the meeting is set to start. Only when I'm panting in the reception area do I realise I haven't prepared in the slightest. Then again, I hadn't prepared yesterday yet here I am for a second meeting.

My breathing returns to normal just as the receptionist orders me up to Karen Loxton's office.

As I head up the stairs, I can't quite decide if I'm more nervous meeting Karen now I don't have Eddie by my side. For possibly the first and only time in my life, I kind of wish he was here. Too late now.

I reach the top of the stairs and take a moment to compose myself. A dozen hesitant steps and I rap on the door to Karen's office.

"Come in."

I open the door to find her seated behind a desk.

"Good to see you again, Adam. Come take a seat."

She immediately returns her attention to a computer monitor and doesn't even offer a handshake when I sit down. Silent seconds tick by before I receive Karen's attention.

"Right. Crystalene," she says flatly.

"Yes?" I reply expectantly.

"It's a very effective product and I love the branding. The environmental aspect is a definite advantage too, especially as many organisations are now trying to be greener."

"Thank you, Karen. I appreciate the positive feedback."

"Don't get too excited."

"Oh."

"Now, correct me if I'm wrong, but I get the impression you don't have a proper production facility?"

My gut reaction is to tell her I do, but what if she wants to see it? I don't think she'll be impressed with a tour of the garage.

"Not as such. This has all happened incredibly quickly, Karen, and I'm still looking at options."

"And that's a problem for me."

"Can I ask why?"

"Put simply: volume. I'm not interested in selling a few dozen litres of your product a week, or any product for that matter. I'm interested in products where I can sell hundreds, if not thousands of units a week. I didn't get where I am today by thinking small."

"But I can produce a hundred bottles a day, easily."

"And what about your other customers? What if they want a

hundred bottles a day?"

Shit.

When you've spent most of your adult life screwing things up, it pays to keep your expectations low. Perhaps deep down I never thought this business would amount to much more than a replacement for the window cleaning round. Even Mungo's business plan only estimated I'd sell a maximum of a thousand bottles a week, and that wouldn't happen for at least a year. I suppose this is a good problem to have, but it's still a problem.

"Truth be told, Karen, the short term plan was just to sell enough to give myself a half-decent income."

"You do realise the market leader in this sector ships over half-a-million litres of product in the UK alone each year?"

"Oh. No, I didn't."

"And your product is better than the market leader."

"Is it?"

"Yes, which is why I'm disappointed we won't be able to stock Crystalene."

If disappointment were a hat, I'd be wearing a sombrero.

"That's, um … a shame."

"Listen, Adam. It doesn't mean we'll never stock Crystalene, but you need to think big, and get the production side of the business sorted so you can sell in large quantities. But, as it stands, I can't risk stocking a product with obvious supply issues."

"I understand."

She stands up and offers a belated handshake.

"Good luck. Come back and see me when the business is in a better place."

And so I skulk away, without using even half of the fifteen allocated minutes. Karen Loxton is nothing if not brutally efficient.

As I wander through the trading estate, my emotions swing back and forth between pride and disappointment. After Mr Bradshaw's endorsement, Karen's glowing feedback is further cause for positivity. However, what's the point of having a great product if I can't make enough of it to meet the demand?

By the time I reach Alan, I conclude there's not much I can do to change the situation. Premises of any kind are beyond my current finances, and as for the kind of machinery required to automate the production process, that's so far on the horizon I'd need a pilot's licence to reach it. So, for now, I'll have to be content selling small amounts in the hope it's enough to scratch a living. That, however, can't be forever because I don't have forever.

I take a seat behind Alan's wheel and carefully extract the scan photo from my pocket. Resting it on the steering wheel, I make a promise.

"By the time you arrive, I'll have this sorted. Daddy won't let you down."

Over the years I've made hundreds of promises and broken far more than I've kept. Whatever it takes, this one will not be broken.

It would have been the easier, obvious option to spend the rest of the afternoon dwelling on Karen Loxton's bad news, rather than the good. However, fuelled by a promise, and the positives from my brief meeting, I morph into a selling machine. Admittedly, I'm an underpowered selling machine and don't always fire on all cylinders but I return home just after six o'clock with orders for eighty bottles.

I don't even bother heading up to the flat for fear I'll flop down on the sofa and never get up again. Instead, I head straight into the garage and crack on with the mixing, bottling, and labelling.

Two hours later, I pull the garage door shut.

Exhausted and frozen to the bone, I traipse up the stairs and unlock the front door. My sense of satisfaction from a productive day fizzles away when I remember the earlier conversation with Kate. This is one problem I can't ignore, as much as I'd love to. Reluctantly, I decide to tackle Mungo before another tray of microwave mush, and pad through to the lounge. I'm greeted by the same scene I left over eight hours ago.

I don't have the energy to complain about the mess, or the smell.

Mungo barely gives me a glance as I collapse on the sofa.

"Yeah, good evening to you too, Mungo."

"I am watching television."

"So I see, but we need to talk."

"You might need to talk. I need to find out who Dylan's real father is."

I turn to the TV, and an episode of a soap Daisy used to watch.

With little energy and even less appetite for a drawn-out discussion, I reach for the remote control and switch the TV off.

I suddenly have Mungo's full attention. "Turn it back on this instant," he snaps.

"I'll turn it back on as soon as you tell me where we are with Ethan."

"It is in hand, as I have already told you."

"That's not good enough, Mungo. Kate is going out of her mind and I can't give her any answers."

"You should tell her what I have already told you. It could take several days for Ethan Montgomery to accept my proposition."

"And I'll ask you what I've already asked—why the hell would he?"

"He will. That is all you need to know."

"But what if he doesn't?"

"Which part of *he will* did you not grasp?"

Tiredness and irritation are not a good mix, and I have to literally bite my lip in order not to react. Mungo's behaviour might have changed but his stubbornness hasn't.

"Fine, here," I spit, chucking him the remote control. "Enjoy the rest of your shitty programme. I've got to call my sister and tell her what I've found out — which is pretty-much fuck all. Thanks, Mungo."

I don't hang around to discover who Dylan's real father is.

My ready meal is even more unappetising than last night's. No surprise considering the bitter taste in my mouth. I sit and chew on rubbery pasta while trying to think of another way to deal with Ethan; ideally without Mungo's involvement.

I'm no further forward by the time I throw the tray in the bin.

Whichever way I look at the problem I find the same road block in that Ethan has twisted the law to work in his favour. My self-esteem may have improved but I'm not deluded enough to think I've any chance against his legal expertise. All I'm left with, besides indigestion, are two options: hire a better solicitor than Ethan, which neither Kate or I can afford, or club the tosser to death with one of his own golf trophies.

Basically, I've got nothing, and there's no point calling Kate and telling her nothing. All I can do is sleep on the problem and pray by some miracle a good night's sleep brings inspiration.

I'm so tired I decide to take a bath rather than a shower. As I hunt for the bubble bath, I unearth one of Daisy's forgotten bath bombs in the cupboard under the sink. I unwrap it and hold it to my nose, drawing in the warm scent of vanilla and coconut. Closing my eyes, I inhale again. The scent recreates a memory of Daisy, fresh from the bath, standing just in front of me and wrapped in a fluffy white towel. Her still-wet skin reflects the light from the flickering candles she always placed around the bath. Such scenes usually ended one way—a mischievous glint in her eye as she slowly peeled the towel away.

There's only so long you can let your own imagination torment you. I open my eyes and return the bath bomb to the cupboard.

I pour a glug of bubble bath into the tub and get undressed.

It's been a long time since I last took a bath and I'd forgotten how wonderful it is to just lie in absolute silence with no distractions. Keen not to let a busy mind spoil my blissful relaxation, I close my eyes and focus simply on breathing in and out. Slowly I slip further beneath the blanket of foam and before I know it, sleep arrives.

There is one inherent problem with sleeping in the bath. I discover that problem as I wake with a start in a tub full of tepid, murky water.

However, my sudden awakening wasn't down to lying in a pool of my own filth. It was caused by the shrill sound of the doorbell.

I clamber out of the bath and quickly dry myself off. I've barely got my first leg into a pair of jogging pants when the doorbell rings again. It's at that point I notice the time—almost eleven o'clock. I've been asleep in the bath for over two hours. Although my fingertips look like dried prunes, at least I avoided drowning.

The doorbell rings again, and whoever it is calling at such an anti-social hour, is keen to be heard as they keep their finger pressed on the bell for seven or eight seconds.

"Yeah, I heard you the first time," I mumble, throwing on a sweatshirt.

I stomp into the hallway and throw the front door open; intent on giving my unwelcome visitor a lesson on social etiquette, or telling them to fuck off.

The latter becomes more appealing when I find Ethan stood on the landing.

"What the hell do you want?" I hiss.

It's the most obvious question but as I take a second to absorb his dishevelled appearance, a more relevant question needs to be asked.

"And why do you look like you've been living in a hedgerow?"

"Where is he?" he rasps, blinking wildly.

"Who?"

"Him … Doctor … him. Where is he?"

"Are you pissed?"

He sounds pissed.

"No, I'm not. I'm … where is he?"

"In bed I'd imagine and, if you don't mind, that's exactly where I'm heading."

I start closing the door but Ethan stumbles forward and plants his foot in the way.

"Let me in," he pleads. "I need to see him."

"Yeah, well. My sister needs to see her daughter but some wanker is stopping her. How's that for karma?"

I expected some protest, some comeback, but what I didn't expect was Ethan crumbling to the floor and sobbing. That is, however, precisely what he does.

"Please," he begs. "I can't take any more."

My sympathy is in short supply. "What the hell are you whining about?"

He looks up at me, a broken man with eyes like a panda.

"I … I can't …" he pants.

"Spit it out, will you? As rewarding as it is, I've got better things to do than stand here watching you have a breakdown."

"I haven't slept in …" he mumbles, glancing at his watch. "Almost ninety hours."

"What has that got to do with Mungo? Go get some sleeping pills."

"They don't work. Nothing stops the …"

His voice trails off and I can't be sure but I think he might be either having a seizure or soiling himself. I couldn't care less which—I just want him to go away.

"Stops what?"

"Nightmares. I … I can't sleep because of the nightmares."

"Oh, good grief. And what do you expect Mungo to do about it? You want him to pop round and read you a bedtime story?"

He tries to muster some composure and clambers to his feet, using the wall to keep himself upright.

"No," he pants. "I want him to make them stop."

"You're off your head, man. What makes you think he can do that?"

"Because … he's in every one of them."

40.

In our final year of school, our form went away on an activity weekend. Alton Towers it was not.

Abandoned in the middle of nowhere, we spent two days hiking through an endless forest, falling from rope swings and, on the last day, screaming our way along a ridiculously high zip wire. It was on that zip wire, or half way along to be precise, Joe's loose-fitting jeans slipped from his waist and settled around his ankles. With his hands gripping on for dear life, there was nothing he could do about it. Joe's embarrassment was compounded by the fact he'd forgotten to pack clean underwear, and the consequence of his tardy packing meant he descended the final hundred feet with his teenage genitalia on full display.

I have never laughed so hard, until now.

"Oh, that's priceless," I cry, wiping the tears away. "Mungo is a bloody nightmare at the moment, I'll grant you that, but I think you need to change your meds, Ethan."

"It's true," he whines. "He's done something to me."

I'm about to slam the door on this nonsense when another door opens behind me. Presumably roused by Ethan's commotion, Mungo saunters up and stands by my shoulder.

The look on Ethan's face warps from exhaustion to terror.

"He's here to see you, Mungo. Apparently you've been giving him nightmares."

Ignoring my sarcasm, he casts his eye over Ethan.

"Let him in," Mungo orders.

"Are you kidding me?" I respond. "I'm knackered, and you haven't heard the crap he's been spouting. I think he's out of his mind on drugs or something."

"Let him in," Mungo repeats. "It is in your sister's best interests."

He then turns around and heads back along the hallway to the lounge, leaving me with a now-hyperventilating Ethan.

"Fucks sake. Come in."

I turn and stomp into the lounge. Mungo is already on the sofa, looking surprisingly relaxed considering the crazy accusations being thrown his way.

Ethan stumbles in and collapses into an armchair, as far away from Mungo as possible.

"This better be good, Mungo," I growl. "I don't want that

piece of shit in my flat any longer than necessary."

He stands up and a twisted smile forms on his face as he approaches Ethan.

"How are you feeling, Ethan Montgomery? A little tired?"

"I … I … can't sleep."

"No, I suspect not."

"What … what did you do to me?"

"What I told you I would do if you failed to accept my proposition."

"You … you spiked my wine … what did you put in it?"

"I did no such thing."

"I … what … did you hypnotise me then? You … you …"

Confusion bites as Ethan struggles to find words. Seeing him here now, rather than in the dim light of the hallway, I get to appreciate just how bloody terrible he looks. His shirt and trousers are crumpled, his hair a greasy nest, and his cheeks shadowed with stubble—a complete contrast to his usual pristine appearance.

I shouldn't really be surprised he looks so awful. I know first-hand what sleep deprivation can do.

Back in the days before Daisy came along, I once stayed up all night playing poker. I lost my last hand at half-seven and went to work an hour later; it was bearable for three or four hours but by lunchtime I felt horrific. Somehow, I made it to the end of the day but by that point I just wanted to curl up and die. If, as he claims, Ethan has been awake for three days, it's no wonder he's a gibbering mess.

It doesn't, however, explain why he hasn't slept for three days. And if Mungo does have anything to do with it, he isn't saying how, or why.

"Is this what you meant when you said he'd eventually comply?" I ask.

"Yes, although I thought it might take longer. Ethan Montgomery is clearly a weak man."

Now I want some answers.

"What have you done to him?"

I don't expect a straight answer but after a moment without any response, the victim himself decides to answer on Mungo's behalf.

"When I fall asleep … they come."

"They?"

"The nightmares. Awful, awful nightmares. They're … terrifying, I wake up in minutes."

"We all have nightmares, Ethan."

"No … not every single time you close your eyes. Every … single … time."

I've had enough nightmares over the years to know how you can suddenly be dragged kicking, and sometimes screaming, from the depths of sleep. I wouldn't wish it on my worst enemy, but Ethan is in a special category of his own—the worst of my worst enemies. My sympathy is negligible.

"This is all very interesting, Ethan, but I'd say your lack of sleep is messing with your mind. I don't know, but it's probably stress or something."

"No … no, it's him I tell you," he cries, pointing to Mungo. "He's in my nightmares."

I look across at Mungo and he lets out a long sigh.

"This is tiresome," he announces, glaring down at Ethan. "Are you willing to accept my proposal?"

"I … no … I can't."

"That is your choice but you should be aware chronic sleep deprivation will, in time, kill you."

"No … no … please stop it," Ethan begs. "I can't take any more."

"Then you have one choice, Ethan Montgomery. By eight o'clock tomorrow morning, you will hand over both your marital home and custody of your daughter to Kate Montgomery. Once you sign a legally binding contract regarding your other assets and the maintenance arrangements I proposed, the nightmares will end."

Knowing Ethan as I do, I can't believe he'd let a few nightmares scare him into signing a deal which would cost him so dearly. True to form, he lets his head fall back in the chair and he stares at the ceiling, perhaps hoping he can drag a legal counter from the midst of his addled mind. Seconds tick by and eventually, his eyelids droop, and then close. His breathing slows as his head lolls slightly to the left.

"Great," I groan. "He's fallen asleep."

"Just wait."

"For what?"

"You will see."

I decide I'll give Mungo precisely one minute and then I'm going to end this charade.

Forty seconds into that minute, Ethan stirs.

"No … no … no," he murmurs in his sleep. "Please, God … don't … don't take me in there."

"He's dreaming about Primark," I suggest.

"Quiet," Mungo snaps.

Ethan's stirring becomes more pronounced as his arms and legs twitch. Then, without warning, he lets out an ear-piercing scream.

"Noooo …"

With his breathing now frantic, he sits bolt upright and his bloodshot eyes dart left and right until they fix on Mungo.

"I'll do it," he gasps. "I'll do it, but please … make it stop."

"Go home, Ethan Montgomery, and call your estranged wife. Do as I requested and your nightmare will be over."

Ethan looks up and nods; his face ghostly white.

"But be warned," Mungo adds. "I do not offer second chances."

Whatever parlour trick Mungo just deployed, it appears to have dramatically shifted Ethan's stance. Mustering the little energy he possesses, he clambers from the chair. Taking a second to find his balance, he then stares at Mungo.

"You're evil," he murmurs.

"Thank you," Mungo replies flatly. "Now kindly fuck off."

The look in Mungo's eye is the final straw for Ethan. He turns on his heels and staggers out of the lounge. Still stunned by the events, I stand inert and listen as his haphazard footsteps continue down the hallway until the front door slams shut.

"I am going back to bed," Mungo declares, and starts shuffling away.

"Whoa! Hold on just a minute. What the hell just happened?"

He stops, and his shoulders slump.

"I said there was a plan," he sighs, wearily. "The plan was successfully implemented and, within approximately twelve hours, the situation will be fully resolved. What is not to understand?"

"Err, quite a bloody lot, as it goes. You can't expect me not to have questions after … whatever that was."

"What I expect, Adam Maxwell, is gratitude rather than an interrogation."

"But …"

"I suggest you get some sleep. You have a busy day tomorrow."

"I just …"

"Goodnight."

He shuffles away, leaving me to stew in a soup of questions.

With my mind too busy for sleep, I slump down on the sofa and try to make sense of the last twenty minutes.

Once I manage to wade past all the questions and the confusion, I find one emotion left standing alone: relief. Now, I don't know how Mungo did it, but all that really matters is that tomorrow Kate will be reunited with Bella. Granted, seeing Ethan for the pathetic piece of shit he is was a welcome bonus, but a problem which felt unsurmountable has finally been put to bed.

On reflection, I can see why Mungo was irked at my lack of gratitude. He has fixed a major problem for Kate, and in turn, for me.

Still, I'd kill to know how he did it. Perhaps Ethan was right and it was some kind of hypnosis trick. I once saw a stage hypnotist on TV, and he somehow hypnotised a rotund, balding, middle-aged man into thinking every woman found him sexually irresistible. Toe-curling stuff, but seeing that poor bloke act with such wanton delusion isn't so far removed from Ethan's conviction his nightmares are being invaded by my lodger.

The more I think about it, the more I realise I'm too tired to really give a shit.

Bedtime.

41.

It's now easy to see why Daisy became so exasperated with my untidiness.

Seven in the morning and I'm in the lounge clearing away empty coffee cups and hoovering discarded peanut shells from the carpet. Despite repeatedly banging on Mungo's bedroom door, and yelling a few choice words, the culprit remains absent from the scene of his crime.

"Lazy shit," I grumble to myself as I wash up the cups.

With the flat tidy, I take a shower and then sit down with a coffee to plan my day. There are several items I can cross off, from what I've now labelled my 'wobble list'. A glance at the kitchen clock tells me Kate should be reunited with Bella any minute; fingers crossed I can strike that most pressing of items from the list.

The next item is Daisy.

I was in such a rush when I left the hospital yesterday, I foolishly forgot to schedule the promised coffee. Should I text her now, or leave it a few days? I don't want to be a pest, but equally I don't want to leave it so long it looks like I don't care.

Christ. Why is there no rule book for this kind of thing?

In lieu of no obvious decision, I move on to the next item on my list: Mungo. I urgently need a proper chat about his decision to move out. Now my irritation at his slovenly ways has eased, I'm still not sure I want him to go. For all the nasty habits he's picked up of late, last night alone was proof I still need him around. How I persuade him of that will have to remain on the wobble list for the time being.

For now though, I've also got a business to run. Well, two to be precise.

With my prospects of producing enough Crystalene to replace my window cleaning income now a pipe dream, I'm set to be a window cleaner in the morning, a salesman in the afternoon, and an overworked production operative in the evenings. On the plus side, by the time the baby arrives I should have saved enough money to buy whatever he or she needs. Sadly, the one thing I really want to provide—a stable home life with two parents—can't be bought.

The dull ache offers a reminder: I might now be walking in the right direction, but the road ahead is long, and the final destination anyone's guess. If I think about that too long, the temptation would be to turn around and head back to where I was. I know it's not an option. Not now.

Got to press on.

I head out to a morning so cold, even a Geordie would consider donning a vest.

Despite my best efforts, I only manage to complete four houses before hypothermia becomes a real concern. It pains me to give up but at least I gave it a go. In the past, I wouldn't have stepped more than a few yards beyond the front door on days like this. And on the upside, at least I've now got a productive use for the spare hours.

I return to Alan and check my phone. One missed call from Kate. I ring her back hoping for good news.

"Adam, you'll never guess where I am," she answers, excitedly.

"A cheese factory in Hull?"

"Very funny. No, I'm actually stood in *my* kitchen."

"Your kitchen?"

"Yep. *My* kitchen in *my* house. Let's try again and see if you can guess what happened this morning. I bet you can't."

I bet I can.

"I reckon Ethan asked you over and gave you the house and full custody of Bella."

"What?" she gasps. "How did you know?"

"He paid me a visit last night."

"Did he? So this sudden capitulation is down to you?"

"As much as I'd like to take the credit, it was all down to Mungo."

"You mean he actually did have a plan?"

"Apparently so, and it clearly worked. Has Ethan agreed to a divorce settlement?"

"He said the papers are being couriered over within the hour. He's being uncharacteristically generous too."

"Good. Was he okay this morning when you saw him?"

"Um, not really. He looked like he hadn't slept in days and most of what he said was gibberish."

Seeing as I don't understand it myself, there's no point even trying to explain the real reason behind Ethan's bedraggled appearance and sudden change of heart.

"Perhaps his conscience has been keeping him up at night, sis."

"Maybe, but I don't really care. All that matters is I've got my baby back, and I can now start planning our future."

"Honestly, I'm made up for you. I really am."

I hear a slight sniffle and the line goes quiet for a second. Unlike our previous calls, I'd guess any tears are likely to be of relief or joy.

"Thank you, Adam," she eventually croaks. "You'll never know just how grateful I am, to you and Doctor Mungo."

"Hey, that's what big brothers are for. And I'll pass your thanks on to Mungo."

"I'd rather do that myself in person. Why don't you and the doctor come over for dinner next week, once I've got myself sorted out? I think it's the very least I can do."

"We'll see. Mungo isn't really the sociable type, but I'll ask."

We say our goodbyes and I throw the phone on the passenger's seat. One problem well and truly put to bed, although Kate's dinner invitation only highlights another: I don't even know if Mungo will be around next week.

As I try to wake Alan, I make a decision. Mungo was the one who told me I shouldn't procrastinate, and I need to take responsibility for getting shit done. Well, seeing as I've now got some extra time in my schedule, I'm going to take Mungo's advice, as the man himself is now top of my wobble list.

On cue, Alan spits into life.

I use the six-minute journey to plan what I'm going to say, once I've thawed out. There's little chance of finding warmth before I arrive home, with Alan's woeful heater barely reaching lukewarm.

Half-expecting to find the TV blaring, I'm surprised when I open the front door to silence.

"Mungo," I yell. "Are you in?"

There's no response so I bang on his bedroom door and call his name again.

Still nothing.

I'm about to bang the bedroom door for a second time when a more obvious option becomes apparent. I grab the handle and turn it, or at least try to turn it, but it doesn't budge. My flat has many faults but this door handle has never been one of them. I try again but there's no give whatsoever—as if it's been welded shut. The only conclusion I can draw is that Mungo had a lock fitted at some point, although there's no obvious sign of one.

Not to be thwarted, I pull out my phone and find Mungo's number. I've never seen him use his phone so it wouldn't

318

surprise me if it's switched off. I prod the call button and after a worrying few seconds of nothing it rings.

"Yes?" he answers in his usual curt manner.

"It's Adam. Where are you?"

"The Red Lion public house."

"Oh, right … what? You're in the pub?"

"Yes, I am. Angry Pete has just introduced me to Jägerbombs."

"Err …"

Too many admissions in succession scramble my mind. Mungo's behaviour has certainly been erratic but this is on a whole different level.

"Sorry, Mungo. Can I just get this straight: despite the fact it's not even lunchtime yet, you're in the pub knocking back Jägerbombs with the psychotic halfwit you humiliated last week?"

"That would be a fair summation."

I can only think of one question.

"Why?"

"Why not?"

"Because … actually, stay right where you are. I'll be there in five minutes."

I thought my greatest challenge would be convincing Mungo to stay, but now I find myself having to drag him away from his own chaotic behaviour. This is not what I need right now.

As I pace through the streets, my mind recounts Dr Rowe's advice last week: *hope for the best but prepare for the worst*. It's hard to imagine how Mungo's behaviour could get any worse. Then again, if Handy Mandy is also in the Red Lion …

As prepared as I'm likely to be, I crash through the door to the public bar.

Unsurprisingly, for this time of the day, the bar is empty besides Mungo and Angry Pete. They both turn in my direction as the door clatters shut.

"Ah, Adam Maxwell," Mungo calls across. "Come and join us."

I make brief eye contact with Angry Pete as he tries, what I can only assume, is his version of a smile. Warily, I wander over and join them.

"You remember Angry Pete?" Mungo asks.

"Um, yeah."

We swap nods.

"Angry Pete and I have resolved our differences," Mungo continues. "It was a misunderstanding."

"Yeah, it was," Angry Pete adds. "Sharon's tits weigh about eleven-hundred grammes each, so Mungo reckons."

"Good to know. Can I have a word, Mungo?"

"You may."

"In private."

"Fine. Let me get you an alcoholic beverage."

"No, thanks."

"You do not want a pint of lager? Or maybe you would like to try a Jägerbomb?"

"I don't want a bloody drink," I snap. "Unlike you, I've got shit to be getting on with."

His reaction is not what I expected as he beams a broad smile.

"Very well. Let us talk."

We leave Angry Pete at the bar and take a table across the room. There are so many questions buzzing around my head I'm not sure where to begin. Fortunately, Mungo takes the initiative.

"You are concerned about my behaviour?"

"Do you blame me? Downing drinks with Angry Pete at this time of day isn't sensible; for anyone, let alone you."

"Sensible is an interesting word," he muses. "The dictionary definition is: to have, or show, good sense or judgement."

"I know what sensible means, thank you."

"You do now. That certainly was not the case, though, was it?"

He's done it again.

"Don't turn this around and make it about me, Mungo. You're the problem here."

"I suppose I am, and that is good news."

"How can it possibly be good news?"

"Because it means your therapy is about complete."

To this point I'm still unconvinced I've had any kind of therapy and, if I have, I'm equally unconvinced it's worked.

"What bloody therapy? Unless I've missed something, there hasn't been any."

"And yet here we are in a public house, and you have just declined an alcoholic beverage."

"Eh? I haven't got time to sit around drinking beer. So what?"

"If you consider the significance of that statement, you will have your answer."

I don't have the patience to deal with his cryptic bullshit; not when the major issue is still to be resolved.

"Just forget my therapy for now. I want to talk about you leaving."

"And as I said, there is nothing to discuss."

"Well, there is. There's your rent money for starters. Shouldn't you give notice or something?"

"The money is of no use to me. Keep it."

"What? All of it?"

"It is my decision to leave, so yes."

It's a generous gesture but the money was never my primary concern.

"But … I don't want you to leave."

The very last word you'd use to describe Mungo would be tactile. It therefore comes as a surprise when he reaches across the table and places his hand on my arm.

"It is not a matter of want," he says softly, fixing me with his turquoise eyes. "It is a matter of necessity."

"I don't understand."

"What you, or I, want, is irrelevant. It is impossible for me to stay because I do not belong here."

For one fleeting moment I thought he was being sincere, compassionate almost. But no.

"Alright," I groan, "I'll play along. Where do you belong then?"

He raises his hand from my arm and with the tips of his fingers, gently taps my temple twice.

"Somewhere, but not in there."

"Jesus wept. How many Jägerbombs have you had?"

"Four, or is it five. I can't recall."

"Well, that explains it then."

I get up from the table. "I'll talk to you when you're sober."

"I doubt you will find the answers you seek, even if I am not under the influence of alcohol."

"Brilliant. And God only knows why I'm asking this, but when exactly will my therapy be complete?"

"Soon."

"I'll tell you something for nothing, Mungo. If you carry on the way you're heading, it can't come soon enough."

"And if you carry on the way you're heading, it will be soon enough."

I roll my eyes, and I'm about to walk away, but there's still something I have to say. Something I should have said last night.

"Just for the record, I much preferred the Mungo who helped me out last night. I never said thank you."

"For?"

"Dealing with Ethan. He kept his word and Kate is back home now."

"I know."

"How?"

"Let us just say Ethan Montgomery is currently enjoying a long overdue sleep."

"Yeah, you're definitely pissed. I'll see you later."

Another snippet of Mungo's advice follows me back across the room and out the door: there's no sense in worrying about things I can't control, and I sure as hell can't control the man who gave me that advice.

As I wander back to the flat, I come to the conclusion it would be better to assume Mungo will be gone next week. It pains me to admit it, but we've reached a tipping point, and I fear he'll become more of a hindrance than a help if his behaviour continues to deteriorate.

It seems some plates are destined to crash, no matter how hard you try to keep them spinning.

By the time I open the flat door, I've recalibrated my thoughts. What Mungo does next is what Mungo does next. He appears to have made a decision and so should I. In roughly six months' time I'll be a father and that is all I can afford to focus on; with or without my errant lodger in tow.

Head sorted, I return my attention to the day I originally had planned, and the need to find more customers. A two-minute shower, a change of clothes, and I'm all set to leave, until my phone rings. I prod the screen to accept a call from a local number I don't recognise.

"Good morning, sonny," a voice booms. "George Bradshaw."

I'm not sure if I find his use of the word 'sonny' endearing or patronising. Either way, he's a customer so best I let it go.

"Morning, Mr Bradshaw. What can I do for you?"

"I need some more stock. Can you drop a dozen bottles over this afternoon?"

"You've sold out already?"

"Why do you sound so surprised? I'm not running a charity here, you know. This is a shop—people come here to buy products that do a job. Yours obviously does, so customers have bought it."

"Right, erm, great. I'm actually about to hit the road so I can pop over now if it's convenient?"

"Righto. See you shortly."

He ends the call.

As pleased as I am to hear Crystalene is selling well, the numbers don't bring quite the same pleasure. I'll earn just over ten quid from his order, and that's before I've spent half-an-hour delivering it. It's a different angle on the same problem—one I've already wrestled with and can't currently solve. Still, I guess ten quid is better than nothing, and certainly ten quid more than I would have earned in the past while sat on my arse in front of the TV.

This beggar can't afford to be choosy.

I head back downstairs and hump the remaining stock into Alan whilst trying to ignore just how little fruit my labour will bear.

Make. Sell. Repeat. It's going to be a long six months.

42.

The bell chimes my arrival as I leave the present day and step into a bygone age. Again, there are no customers and no sign of Mr Bradshaw. If I were a shoplifter with a ready market for mothballs or masonry nails, I could have a field day.

I plod over to the counter and place the box of Crystalene down.

"Hello," I call out. "Mr Bradshaw?"

I hear footsteps and George Bradshaw emerges from the archway.

"Ah, that was quick," he comments. "I do like a man who keeps his word."

Conscious of not wasting too much time, I reply with a smile and hand him a delivery note.

"I appreciate the order, Mr Bradshaw. Give me a call when you need more."

I offer him a handshake which he ignores.

"How's it going then?" he asks.

I can only guess the old fella is either lonely or bored, but I really don't have time for idle chit chat. Every wasted second chips away at my already meagre profit margin.

"It's going okay, thank you."

"Is it selling well?"

"Fairly well."

I kind of hoped my clipped answers would get the message across, but no. Mr Bradshaw throws another question.

"What are your plans?"

Is he asking me out on a date?

"Err, plans?"

"Yes, plans for growing the business. I assume you can't be making much money selling a few dozen bottles here and there."

"Oh, right," I cough. "It's really early days."

"But you do have a plan?"

I should just lie, and leave.

"Not really."

He plucks a bottle of Crystalene from the box and studies it with more interest than a bottle of cleaning solution warrants.

Unsure what to do, I shuffle on the spot until he returns the bottle to the box and asks another question.

"Have you got ten minutes for a cup of tea?"

As Mungo made clear, time is finite, and it's the one resource I can't afford to waste. I'm about to decline Mr Bradshaw's offer when I pause for a second and ask a question of myself. Would spending ten minutes with a once-successful businessman really be time wasted?

At worst, he might bore me witless for ten minutes but, maybe, I might pick up the odd nugget of good advice.

"Sure. Thank you."

"The kettle has just boiled. Give me a minute."

He shuffles back through the archway and returns a moment later with a tray. Clearly George Bradshaw is a traditionalist so I'm not surprised to see cups and saucers rather than mugs. He's even laid on a plate of custard creams. The biscuits alone validate my decision as no time involving custard creams could ever be considered wasted.

He nudges one of the cups in my direction together with a bowl of sugar cubes.

"So, sonny. Do you know who I am?" he asks out of nowhere.

It's the kind of question usually uttered by z-list celebrities when they're denied access to a nightclub but, on this occasion, there's no hint of arrogance or ego behind it.

"I do now, but not when I first came in."

"No," he chuckles. "I didn't think so."

"Why do you say that?"

"Because you were fearless. In all my years, no sales rep has ever offered me a wager, let alone talked to me the way you did."

"Sorry, I didn't mean to offend you."

"You didn't, and never apologise for playing to your strengths. I was impressed. If you hadn't shown a bit of spunk, I wouldn't have heard you out."

I feel my cheeks flush. Primarily because I'm not used to receiving compliments, but partly because I've never been accused of showing spunk before.

"Thank you."

"Now, let's talk about your plan, or lack of one."

"Okay."

"You've got a decent product so you must have a vague idea of where you want to take it?"

"I kind of do, but it's an idea that feels a long way away at the moment."

"Go on."

Seeing as I have no more than a tenner's worth of custom to lose, I explain what happened in my meeting with Karen Proctor, and the truth about my production methods. Mr Bradshaw listens intently while nibbling on a custard cream.

"You see," I conclude. "Selling Crystalene isn't my major concern. Producing it in sufficient quantities and bottling it is where my problem lies."

"That's not a problem," he replies dismissively.

"Isn't it?"

"Of course not. You've got two options. You could licence the product to a major player and they'd handle all the production, or you could find an investor and fund a production facility of your own."

Neither of these options were mentioned in Mungo's business plan which means I'm now on my own. Do I admit I don't have the first clue what he's talking about, or do I wing it?

I choose a third option and reach for another custard cream while nodding slowly, as if pondering his options. My hope is Mr Bradshaw will fill the silence by expanding on his statement. A risky, but necessary ploy.

"I could have a word with my lad if you like?" he casually adds.

"Your lad?"

"Stuart. He's now the CEO of Barton Bradshaw and I could float the idea of licencing Crystalene to him."

I almost choke on my biscuit.

"Sorry," I splutter. "What, um, exactly would that entail?"

"It'd be a standard licencing agreement. Basically Barton Bradshaw would manufacture, distribute, and market the product as they do with their own lines. You'd earn a small royalty payment on every unit sold."

I heard what he said, quite clearly, but the casual manner in which he said it doesn't quite tally with the significance. I need to play this cool.

"And what could I expect to earn from that kind of arrangement, you know, roughly speaking?"

"Hard to say, but I think you'd safely creep into the six-figure income bracket."

Six. Fucking. Figures. A hundred grand? Two hundred grand? Does the specific number really matter? What does matter is containing my excitement, and resisting the urge to run around the shop as if I'd scored the winning goal in a cup final.

I swallow hard and scrape together just enough composure

to continue.

"Right. I'd certainly be interested in speaking to Stuart, then."

"Not so fast, sonny," he chortles with a little too much glee for my liking. "I said I *could* have a word with Stuart. I didn't say I would."

The decimal point slides a few places to the left in that six-figure income, and that irks.

"So, why say it then?"

Despite my best efforts to stifle it, I can hear the agitation in my voice.

"I was just floating the idea. As options go, it's not one you should seriously consider."

"I shouldn't consider the option of earning a six-figure income? With respect, Mr Bradshaw, I don't think you realise how that kind of money would change my life."

"You'd be surprised. Back in the day, when I first started, I didn't have a pot to piss in. All we had were three products and an empty order book."

"Surely you know what it's like then? I just need a break."

"You don't need a break. You've already got what you need, and it's all I needed to build my business."

Whatever he thinks I've got, I'm clueless, and my confused frown says as much.

"You've got belief, sonny," he confirms. "And that's all you need."

"Belief?"

"Yep. Let me ask you a question: do you think your product is the best out there?"

"Err, it's better than anything else I've ever used."

"And that's why the second option is the way to go. I'll give you the advice I wish someone had given me before I floated Burton Bradshaw—keep control, at all costs."

I adopt an expression as vacant as a Skegness hotel in February

"Listen," he sighs. "Licencing is an easy option but you'd be handing over control of your product for at least a decade. This industry can change in a heartbeat and if you don't have control, you can't change with it. That's why I don't think it's your best option."

"Understood, I think, but surely I'm back to square one then? I don't have the money to fund a proper production facility."

"Indeed. And that's why you need an investor."

The wires connect and a lightbulb glows.

"Ohh, I see."

"No, you don't," he chortles. "I'm not that investor."

The lightbulb pops.

"Great," I huff. "So, I really am back to square one."

"You're nowhere near square one. You have an excellent product and you have belief. Trust me; that's all you need."

His advice is beginning to sound as vague as some of Mungo's.

"Yes, but …"

"No buts," he interjects. "Stop wasting your time trying to flog a few dozen bottles to the likes of me, and start using that time to find an investor."

It would be so easy to grasp the negatives from my conversation with George Bradshaw. I've had a six-figure carrot dangled in front of my face, only for it to be snatched away, and I've been told to find an investor, which I fear will be as complex and risky as purchasing lingerie. However, I don't feel as negative as I might.

"Do you really think I could persuade someone to invest?"

"You persuaded me to hear you out, didn't you? Some of the best sales reps in the land haven't managed that."

"But, where do I start?"

"Do the numbers. Work out how much you need and how much of your business you're willing to trade in exchange for funding. If you want my advice, keep things lean to start with. You don't need expensive premises and you don't need brand new equipment. If you're sensible you can get a facility set up for maybe forty grand, or even less."

Forty grand sounds like a vast sum of money but I guess everything is relative. To a man like George Bradshaw, it's probably the cost of a week's holiday.

As I ponder my next move, Mr Bradshaw empties his teacup.

"Anyway, sonny," he says. "I've got things to be getting on with."

"Right, yes. And thank you, Mr Bradshaw. I appreciate your advice."

"You're welcome, and I expect to see Crystalene in the shops before autumn."

I'm not sure if he's being flippant or genuinely believes it's a possibility, but I'm willing to hope for the latter.

With a parting nod, he picks up the tray and turns to the archway. I'm about to leave, but there's one burning question I'll probably never get the chance to ask if I don't ask it now.

"Why do you do it, Mr Bradshaw?"

"Do what?" he replies, turning to face me.

"Run this shop? I know you don't need the money, so why?"

"Even if this place made a profit, which it doesn't, not everything in life can be measured in pounds and pence."

"I'm not with you."

"You'll understand one day, when you've built your own little empire. You'll get yourself an overpriced sports car, you'll holiday in five-star hotels, and you'll buy a house the size of a castle, but then you'll realise none of that stuff really matters at the end of the day."

"What does matter then?"

"Love. Simple as that."

"Love?"

"Aye, and The Beatles were right when they said money can't buy it."

"I'm not sure how that explains why you're running this shop."

Really, it's none of my business and I'm not expecting an answer but after a wistful sigh, I get one.

"When my father passed away, I was busy with my own business, so my wife offered to run this place so it would stay in the family. This became her little empire."

Mum already mentioned Mrs Bradshaw is no longer of this earth but the sadness in his eyes confirms it.

"Maybe I'm just a daft old bugger," he continues. "But when I'm in here, I feel close to her."

"Not that my opinion is worth much, Mr Bradshaw, but I don't think you're daft."

"Just an old bugger then?" he smiles.

"Oh, no, that's not …"

"I'm kidding with you. And remember what I said about not measuring everything in pounds and pence. At the end of every tough day, and there will be plenty of those, it won't be your accountant waiting at home with words of comfort and a hug."

The words linger but the man doesn't. Mr Bradshaw smiles, and then heads back through the archway.

I may have only made a tenner but I exit the shop with a priceless new perspective, and a different path to tread.

43.

Apparently, time flies when you're having fun. I wouldn't say I'm having fun as I sit and stare beyond Alan's dashboard, but forty minutes still passes in a heartbeat. I daren't drive yet because my mind is too distracted, so I remain parked outside Bradshaw's Hardware.

It's strange how the human mind works, and mine is possibly stranger than most. During my introspection, a random, and seemingly irrelevant memory gate-crashed my thoughts. It was a few days after Daisy and I first moved into the flat, and we took a trip to IKEA. We returned with two flat-pack bookcases, and their entire stock of scatter cushions.

Keen to demonstrate my DIY skills, I unpacked the first bookcase and, in accordance with man-law, started assembling it without referring to the instructions. I got so far but had to eventually concede defeat when Daisy noted the shelves were wonky. I read the instructions three times and still couldn't fathom out where I'd gone wrong. Much frustration ensued, until two hours later when I found a second page of instructions—still in the box.

I might be wrong, but I reckon Mr Bradshaw has just presented me with a second page. Perhaps I now possess all I need to reassemble my life.

I make a call.

"Daisy. Hi, it's me."

"Over twenty-four hours," she chuckles. "I was beginning to think you'd forgotten about me."

Just hearing her voice makes my heart flutter. I need to keep calm, and stick to my half-baked plan.

"Sorry, but I've been a bit busy."

"I'm joking. It's fine."

I take a breath and compose myself.

"Look, I was wondering if you're free for dinner tonight?"

"Um, maybe."

Despite the hesitancy in her voice, at least she didn't flatly refuse my invite.

"Don't worry. I'm not going to do or say anything stupid. I know where we are, and I respect your decision."

"You do?"

"Yes, and I promise this is nothing to do with changing your mind about us. It's about the future—our baby's future."

"Okay, fine. Where and when?"

"Seven o'clock, at Oscar's Bistro."

"Oscar's? That's an improvement on those dreadful buffet restaurants you used to take me to."

She has a point, but tonight is about making an impression rather than stockpiling prawn toast.

"So, you'll be there?"

"I will."

"Great, and bring Eddie."

My request is met with stunned silence.

"Sorry, did I hear that right? You want me to bring my dad?"

"Yes."

"I don't need a chaperone, Adam."

"This concerns him as much as you, so please just bring him along."

"I can ask him."

"Don't ask him, Daisy—tell him, please. This is important, for all of us."

It would be fair to say I've always lacked assertiveness, and my demand clearly takes Daisy by surprise.

"Okay, okay," she blusters. "He'll be there."

"Great. See you later."

I hang up before she gets to ask the questions I know she'll be dying to ask.

With phase one initiated, I head back to the flat to work on my battle plan.

I arrive home to a pile of mail but no flatmate. If he's still in the Red Lion I dread to think what state he's in, but we all have to learn the hard way, I guess. I scoop up the mail and frown at the top letter—a utility bill. Daisy always handled the bills, for obvious reasons, but the letter from the utility company is now in my name. I tear it open.

"Holy shit."

Having shirked the responsibility of utility bills for most of my adult life, it comes as a shock to learn gas and electric are so bloody expensive. Maybe that's why Daisy was so keen on candles. I stick the bill to the fridge and immediately turn the heating off.

Armed with just a laptop and a mug of coffee, I sit down at the kitchen table and open a blank spreadsheet. It's still a blank spreadsheet by the time I finish my coffee. I need help. Of the two people who could provide that help, one of them is currently intoxicated and the other lying in a hospital bed. There's no real decision to make, so I call Mum's mobile.

"Hi, Mum. I don't suppose you're at the hospital?"

"And a good afternoon to you too, son. Yes, I am."

"Great. Can I have a word with Dad?"

"You don't want to talk to your mother then?"

"Can you help me with spreadsheets and financial data?"

"I'll pass you over."

A series of muffled sounds follow before I hear Dad's voice.

"Alright, son. How are you?"

"Good thanks, Dad. Enjoying your final day of hospital food?"

"Put it this way: if I never eat scrambled eggs again, it'll be too soon."

Before I get to discuss the purpose of my call, Dad takes the opportunity to complain, in detail, about every meal he's been served over the last five days. Many minutes pass before he steps off his soapbox.

"Anyway, Dad, I need your advice."

"About?"

I relay my conversation with George Bradshaw and what he suggested.

"So, you're serious about this business?" Dad asks.

"Deadly. I've got to make this work."

"Okay, well, there's nothing complicated about preparing a financial plan. The best way to think of it is like running a car, or a van in your case."

"Go on."

"You have two types of cost in business: capital investment and ongoing."

I'm already fighting the urge to switch off.

"Your capital investment costs would be, for example, the price you pay for any machinery, and your ongoing costs would be rent, rates, insurances and the like."

"Um, okay."

"I've lost you already, haven't I?"

"Kind of."

"Think of it another way. When you bought your van, that was a capital investment because it was necessary to deliver your service, and you only paid for it once."

"Financially, yes. Emotionally, I'm still paying for it."

"I thought you were taking this seriously?"

"Sorry. Carry on."

"Your ongoing costs are expenses, like diesel and road tax."

"Okay, got that."

"Now, think of what you need to set up and run a production-based business, and break it down into separate areas. Firstly, there's the premises, and I'd suggest contacting a few local estate agents to get an idea of rents. You'll also need to factor in, like with any property, the other ongoing expenses such as insurance, utilities, rates, repairs, etc."

Probably best not to tell him I've only just discovered the true horror of household expenses.

"Gotcha."

"Then there are the manufacturing expenses. You'll need to buy the bottling machinery, which would be capital investment, but it will almost certainly need regular servicing, and consumables such as lubricants, and those are ongoing costs."

"That makes sense, I think."

It takes another twenty minutes of explanation, and all Dad's patience, before I get the full picture.

"And that's all there is to it," he concludes, wearily. "Once you put all the numbers into a spreadsheet, you'll be able to determine how much investment you need up front, and how much cash you'll need to maintain the business each month. It really is no different to your window cleaning round—just on a larger scale."

"Thanks, Dad."

"And most importantly, once you know how much you're spending, you'll know what quantities you need to sell in order to make a profit. That's the most important part, so don't forget to factor those numbers in."

"Understood."

With a final thank you, I end the call abruptly as I can already sense the information slipping away.

Although it feels something akin to a school project, I furiously scribble a list of the specific information I need, together with some initial thoughts on where I can get it. It takes a while, but the process helps to corral all of Dad's advice together. Using Mungo's original business plan as a template, I then organise my lists into a series of tasks. I'm sure it's not how these things are usually done but it works for me, and delivers a timely boost to my confidence as I make the first of many phone calls.

After three long hours, the spreadsheet begins to take shape.

Despite a few gaps in my data, there is a surprising sense of satisfaction in seeing the actual numbers required to set up a basic production facility. It must be said, those same numbers are also terrifying when I think of them as debts and liabilities rather than just digits on a spreadsheet. Is it normal to feel so arse-clinchingly petrified at this stage of launching a business?

I take a break for a coffee, and remind myself I built the window cleaning business up from nothing and, although it's not on the same scale, I made that work.

Bolstered by caffeine and positive thoughts, I'm about to resume my quest for data when I hear the front door open. The allure of the Red Lion appears to have finally worn thin.

"Mungo? Is that you?" I call out; perhaps needlessly considering it's unlikely to be anyone else.

My call, however, is not answered by a monotone voice, but a shrill peel of laughter which sounds vaguely familiar.

"Shit. No."

I dart out to the hallway and confirm my fears.

"What the fuck?"

I can't be sure who is supporting who, but two, clearly-pissed, figures are leant against one another with arms draped around each other's shoulders. One of those figures is Mungo and the other is Handy Mandy; the Red Lion's resident alcoholic and purveyor of car-park hand jobs.

"Alright, Adam," she cackles. "I like your flat."

I look her up and down. Perhaps once, some time back in the eighties, Mandy might have been an attractive woman. Time and alcohol have taken their toll, though, and no amount of hair bleach or lurid makeup can turn back the clock.

"What are you doing here, Mandy?"

"She is here to consume alcoholic beverages," Mungo slurs, waving a bottle of gin.

"Oh no she's not," I blast. "I'm not having you two getting up to God knows what under my roof."

"I promise we'll be good as gold, darlin'," Mandy coos in a misguided charm offensive.

Ignoring her, I turn my attention to Mungo. "You and I need to talk. Now."

"What about me?" Mandy squawks.

"Go and sit in the kitchen," I order, pointing the way. "And don't steal, eat, or even touch anything."

She snatches the gin bottle and staggers down the hallway, giggling to herself. With my unwelcome guest out of the way, I step towards Mungo and straight into a fog of alcohol fumes.

"Christ, Mungo. What have you been drinking?"

"Is that a rhetorical question?" he replies, leaning up against the door. "Or do you need to know specifically?"

Despite his inability to stand unaided, at least he's vaguely coherent. Small mercies.

It would be so easy to lose my shit but, having been in Mungo's shoes more times than I care to remember, I know you can't win an argument with a drunk. Beyond venting my annoyance at the interruption, yelling at him won't achieve anything so I try to remain calm.

"This has got to stop, Mungo, for your sake as much as mine."

"This?"

"Yes, your behaviour. I can just about cope with your untidiness, but getting pissed and bringing the likes of Handy Mandy home is too much, even for me. What the hell were you thinking?"

"Very little thought went into my decision. Just an awful lot of alcohol and poor judgement."

"And that's what I don't understand—why you're acting up like this. Has something happened you're not telling me about?"

"There is a lot I have not told you about."

"Now might be a good time to tell me, then. It's pretty obvious something isn't right."

"On the contrary. Everything is right."

"Clearly, you and I have a very different idea of what's right."

"It matters not, Adam Maxwell," he says dismissively while trying to stifle a burp. "My errant behaviour will stop soon enough, because I will not be here."

"You're still set on leaving?"

"I always was. There is no need for me to be here now."

Exasperated, all I can do is shake my head.

"Whatever," I sigh. "But while you're still here, at least show some respect. You can start by getting rid of Handy Mandy."

"Very well," he groans.

Steadying himself with an outstretched arm, he takes a few wobbly steps and I move aside so he can go fetch his drinking buddy. As he passes, he suddenly stops and looks up at me.

"How did you ever manage to live like this?" he murmurs.

"Like what?"

"Without rational thought or even a modicum of common sense."

As he awaits an answer, the sheer gravity of his question hits home. How did I live like that, and when did my issues become past tense?

The realisation painted across my face prompts a smile from Mungo.

"As I said, your treatment is virtually complete."

He staggers on and disappears into the kitchen, leaving me to dissect my thoughts. It doesn't take long to draw a conclusion.

"Shit," I whisper to myself.

He might be drunk but he might also be right.

44.

She did not go quietly.

In the end, Mungo had to give her twenty quid in the hope she'd fuck off to the nearest off licence. Mandy, true to form, took it as advance payment. I'll give Mungo his dues, though. For a small man, he did well in resisting Mandy's efforts to forcibly deliver an unwanted hand job. She eventually backed down, but not before exposing her left tit, and then throwing up on the kitchen floor; both times severely testing my own gag reflex.

To his credit, Mungo cleaned up the mess before disappearing into his bedroom; presumably to head off the mother of all hangovers before it could take hold.

Now peace has been restored, I can continue working on my financial plan and some equally important research.

I become so engrossed in my task, it comes as a shock when I eventually look at the clock, and discover it's almost six—an hour before I'm due to be at Oscar's Bistro.

After a final check on my afternoon's work, I allow myself a satisfied smile and print off five spreadsheets. If I didn't know I was the author, I'd say the documents appear almost professional. However, much like when you leave home in a rush, there's still a nagging doubt I've forgotten something. Too late now, even if I have.

I take a quick shower and head into the bedroom. A suit feels too formal so I decide to wear a fitted linen shirt Daisy bought me, together with my best pair of jeans. It's a look I think they call smart casual. A splash of aftershave and a spot of wax to tame my unruly hair, and I'm ready to go.

Slipping on the only smart jacket I possess, I grab the spreadsheets and tuck them into the inside pocket. A final glance in the hallway mirror and I'm set.

I barrel down the stairs and out into the cold night air; all the while going over what I'm going to say when I finally sit down at the table. I know, for sure, I'm taking a leap of faith with this plan, and it could spectacularly backfire, but I reckon the potential rewards outweigh the risk. Of the many reckless decisions I've made throughout my life, I'm sure this is more a calculated risk than a wild, ill-conceived punt.

I'll know for sure in a few hours, but one thing I already

know is I could do with a few drinks to calm my nerves. I decide to walk into town.

Five minutes into the walk and I'm already having regrets as my ears and cheeks sting. Strangely, the concern over possible frostbite proves a welcome distraction from worrying about how the evening will go. It's only when I turn into the High Street, and Oscar's Bistro comes into sight, the worrying returns.

Checking my watch, I'm relieved to see I'm fifteen minutes early. At least there's time to grab a drink and settle my nerves before Daisy and Eddie arrive.

I push the door open and walk straight into a wall of warm air; heavy with the aroma of dishes I know will cost more than my weekly shop. On the upside, a quick glance around confirms Oscar's is a definite improvement on my usual culinary haunts. I'm no expert on interior design, but somebody clearly is, and the muted decor feels just the right side of relaxed.

"Can I help you, sir?"

A waiter approaches me—Greg, according to his name badge. Greg clearly subscribes to *Hipster Monthly* judging by his finely sculpted hair and beard.

"I've got a reservation for seven, in the name of Maxwell."

Greg steps over to a lectern by the door and prods a screen.

"It says here you've booked for three," he says.

"No, it was definitely seven. Why would anyone want a meal at three in the afternoon?"

"No, sir. Three people."

"Oh, gotcha. Sorry. A table for three at seven o'clock, yes."

I need alcohol perhaps more than I realised.

Greg leads me across to a table by the window and asks if I'd like a drink. My default answer would be to order a pint of lager, and that's what Daisy will expect to see when she arrives. Actually, that's not strictly true. Daisy will be expecting me not to be here on account I'm usually late for everything.

"I'll have a bottle of white wine, please."

"Would you like to see the wine menu?"

The only reason I'd need to see a wine menu is to check the prices. The names alone would be meaningless to a lager lout like me.

"Um, no. Just a bottle of house white, please."

Judging by the look on Greg's face, I think I've inadvertently outed myself as a poor tipper. He floats off and returns a minute later with a bottle of wine which will probably be cheap in every way but price. He pours half a glass and confirms he'll be back once the rest of my party arrive.

One sip confirms why I don't drink wine—a bouquet of chip-shop vinegar with subtle hints of witch's piss. Still, alcohol is alcohol, so I bravely neck half the glass and try not to let the disgust show on my face.

I could murder a pint. I must resist.

Despite finishing the glass, the alcohol has barely had time to cast its magic when the door swings open, and in walk Eddie and Daisy. Seeing them both together, you'd never guess such a stunning creation could possibly be the fruit of Eddie's grizzled loins. They are, in every sense, beauty and the beast.

I stand and wave to catch Daisy's attention. She smiles and waves back before making her way over. Eddie ambles behind; looking every bit like he doesn't want to be here.

If composure were a living entity, I'm sure it would have barged past me and made a beeline for the door by now. Daisy looks incredible in a short, ruby-red dress, which somehow manages to look stylish yet sassy. Eddie looks like Eddie.

"You're here," she chirps. "There's a good start."

She steps over and kisses me on the cheek; the sweetness of her perfume triggering memories of better times.

"You look fantastic," I gush.

"I don't feel fantastic. I feel frumpy and fat."

I avoid the minefield by answering with a smile and a shake of the head. My smile is returned as we take our seats with Daisy opposite me and Eddie next to her.

I'd be quite content to simply sit and stare at Daisy all evening but Eddie has other ideas.

"Let's have it then," he grumbles. "Why have I been dragged here this evening?"

This is the moment. Everything I practised this afternoon comes down to what I say next. And, I guess, everything I practised this afternoon comes down to what I've learnt over the last two weeks. I must keep control of the conversation—I can't afford to be bullied or intimidated by Eddie.

"Let me get you some drinks first. Wine, Eddie?"

I don't wait for an answer and pour the admittedly awful wine into his glass. He's already wearing a deep scowl so I'll have no way of telling just how awful he finds it. He takes a sip. His expression remains the same, but he doesn't spit it out. A good start.

I spot Greg a few tables away and wave him over.

"What would you like, Daisy?"

"Just a sparkling water, please."

As Greg arrives, I order Daisy's drink and ask for the menus. With the formalities out of the way, it's time to begin my charm offensive.

"Have you had a good day, Eddie?" I ask with as much sincerity as I can muster.

I know what he wants to say. He wants me to cut the bullshit and get to the point. However, the reason I wanted both of them here is because Eddie can't deploy his charmless aggression with his daughter next to him.

I'm sure she thinks I didn't notice, but Daisy nudges Eddie's leg under the table, and he eventually has to return a polite answer.

"Yes, I have," he replies through gritted teeth. "Thank you."

"Great. And how's that bump doing?" I ask, turning to Daisy.

"The bump is doing really well. We were talking about names on the way over, weren't we Dad?"

"Yes, sweetie. We were."

He smiles but his eyes tell a different story.

"And, have you come up with anything?" I ask.

It's my turn to speak through gritted teeth. This is my child too, yet apparently I get no say in choosing their name. I take a sip of wine in the hope it quells the irritation now bubbling away.

"If it's a girl," Daisy replies. "I love the name, Darcy."

"I like that. And if it's a boy?"

Please be Spartacus. Please be Spartacus.

"We're not sure, are we Dad?"

"No."

Somewhere from my seething pit of irritation, a bubble of inspiration rises. It's a risky play, but Daisy was particularly close to her paternal grandfather, who passed away last year. I'm sure she'll love the idea, but I've got no idea how Eddie will feel about his grandson being named after his late father.

"What about Frankie?"

My suggestion is met with silence.

Daisy looks at her father as he takes a gulp of wine.

"Funnily enough, Dad, I was going to suggest naming him after Granddad but I wasn't sure how you'd feel about it."

Eddie places his glass down and stares at it. This could go either way.

"I think …" he says in a low voice. "Your granddad would

341

be chuffed to bits."

Daisy places her hand on Eddie's. "Frankie it is then."

She then turns to me and silently mouths a thank you. I might have brought Daisy on side but I suspect Eddie is still some way off.

"Shall we order?" I suggest, trying to move the conversation away from dead grandparents.

We each study a menu, although I'm more concerned with the exorbitant prices than the fare.

"We're skipping starters, I hope," Eddie mumbles, for which he receives another nudge under the table.

That'll save me the best part of thirty quid so I'm not going to argue.

"Sure. If you like."

Greg returns and we place our orders; mine being the cheapest item on the menu. Daisy orders a relatively inexpensive salad but Eddie, looking pleased with himself, orders a fillet steak.

Greg then warns us there could be a wait of up to thirty minutes. I look around the half-empty restaurant. The sceptic in me says our wait has nothing to do with an overworked chef and a lot to do with us supping more of their expensive wine. This would have once irked me but, having spent all afternoon crunching numbers, I can see how squeezing an extra bottle of wine from every customer must add up. It's a clever ploy, but not one I'm going to fall for.

"And we'll have a bottle of Château Doisy Daëne," Eddie adds.

Bollocks.

Greg perks up, which is a bad sign. Whatever Eddie just ordered, I'm guessing it won't be cheap but, if it keeps him happy, it'll be money well spent.

"So, are you going to tell us why we've been summoned?" Daisy asks with a wry smile.

"And it better be a bloody good reason," Eddie adds. "I'm missing the football for this."

I sit back in my chair and try to outwardly display a confident facade; a far cry from the indecision currently pitching and yawing in my head. I guessed this might happen and devised a back-up plan which is weak but carries minimal risk of conflict or rejection. Once I open my mouth, the decision will be made— I either fold, or go all-in.

"I have a proposition for you, Eddie."

All-in it is.

"Right," he snorts. "This should be good."

Another nudge under the table.

"I met with Karen Loxton yesterday afternoon."

"I know," he shrugs. "She told me."

"Oh, right. So, you know she won't place an order because I can't supply the volumes of Crystalene she wants?"

"Are you going somewhere with this?"

"Wait," Daisy interjects. "What is Crystalene?"

"It's, um, my cleaning solution."

"Oh, I like the name. How did you come up with it?"

Do I tell her? Fuck it.

"Let's just say your middle name might have been an inspiration."

She fixes me with her blue eyes. "You named your cleaning solution after me?"

Is she annoyed? I honestly can't tell.

"That's really kind of sweet," she adds.

I smile with relief just as Eddie butts in.

"Technically, then, you named it after Crystal Gayle."

"Who?"

"You've never heard of Crystal Gayle?" he gasps.

Eddie then adopts an expression I don't think I've ever seen before as he froths with enthusiasm.

"Crystal Gale is one of my all-time favourite singers," he gushes. "I wanted Daisy's first name to be Crystal but her mother was having none of it so we compromised."

"Oh, right," I reply, doing my best to appear interested. "Would I know any of her songs?"

I've not yet had cause to regret anything I've said thus far. Now I have, as Eddie recounts every one of Crystal Gale's singles.

"Surely you know *Don't It Make My Brown Eyes Blue* and *Talking in Your Sleep*?"

I can't say I've heard of the first song, but I know the second; and only because I used to talk in my sleep, so it was vaguely relevant.

"I bloody love that track," Eddie coos, as I confirm I know at least one of his heroine's songs.

I can only imagine how many times Daisy has heard her father reminisce about how, back in the early eighties, he and her mother used to listen to Crystal Gale's albums in their tiny flat, but she sits and listens patiently as Eddie recounts the tale for my benefit.

It would be so easy to switch off and let my mind drift elsewhere, and it takes a real effort not to, but I'd be a fool not to grasp this opportunity. Eddie's demeanour has completely changed since we strayed onto this subject and I need him to remain in his happy place.

All I have to do is somehow swing the conversation back to the reason I'm here.

"What was the flat like, Eddie?"

"It was a complete shit hole but it was all we could afford back then."

"So, how does someone go from living in a shit hole of a rented flat to running a successful business?"

"Through hard graft and by taking risks. Oh, and necessity."

"Necessity?"

"It's easy enough to coast through life but once you become a father you have responsibilities. I took mine seriously so worked all hours to build a better life for my girls."

He glances across at Daisy and I can see the pride in his eyes. This is my opportunity. If he's ever likely to take me seriously, now is the time.

"I've got responsibilities now, Eddie."

His sneer returns as he realises where I'm taking the conversation.

"Don't you dare compare my life to yours, sunshine. I never treated my Tina the way you've treated Daisy."

"And that's why you don't want me in her life?"

"Well done. You've finally got the message."

I look across at Daisy just as she closes her eyes. I don't blame her—she's caught between the two of us and if she says anything, it's bound to upset one of us. In her shoes I think I'd hedge my bets and keep my mouth shut too.

"Fair enough, Eddie. I've got the message, but I still want you to hear my proposition."

"Why should I?"

"Because it's a win-win for you. You're a smart man so why wouldn't you?"

With no sign of our food and his daughter mute, Eddie only has one option.

"For crying out loud," he huffs. "Get on with it, then."

"Okay, I met with George Bradshaw this morning."

"And?"

I need to word my reply carefully, so I take a sip of wine to buy a few seconds.

"He said I could speak to his son, Stuart, about Barton Bradshaw licencing Crystalene."

Technically, my statement is one hundred percent factual. I don't think I'll share what happened later in the conversation, though.

"What? He said that?"

"On my unborn baby's life."

In an instant, the winds of scorn are taken from Eddie's sails.

"The old man must be going senile," he scoffs. "But I'm guessing you agreed?"

"George Bradshaw is anything but senile, but no, I didn't agree to see Stuart."

Again, technically correct.

"Are you insane? What sort of idiot turns down that kind of opportunity?"

"The sort of idiot who has a better idea."

I take another sip of wine as both father and daughter stare at me in disbelief.

"And that brings me back to my proposal," I continue. "I'm looking for an investor so I can set up my own production facility."

The cogs in Eddie's head whirl, and then jar.

"No bloody way," he coughs. "If you think I'm going to invest in any business you're involved with, you're an even bigger fool than I thought."

"Go easy, Dad," Daisy then scolds. "At least hear him out."

Eddie folds his arms and draws a long sigh. "Fine."

"I said this was a win-win, and I meant it. I'm willing to give twenty percent of my business in return for thirty-eight thousand pounds of investment."

"Is that it? I hand over thirty-eight grand of my hard-earned money and end up with twenty percent of fuck all when the business fails, which it will if you're running it?"

A more forceful nudge is administered under the table.

"That's the win-win part, Eddie," I calmly reply. "You see, if you're wrong and I make a success of the business, you'll get your money back plus twenty percent of future profits. If I fail, it'll prove I really am the hopeless waste of space you think I am. You'd then have every right to cut me out of Daisy's life, and the baby's. Your views will be vindicated and I'll be off the scene, and that's what you really want, isn't it?"

I dip into my jacket pocket and withdraw the sheets of paper.

"But before you decide, just spare me a minute to look at the numbers."

After a glare from Daisy, Eddie reluctantly snatches the paper from my outstretched hand and unfolds the sheets.

"What is this?" he mumbles.

"It's a financial plan. It outlines how much I need to invest to get the production facility up-and-running but, more importantly, also the potential profits I could expect once Crystalene is produced in bulk."

My expectations remain low as Eddie studies my afternoon's work. I feel like a schoolboy having his homework assessed by that one demanding teacher everyone considered an arsehole.

"I'm just popping to the bathroom," Daisy announces, perhaps not wishing to witness my rejection.

With Daisy gone and Eddie scowling at the papers, I pour a glass of the wine he ordered and take a sip. It comes as no surprise to discover very expensive wine tastes just as fucking awful as any other wine.

"You produced these numbers?" Eddie eventually asks.

"I did, although Dad helped."

It's a stretch to say Dad had any involvement in the actual numbers but it won't do my cause any harm to say they were compiled with the assistance of a qualified financial advisor.

He folds the sheets up and sits back in his chair.

"I've got one question," he says.

"Go on."

"Why me? Why not borrow the money from your parents, or the bank, or anyone else for that matter?"

It's not just a good question. It's *the* question.

45.

I hoped, prayed even, that Eddie would ask why I chose him as a potential investor. Of all people, logically he would be the least likely. However, I've learnt that judgements based upon logic alone are no better than judgements based upon emotion alone—there has to be balance. Now I intend to deploy both and force Eddie into a corner from where there is no escape; least not without appearing either a fool or a heartless shit.

I pause for effect, and summon the most earnest expression I can.

"The reason I asked you is simple, Eddie. There's one thing I want more than your money—your respect."

"My respect?" he snorts. "After the way you've treated my girl? You've got to be kidding me."

"I don't deserve a second chance, then?"

"I don't do second chances."

Eddie is nothing if not consistent, and I didn't expect him to roll over so easily.

"Fair enough, but let me ask you a question. If anyone else but me had put that proposition to you, and knowing there's a ready market for the product, would you consider investing?"

"Maybe. Probably."

"So, to be clear, you're prepared to walk away from a perfectly sound investment opportunity, one where you can't lose, because of sheer bloody-mindedness?"

His reply comes in the form of a stern glare. I push on.

"Look, Eddie. I'm presenting you with cold hard facts which you're choosing to ignore. And you're ignoring them despite everything I've already achieved in such a short space of time. You're choosing to ignore them despite reading a sound financial plan, and despite people you know in the industry being impressed with the product."

He looks around, perhaps in the hope either our food or Daisy arrives so he can change the subject. He's out of luck on both counts and I continue with my questioning.

"You got a second chance, didn't you Eddie?"

"What are you waffling on about?"

"There was a reason you were living in that shit hole of a flat, wasn't there?"

"Eh? I … what?"

I didn't just spend the afternoon compiling spreadsheets. I also took Mungo's advice and conducted some research on my potential investor. As luck would have it, the company history page on the Wallace Engineering website made for interesting reading.

"Before you set up Wallace Engineering, you had a business manufacturing vacuum pumps, didn't you?"

"Who told you that?" he snaps defensively.

"Nobody told me, but you do mention it on your company website and I just did a little online research. And whilst you did mention your previous business, you didn't mention it folded with significant debts. I'm guessing you were living in that flat because you lost everything."

Eddie's face turns an interesting shade of crimson but words appear to have escaped him. I can't begin to imagine what's going through his mind as he wrestles with the Adam Maxwell he knew and the one seated in front of him now.

"Very clever, Sherlock. I'll take my hat off to you," he eventually concedes. "You've found out I've got a business failure in my closet. So what?"

"I only mention it because Daisy once told me you started Wallace Engineering with a loan from your dad."

"This is getting tedious. Can you just get to the point, or better still, find out where our bloody food is?"

"Alright, I'm nearly done. One final point and then I'll shut up."

"Make it quick."

"I happened to notice your dad was also on the list of debtors for the vacuum pump business. He tried to help you out once and lost a tidy sum. Still, he gave you a second chance, didn't he?"

He fixes me with a glare but I can't tell if I've touched a nerve or not; being his default expression is mildly annoyed. It's also impossible to tell if he's grasped the point I'm trying to make, but I'm not taking any chances and deliver my closing argument.

"Now, correct me if I'm wrong, but I'd guess you were desperate not to fail again, because it wasn't just your dad's money you wanted to earn back, but also his respect. In your shoes, I know I would."

Case made, I sit back in my chair and take a well-earned glug of wine. My timing is spot on as Daisy makes her way over from the far side of the restaurant. Perhaps I've got time for one final appeal to Eddie's better nature.

"I can't change the past, Eddie. I made mistakes, sure, but I'm trying my best to make amends, so don't I deserve a second chance too?"

"I'm going to the bathroom."

"Really? That's all you've got to say? All I wanted …"

"Leave it," he growls. "I've heard enough."

He gets up and ambles away without another word; and barely acknowledges Daisy as she returns to the table.

"What have you said?" she asks, retaking her seat. "Dad didn't look happy."

"Has he ever looked happy?"

"Please, Adam," she sighs. "Don't tell me you two have been at loggerheads again? You have no idea how hard it was convincing him to come along this evening."

"I didn't say anything he didn't already know," I mumble, struggling to hold back my dejection.

"What does that mean?"

"Look, all I wanted to do this evening was to prove I'm not a waster, and I tried my best but it wasn't good enough. Your dad has made his mind up about me and he isn't going to change it; no matter what I do."

With an exasperated sigh, she closes her eyes and shakes her head. I don't blame her for expecting the worst of me—truth is, that's all I've ever given her. I could, I suppose, launch into an explanation of what I said to Eddie, but what's the point? I'm not going to apologise for trying. I gave it a go but some bridges are just too badly burnt, it seems.

Calculated or otherwise, my risky plan has failed and I could do without the ignominy of dinner and forced conversation.

"I think I'll make a move," I say. "You enjoy a meal with your dad. I'll settle the bill on my way out."

I get up and slip my jacket on.

She looks up, her eyes moist. "Why do you keep doing this to me?"

Before I can answer, she corrects herself. "Why do I *let* you keep doing this to me?"

"Sorry, what have I done?"

"What you always do, Adam. You give me hope and then break my heart. Every. Single. Time."

My lips move but I catch the words just before they escape. There are only so many times I can say I'm sorry.

It's all I can do to stare at her like the fool I am, although I

349

can now see beyond her obvious beauty. I can see the anguish and the pain I've inflicted upon her; not just in the last few weeks but since the day we met. I knew from that day I didn't deserve a girl like Daisy, and I know now she doesn't deserve to suffer any longer.

"I think it might be for the best if we have a clean break. I'll move away if it makes it easier."

"Easier?" she scoffs. "You really are fucking unbelievable."

Okay, she swore. This isn't good.

"I want to hate you, Adam. God, I want to hate you so damn much, but you can't even make that easy for me."

"Tell me then. What *can* I do to make your life easier?"

She plucks a napkin from the table and wipes away a stray tear.

"Make it stop; all of it. The sick feeling in my stomach, the sleepless nights, the tears, the frustration, the constant battle raging in my head all hours … I can't take any more."

Her words crash like waves in a storm: relentless and savage.

"Above all, though," she gulps. "Tell me how I can stop loving you, because I want that more than anything."

It's a question without an answer, as I well know. You can take just about every emotion and control it to some degree. You can undertake therapy or take medication, or both. You can run away from fear, hide from loneliness, and battle anxiety. Love, however, is an unrelenting, all-consuming bastard of an emotion. It doesn't play by any rules nor does it know any bounds. It is captivating. It is cruel. It is everything in-between.

It is also the one emotion over which I will never have control. And nor will Daisy it seems.

There is nothing I can say to her. No pearls of wisdom and no quick fix. Her problem is my problem and my problem is her problem.

"I honestly think the only way either of us can move forward is to sever all ties."

"What?"

"This is doing neither of us any good, is it?"

"And what about the baby?"

"I've got a choice: keep making your life a misery, and probably theirs too if my track record is anything to go by, or walk away. And, it's clear Eddie doesn't want me around, so perhaps it'd be best for all concerned if I just fuck off for good."

There's no gallantry in my offer; I simply know when I'm

beaten. The last two weeks have taught me so much but, despite my best efforts, I've fallen short when it mattered most. A plucky, yet, ultimately unsuccessful, bid to reinvent myself; to make something of myself.

Perhaps I am destined to fail, no matter what Mungo might think.

I take a final glance into those blue eyes as a hand grips my heart and crushes it. A sentence then forms in my head—the hardest sentence I'll ever utter.

"I think we both know it's for the best if I'm not around."

I can't even bear to look at her. I turn away and take three steps when a voice booms.

"Where are you going?"

Ten seconds earlier and I'd have avoided Eddie.

"You've got what you wanted," I rasp, my voice near breaking. "I'm going."

"Wait."

He steps past me and grabs my now-pointless financial plan from the table.

"The numbers are wrong," he says flatly, handing the crumpled sheet to me.

"Doesn't matter."

"You don't want to know where then?"

My sullen expression should be answer enough. I don't have the appetite for more conflict but Eddie appears keen to rub my nose in it.

"You've allocated eighteen grand a year on rent for the premises."

"I said, Eddie, it doesn't matter."

"And twenty grand on the bottling machine," he adds, seemingly oblivious to my indifference.

"I'm going. I'll get the bill."

"Sit down."

"Why? So you can find a dozen different ways to tell me what a waste of space I am. Thanks, but no thanks."

"Sit down. Please. I just want two minutes."

His uncharacteristically polite request throws me and, without thinking, I retrace my steps and flop back on the chair; all the while trying to avoid eye contact with Daisy.

Eddie retakes his seat and empties his wine glass.

"So, you don't want to know how I could save you a small fortune?" he asks.

It feels like he's offering a quote for landscape gardening as

I stand in the crumbled ruins of my home after an earthquake. I nod, not really caring one way or another.

"For starters, I've got sixteen hundred square feet of free space at the back of my warehouse."

"Right," I sigh. "That'd make a decent squash court."

"Or a production facility."

"Eh?"

Rather than expand on his statement, he turns to Daisy and takes her hand.

"I'm sorry, sweetheart."

Her confused expression mirrors mine.

"I've been selfish," he continues. "And while you were in the bathroom, Adam told me a few home truths which made me realise I've not been fair either."

"He did?" she replies, still confused.

Eddie then turns to me.

"Listen, Adam. I'm not going to pretend you don't still have a lot to prove, but you said you wanted my respect—you've now got it. I can't fault what you've done with your business and it took some balls to point out my hypocrisy. Most men would have given up by now so, if nothing else, you've proven what a determined son-of-a-bitch you are. If you're just as determined to prove yourself a good father, I think that nipper will be alright."

"Um, thanks."

"And you wanted a second chance so I'm willing to give you one … but not as an investor."

The man giveth. The man taketh away.

"And the reason I'm not prepared to invest is because I've got a better idea," he continues. "I can give you the space in my warehouse, rent-free for a year, and I can help you fund the machinery you need by way of a loan. And, you can start making repayments after six months, by which point you should be clearing a healthy profit if your forecast is accurate."

"I … I honestly don't know what to say, Eddie."

And I don't.

"I'm going to level with you," he adds. "I'm doing this more for my daughter and grandchild than I'm doing it for you. But, credit where it's due—you've somehow pulled yourself together in the last two weeks so, whatever prompted that change, I bloody well hope you keep it up."

I'm about to offer him my word when he suddenly gets to his feet.

"I think I'll be off now," he then announces.

"You're going?" Daisy blurts. "But you haven't even eaten."

"To be honest, sweetie, I'd rather have a pie and a pint in the pub down the road. And besides, I think I've interfered enough—you two need to talk, without me here."

He then turns to me. "Give my secretary a call in the morning and set up a meeting. Let's see if you're as good as your forecast predicts."

I'm relieved to see a wry smile rather than a sneer. He's right, in that I've still got a lot to prove but I've got the chance, and that's all I ever wanted.

"Will do, and thanks again, Eddie. Genuinely."

I stand up and shake his hand before he plants a kiss on Daisy's forehead.

"Enjoy," he says, and ambles away.

Perhaps it's the shock at Eddie's change of heart, or perhaps because the door I was about to slam shut is now ajar, but we sit and stare at one another in silence. The now homeless fillet steak arrives barely a minute later.

"Seems a shame to waste it, don't you think?" I remark.

Daisy finds a smile, and reaches for what was Eddie's plate.

"I didn't mean the steak," I confirm. "I meant the opportunity."

"And what opportunity would that be?"

I choose my words carefully. It'll take more than her father's blessing and a Caesar salad to mend the damage I've caused.

"For us to forget the past and look towards the future."

"And what sort of future did you have in mind, for us?"

"Honestly? I don't care. Any kind of future which involves you and our baby is good enough for me."

"And what about *Bad Adam*? Where does he sit in this future of yours?"

"You know, I don't think we'll be seeing *Bad Adam* again. In fact, I'm pretty sure of it."

And, I am.

46.

You know you've outstayed your welcome in a restaurant when they give you the bill, even though you haven't asked for it.

I walked Daisy back to her car and we continued to chat about the baby, and the business, and everything else apart from the elephant which followed us back to the car park. I was never going to push my luck and suggest there's a chance we might start again, and I guess Daisy felt the same, although for very different reasons.

Nevertheless, we said goodbye with the longest of hugs and an agreement we'd focus on the baby, for now, and see where that takes us. No commitments, no promises, and definitely no rash decisions—we've both had our fill of those.

I watched her drive away, and for the first time in a long while, I felt truly content; like slipping into a warm bath content.

Even now, as I skip up the street towards the flat, my head is full of nothing but positive emotions. My wobble list is all but clear, and while I know there will be an entire dinner service of new plates spinning next week, I've never felt more ready for the challenge.

By the time I unlock the front door, another conclusion also arrives. The 'how' is unimportant, but I do feel my therapy is now complete; if indeed there was any actual therapy. It doesn't matter. Nothing of the past matters, now I can see a future.

"Mungo?"

Flickering lights creep from a crack in the lounge door. He's obviously watching TV.

I bowl through to the lounge to find him slumped on the sofa with a whisky tumbler in hand.

"Haven't you had enough booze for one day?"

He looks up at me and smiles. "I'm celebrating."

"Ironically, so am I, so you might as well pour me one."

"You will need a glass."

I head into the kitchen and return with one of the few glasses not in the sink.

"I see you couldn't manage the washing up. Thanks for leaving it."

"You are welcome."

He sits up and pours me a generous tot of whisky, before

adding an equal measure to his own glass. I take a seat at the other end of the sofa and sip the malty amber liquid.

"What are you celebrating?" he asks.

I give him the edited highlights of my evening.

"I've got to say, Mungo, I've never felt like this before. I can't put my finger on it, but it feels like something has finally clicked in my head."

"You think that is just chance?"

"You're going to tell me it's a result of your therapy, aren't you?"

"In a way, it is, but I have only given you what was already yours. You were simply not aware it had gone."

"Well, it could be the three glasses of diabolical wine, and a whisky, but that makes no sense whatsoever. I don't much care, though. Whatever you did or didn't do, I honestly feel like I've turned a corner."

I raise my glass and clink it against Mungo's.

"Cheers, my friend."

"It was my pleasure, Adam Maxwell ... my friend."

We both take a sip of whisky and savour the moment.

"So, tell me, what are you celebrating?"

"The end," he replies, wistfully.

"The end of what exactly?"

He swills the whisky around the glass while musing on a reply.

"This is an interesting fact," he then announces. "Were you aware it is a tradition amongst authors to take a drink when they have completed a manuscript?"

"Having never written a book, no. Come to think of it, I can't remember the last time I even read a book."

"Twenty-four years ago."

"What?"

"We never did clear up that hearing issue of yours. I said, you last read a complete book twenty-four years ago. I believe you were nine years of age."

"How on earth would you know that?"

"Call it an educated guess."

"Call it what you like but I don't think that's right. I must have read books at school."

"In their entirety?"

I cast my mind back to English lessons in primary and secondary school. I vaguely remember the titles of a few books: *Stig of the Dump*, *A Kestrel for a Knave*, and *Animal Farm*. I also remember just how much I detested anything by Shakespeare, but did I actually finish any book? The fact none of them left a lasting impression, coupled with my woeful English grades, suggest maybe I didn't.

"You should start reading books again," Mungo continues. "It expands one's mind."

"Yeah, we'll see. Anyway, you were saying you've finished writing a book?"

"Not a book. An assignment, of sorts."

"Care to elaborate?"

"Not really. Let us just say it was long, painstaking, and not what I had originally planned."

"And does this assignment have anything to do with you leaving?"

"It has everything to do with my leaving. It was always an inevitability."

"Are you going to tell me exactly when, or where you're going?"

"Very soon," he sighs. "And where I go remains to be seen. You are not the only one who has learnt lessons of late, Adam Maxwell."

I sit back and try to imagine how empty the flat will feel once I'm on my own again. I don't think I like the idea much, but maybe it won't be a long-term problem. I can only hope.

"Would you care for a stroll?" Mungo suddenly asks, out of the blue.

"Err, I didn't have you down as a stroller."

"Now feels an appropriate time to start."

Do I really want to head back out into the cold? Not really, but accompanying Mungo on a few laps around the block is the least I can do, I suppose.

"I'll get my coat."

I make a quick visit to the bathroom whilst Mungo disappears into his bedroom. We reconvene in the hall with Mungo sporting the same outfit he was wearing when he first arrived at my door—top to toe black.

"I'm glad to see the you've run out of awful jumpers," I jest.

"We have journeyed full circle. This attire feels appropriate."

"Indeed. Let's go then."

We head down the stairs and into the night.

It's so cold it reminds me of a job I had in my early twenties. I worked in a wholesale warehouse; the kind of place where small grocery shops buy their stock. I was given the job of restocking the freezers and the stock room was essentially just a walk-in ice box, but larger than my flat. I hated that job and I hated the cold, which is why I constantly skived off to the toilets at any given opportunity. They sacked me after three weeks.

Trying to be positive, at least tonight's cold is accompanied by a clear sky, dotted with shimmering stars, rather than fluorescent lighting.

"It's a bit parky, isn't it?" I remark, teeth chattering.

"Cold? Yes, it is."

We head right without thought to a destination, or much in the way of conversation. Mungo seems happy enough; occasionally looking up at the stars as we traipse through one dark street after the next.

With little else to occupy my mind, I think back to the first time I walked the streets with Mungo at my side—the night we went to the Red Lion. I remember it so well, even to the point I know he was walking on my left. Now, he's walking on my right, and in some way that feels symbolic as it could be argued we've swapped positions in more than just a physical sense. Mungo is now irresponsible, unpredictable, and annoyingly lazy. It's taken a while, but I can now see that's who I once was.

"Listen, Mungo. I know you're not big on gratitude, but I don't want you to leave without knowing how grateful I am. This … whatever it's been … has completely changed my life."

"There is a good reason I do not deserve your gratitude."

"And that reason is?"

I ask with no expectation of a straight answer.

"I have given you nothing. All I have done is reinstate the man you were always meant to be."

"That's not true. I've changed, and that's because of what you've taught me, and what you've done for me."

He comes to an abrupt halt and grabs my arm.

"Let me ask you a question, Adam Maxwell. The situation with Ethan Montgomery: should your sister be grateful for taking what is rightfully hers?"

"No, of course not."

"Then neither should you."

He releases my arm and walks on.

I was right. Either due to alcohol or his inherently cryptic nature, Mungo doesn't provide anything like a straight answer to my question. I guess I don't really care, or it even matters much now. As he told me himself: not every question has an answer.

I catch up with him and chance a less meaningful question.

"Are we heading anywhere in particular?"

"Figuratively or specifically?"

"Specifically. It's chuffing cold out here."

He raises his arm and points above the rooftops on the opposite side of the street.

"Up there," he replies."

"The multi-storey car park?"

"Yes."

"Okay. Why?"

"A better view of the sky."

I look up. I'm doubt being a few hundred feet closer is likely to change the view much.

"Really?" I huff. "It's bound to be locked up at this time of night."

"We will see, but it is not necessary for you to accompany me."

It seems I have a decision to make — one of those decisions which up until recently, has marred my life.

No more.

"Wait, Mungo."

He comes to a halt.

"You're not going to do anything illegal, are you?"

"Opening an unlocked door would not be classed as illegal, you would agree?"

"I guess not."

He sets off again.

A large part of me wants to turn around and head home but I don't trust Mungo not to do something reckless or stupid. The irony follows us all the way to a fire door at the rear of the car park.

"That's looks locked," I suggest, as Mungo approaches the sturdy-looking door.

He grasps the handle, turns it, and pulls the door open.

"Clearly not," he replies.

He steps into the dimly lit stairwell and I reluctantly follow.

Much like a dog, my sense of smell, rather than my vision, forms a view of our surroundings. Monotone concrete walls and stairs, but a pungent odour of petrol fumes and piss.

Mungo heads up the stairs and I follow.

Flight after seemingly never-ending flight until we reach the twelfth and final floor.

"Give me a sec," I gasp. "I'm not as fit as I thought I was."

Haunched over while I catch my breath, I look across at Mungo. Remarkably, considering he's been on the booze all day and we've just stormed twelve flights of stairs, he looks as unruffled as the day he first appeared at my door.

"Okay," I pant. "Let's go look at the bloody sky."

He pulls open the door to the upper floor of the car park and I stagger after him. Trying to remain positive, at least my exertion should keep hypothermia at bay a while longer.

We walk out to a view of empty tarmac and an ink-black sky. Mungo makes his way towards the four-foot-high perimeter wall and I plod along behind him.

We reach the edge and stare out at the lights of the town centre, and beyond.

"Not a bad view," I remark.

He looks up to the sky. "I prefer the view above."

I mirror his action and look up into the vast blackness. The complete lack of cloud cover does nothing for the temperature but a lot for the view, with a dozen stars shimmering brightly and surrounded by countless faint dots of light. It's funny, but it's probably the first time I've looked up at the night sky and really thought about what I'm looking at. I conclude there's nothing quite like staring into the infinite void of space to make you feel insignificant.

I share my conclusion with Mungo.

"It is where we all begin," he replies. "And where we all end."

"That's very deep."

"Yes. Yes, it is."

He then lowers his gaze and fixes me with his turquoise eyes.

"I am glad we finally got to meet, Adam Maxwell."

"Finally? I wasn't aware we'd been waiting?"

"Your journey has been short, but productive. Mine has been long, and difficult. It has taken me many years to find a way here."

"Roadworks on the M25?" I snigger.

He doesn't laugh.

"Come on, Mungo," I groan. "You asked for that. If you didn't continually talk in metaphors, I might actually understand what you're trying to say."

After a thoughtful pause, I receive a belated, yet unexpected, response.

"A question, my friend," he smiles, placing his hand on my

arm. "Are you familiar with the poet and playwright, Oscar Wilde?"

It takes a moment to get past his sudden display of warmth, and seemingly random question.

"Err, I've heard of him, yes."

"Wilde once said: 'The truth is rarely pure, and never simple.'"

"Your point being?"

"My truth is far from simple, and despite my current state of mind it would be an ill-judged decision to say any more."

My need to argue isn't as strong as the sincerity in his eyes. I don't respond because there's no response worth offering—Mungo is, after all, Mungo.

I return a smile and we simultaneously look back to the heavens.

As we gaze up in silent contemplation, a biting wind whips across the tarmac and encircles us. I physically shudder as the cold shifts from uncomfortable to painful.

"Mungo, I think it might be time to head home," I chatter. "I'm frozen to the bone."

"I agree. Time to go home."

Desperate to escape the stinging cold, I don't need further confirmation. I dig my hands deep into my jacket pockets and hurry back towards the stairwell door.

I get half way, and I don't know why, but I glance over my shoulder.

My legs come to an involuntary halt. I turn around and blink to check I'm not mistaken.

Twenty feet from my position, Mungo's diminutive frame is silhouetted against the night sky as he stands atop the perimeter wall, facing out towards the town.

It takes but a second to question why he's decided to indulge in some impromptu parkour. I could stand inert for hours and not find an answer but I don't have the will or resistance to endure the cold any longer than a few minutes.

"For God's sake," I mumble to myself.

I take six steps back towards the wall, and I'm about to yell at him when the words catch in my throat.

Definitely not a leap. Not even a hop. A step, maybe—no different to that between a train carriage and the platform. And the casual way Mungo steps off the wall is a stark contrast to the chaos of activity in my head. Before I can decide to scream, to move, or to even take a breath, gravity yanks him away.

If I were stood on a glacier, the cold wouldn't find a way past my shock. It engulfs me, consumes me, to the point I'm conscious of nothing other than my own laboured breathing and pulsing heartbeat.

My brain delivers a shot of adrenalin. My vocal chords are the first to benefit.

"Mungooo!" I scream.

My limbs take their turn and I spring towards the wall and peer over. I know the geography of the town well enough, and I stare down with no great surprise—an unlit alleyway parallel to this side of the car park. It would be hard to see anything during the day. At night, hopeless.

"Fuck! Fuck! Fuck!"

What do I do?

I pace along the wall and peer over every four or five steps. I can't see anything.

Rational thought is clouded with panic, fear, and residue shock.

Cannot think straight. I pace along the wall again. More checks. I really can't see anything.

I should go down there … or should I? Can I face finding Mungo's broken body? Would that image haunt me for the rest of my days? What if he survived the fall?

Fucking questions.

What do I do? What do I do?

Think. Think.

I stop pacing. I dig a trembling hand into my jacket pocket. My phone. I jab the screen. Three numbers and the call icon. Stay calm.

"Police. No, wait … ambulance."

A voice asks questions and I return breathless answers whilst peering over the wall again. I definitely can't see anything.

The questions keep coming but I'm out of answers and end the call.

My legs buckle and I slump to the floor with my back against the wall. A thought occurs: perhaps I didn't see what I thought I saw. I scan my surroundings in the hope of finding Mungo waiting to go home.

Just tarmac, sky, and stars. I know what I saw.

More questions.

Why the hell would he step off the wall and fall to an almost certain death? Did he seem suicidal? Did I miss some obvious

361

sign?

Ignoring the futility, I replay our conversation over and over; dissecting every word, every action.

What's the point?

The faint wail of sirens interrupts my inquisition. I find some respite; knowing help is on its way.

The sirens grow louder. Then, louder still until their echo surrounds me.

I can't stop shaking.

The stairwell door bursts open and two police officers scan the tarmac. They spot me and hurry over.

"Mr Maxwell?"

As if my mind wasn't already being crushed under the weight of a million questions, they pile more on. Who am I? Where do I live? What exactly happened? What did I see?

A radio crackles. One of the officers excuses himself and wanders off towards the stairwell.

His colleague continues the interrogation. How did we get up here? Were there any other witnesses? Am I sure the jump was intentional?

The other officer returns and swaps nods with his younger colleague before asking a question of his own.

"How do you know the victim, Mr Maxwell?"

"Victim?"

The word leaves my mouth as a gasp.

"He's … dead?"

He gives me a look I've seen more times than I care to recall. The stupidest of stupid questions.

"I'm afraid so."

As I struggle to breathe, they continue to ask questions; clearly unaware there's more than one victim here. I remain mute as the same question loops over and over in my head: why, Mungo? Why?

At some point they give up and the older officer retreats a few steps. He talks into his radio but I don't hear or care what's being said. Two paramedics arrive and swap places with the police officers; both men look relieved I'm no longer their problem. They head off while I sit listless as the paramedics diagnose the severity of my shock. They suggest I return to the hospital with them but that's the last place I want to be.

"No hospital," I murmur, getting to my feet.

They argue, but it's hard to make your point when there's nobody around to hear it.

I descend the stairs and exit the stairwell to find the strobing blue lights of two police cars and an ambulance. The two officers are knelt down, some fifty feet away and studying something on the ground. Bile rises in my throat when I conclude what that something is, or was.

I can't stay here.

One final glance up at the sky and I depart the scene. On autopilot, I drift through the quiet streets towards home; the same journey I made earlier, but with one significant difference.

By the time I arrive back at the flat, an old friend has joined me. I thought I'd seen the last of the dull ache, but no. I head into the lounge and snatch the whisky bottle from the coffee table.

The burn is exquisite.

I flop on the sofa and take another long pull. The dull ache joins me; jabbing and clawing at my heart.

"Please, please," I beg. "Just go away."

I recognise the grief in my voice. I've travelled so far yet here I am, back where I started. Why the fuck would Mungo do this to me?

Now the shock has passed, grief can make its presence felt. Another glug of whisky, but I know there will never be enough.

Tears well, and I blink to clear the mist from my eyes.

Only then do I notice it—a white envelope on the coffee table. Was it there earlier? I place the whisky bottle down and swap it for the envelope.

My full name is inked on the front in a style of handwriting close to calligraphy. If this is, as I suspect, Mungo's suicide note, the precise, elegant writing style doesn't tally with someone who is about to throw themselves from the twelfth floor of a car park. Surely, a suicide note is written in a frantic, desperate style; much like the author's mind.

I tear it open, and find a letter written in the same precise handwriting …

I apologise.

There was no other way, Adam Maxwell. I could not stay and I cannot return—you had to be left in no doubt of either fact.

I must confess: I have never written a letter before; much less a letter of such magnitude. It is challenging, to find words which might explain my actions. One might argue it was a fitting finale to my reckless behaviour. Small comfort, I am sure, but it was the only way. And while I doubt you will ever truly understand, I hope you can accept my decision. You must move forward. If you do not, it will be an insult to my memory.

I know you will feel angry, shocked, and perhaps even mournful, but do not mourn what you no longer need because that would not be logical. I would hope you have come to trust my judgement and I will therefore ask you to trust me one final time: you have achieved much, but those achievements will be in vain if my departure consumes your thoughts. I would therefore ask you not to grieve, but to celebrate my departure for it is your final release.

There is little left to say so I will leave you with one final piece of advice: never buy a jumper in haste.

Forever your friend

Mungo

An unexpected but welcome wave of serenity washes over me as I read the letter again and again. Quite why, I have no idea.

Then, without really thinking about it, I get up and grab the whisky bottle.

I hold it aloft. "To you, Mungo Thunk."

I take a swig and then do what feels appropriate; what feels like the right decision. I head into the kitchen, pour the rest of the whisky down the sink, and make a start on the washing up.

SEVEN MONTHS LATER ...

47.

The three of us vie for position at the barbecue. Three men, all captured by the primal need for fire and cremated meat.

"They're burning, Dad," I remark.

"And yet, still raw on one side," Joe adds.

"Alright, alright," Dad huffs. "I do know how to cook sausages."

The biting winds and frigid mornings of January are but a distant memory as we bask in the August sunshine. The weather could not be more perfect for the last ever barbecue at my parents' house. It was Mum's idea, to throw one final hurrah in the garden Kate and I used to play in as kids. In just over two weeks, another family will move in and a new chapter will begin for my parents; thirty miles away on the coast.

There's much to celebrate but I can't deny there is an undercurrent of lament, perhaps sadness. Just as the seasons change, so do our lives, I guess.

A pair of arms encircle my waist from behind.

"Are they supposed to be that colour?" Daisy asks.

"Don't you start," Dad chuckles. "You know what they say about too many cooks."

"I'm struggling to see one cook," she giggles.

I turn and plant a kiss on Daisy's forehead.

"What have you done with the little guy?" I ask.

"He's having a cuddle with his other granddad."

Frankie was born five weeks ago, after a seven hour labour that I witnessed from beginning to end. I had prepared well, or so I thought, but no amount of reading can possibly prepare you for the reality of childbirth. In many ways, it reminded me of a long flight. The excitement and anticipation, then long periods of boredom interspersed with turbulence, over which you've no control. And much like the toilets on a plane, there are some things you witness and wish you hadn't.

It's the final half hour that really matters, though. The intense and nervy final descent into parenthood; followed by unbridled joy when the journey is finally over. However, judging by her screams throughout I think it'll be a while before Daisy boards that particular plane again. I guess childbirth probably stings a bit, but I kept that view to myself.

I grasp Daisy's hand and we leave Dad and Joe to argue

over sausage-burning duties.

"This is great, isn't it?" she coos, as we make our way over to the patio.

"It's perfect," I smile back.

It's a white lie. Granted, it's hard to imagine how my life could be any better, but the man who helped me forge this perfect life is no longer part of it. It'll be a long time before I reconcile that fact.

Even now, it's hard not to dwell on Mungo's final day, but focusing on the happy faces seated around the patio table certainly helps. Besides Mum, there's Kate and Bella, and Eddie and his wife, Tina. There's also Kate's best friend, Donna, who also now happens to be Joe's girlfriend—if two people were ever made for each other, it's Joe and Donna. I couldn't be happier for my now-solvent best mate.

"How are they getting on?" Eddie asks. "I'm starving."

I release Daisy's hand and squat down beside his chair.

"They're nearly ready," I reply, stroking Frankie's cheek as he lies in his granddad's arms.

"He's definitely got the Wallace eyes," Eddie says, proudly.

It's true he has his mother's eyes, for sure. Big and blue and beautiful.

"He does," I reply. "And he's already got more hair than his granddad."

"I'll give you that," Eddie chuckles.

I lean over and gently kiss my son's cheek. I'm not sure five-week-old babies have any conscious thoughts, but I pray he knows how much I adore him.

"You understand now?" Eddie beams.

I look up. "Huh?"

"I bet you'd give your life to protect this little man. Do you understand now why I was so protective of my little girl?"

I don't have to answer. He knows, I'm sure.

"Anyway," he continues. "I received the cheque on Friday. Thank you."

"It should be me thanking you. Your lending rates are much more competitive than the bloody bank; as I've just discovered."

The true cost of bank lending charges are not the only lesson I've learnt since that fated evening in Oscar's Bistro. After six weeks of fourteen-hour days, the first bottle of mass-produced Crystalene rolled off the production line. Over those six weeks there were tears, there were tantrums, and I'd be lying if I said there weren't moments I almost gave up. Credit to Eddie, though, as he was always there to kick my arse when it needed kicking.

After belatedly securing an order with Karen Loxton, I continued in my quest to find other retailers able to shift larger numbers of Crystalene. As it stands, I now have a contract with a major DIY chain and a supermarket, along with almost twenty smaller, but not insignificant, retailers. That success allowed me to repay Eddie's loan in full last week, and I'm now looking to secure funding for larger premises and better machinery as the current set-up is already nearing capacity.

Several people have suggested I add other lines to the Crystalene brand but I think once I hit a certain turnover, that'll be it for me. I will never forget George Bradshaw's advice about striking the right balance with empire building and spending time with my family; primarily because he's repeated it every time I've popped in to the shop for tea and biscuits. All I want is a business which allows me to enjoy a comfortable life, and that comfortable life really begins in a few months' time when my little family move out of our rented house and into a modest detached house we've just agreed to buy. It's no castle, but it's a home, and that's all the three of us need.

"Have you decided on the dress yet?" Mum asks Daisy.

"I think so, Carol, and it's been a lot easier this time," she laughs. "What with the limited baggage allowance."

In December, Daisy and I will finally make our trip to New York, along with our close family and friends. We'll leave Heathrow as Adam Maxwell and Daisy Wallace, and return as Mr & Mrs Maxwell. When I proposed, again, and Daisy accepted, again, I promised her we'd do it in style, but we wouldn't be suffering the military-grade planning this time. I think Daisy quite likes the new, assertive version of me because she agreed on the spot.

Funnily enough, I haven't been tasked with making the travel arrangements. I can't imagine why.

"I've been made redundant," Dad huffs, sidling up to me.

"By who?"

"Young Joe and his lady friend have taken over cooking duties."

"Trust me, Dad, you're better off out of it. I think Donna is assessing Joe's domestic skills."

"You're probably right," he chuckles.

Looking at Dad now, you'd never guess he was the same man who suffered a severe stroke six months ago. I guess Mum's new healthy eating regime, coupled with his abstinence from alcohol, have paid dividends.

"I don't suppose I could borrow you for five minutes?" he asks.

"Sure. What for?"

"I just need a couple of boxes brought down from the loft. They're a bit on the heavy side and you know what your mother is like—she still frets I'm overdoing it."

"No worries."

We make our excuses and Dad leads me up the stairs to the landing. Using a pole, he opens the loft hatch and tugs the ladder down.

"You still remember how to climb a ladder, right?" he jests.

It's been a while—over four months—since I last climbed a ladder of any kind. Once the production facility was up-and-running, it became clear I couldn't continue to run both businesses.

I always assumed the day I jacked it in, I'd simply tell my customers to find another window cleaner and that would be that. However, after thinking about it, I realised there had to be some value in a business turning over a reasonable profit. After calling all three of my local competitors, a minor bidding war commenced, and I actually sold the round for ten grand. Part of that money provided a deposit for our rented house, and a not-insignificant chunk went on paying for all the paraphernalia Frankie needed, and an awful lot he didn't need but Daisy wanted anyway.

"Yeah, I think I still remember," I reply, grasping the ladder.

A minute later, I can see why Mum didn't want Dad shifting the boxes.

"Christ. What the hell have you got in here?" I puff, struggling back down the ladder with the first box.

"Probably a load of old crap but your guess is as good as mine, son. They've been up there for at least twenty years."

I drop the first box on the landing and repeat the journey; the second box being marginally lighter, thankfully.

"Where shall I put them?" I ask, as Dad closes the hatch to the now empty loft.

"We're using the second bedroom to store everything. Stick them in there."

The second bedroom Dad is referring to is my old bedroom. It stopped being Adam's bedroom a few months back, when my parents gratefully acknowledged I'd never need it again.

I lug both boxes into the bedroom and stand for a moment to take one final look around. I can still see the tiny pinholes in the ceiling where I used to hang the model aeroplanes I made with Dad. And the walls are dotted with similar holes from the drawing pins used to mount posters. Sadly, the model Hawker Hurricane and poster of Pamela Anderson in a red swimsuit are long gone. I miss them both, for very different reasons.

"Reminiscing, eh?" Dad remarks.

"There was a time I hated this room but I think I'm going to miss it."

"There's a lot about this old house we're going to miss," he says wistfully. "So many memories, but now it's time to make some new ones."

"Better late than never," I smile.

"Yep. We should have done this years ago."

"What stopped you?"

"This bedroom."

"Sorry?"

Dad takes a seat on one of the boxes I moved from the loft.

"Every time we thought about moving, you'd turn up after your latest calamity and move back in. I guess we didn't want to take away your last place of refuge."

It's been a while, but I still recognise the heavy burden of guilt.

"I ... I didn't realise. I don't know what to say, Dad."

"Nothing to say. That's the sacrifice you make as a parent; as you'll find out in time."

Whether he intended it or not, his confession provides an explanation.

"Is that why Mum has always been so frosty with me; because my behaviour stopped you getting on with your lives?"

"Would you blame her?"

I suddenly recall my mother's face that night at the intensive care unit. To think: she'd postponed the life she wanted for so long, and the man she intended to share it with was stood at death's door. Her future, their future, was slipping away before her very eyes. I don't think I could have lived with that guilt if the worst had happened.

"But, for the record," Dad continues. "It was your mother who insisted we stay here."

"Eh?"

"You know I'm a pragmatist, son. I thought the only way for you to take some responsibility was to remove your last resort.

As long as you had this bedroom to return to, you always had a 'Get out of Jail' card. I didn't think that was helping anyone, but your mother couldn't take it away. You've her to thank for all the times you were able to turn up here when there was nowhere else to go."

I slump down on the other box.

"Jesus, Dad. I didn't know."

"I didn't tell you to make you feel guilty, son. I just wanted you to know that no matter how many times you've broken her heart, she loves you. And despite what you think, she's always been proud of you."

If guilt had mass, I'd be lying crushed on the carpet by now.

"I've been a bigger idiot than I realised, haven't I?"

"Absolutely not," he chides. "An idiot wouldn't have turned his life around the way you have."

"Thanks. I still feel bad though."

"What's the point in wasting a day feeling bad? I, of all people, know we need to squeeze every ounce of joy we can from each day. When you go back out to the garden, take a look at your mother's face. You'll see the happiest, proudest woman alive, and that's all that matters now. Bollocks to the past."

Dad leans across and ruffles my hair; his trademark show of affection for as long as I can remember. It has never felt more reassuring.

"Anyway, son. Do you fancy seeing what treasures lie in these boxes? You never know: we might unearth an old Picasso or two."

I'd be happy unearthing a poster of a Baywatch star in a red swimsuit.

"Yeah, go on. I don't think they'll miss us for five minutes."

We get to our feet and Dad rips the tape from the first box. As he pulls the flaps back, the scent of decades-old paper and dust escapes.

"My, my," Dad mumbles as he extracts a pale blue notebook.

"What's that?"

He turns it over and shows me the printed name and class number on the front.

"Ohh. Let me see."

The notebook in question is actually one of my textbooks from infant school. Dad hands it over, and as I flick through the yellowed pages, a surreal yet warm glow takes hold, knowing my seven-year-old hand was responsible for the scrawly handwriting.

"I can't believe you kept this," I gush.

"I can't take the credit, son. It was your mother."

He then extracts a three inch pile of textbooks in varying pastel colours.

"In fact," he adds. "It looks like she kept all your old schoolbooks."

I take the pile of dog-eared books and scan the covers. Despite my name being printed on each one, I can't say I remember any of the books. Perhaps once I've had a chance to sit down and look at them properly, I might be able to find some memories.

"I guess this proves your point, Dad."

"I hope so."

"Can I keep them?"

"Too bloody right you can," he laughs. "The less crap we have to move, the better."

Still chuckling to himself, he delves back into the box.

"Good Lord," he then gasps. "I wondered where this had got to."

It's not an old Picasso or a poster he pulls from the box, but a tatty-looking book.

"What is it?"

"This, son, is the closest thing we have to a family heirloom."

He holds the book aloft, as if he'd just unearthed a lost biblical script.

"This book has history," he says with some reverence. "It originally belonged to your great-grandfather, and it's been passed down from father to son."

"Oh, I see. I'm guessing it skipped a generation when it was my turn?"

His expression slips from sunny to serious.

"You don't remember it?"

"Err, no. Should I?"

"Probably not, thinking about it. But you did read it when you were a lad."

I turn my attention from Dad to the cover. Some offspring are bequeathed houses and large sums of cash, but my inheritance is a forgotten book with a faded blue cover and a sketchy, poorly-drawn picture of an impish creature on the front. Even the title sounds lame: *The Naughty Never Sleep*.

"You honestly don't remember reading it?" Dad confirms.

"Nope. Not at all."

"Well, you did, and you weren't supposed to."

"Why? It's just a book."

"It was written a long time ago, son, and let's just say authors had a very different idea of what kids should be reading."

"You let me read soft porn?"

"If only," he puffs. "It would have saved us months of grief."

"Come on then—I'm intrigued now."

"I think you were about eight or nine. I always read you a bedtime story but maybe you were too old by that point. One night, in the summer I think, I finished a story as usual, and said goodnight. Once I left your bedroom, you decided to continue reading on your own."

"Aren't kids supposed to show an interest in reading?"

"Yes, but of all the books you could have chosen, you decided to read this one. It was my fault, I suppose. I shouldn't have left it in your room but it was hidden on the top shelf of your bookcase. You found it and decided to read it—that's when the problems started."

"Problems?"

"The nightmares, son. Awful they were. You'd wake up screaming in the middle of the night, maybe three or four times a week. And that went on for months."

"Really? I honestly have no recollection."

"You can thank the therapist for that."

"Shit, really? I had therapy?"

"Hypnotherapy, and we had no choice. According to the therapist, the book must have scared you so badly you were virtually traumatised, and it took almost three months of therapy before the nightmares ended."

"Christ, I honestly don't remember any of this."

"I think that was the point of the therapy; to wipe away the entire event so you couldn't remember reading the sodding book. But I was never comfortable with it and … I don't know … I felt you were never the same child afterwards."

"In what way?"

"It's hard to put my finger on it, but it was like something was missing. And, thinking back, it was about that time your behaviour changed. You went from a bright, well-behaved lad to—how can I put this—a pain in the arse."

Dad hands me the book.

"Anyway, it's yours now, but for the love of God don't let Frankie read it until he's a teenager."

"Thanks."

I make a mental note to list it on eBay the moment I get home.

"What's so bad about it, anyway?" I ask. "And why did it scare me so much?"

"Probably the main character, son. He was a malevolent imp who would invade the dreams of naughty kids and cause all kinds of mayhem."

"What kind of mayhem?"

"If memory serves, the imp was only ever supposed to frighten the kids into changing their naughty ways, and he'd do that by haunting their dreams. But this particular imp had a curious streak and while he was in each child's head, he decided to borrow elements of their psyche."

"Curious about what? I can't imagine there's much in a kid's head worth borrowing."

"He desperately wanted to experience what it was like being human. So, if he wanted to know what courage felt like, he'd borrow a child's bravery. If he wanted to humour himself, he'd borrow a child's wit. However, the human emotions were far too strong for an imp and he became totally consumed by each one. In the end, he had no choice but to return what he borrowed, but the kids were pretty messed up by that point. I think the moral of the story was not to be naughty in the first place but it's not a tale with a happy ending."

"Bloody hell. No wonder I needed therapy."

"Exactly, and you were convinced that imp was invading your dreams and that's what the therapist had to deal with—to banish the imp from your mind."

"Hey, perhaps the imp borrowed my common sense," I chuckle. "And the therapist banished him from my memory before he could return it."

"Hah," Dad snorts. "That might explain a lot."

Fortunately, we can now both laugh but I suspect there was a time neither of us found the imp funny.

"Did this imp have a name?" I ask.

"Oh, heaven knows. Must be forty years since I read it."

I flip open the first page and scan the four or five paragraphs, for no other reason than blind curiosity.

At some point in the third paragraph, triggered by two words, they come—a barrage of memories; each one striking with the force of a tsunami.

Twenty-four years after it slid from my duvet, the book slips from my hand and falls to the bedroom floor.

"You alright, son? You look like you've seen a ghost."

"The imp … his name," I gasp, barely able to find a breath. "It was … no, it can't be."

"Ohh, now I come to think of it, he shared a first name with that doctor friend of yours. What was it … Mungo? Yes, Mungo Thunk."

THE END

But before you go ...

I genuinely hope you enjoyed *Meeting Mungo Thunk*. If you did, and have a few minutes spare, I would be eternally grateful if you could leave a review on Amazon. If you're feeling particularly generous, a mention on Facebook or a Tweet would be equally appreciated. I know it's a pain, but it's the only way us indie authors can compete with the big publishing houses.

Stay in Touch ...

For more information about me and to receive updates on my new releases, please visit my website...

www.keithapearson.co.uk

If you have any questions or general feedback, you can also reach me, or follow me, on social media...

Facebook: www.facebook.com/pearson.author
Twitter: www.twitter.com/keithapearson

Printed in Great Britain
by Amazon